"A seamless melding of the mundane and the fantastic."
—*Winnipeg Free Press*

"A solid thriller, full of suspense and peppered with villains of various talents and their adversaries, the decent folk who constantly try to thwart their evil intentions. Though de Lint may be a master of contemporary fantasy, he also brings to life the human frailties of his characters and the spirit with which they cling together. 'What I do know,' says one character, 'is that we've all got our hidden currents, no matter how wide and friendly the river seems. Start casting deep enough and who knows what you'll dredge up.' The reader does not have to be strictly a fan of either thrillers or fantasy to thoroughly enjoy this delightful tale."
—*The Washington Post*

"De Lint's elegant prose and effective storytelling continue to transform the mundane into the magical at every turn. Highly recommended."
—*Library Journal*

"As page-turning and intelligent as usual for de Lint, who clearly has no equal as an urban fantasist and very few equals among fantasists as a folklorist. First-rate."
—*Booklist*

SOMEPLACE TO BE FLYING

CHARLES DE LINT

TOR®
fantasy

A TOM DOHERTY ASSOCIATES BOOK
NEW YORK

This is a work of fiction. All the characters and events portrayed in this book are either products of the author's imagination or are used fictiously.

SOMEPLACE TO BE FLYING

Edited by Terri Windling

A Tor Book
Published by Tom Doherty Associates, Inc.
175 Fifth Avenue
New York, NY 10010

Tor Books on the World Wide Web:
http://www.tor.com

Tor® is a registered trademark of Tom Doherty Associates, Inc.

ISBN: 0-812-55158-3
Library of Congress Card Catalog Number: 97-37433

First edition: February 1998
First mass market edition: March 1999

Printed in the United States of America

0 9 8 7 6 5 4 3 2 1

For Kiya
yippee-ki-yi-yay

CONTENTS

So I asked the raven as he passed by,
I said, "Tell me, raven, why'd you make the sky?"
"The moon and stars, I threw them high,
I needed someplace to be flying."

—Kiya Heartwood,
from "Wyoming Wind"

If men had wings and bore black feathers,
few of them would be clever enough to be
crows.

—Rev. Henry Ward Beecher (mid-1800s)

it's a long long road
it's a big big world
we are wise wise women
we are giggling girls
we both carry a smile
to show when we're pleased
both carry a switchblade
in our sleeves

—Ani DiFranco,
from "If He Tries Anything"

~1~

POETRY IN A TREE

Everything is held together with stories. That is all that is holding us together, stories and compassion.
—BARRY LOPEZ,
FROM AN INTERVIEW IN *POETS AND WRITERS*,
VOL. 22, ISSUE 2 (MARCH/APRIL 1994)

1.

Newford, Late August, 1996

The streets were still wet but the storm clouds had moved on as Hank drove south on Yoors waiting for a fare. Inhabited tenements were on his right, the derelict blight of the Tombs on his left, Miles Davis's muted trumpet snaking around Wayne Shorter's sax on the tape deck. The old Chev four-door didn't look like much; painted a flat gray, it blended into the shadows like the ghost car it was.

It wasn't the kind of cab you flagged down. There was no roof light on top, no meter built into the dash, no license displayed, but if you needed something moved and you had the number of the cell phone, you could do business. Safe business. The windows were bulletproof glass and under the body's flaking paint and dents, there was so much steel it would take a tank to do it any serious damage. Fast business, too. The rebuilt V-8 under the hood, purring as quiet as a contented cat at the moment, could lunge to one hundred miles per hour in seconds. The car didn't offer much in the way of comfort, but the kinds of fares that used a gypsy cab weren't exactly hiring it for its comfort.

When he reached Grasso Street, Hank hung a left and cruised through Chinatown, then past the strip of clubs on the other side of Williamson. The clock on his dash read 3:00 A.M. The look-at-me crowd was gone now with only a few stragglers still wandering the wet streets. The lost and the lonely and the seriously screwed-up. Hank smiled when he stopped at a red light and a muscle-bound guy crossed in front of the cab wearing a T-shirt that read, "Nobody Knows I'm a Lesbian." He tapped his horn and the guy gave him a Grasso Street salute in response, middle finger extended, fingernails painted black. When he realized Hank wasn't hassling him, he only shrugged and kept on walking.

A few blocks farther, Hank pulled the cab over to the curb. He keyed the speed-dial on the cell phone and had to wait through a handful of rings before he got a connection.

"You never get tired of that crap, kid?" Moth asked.

Hank turned the tape deck down.

"All I've got left is that six o'clock pickup," he said by way of response. The only thing Moth considered music had to have a serious twang—add in yodeling and it was even better—so there was no point in arguing with him. "Have you got anything to fill in the next couple of hours?"

"A big nada."

Hank nodded. He hated slow nights, but he especially hated them when he was trying to raise some cash.

"Okay," he said. "Guess I'll head over to the club and just wait for Eddie outside."

"Yeah, well, keep your doors locked. I hear those guys that were jacking cars downtown have moved up to Foxville the past couple of nights."

"Eddie told me."

"Did he say anything about his people dealing with it?"

Hank watched as a drunk stumbled over to the doorway of one of the closed clubs and started to take a leak.

"Like he's going to tell me?" he said.

"You got a point. Hey, I hear that kid you like's doing a late set at the Rhatigan."

Hank almost laughed. Under a spotlight, Brandon Cole seemed ageless, especially when he played. Hank put him in his mid-to-late thirties, but he had the kind of build and features that could easily go ten years in either direction. A tall, handsome black man, he seemed to live only for his sax and his music. He was no kid, but to Moth anybody under sixty was a kid.

"What time's it start?" he asked.

He could almost see Moth shrug. "What am I, a press secretary now? All I know is Dayson's got a couple of high rollers in town—jazz freaks like you, kid—and he told me he's taking them by."

"Thanks," Hank said. "Maybe I'll check it out."

He cut the connection and started to work his way across town to where the Rhatigan was nestled on the edge of the Combat Zone. The after-hours bar where Eddie ran his all-night poker games was over in Upper Foxville, but he figured he could take in an hour or so of Cole's music and still make the pickup in plenty of time.

Except it didn't work out that way. He was coming down one of the little dark back streets that ran off Grasso—no more than an alley, really—when his headlights picked out a tall man in a dove-gray suit, beating on some woman.

Hank knew the drill. The first few times he took out the spare car, Moth had stopped him at the junkyard gate and stuck his head in the window to reel it off: "Here's the way it plays, kid. You only stop for money. You don't pick up strays. You never get involved." One, two, three.

But some things you didn't walk away from. This time of night, in this part of town, she was probably a hooker—having some altercation with her pimp, maybe, or she hadn't been paying attention to her radar and got caught up with a john turned ugly—but that still didn't make it right.

He hit the brakes, the Chev skidding for a moment on the slick pavement before he got it back under control. The baseball bat on the seat beside him began to roll forward. A surge of adrenaline put him into motion, quick, not even thinking. He grabbed the bat by its handle, put the car in neutral, foot coming down on the parking brake and locking it into place. Through the windshield he could see the man backhand the woman, turn to face him. As the woman fell to the pavement, Hank popped the door and stepped outside. The baseball bat was a comfortable weight in his hand until the man reached under his jacket.

Hank could almost hear Moth's voice in the back of his head. "You get involved, you get hurt. Plain and simple. And let me tell you, kid. There's no percentage in getting hurt."

It was a little late for advice now.

The man wasn't interested in discussion. He pulled a handgun out from under that tailored dove-gray suit jacket and fired, all in one smooth move. Hank saw the muzzle flash, then something smashed him in the shoulder and spun him around, throwing him against the door of the Chev. The baseball bat dropped out of numbed fingers and went clattering across the pavement. He followed after it, sliding down the side of the Chev and leaving a smear of blood on the cab's paint job.

Moth is going to be pissed about that, he thought.

Then the pain hit him and he blacked out for a moment. He floated in some empty space where only the pain and sound existed. His own rasping breath. The soft murmur of the cab's engine, idling. The faint sound of Miles and Shorter, the last cut on the tape, just ending. The muted scuff of leather-soled shoes on pavement, approaching. When he got his eyes back open, the man was standing over him, looking down.

The man had a flat, dead gaze, eyes as gray as his suit.

Hank had seen their kind before. They were the eyes of
the men who stood against the wall in the back room of
Eddie's bar, watching the action, waiting for Eddie to
give them a sign that somebody needed straightening out.
They were the eyes of men he'd picked up at the airport
and dropped off at some nondescript hotel after a stop at
one of the local gunrunners. They were the eyes he'd seen
in a feral dog's face one night when it had killed Emma's
cat in the yard out behind her apartment, the hard gaze
holding his for a long moment before it retreated with its
kill.

The man lifted his gun again and now Hank could see
it was an automatic, as anonymous as the killer holding
it. Behind the weapon, the man's face remained expressionless. There was nothing there. No anger, no pleasure,
no regret.

Hank couldn't feel the pain in his shoulder anymore.
His mind had gone blank, except for one thing. His entire
being seemed to hold its breath and focus on the muzzle
of the automatic, waiting for another flash, more pain.
But they didn't come.

The man turned away from him, cobra-quick, his
weapon now aimed at something on the roof of the cab.
It hadn't registered until the man moved, but now Hank
realized he'd also heard what had distracted the killer. An
unexpected sound. A hollow bang on metal as though
someone had jumped onto the roof of the cab.

Jumped from where? His own gaze followed that of
his attacker's. One of the fire escapes, he supposed. He
knew a momentary sense of relief—someone else was
playing Good Samaritan tonight—except there was only
a girl standing there on the roof of the cab. A kid. Skinny
and monochrome and not much to her: raggedy blue-
black hair, dark complexion, black clothes, and combat
boots. There seemed to be a cape fluttering up behind her
like a sudden spread of black wings, there one moment,
gone the next, and then she really was just a kid, standing

there, her weight on one leg, a switchblade held casually in a dark hand.

Hank wanted to cry a warning to her. Didn't she see the man had a gun? Before he could open his mouth, the killer stiffened and an expression finally crossed his features: surprise mixed with pain. His gun went off again, loud as a thunderclap at this proximity, the bullet kicking sparks from the fire escape before it went whining off into the darkness. The man fell to his knees, collapsing forward in an ungainly sprawl. Dead. And where he'd been standing . . . the girl. . . .

Hank blinked, thinking the girl had somehow transported herself magically from the top of the cab to the pavement behind the killer. But the first girl was still standing on the roof of the cab. She jumped to the ground, landing lightly on the balls of her feet. Seeing them together, he realized they were twins.

The second girl knelt down and cleaned her knife on the dead man's pants, leaving a dark stain on the dovegray material. Closing the blade, she made it disappear up her sleeve and walked away to where the woman Hank had been trying to rescue lay in the glare of the cab's headlights.

"You can get up now," the first girl said, making her own switchblade vanish.

Hank tried to rise but the movement brought a white-hot flare of pain that almost made him black out again. The girl went down on one knee beside him, her face close to his. She put two fingers to her lips and licked them, then pressed them against his shoulder, her touch as light as a whisper, and the pain went away. Just like that, as though she'd flicked a switch.

Leaning back, she offered Hank her hand. Her skin was dry and cool to the touch and she was strong. Effortlessly, she pulled him up into a sitting position. Hank braced himself for a fresh flood of pain, but it was still gone. He reached up to touch his shoulder. There was a hole in his shirt, the fabric sticky and wet with blood. But there was no wound. Unable to take his gaze from the girl, he explored with a finger, found a pucker of skin where the bullet hole had closed, nothing more. The girl grinned at him.

All he could do was look back at her, stumbling to frame a coherent sentence. ''What . . . how did you . . . ?''

''Spit's just as magic as blood,'' she said. ''Didn't you ever know that?''

He shook his head.

''You look so funny,'' she went on. ''The way you're staring at me.''

Before he could move, she leaned forward and kissed him, a small tongue darting out to flick against his lips, then she jumped to her feet, leaving behind a faint musky smell.

''You taste good,'' she said. ''You don't have any real meanness in you.'' She looked solemn now. ''But you know all about meanness, don't you?''

Hank nodded. He got the feeling she was able to look right inside him, sifting through the baggage of memories that made up his life as though it were a hard-copy résumé, everything laid out in point form, easy to read. He grabbed hold of the cab's fender and used it to pull himself to his feet. Remembering that first image of her he'd seen through his pain, that impression of dark wings rising up behind her shoulders, he thought she must be some kind of angel.

''Why . . . why'd you help me?'' he asked.

''Why'd you try to help the woman?''

''Because I couldn't not try.''

She grinned. ''Us, too.''

''But you . . . where did you come from?''

She shrugged and made a sweeping motion with her hand that could have indicated the fire escape above his cab or the whole of the night sky. ''We were just passing by—same as you.''

He heard a soft scuff of boots on the pavement and

then the other girl was there, the two of them as alike as photographs printed from the same exotic negative.

The first girl touched his forearm. "We've got to go."

"Are you . . . angels?" Hank asked.

The two looked at each other and giggled.

"Do we look like angels?" the second girl asked.

Not like any kind he'd ever seen in pictures, Hank wanted to say, but he thought maybe they were. Maybe this is what angels really looked like, only they were too scruffy for all those high-end Italian and French artists, so they cleaned the image up in their paintings and everybody else bought it.

"I don't know," he said. "I've never seen real angels before tonight."

"Isn't he cute?" the first girl said.

She gave Hank another quick kiss, on the cheek this time, then the two of them sauntered off, hand in hand, like one of them hadn't just healed a gunshot wound, like they weren't leaving a dead body behind. Hank glanced down at the corpse, then looked back up the alley where the girls had been walking. They were gone. He leaned against the cab for a moment, dizzy. His hand rose to touch his shoulder again and his fingers came away tacky with the drying blood. But the wound was still only a puckered scar. The pain was still gone. He'd be ready to believe he'd imagined the whole thing if it weren't for the blood on his shirt, the dead man lying at his feet.

Straightening up, he finally walked around the corpse, crossing the pavement to join the woman he'd stopped to help. She sat on the pavement, back against the brick wall behind her, the lights of the cab holding her like a spotlight. He saw the same dazed expression in her features that he knew were on his own. She looked up at his approach, gaze focusing on him.

"You okay?" he asked.

"I don't know. . . ." She looked down the alley in the direction that the girls had taken. "She just took the pain away. I can hardly hold on to the memory of it . . . of the

man . . . hitting me. . . ." Her gaze returned to Hank.
"You know how when you're a kid, your mother would
kiss a scrape and you'd kind of forget about how it
hurt?"

Hank didn't, but he nodded anyway.

"Except this really worked," the woman said.

Hank looked at the blood on his hand. "They were
angels."

"I guess. . . ."

She had short brown hair and was holding a pair of
fashionable glasses with round tortoiseshell frames. One
of the lenses was broken. Attractive, late twenties to early
thirties, and definitely uptown. Well dressed. Low-heeled
shoes, a knee-length black skirt with a pale rose silk
jacket, a white shirt underneath. After tonight the outfit
was going to need dry-cleaning.

Secretary, he decided, or some kind of businesswoman.
A citizen, as out of place here as he'd be in the kinds of
places where people had a life on paper and paid taxes.
Met her Mr. Goodbar in some club tonight and things
just went downhill from there. Or maybe she was working, he thought, as he noticed the camera bag lying in
some trash a few paces away.

He rinsed his hand in a puddle, wiped it clean on his
jeans. Then he gave her a hand up and fetched the bag
for her. It was heavy.

"You a photographer?" he asked.

She nodded and introduced herself. "Lily Carson.
Freelance."

Hank smiled. He was freelance, too, but it wasn't at
all the same kind of thing. She probably had business
cards and everything.

"I'm Joey Bennett," he said, shaking the offered hand.
They might have gone through an amazing experience
together, but old habits were hard to shake. Joey Bennett
was the name that went with the I.D. he was carrying
tonight; Hank Walker didn't exist on paper. Not anymore.
"You need a lift somewhere?"

Her gaze traveled to the corpse. "We should call the police."

She was taking this well. He reached up and touched his shoulder. Though he wasn't exactly stressing out over it either. Those girls had done more than take away her bruises and the hole in his shoulder.

"You can call them," he said, "but I'm not sticking around."

When she gave him a surprised look, he nodded toward the Chev. "Gypsy cab."

"I don't get it."

"Unlicensed."

Now she understood.

"Then we can call it in from a phone booth somewhere," she said.

"Whatever."

Hank just wanted away from here. He'd sampled some hallucinogens when he was a kid and the feeling he had now was a lot like coming down from an acid high. Everything slightly askew, illogical things that somehow made sense, everything too sharp and clear when you looked at it but fading fast in your peripheral vision, blurred, like it didn't really exist. He could still taste the girl's tongue on his lip, the earthy scent she'd left behind. It was a wild bouquet, like something you'd smell in a forest, deep under the trees. He started to reach for his shoulder again, still not quite able to believe the wound was gone, then thought better of it.

"We should go," he told her.

She didn't move. "You've been hurt," she said.

He looked down at his bloody shirt and gave a slow nod. "But they . . . those girls . . . just took it away. I caught a bullet in the shoulder and now it's like it never happened. . . ."

She touched her cheek. There wasn't a mark on it now.

"What's happened to us?" she said. "I feel completely distanced from what just happened. Not just physically, but . . ."

She let her hand drop.

"I don't know," he said. "I guess it's just the way we're dealing with the stress."

She nodded, but neither of them believed it. It was something the girls had done to them.

He led her to the passenger's side of the cab and opened the door for her. Walking around back, he stopped at the trunk and popped it open. Between the coolers of beer and liquor on ice, he kept a gym bag with spare clothes. Taking off his shirt, he put on a relatively clean T-shirt and closed the lid of the trunk. He paused for a moment as he came around to the driver's side of the car, startled by the body lying there. He kept fading on it, like it didn't really exist, like what had happened, hadn't. Not really. He remembered the girl's lips again, the taste of them, the faint wild musk in the air around her. Her breath, he thought suddenly, had been sweet—like apples.

His attention returned to the corpse. Frowning, he nudged a limp arm with the toe of his boot, moving it away from the Chev's tire. Last thing he felt like doing was running over the thing. He picked up the baseball bat from where it had fallen and tossed it onto the backseat.

"Where to?" he asked when he joined Lily in the front of the cab.

She gave him an address in Lower Crowsea. Yuppie territory. He'd figured right.

She was quiet until they pulled out onto a main street and headed west. When she spoke, he started, almost having forgotten she was there.

"How come you don't get a license?" she wanted to know.

Hank shrugged. He turned the cassette over and stuck it back in, volume turned way down now.

"This isn't that kind of a cab," he said.

He put an inflection in the way he spoke that he hoped

would let her know this wasn't something he felt like discussing. She took the hint.

"Who's that playing trumpet?" she asked.

"Miles Davis."

"I thought so. And Wayne Shorter on sax, right? I love that stuff they were doing in the mid-sixties."

Hank gave her a quick look before returning his attention to his driving. "You like jazz?" he asked, pleasantly surprised.

"I like all kinds of music—anything that's got heart."

"That's a good way to put it. Miles sure had heart. I thought a piece of me died when he did."

They were on Stanton Street now, the sky disappearing overhead as they entered the tunnel of oaks where the street narrowed and the big estates began. A few more blocks west, the houses got smaller and closer to the road. Most of these had been turned into apartments over the years, but they were still out of Hank's price range. Everything was pretty much out of his price range. He took a right on Lee Street, then another on McKennitt and pulled up to the curb in front of the address Lily had given him.

"Nice place," he said.

Her building was a three-story brick house with a tall pine and a sugar maple vying for dominance in the front yard. Hank looked at the long front porch and imagined being able to sit out on it in the evening, drink in hand, looking out at the street. A pang of jealousy woke in him, but he let it go as quickly as it came. Only citizens had that kind of a life.

"I don't own it," Lily said. "I'm renting a second-floor apartment."

"But still . . . it's a nice place, in a good neighborhood. Safe."

She gave him a slow nod. He put the Chev in neutral, engaged the hand brake, and turned to look at her.

"So who was the guy?" he asked.

"I don't know." She hesitated for a long heartbeat,

then added, "I was out looking for animal people when I ran into him."

She had to be putting him on. It was that, or he hadn't heard her properly.

"Animal people?" he asked.

"I know what you're thinking. I know how crazy it sounds."

"It doesn't sound like anything to me yet," Hank said.

"The only reason I brought it up is I thought maybe you'd know what I was talking about. They're supposed to live on the edges of society—sort of a society unto themselves."

"Outsiders."

She nodded. "Like you. No offense, but you know, with this cab and everything."

"No offense taken," Hank assured her. "I've been an outsider all my life. I guess I was just born that way."

It wasn't entirely a lie. When you didn't get nurturing from day one, you learned pretty quick to depend on yourself.

"I thought you might know about them," Lily went on. "Or maybe know where I can find them."

He'd heard of them, but not as anything real. They were only stories.

"Animal people," Hank repeated.

He was thinking now might be a real good time to get her out of the cab and put all of this behind him. It was getting close to six when he had to pick up Eddie anyway, so he had an excuse, but he couldn't let it go. The whole thing was too intriguing. A good-looking, straight citizen like this, out walking the streets of the Combat Zone looking for animal people like Jack was always talking about. He knew what Moth would say, what he'd do, but he wasn't Moth. Moth wouldn't have stopped in the first place—not unless he'd known her. Then Moth would have given his life for her, just as he almost had.

"What exactly are they supposed to be?" he asked.

"The first people—the ones that were there when the

world began. They were animals, but people, too.''

''When the world began.''

This was way too familiar, he thought as she nodded. At least Jack knew they were only stories.

''That'd be a long time ago,'' Hank said, humoring her.

''I know. Lots of us have their blood in us—that's what gives us our animal traits.''

''Like the Chinese calendar?''

''I suppose,'' she said. ''The thing is, there's been so much intermarrying between species—you know, us and real animals—not to mention us killing them off when they're in their animal shapes, that there aren't many pure animal people left. But there *are* some, living on the edges of the way we see the world, the way we divide it up. They're like spiritual forces. Totems.''

Hank didn't know what to say.

She sighed and looked out the windshield. ''I told you. I know how crazy it sounds.''

Hank knew crazy, and this wasn't it. Crazy was Hazel standing out in front of the Williamson Street Mall, trying to tell anybody who'd listen about the video games going on inside her head, how right now, Mario the Plumber was walking around inside her stomach. Or No Hands Luke who was convinced that aliens had stolen his hands and would only pick things up with his wrists held together. But he thought he knew where she'd picked up this business with the animal people.

''Do you know a man named Jack Daw?'' Hank asked.

She turned so that she was facing him. ''Do you know him, too?''

Everybody on the street, or who worked it, knew Jack. The only thing that surprised Hank was that a citizen would know him. Jack didn't exactly fit into the cocktail hour/espresso bar set. He lived in an abandoned school bus up on the edge of the Tombs near Moth's junkyard, had the place all fixed up inside and out: potbellied cast-iron woodstove, bed, table and chairs to eat at, big old sofa outside where he'd sit in the summer when he wasn't out and about, cadging coins and telling stories. There were always crows hanging around that old bus, feeding off the scraps he fed them. He called them his cousins.

"How'd a woman like you meet someone like Jack?" Hank asked.

The smile she gave him transformed her features, taking them from attractive to heart-stopping. Easy, Hank, he told himself. She's way out of your league.

"So what kind of woman am I?" she wanted to know.

Hank shrugged. "Uptown."

"Are you always so quick to label people?"

"You've got to be—in my business."

"And you're never wrong?"

Hank thought about the man that right now was lying dead in an alley back in the Combat Zone. If things had played out like he'd expected, the guy would have taken off and still be running.

"Once or twice," he said.

She nodded. "Well, I meet a lot of different kinds of people in my business. I'll take a man like Jack over politicians and the moneymen any day."

Hank studied her for a long moment.

"I guess you're okay," he said finally.

She gave him that smile of hers again, lots of wattage, but genuine. "That's what Jack said, too."

"So how'd you meet him?"

"The way I usually meet interesting people: I was working on a story."

"You said you were a photographer. Doesn't somebody else write the stories?"

"It all depends. Sometimes I sell a story, sometimes just the pictures, sometimes both. It really depends on whether I've got an assignment, or come up with the idea for the piece myself."

"And this one you came up with."

"It wasn't about Jack, but I ran into him and . . . he's really interesting."

That he was, Hank thought. He'd listened to more than one of Jack's stories himself, late at night, fire burning in one of the junkyard oil drums, the sky so big and clear up above that you'd never think you were in the middle of the city. The things he talked about sounded almost plausible and stuck with you—at least until you thought about them in the daylight.

"Jack tells those stories to everybody," he said. "That's what he does. Mo—" He caught himself. "A friend of mine says it's Jack's way of explaining the world to himself. You can't take what he says literally."

"No. Of course not. It's just . . ." Her gaze went away again, not simply out the windshield, but to someplace Hank couldn't see. "I need to believe in something like animal people right now."

Hank didn't ask her why. He just gave her the same advice he'd been given by an older kid in juvie hall.

"Believe in yourself," he said.

"I do," she said, her voice soft, as though she were sharing a secret. "But it doesn't always help."

Before Hank could think of a reply, she shook her head, clearing it, and turned to look at him. Wherever she'd gone, she was back now. She reached into her pocket and pressed a business card into his hand.

"Call me sometime," she said.

Hank smiled. He'd been right about the card, too.

"Sure," he lied.

He glanced at the card before he dropped it on the dash. She played it safe. The card had her name on it, phone number and email address, and one of those "suite" addresses that people used when they didn't want to make it look like they had a P.O. box.

"Are you still calling the cops?" he asked.

She shook her head. "I wouldn't know what to say. Two girls came out of nowhere and killed an armed man and all they had were pocketknives? Besides, I think maybe he got what he deserved. He was going to kill you."

Not to mention beating on her, Hank thought. But it was hard to get worked up about it anymore. They should both still be in shock, dead or on their way to the hospital at the very least, but the whole thing seemed surreal now, as though it had happened to someone else, or a long time ago. He could see she felt the same way.

"I think those girls were animal people," she added.

Hank flashed on the afterimage of wings he thought he'd seen when the first girl had landed on the roof of the cab. He touched his shoulder, feeling the wound that was only a scar.

"They weren't like anything I've ever seen before," he said.

She nodded. "Thanks again—for everything. Most people wouldn't have stopped to help."

"Yeah, well . . ."

"And call me."

"Sure," he said, just as he had the last time, only this time he thought maybe he might.

He watched her go up the walk to her building, the branches of the pine and maple entwining above her, waited until she was inside before he put the Chev in gear and pulled away from the curb. He got the sense she wasn't like Andrea, the last uptown woman he'd dated, that she didn't look at him as a project, something to clean up the way other people went to garage sales, buying junk that they could polish into antiques.

But then, Andrea hadn't been the kind to go out walking the streets at night, looking for animal people.

He knew what Moth would say: You've got to ask yourself, what's in it for her? Because everybody's playing an angle, working the percentages. That's just the way the world turns, kid. Look out for yourself, because nobody else'll be doing it for you.

Except for a couple of kids with switchblades who could rub spit on a gunshot wound and make it go away like it had never happened.

Animal people.

Bird girls.

He wasn't sure whether he would tell Moth about what had happened tonight. Moth wasn't going to believe it anyway. Hank had been there himself and he wasn't really all that sure what had happened. It felt too much like he'd dreamed the whole thing.

But as he took a sharp corner and Lily's business card began to slide down the dash, he grabbed it and stuck it in the pocket of his jeans.

2.

Lily waited just inside the front hall, studying the cab through a slit in her landlady's lace curtains until it pulled away. Without her glasses, the receding taillights and the red reflections trailing behind them on the wet street smeared and blurred. She waited until the cab turned a corner, then moved away from the window.

Well, she'd certainly made a good impression on Joey Bennett, she thought. She leaned her back against the wall, shoulders slumped. What could she possibly have been thinking, talking to him about the animal people? He probably thought she was ready to check into the Zeb where the shrinks could deal with her.

When Jack was telling his stories, she hadn't believed in the animal people either. Not really. But she wanted to. She wanted to because, for all that she clearly knew the difference between what was real and what wasn't, those strange animal spirits of his still called out to her. When he spoke, she could almost see them lift their heads to peer at her from the spaces where he took a breath, the idea of their existence resonating against something that ran deep in her own blood. But that didn't mean she actually believed in them.

I was out looking for animal people. . . .

She cringed as she remembered saying that. She hadn't needed her glasses to read the look on Joey's face, the polite way he didn't come right out and tell her he thought she was nuts. But he didn't have to.

Jack could get away with it, telling those stories, believing in animal people. He was such a character, living in that old school bus of his, the way he put himself in so many of his stories, as though he'd actually been there when they happened, no matter how tall the tale.

Lily understood the temptation, perhaps too well. She might even call it a need because, while she didn't know Jack well enough to be able to say why he did it, she was familiar enough with the process. The stories he related were like the ones she and Donna used to tell each other when they were kids, the two of them thrown together because no one else in the neighborhood wanted to play with the fat kid with the Coke-bottle glasses or her gimpy friend. They were both voracious readers, as much by circumstance as by choice, and the stories they made up were a natural outgrowth of all that reading, born out of the need of two tomboys, trapped in bodies that didn't look or work properly, having to make up a place where they could fit in. Because the real world didn't have such a place for them.

All these years later, Donna still had her limp. She'd moved to the East Coast where she worked as an editor for a small publishing house and was doing well for herself, though she often mentioned missing Newford when she wrote. Lily was no longer fat; in fact, if anything, she was slightly underweight, but inside she was still that tubby little kid and she still wanted to believe. She thought maybe Donna felt the same; that what Donna really missed was being able to believe. But that was something they never talked about in the email they sent each other every day.

Lily sighed. Pushing herself away from the wall she made her way upstairs and let herself into her apartment. She didn't know why she even cared what Joey thought of her. It wasn't likely she'd ever hear from him again— she'd recognized that look in his eyes when she'd asked him to call her. It was the same look men always got when they promised something they never meant to do. "I had a great time tonight. We should do it again. I'll call you." And then you waited all week before you realized it wasn't going to happen. And you never learned. You always thought, maybe this time it'll be different.

Joey wasn't her type, anyway. He was too good-looking, in a tough sort of a way, rough around the edges, perhaps, but so sure of himself. Like the cool, rebel kids she'd always admired from a distance in school, the ones who never had to worry about whether people liked them or not, who just strode through life, pulling everybody else along in their wake. Things didn't happen to them, they made them happen. They were in control of their own destinies.

What a load of crock, she thought, dropping her camera bag on the sofa. Because really, wasn't there something pathetic about a grown man making his living by driving an illegal cab in the middle of the night? What kind of a "destiny" was that? The destiny of a loser.

She sighed. It was a nice try, but putting him down didn't work. She felt attracted to him. It wasn't even the mystique, that edge of danger that clung to him like an aura. It was . . . the unexpected kindness in him, she realized. The way he'd stopped to help her without any consideration of the danger he'd put himself into. He could have been killed. He could have . . .

She sat down on the sofa beside her camera bag. Kicking off her shoes, one by one, she leaned back against the cushions. Closed her eyes.

He'd been shot. She remembered that. She remembered how loud the gun had sounded and seeing the bullet hit him, how the impact had slammed him against his car, remembered the blood that smeared the side of the door and soaked his shirt. But then those girls had come with their little penknives, almost as if they'd stepped out of one of Jack's stories, and her attacker was dead. She and Joey were all better, wounds healed, neither of them traumatized, and the man with the gun was dead. Just like that.

She knew she should be feeling something about what had happened but it really was like a story—not like anything that had happened to her outside of her imagination. She'd been prowling about in those lanes and alleyways for hours, feeling like a cat, invisible, very proud of herself for not being scared, feeling like one of the animal people she was looking for.

Then her attacker had appeared. He'd come up to her out of nowhere, sliding from the shadows, demanding she hand over her camera bag, and she, still in her story, feeling impossibly brave and sure of herself, had simply told him off. That was when he hit her. As random an act of violence as Joey's kindness had been. He hit her and kept hitting her until . . .

She sat up slowly, fingers exploring her face, the back of her neck, her shoulders.

There was no swelling, no pain. She knew if she got up to look in the mirror, there wouldn't even be a bruise.

She remembered the girl kneeling down beside her, her face so close, and even without the aid of glasses, oddly in focus: the sharp features below that ragged thatch of black hair and those dark, dark eyes. The smell of her like cedars and wet oak leaves and something sweet. Apple blossoms.

And she'd said something so odd, just before she'd taken the pain away. No, not said. She'd half-sung, half-chanted a few lines that returned to Lily now.

The cuckoo is a pretty bird, he sings as he flies.
He sucks little birds' eggs, and then he just dies.

She was sure they were from some song, though not one Lily knew. Sucks little birds' eggs. What was *that* supposed to mean? She tried repeating the words aloud, but they remained doggerel, as enigmatic as the girl singing them to her had been.

That girl. Those girls.

They were real.

The memory of them and what had happened kept trying to slide away from her, to lose its immediacy and become just another story, something she'd heard somewhere once, not something that had happened to her only hours ago. She wouldn't let it happen. She hung on to the memory, refusing to let it go.

She'd really found them.

Jack's animal people were real.

3.

The red-haired woman came by Jack's place early in the morning, as she often did. She called a greeting to the crows who watched her suspiciously from the roof of the old school bus. One of them cawed halfheartedly, then turned its head away and began to preen its glossy black feathers. The others continued to watch her, black eyes swallowing light. She supposed they'd never learn to trust her.

Kneeling by the steps of the bus, she reached under and pulled out the Coleman stove that Jack kept there. He had a woodstove inside the bus, but it was too warm to use it for cooking at this time of year and Jack didn't have any wood for it anyway. It took her a few tries to get the naphtha stove going, but soon she had a steady flame on the right burner. The left one didn't work anymore. She filled a battered tin coffeepot with water from the rain barrel, added ground coffee to the brewing basket from a plastic bag she was carrying in her jacket pocket, and put the pot on the stove. Once the coffee was brewing, she settled herself on the sofa out in front of the long length of the bus and leaned back, hands behind her head.

After a few moments she heard a stirring inside, then the smell of the coffee brought Jack out to join her on the sofa. He was a tall, gangly man, all long legs and arms, smooth-shaven and raven-haired, with skin a few shades darker than her own coffee-and-cream complexion. His cowboy boots were black. His jeans were an old and faded gray, shirt black, as were the flat-brimmed hat and duster he invariably wore. He had his hat on this morning—like Dwight Yoakam, she doubted he ever took it off in public—but he'd left his coat inside for now.

As soon as they saw him, the crows on the roof began to squabble, filling the air with their racket.

"Hush, you," Jack called over his shoulder. "Go make yourselves useful somewhere."

Still squabbling, the small flock erupted from their roost and flew out across the empty lots that lay between the bus and Moth's junkyard on the edge of the Tombs. Jack shook his head as they watched them go.

"Going to tease the dogs," he said. "Silly buggers."

Katy smiled. "Someone's got to do it. Moth lets those dogs get too lazy. Do you want some coffee? I think it's just about ready."

"You're spoiling me."

"I guess someone's got to do that, too."

"I won't say no."

She got up from her seat to get mugs from inside the bus, filling them on her way back to the sofa. They both drank it black. Squatting was easy to accomplish in the Tombs—regular citizens didn't venture into its sprawl of abandoned factories and tenements and all you had to do was roll out your bedding to stake a claim—but amenities, even such simple ones such as sugar and cream, simply didn't exist unless you brought them in yourself.

Jack took a few sips of coffee and smacked his lips in appreciation. Taking out a pipe, he went through the ritual of filling it, tamping the tobacco down just right, getting it lit. He drank some more coffee. Katy watched the air show the crows were putting on above Moth's place, dive-bombing the junkyard dogs, swooping and darting

in among the wrecked vehicles. The dogs howled their
frustration.

"You're feeling sorry for them," Jack said.

"Them and me. But at least those dogs of Moth's have
a place to be—somewhere they fit in."

"Anytime you need a place to stay . . ."

Katy sighed. "It's not that. It's just . . . she's coming.
I don't know how I know, but I do."

Jack nodded to show he was listening, but let her talk.

"I won't be able to stay away from her. I know I
promised her before, and it was hard, but I could manage
it because we had a few thousand miles between us. But
now she's coming here." She looked at Jack. "So it's
like the promise is broken, isn't it? She broke it."

"You're going to have to work that one out for yourself," Jack told her.

"Maybe her coming means she's changed her mind."

"Could be. You could ask her."

Katy shook her head. "Anybody else, but not her."

"You've got nothing to be afraid of," Jack said.

"She can kill me."

Jack wouldn't let her run with that. "You can't die."

Because she'd never been born. But Jack was wrong.
She wasn't like some of the animal people in his stories
who kept coming back and back, their lives a wheel
where most people's were a simple line from point A to
B. She could die. She knew that, no matter what Jack
said.

"Maybe the crow girls could help me," she said.
"You could introduce me and I could ask them."

Jack laughed. "You know how it goes. They do any
damn thing they please. But ask them right and maybe
they'll help you. Point you down a road, anyway. Could
be where you want to go. Could be where you need to
go. That's not always the same place, you know."

Katy sighed again. "Tell me a story," she said.

"What kind of story?"

"Something about the crow girls."

"The crow girls," Jack repeated.

He leaned his head back against the sofa, which made his hat push up and fall down over his eyes.

"I can do that," he said.

4.

This is how it was in the long ago: Everyone respected the crow girls. Didn't matter where you were, walking the medicine lands or right here in this world with the roots and dirt underfoot. You could look up and call their names, and there they'd be looking back down at you, two pieces of magic perched high up in a forever tree, black feathers shining, dark eyes watching, heads cocked, listening.

Some people say Raven was older, and wiser, too, but the crow girls were kinder. Any mischief they got into never hurt anyone who didn't deserve it. Knew all the questions and most of the answers, always did. Never had rules, never told you what to do, but they would teach you how to find your own answers, if you asked nicely enough.

Now no one remembers them. Not that way.

I think maybe we started to forget when we stopped looking up. Instead of remembering there was a world of sky up there above our heads, we'd sit on the ground and look at our feet. We'd get together around the trunk of some old tree and tell stories, consider how it was that the world began, try to make sense of how we got here and why— same as people do now, except we did it first, because we were here first. Back then, we were the people. Animal people. Same as you, but feathered and furred and scaled. Those stories you tell each other, you got them from us, all of them. First World, the Garden, the Ocean of Blood, the Mother's Womb.

Everybody would take a turn, make up how they thought it was. Except for Raven and the crow girls. They didn't have to speak. They didn't have to make up stories. Because they knew. They were there, right from the beginning when the medicine lands came up out of the long ago and this world began.

Only the corbæ remember that first story. But Raven and the crow girls never needed to tell it and no one ever really listens to me. Problem is, I didn't always remember it. It took me a long time, trying on different sets of words the way some of us try on skins, until I finally got past guessing and into re- membering. I guess I ended up like that little boy crying wolf, told so many stories that when I finally got hold of the real ones, no one was ready to listen to me anymore.

No, that's not true. People listen. They just don't believe.

5.

Didn't he go on, Moth thought as they sat around listen- ing to another of Jack's stories later that night. But this was a good one. Moth had heard it before. All about how you didn't fall from grace, but into it.

Jack continued the tale:

"Cody, he's looking around. Trying to get the corbæ to understand, but they're not listening. Those crows don't listen to much except for what they've got to say themselves.

" 'See,' Cody, he tries again, 'If you're going to be pure and good, you can't be sexy. You can't be creative. You can't think for yourself. You want to get along with the big boss, you've got to be an obedient little sheep.'

"Raven, he laughs. 'You think we don't know that?' he says.

" 'Maybe some of you still do,' Cody says right back. 'But most of you forgot.' "

Moth nodded. Cody and the crowfolk never got along in Jack's stories. Canid and corbæ, they were like oil and water. Sometimes Jack told a story from one viewpoint, sometimes from the other, but it always came back to how most of the time they agreed, they just didn't know it, which didn't make them all that different from ordinary folks. 'Course there was one thing hardly anybody agreed on: Everybody thought sex and knowledge was what got folks booted out of paradise, but like so much else, the churchmen got it wrong. People didn't find the potential for paradise until they left the garden and started thinking for themselves. Screwed up more often than they didn't, but hell, everybody made mistakes. Another word for that was "experience." The only reason any of them were here tonight was because of some mistake or other.

Take Benny; he never could hold down a life. Man had a serious gambling jones, would bet on a traffic light if he could find the percentage in it. One day he lost the big one—had the moneymen on his ass and the next thing he knew, job, house, family were all gone, just like that, whole life changed from one day to the next. Says his mama used to take him to the track when he was a kid, that's where he caught the fever, but Moth didn't see that as an excuse. A man had to take responsibility for his own life at some point. Benny had been a good-looking man once, before the alcohol poisoning settled in. He could clean himself up. He just wasn't ready yet. Maybe he never would be.

Anita, now she was a piece of work. On one hand, she was a first-class accountant—did Moth's books for the junkyard, the ones he showed the feds and the real ones— on the other, a sensei-level mechanic. If she couldn't fix it, sometimes with no more than bobby pins and duct tape, well, it probably couldn't be fixed. A stand-up woman. Stuck to her man through a lot of bad times, put him through law school, the whole number, then got dumped for a trophy wife when he made partner.

A handsome woman, but not pretty enough to be an important lawyer's wife. The man didn't even see that she'd be looked after. Took her for everything and laughed when she tried to fight back. Moth didn't think she'd ever fully recovered from the betrayal. But she wasn't one to quit. When her husband stole away her old life, she turned around and made herself a new one, worked in a diner where Moth first met her while she took a few of those courses you see advertised on match-book covers. Did so well on them she could've got a job with anybody, but she was through with the high-roller crowd and came to work for Moth instead. She never said why, but Moth knew. He and his crew could give her the one thing nobody else was interested in offering: a sense of family.

Hank, he just got himself born into the wrong family, simple as that. Junkie mother, old man a mean drunk when he wasn't doing time. The only surprise with Hank was that he'd turned out to have as good a heart as he did. In and out of foster homes and juvie hall since he was five, a couple of turns in county, and one stretch in the pen after that. He had more reason to be bitter than anyone here, maybe, but it didn't pan out that way. He was always picking up strays, helping somebody out. Kept what he was feeling locked up pretty tight behind an easy disposition, which Moth didn't think was nec- essarily a good thing, but he understood. Brought up the way Hank had been, you learned pretty quick not to give anything away.

Now Jack, he was the kind of man who, one day, just up and walked away from everything he had. Maybe it was a mistake, maybe it was the only right thing to do. Hard to know for sure without understanding his history, but Moth knew the type. Once upon a time, people might've called him a hobo, now he was just another bum.

Moth leaned back in his lawn chair and shook a smoke

free from the pack he kept in the sleeve of his T-shirt. As he fired it up, he considered the red-haired woman who'd taken to hanging around with Jack the last year or so. They were another kind of oil and water, didn't seem to mix at all, but they broke the rules and got on well, so go figure. Katy had to be a third of Jack's sixty-some years and two-thirds his size, a small street punk to his old-timey hobo with her hair shaved on the sides, long on top before it fell down in dreads going halfway down her back. Hard to tell what she looked like under those green leggings and the oversized purple sweater, but she had a sweet, heart-shaped face and the bluest eyes he'd ever seen.

He didn't know what had put her on the street, but a nice-looking kid like that, it had to be something bad. She might have done time. She had that stillness down pat, the ability to sit so quiet she became pretty much invisible. The only other place Moth had seen that was inside. He'd learned the trick from an old habitual con who'd taken him under his wing—back before he'd discovered the weight room and had needed an edge, just to stay alive. Once he'd put on some muscle and got himself a don't-screw-with-me attitude he didn't much need to be invisible anymore, but it wasn't something you forgot.

Jack was finishing up his story with a new ending: Cody got a few of the foxfolk to help him trick Raven out of his magic cauldron—it looked like a tin can, this time around—and started stirring up some trouble out of it again. 'Course Raven would get it back, but that'd be another story.

Moth took a drag from his smoke and flicked it away. The butt landed in a shower of sparks in the dirt and one of his dogs growled. Judith, the pit bull. Still jumpy after living with Moth for going on three years now. Her previous owner had turned her out on the dogfight circuit before he'd run into an unfortunate accident and Moth had inherited her. Moth never felt sorry for the way things had worked out. Any time he got an attack of conscience,

he just had to take a look at the webwork of scars that
circled her throat and ran like a city street map along her
flanks and stomach.

Beside his chair, Ranger stirred. He was a big German
shepherd, the alpha dog in Moth's pack, ninety pounds
of goofy good humor that could turn instantly serious on
a word from Moth. Ranger checked Judith out, then
turned his attention to Jack, dark gaze fixed on him like
he was thinking of taking a bite out of him. Jack brought
that out in all the dogs, even good-humored Ranger. None
of them ever took to him. "Too much crow in me," Jack
said when Hank mentioned it one time.

Jack and his crows. Moth shook his head. He'd never
seen such a pack of badass birds before, always hanging
around the yard, teasing the dogs. But he let them be
because he could see they were just being playful, keeping the dogs on their toes, not being mean. Moth couldn't
abide meanness.

He leaned down to scratch Ranger behind the ear, then
lit up another cigarette. Hank gave him a look. When
Moth nodded, Hank got up and fetched another round of
beer from inside Moth's trailer. Four bottles. Jack and
Katy were drinking some kind of herb tea they'd brought
along in a thermos. Smelled like heaven, but Moth had
tried it once before. It tasted like what you might get if
you brewed up a handful of garbage and weeds.

"Didn't that story have a different ending the last time
you told it?" Benny asked.

Jack shrugged. "Maybe. But it's a true story. What
you've got to remember is that Cody and Raven never
had just the one go at each other. Things that happen
between them happen over and over again. Sometimes
the one of them's on top, sometimes the other."

"But how true are they?" Hank wanted to know.

Moth caught an odd note in Hank's voice, like the
question was more important than he was letting on.

"True as I can tell them," Jack said.

Anita nodded. "Truth's important."

"But it's not the most important thing we can offer each other," Katy said.

Now Moth was intrigued. Katy never had much to say of an evening. She'd sit there, smiling, listening, quiet. Her voice had a husky quality, like she didn't use it often.

"And what would that be?" he asked.

Katy turned to him and Moth was struck all over again by the blue of her eyes. It was like a piece of the bluest summer sky had got caught in them and decided to stay.

"Playing fair," she said.

Moth could go with that. Sometimes the truth did nobody any good, but playing fair—that never hurt. Karma was the big recycler. Everything you put out came back again.

Benny stood up from his lawn chair and added a couple of pieces of an old wooden chair to the fire they had going in the oil drum. It was a good night. The moon was hanging low, like it was playing hide-and-seek with them, just the rounded top showing up from behind the roof of the abandoned factory that loomed over the back end of the junkyard. The sky was clear—not like last night. Moth had been out doing a couple of deliveries and for awhile there he'd thought he might drown every time he had to leave the cab. The dogs were quiet. Nobody prowling around looking to get a piece of the fortune in cash that he didn't have but was still supposed to be stashed somewhere in the yard.

He did have a fortune here, but nobody who came looking for it ever recognized it for what it was. Family.

Jack told another story, one Moth hadn't heard before, then he and Katy headed off into the night, Jack making for his trailer, Katy walking with him across the rubble-strewn yard before cutting off on her own. Nobody knew where Katy slept and Moth had never tried to find out.

Benny was the next to leave. He had a room in the basement of a rooming house over on MacNeil this month. Moth had the feeling he wouldn't make his September rent. Benny'd never had the same address for more than a couple of months for as long as Moth had known him.

"You need me tomorrow?" Anita asked.

Moth shook his head.

"Think I'll visit my sister then. We were talking about taking the kids over to the island for the day and here the summer's almost over."

Her sister wasn't blood family. She'd met Susie while she was still working at the diner, helped her out, got close in the way a crisis can bring people together. It was something neither of them had been looking for and maybe that was why they found it.

"You need any money?" Moth asked.

"Nah, I'm still flush."

She left, walking deeper into the junkyard to the old VW bus she'd been sleeping in all summer, and then there was only Moth and Hank and the dogs, sitting out under the sky, smelling the night air, watching sparks from the fire jump over the rim of the oil drum to die in the dirt.

After awhile Moth turned to Hank. "Terry said you asked him to run Eddie to the bank tonight."

"You don't mind?"

"Why should I?"

"No reason."

Hank picked up a pebble and tossed it against the side of the oil drum. The soft *ping* it made lifted all the dogs' heads.

"You ever wonder about Jack?" he asked, not looking at Moth. "Where he gets those stories of his? Why he tells them?"

Moth shook another smoke out of his pack, lit it. "Helps him make sense of things, I guess. Or maybe it's just something he's got to do. Like Benny has to take a bet."

"I think maybe there's more to it than that."

Moth remembered that question Hank had asked Jack earlier. He took a drag from his cigarette, watched the glow from the oil drum through the gray wreath the smoke made when he exhaled.

"How so?" he asked.

"I saw two of them last night. Bird girls. Like the people in his stories."

He'd known all day that something was bothering Hank, but Moth was never one to push. If Hank wanted advice, needed help, he'd ask. Moth had thought maybe Hank was trying to get some girl off the street again, or wanting to help somebody make bail. Something simple. Nothing like this.

"You want to run that by me again?" he said.

He sat and smoked while Hank told him about the woman he'd stopped to help last night, how he'd been shot, how these two girls came out of nowhere, killed the guy, healed up Hank's shoulder with nothing more than spit.

"The guy shot you," he said when Hank fell silent.

Hank nodded and started to lift his shirt.

"You don't have to do that," Moth told him. "I believe you."

But Hank already had his T-shirt off. Moth leaned closer and saw the white pucker of a scar on Hank's shoulder. They'd been moving scrap to the back of the junkyard yesterday, shirts off, sweating under the hot afternoon sun. Hank hadn't had that scar yesterday.

"Guy was a pro?" he said.

"It wasn't the first time he shot someone," Hank told him. "I could see it in his eyes when he was standing over me—just before the second girl killed him."

"Hard to kill someone like that—blade in the back. Usually takes awhile to die."

"I thought about that—later."

Moth had to laugh. "Maybe she was using spit on the blade, too."

Hank smiled. He put his shirt on again and settled back in his chair.

"You ever hear of anything like this before?" he asked.

"Only in Jack's stories. Maybe you should talk to him."

"I don't know," Hank said. "Jack's not much of a one for straight answers."

"Well, that kind of depends on whether you take him literally or not."

He finished his cigarette as Hank worked that through.

"Jesus," Hank said after a moment. "You're saying his stories are true?"

Moth shrugged. "They're true for him. He makes no secret about that. How that translates into things other folks can experience, I don't know."

"True for him," Hank repeated softly. "And now for me."

"Maybe you should call that woman, too."

Hank gave him a blank look.

"Think about it, kid," Moth said. "The guy was trying to kill her."

"Animal people."

"Say what?"

"She said she was out looking for animal people."

Moth sighed. He looked out across the junkyard. The moon was almost down now and the familiar shapes of the junked cars and scrap had taken on odd shapes and shadows in the starlight. He'd never taken Jack's stories at face value, but right at this moment, he didn't know what to think anymore.

"Sounds like she found them," he said finally.

Hank nodded thoughtfully. "Found something, anyway."

6.

After the events of the previous night, the last place Lily wanted to be was in the basement of some punk club, taking pictures of kids half her age who had way too much attitude and too little sense of personal hygiene. She'd touched a piece of magic last night and this was anything but. The three members of Bitches in Heat made her feel like a tired and worn-out old woman, especially the lead singer/guitarist with her wasted junkie body and practiced sneer. She called herself Vulva de Ville.

This is not innovative, Lily wanted to tell her, having shot hundreds of bands and seen far too much attitude to be charmed by this same-old, same-old anymore. Billy Idol and Sid Vicious were there before the Bitches. And Elvis long before any of them.

The other two members of the band were merely surly, but they had the same emaciated bodies. Looking at the three of them through her camera lens, all she saw was a clot of leather and denim, piercings and tattoos, stringy hair and wasted faces. They were either junkies, or trying too hard, and neither appealed to her. She didn't like capturing that kind of an image on film. It felt too much as though she was pandering to the same asinine art directors who thought bruises on anorexic models would sell clothes or makeup. It was like using child abuse to sell product and the concept repulsed her as much as equating heroin use with having a good time the way bands like this did. You didn't romanticize those sorts of activities, she believed; you tried to eradicate them.

"Hey, this'll be cool," the lead singer said.

Lily had been focusing on the drummer, so she wasn't aware of what de Ville had been up to until she lifted her head from her viewfinder. De Ville had tied off one of her twig-thin arms with a piece of rubber tubing to make the veins pop up and was clowning around with a hypodermic needle.

Lily turned to Rory. "If she starts shooting up, I'm out of here."

"Christ," de Ville told her, the sneer having slid into caricature by this point. "Lighten up why dontcha?" But she tossed the needle onto the cardboard box that stood in front of the sofa and was serving as a table.

"You almost done?" Rory asked.

"A couple more shots," Lily told him. She looked at the band again. "If you could all get together on the sofa and maybe lean a little in toward each other. . . ."

She immediately regretted the suggestion. The three women fell into a tumble on the battered sofa and began groping each other, hands going up T-shirts and cupping crotches, faces attempting lusty sexual expressions that only came off as pathetic leers. Lily sighed, returned her eye to her viewfinder and finished the roll.

"You owe me," she told Rory afterward as they climbed the stairs toward the smoke and noise of the club above.

"No, *Spin* does," he said, pausing in the stairwell so that they could hear each other talk.

Lily stopped beside him and adjusted the strap of her camera bag. She was carrying way too much stuff in there as usual. She doubted she'd used even half of the lenses she'd brought along.

"I'm not talking about a paycheck," she said.

"I know. And you're right—I do owe you for getting you into this. But I wanted the best and so, naturally, the first person I thought of was you."

Lily had to smile. "Flattery's good—but you still owe me."

"This is true."

Lily had known Rory Crowther for years. He was a freelance writer, forever working on the proverbial Great North American Novel, paying the bills with articles and the occasional short story, but mostly with the jewelry he made in his apartment on Stanton Street and sold through various craft stores and at fairs. They first met while working on a piece for *In the City*, Newford's entertainment weekly. Early on in their relationship, they had explored a more romantic involvement than they shared now, but they soon realized that they got along better as friends. Ten years later, they were still loyal confidantes, getting together at least once or twice a week, maintaining their friendship through any number of ultimately unhappy relationships and, in Rory's case, a failed marriage.

They were here in Your Second Home for an article on the reemergence of punk on the Newford music scene that Rory was writing for *Spin* magazine. The club was a blue-collar bar during the day, a music club at night.

When he came by in a cab to pick her up earlier in the evening, she'd told him about what had happened last night, but gave him only a bare-bones version, no more than she'd told Donna in an email she'd sent off this morning: She'd been mugged, but a cab driver had come by in time to help her. Yes, she was fine now, really, and she didn't really want to talk about it anymore. She just wanted to put it behind her.

She had no idea why she was so reticent about sharing the details of her experience with her two best friends, yet had been willing to blurt out to Joey Bennett that she'd been out walking the streets looking for animal people. It wasn't that what had happened was so impossible, or at least it wasn't only that, but she found herself no more able to understand her reluctance than she was able to discuss what had happened in any more detail than she already had.

"Come on," Rory was saying. He nodded his head back down the stairs where Bitches in Heat were probably shooting up now. "It wasn't so bad. Be honest. It was kind of like passing the scene of an accident, wasn't it? You don't really want to see what's going on, but you can't stop yourself from looking."

"I suppose. But you know what kept me shooting?"

Rory shook his head.

"The thought of how, ten or twenty years from now, they'll come across these pictures in a scrapbook or somewhere and realize just how pathetic and foolish they really were."

"If they live that long."

That took Lily's smile away. "If they live that long," she agreed.

They continued up the stairs, a wall of sound hitting them when they reached the top. Helldogz were on stage—it was a canine theme night, Lily supposed, since the third band, who'd played in between the sets by this band and the opening act Bitches in Heat, had been a couple of rappers who called themselves Howl. Helldogz's lead singer reminded Lily of Henry Rollins—he had that same look of pumped-up muscles topped by a buzz cut, neither of which appealed to her—but she liked the raw honesty of his delivery and the band could really play. There was no posing, no pretense, just solid musicianship with something to say, albeit at an earsplitting, Spinal Tap/amps-set-to-eleven volume.

Rory tried to tell her something and she had to shake her head. He repeated it, leaning forward, mouth almost in her ear. "I said, do you want to take any more shots of them?"

She shook her head again. They waited until the song was over, stood through another, then finally went outside where the usual noise of Foxville's Lee Street seemed subdued in comparison.

"Share a cab home?" Rory asked. "Or should we walk?"

Lily knew a moment's nervousness, remembering where walking had got her last night, but she refused to let it take hold.

"Let's walk," she said.

"Okay. But let me be a chauvinist and carry your camera bag for awhile."

"It's all right."

"Sure. That's why you've been fidgeting with it all night. If I know you, it weighs a ton."

Reluctantly, she handed it over. Rory pretended to stagger under its weight, almost dropping to his knees before he laboriously straightened up.

Lily smiled. "You know you've probably gone down

at least thirty cool points so far as these kids are concerned.''

The kids she referred to stood about like a tide of
leather and denim and combat boots, washed up against
the wall of the club, pooling in small clusters along the
curb and down the pavement, hair spiked here, long there,
dark smudges around the eyes of the women, lips bright,
the men stony-eyed, looking tough. Some of them probably were, but for most of them it was a pose.

''Screw 'em,'' Rory said.

He headed south on Lee Street and Lily fell in step
beside him. The farther they got from the club, the quieter
the street became. There was still traffic, but the stores
here were all closed and there were no clubs or restaurants until one reached the Kelly Street Bridge.

''So what do you know about gypsy cabs?'' Lily asked
after they'd been walking for awhile.

Rory shrugged. ''What's to know? The way the city's
got everything regulated these days, it costs a fortune to
get a cab license, that's just saying you can even get
someone to sell one, so some people forgo the formalities
and operate without the blessing of city council. From all
I hear, it's been going on forever.''

Lily nodded to show she was listening.

''Most of them are two-bit affairs,'' Rory went on.
''Just some guy with a car cruising the club strips at
closing time, maybe he's selling beer or liquor out of his
trunk as well. You settle on a price and he takes you
where you want to go. You and me, we never see them—
or at least they don't stop for us—because we don't look
right.''

''How would we have to look?'' Lily asked.

''I don't know. I guess it's not so much a look as an
attitude. These people know each other, even if they've
never met before—you know what I mean?''

Lily nodded. It was probably the same way she could
always tell a serious photographer from someone who
was just snapping a shot.

"Have you ever been in one?" she asked.

"No, but Christy has."

Rory had taken a fiction writing workshop with Christy Riddell a few years ago and they'd hit it off, becoming friends. They didn't write the same sort of thing at all—Christy specialized in collecting urban folklore, writing it up either as short stories or, more rarely, in a more traditional scholarly style—but they both seemed to suffer from the same block of not being able to write anything longer than a novella. Lily had met him a few times and liked him. She knew some people thought there was something a bit standoffish about him, as though he observed the world, rather than let himself be engaged by it and the people in it, but she'd long since discovered it was only a front.

"I wonder if he'd know this Joey Bennett fellow who helped me out last night," she said. "I should ask him."

Rory gave her a considering look. "You know how in fairy tales the princess always falls into the arms of her rescuer?"

"It's not like that," Lily said. "I just didn't get a chance to thank him properly, that's all."

But Rory wouldn't let it go. "Are you okay with this?" he asked. She could hear the worry in his voice. "I mean, you're taking it all pretty well, but getting mugged—it's pretty serious business. I know I'd have the shakes for weeks."

Lily wanted to lie—it would make everything so much easier—but she couldn't. Not to him.

"I . . . I'm not entirely okay," she said. She stopped and turned to look at him. "But I'm not ready to talk about it yet. You understand, don't you?"

She could see him try to hide the hurt that she wouldn't confide in him, but it didn't work. They knew each other too well.

"I'm sorry," she said. "There's just a few things I have to work through. I'm not trying to shut you out. Honestly. It's just . . . I don't even know what it is. I guess that's part of what I have to work out."

She gave him a wan smile, hoping he'd understand, hoping this wouldn't change things between them, but knowing it already had. Oh, why did it even have to have come up?

"It's okay," Rory told her.

They started walking again, an uncomfortable awkwardness keeping pace with them for blocks as they tried to get past the tension that had crept up and settled in between them. Lily was beginning to feel so miserable that, even though it felt like the wrong time, she was ready to tell him anyway. But they had reached her street by then, turned down it, and had arrived in front of her building. She took a steadying breath and let the moment pass.

"I'll drop the color rolls off to be developed first thing in the morning," she said. "The black and whites should be ready by the afternoon, unless I get to them tonight."

Rory shook his head. "Get some rest," he said. He handed her the camera bag. "And, Kit?"

She couldn't find the usual smile that came when he used his pet name for her. Kit, as in Kit Carson, wilderness scout. All she could do was look at him.

"Don't let this get you down," he said. "You need to work something out for yourself, that's all. I really do understand. Okay?"

The words reassured her, but the hug he gave her reassured her more.

"Thanks," she said into his shoulder.

"Hey, what're friends for?"

She meant to go right to bed when she got up to her apartment, but she wasn't tired. So first she developed the rolls of black-and-white film she'd taken earlier in the evening and hung them up to dry on the clothesline she kept in her bathroom for that purpose, then she went into her study and booted up her computer, logging on to her Web server. When she checked for messages, a little box popped up saying, "You Have New Mail!" and she clicked on "OK." The box went away and she scrolled through messages from the photography listserver she was on, deleting each one after she'd skimmed its contents.

The last message was from Donna.

Lily sighed. She still felt a little wrung out from talking to Rory and now here was Donna who'd be asking all the same questions he had. They weren't meeting face-to-face, so Donna wouldn't be able to read her mood the way Rory had, but Donna also wouldn't let up until she was satisfied that Lily was one hundred percent okay.

Sighing again, Lily began to read. As usual, Donna used snippets of Lily's previous message in her own letter. Lily understood how it made replying easier, but it was the one thing she missed about regular mail. She never liked having her own words come back to her this way.

```
Sender: dgavin@tama.com
Date: Thu, 29 Aug 1996 08:31:09-0500
From: 'Donna Gavin' <dga-
vin@tama.com>
Organization: Tamarack Publishing
To: lcarson2@cybercare.com
Subject: Tell me more


>I know what you'll think

My God, woman, what did you expect me
to think? Who in their right mind
goes walking through the Zone at that
time of night and on her own?


>life doesn't really flash before
>your eyes. It's more like everything
>shuts down. You're still *there* but
>you're watching it happen instead of
>having it actually happen to you.
>It's the strangest experience.
```

Please tell me that you won't be doing this anymore. I don't know how
I'm going to sleep tonight, worrying
that you might be silly enough to be
out there again. Read my electronic
lips: the streets are _not_ safe!!

>came out of nowhere and rescued me.
>Joey Bennett one of those 'What're
>you rebelling against?'/'What have
>you got?' kinds of guys. Like John
>Buckman in our final year at Mawson—
>--remember him?-- except Joey doesn't
>have that meanness in his eyes.

I remember too well. He used to walk
along behind me in the halls with
this exaggerated limp and then look
all innocent whenever I turned
around. He wasn't just mean--he was
smirky mean. I still hate him.

Which doesn't endear this Joey Bennett of yours to me. I mean, I'm glad
he was there and everything, but all
I can picture is someone too good-
looking for his own good and creepy.

>I still have no idea why I can be
>calm about all of this.

I can't figure it out either. And
you're being _so_ sketchy with the
details. You tell me this gypsy cabs
driver rescues you, but what happened
to the guy who attacked you? Are you
sure you're okay? What did the police
say? How long were you stuck dealing

with them? Was he charged? Is he out
on the street again?

And really, _what_ were you doing in
the Zone anyway? Don't keep me hanging on with this. I need to know
ASAP.

I'd tell you my news, but I don't have anything that can even compare with yours
and if you want to know the truth, I wish
you didn't either. But I did have lunch
with that fellow named Peter I met at Mir-
anda's party and he asked me to go to a
movie with him next week. And before you
ask, I said yes, except I don't have anything to wear and I'm about to get my period and I think it'll be a disaster.

Write back as _soon_ as you read
this.

Love

D.

Lily had wanted to tell Donna everything, but she
hadn't known where to begin. It was like talking to Rory.
She'd already told both of them about Jack and his stories, but it required a great leap of faith to jump from
stories as they were told, no matter how charming, to the
idea that things in such stories could be real. She wasn't
sure either of them could make the leap—especially not
Rory. One of the things he and Christy were forever arguing about was how Christy wrote his stories of fantas-
tical urban folklore as though the events and things
described in them were real.

Maybe she should talk to Christy about it, except she
couldn't even begin seeing herself do that. If she couldn't

talk to her best friends, how could she bring it up with a relative stranger?

You talked to Joey about it, she thought. And you only just met him.

Yeah, but he was there.

No, like Rory, Donna was simply going to have to wait until Lily had worked things through to the point where she could talk about it, whatever that point might be. At least she had an idea as to where she could start. First thing tomorrow, after she'd dropped off the color film to be processed, she would try to find Jack and talk to him.

She returned her attention to her computer screen, but more than three minutes had passed since she'd touched the keyboard or mouse and the screensaver had long since kicked in. The dark screen drew her gaze, swallowing it until she hit the "Shift" key to bring her program back. Moving the cursor to "Reply," she clicked her mouse. The screen came up with a blank box, the sending information for a reply message to Donna automatically filled in above it.

Don't be mad at me, she thought as she moved her cursor to the top line of the box and began to type.

7.

Hank started the morning by walking through the Tombs. He took a familiar route that wound through empty lots and streets fronted by derelict buildings and eventually brought him to a large, flat stretch of pavement well north of Gracie Street that he'd cleared at the beginning of the summer. It might have been a parking lot once, or the ground floor of a building—there was no way of telling anymore. It didn't really matter. It served his purpose now.

At one rubble-strewn edge he emptied the contents of a small paper bag of dog kibbles onto the pavement, then he walked out into the middle of the open area and stripped down to the exercise shorts he was wearing under his jeans and laced up his running shoes. He did a hundred sit-ups, followed by a hundred push-ups, letting the count hold his thoughts like a form of meditation and clear his head. It wasn't until he was a half hour into his tai chi exercises that the dog showed up.

Hank didn't know what kind of a dog it was—Tombsmutt was the way Moth described it—but there had to be some shepherd in its background, a lot of mastiff, and maybe some ghost wolf in the blood, letting it move like silk in a soft breeze for all its size, silent and almost invisible when still. It stood thirty inches at the shoulder, wide-chested, head massive, body leaner than a mastiff but carrying a lot more bulk than a shepherd. There was nothing gentle about it, but it didn't display any aggressive behavior either—unless you tried to approach it.

After the one glance, Hank ignored the dog, finishing his exercises while the dog ate. When he went for his run, the dog fell in beside him. It wouldn't let him pet it, wouldn't let him near it, but every morning it ate the food he put out and joined Hank for his run.

They took a circuitous route through the streets, abandoned tenements and factories rearing up on both sides. There were squatters in the buildings, runaway teenagers and less innocent inhabitants: junkies, bikers, bums, crazy people who were no longer legally crazy once the public money to keep them in an institution dried up. He didn't see them, not at this time of the morning, but he knew he was watched. Not every day, not from the same building, but the squatters knew him, saw him go by, a man wearing only a pair of shorts with a big mongrel dog loping at his side. Nobody bothered them.

One morning a biker looked up from the Harley he was working on, wiped his greasy hands on his greasier jeans, and wanted to know the dog's name.

"Never asked him," Hank had replied.

The biker had nodded, needing no more explanation, just as Hank didn't need to know what he was doing up so early when most of the bikers slept till noon. He'd never given the dog a name, never gave any of the animals he brought back to Moth's a name. That was Moth's thing. And Anita's.

But this morning he looked at the dog running so casually beside him, and wondered, not about its name, but if it knew anything about animal people.

When he got back from his run, he put on his jeans and T-shirt and went down to Cray's gym to have a shower and shave. The dog was already gone by the time he stepped off the pavement to head back out through the rubbled lots surrounding it.

Jack wasn't home when Hank dropped by the school bus later in the day, but Katy was. He didn't see her at first, though she was right out in the open. He remembered what Moth had said about her invisibility once. He'd known exactly what Moth was talking about, though he'd learned it a lot earlier than Moth had. He had that trick down by the time he was five. Jack had been standing nearby, listening, and said, "Maybe she's a ghost," but he and Moth knew better. There was no such thing as ghosts. Dead was dead. If anything survived the body, neither could think of one good reason that it would stick around.

Katy wasn't a ghost. Even with her penchant for bright colors and that red hair of hers, she simply had it down pat, that knack for not being noticed.

Hank slipped into his own quiet mode when he reached Jack's place, sensing someone nearby but not seeing anyone. He stood there for almost five minutes, blending into the background himself, until Katy came into view, slowly, the way Lewis Carroll had described his Cheshire cat's comings and goings. When Hank finally focused on her, she was out in front of the bus, propped up against an arm of the sofa with her legs stretched out, reading a book called *Practical Bird-watching* and drinking coffee.

"Is there an unpractical kind of bird-watching?" Hank had to ask.

She looked up and smiled. "Sure. Doing it without reading the book first."

She brought her knees up to make room for him and
he sat down. She looked like somebody's punky kid sister
today, no makeup, red hair in a ponytail that was pulled
through the hole in the back of her baseball cap, wearing
purple jean cutoffs and a bright yellow tank top, barefoot.
He'd never noticed the tattoo on her shoulder before:

It looked like a Japanese ideograph. The simple black
lines seemed to retain the essence of brush marks, no easy
feat. He wondered who the tattooist had been and what
the symbol meant.

"Anything in there about bird girls?" he asked instead.

"You mean girl birds, don't you? What species?"

Hank thought about it for a moment. Jack wasn't here
and he needed to talk.

"It gets more complicated than that," he said.

He gave her an abbreviated rundown of what had happened to him the other night. He didn't make himself out
to be a hero, he was just passing by. He didn't talk up
the miracle of a raw bullet hole turning into a scar, just
like that, from one moment to the next, bruises disappearing like they never were, but he did search and find
the right words to describe the birdishness of the girls
who had dropped in from who knew where to help him
out.

"The woman," he said. "Lily. She thought they were
animal people—like in Jack's stories."

Katy didn't even blink an eye.

"You've seen the crow girls," she said. "You're so
lucky."

That sense of stepping outside the world returned to
Hank. Looked like *everybody* had bought into this stuff

and he never knew it. He thought they were all hearing stories, no more, just like him.

"Did you ever run into something you'd never heard of before and then suddenly you hear about it wherever you turn?"

He wasn't even aware he'd been talking aloud until Katy replied.

"Sure," she said. "It's called syncronicity."

"Right."

"It happens way more than people think. What they're calling coincidence is really just patterns coming together. There's people that can see them, but I wouldn't want to be like them. It'd ruin the surprise."

Hank nodded slowly, like he was listening, but in his mind he was backing up their conversation. Bird girls. Crow girls. Sure, why not? If you were going to take Jack's stories at face value, it fit. Those two girls *had* been like a pair of raggedy crows.

"You heard about these crow girls from Jack?" he asked.

She nodded. And now Hank, thinking about it, realized that he had, too, though he couldn't reach out and pick a particular story that he remembered them from. But there was always a pair of them, up to mischief, living on Zen time. According to Jack, people changed, inside where you couldn't mark it, just from seeing them.

Hank touched his shoulder, then let his hand fall. Of course people changed. Once you put these bird girls into the equation, you had to redefine the world.

"You believe everything Jack says?" he asked.

Katy shook her head. "Jack says she can't kill me, but he's wrong about that."

"Who's 'she'?" Hank asked.

"My sister."

"I didn't know you had a sister."

"I don't. At least I don't anymore. It's complicated."

Silence hung between them for a long moment.

"There are no guarantees," Hank said finally. "I guess we all know that. Anybody can get hurt. But maybe what

Jack meant was that we won't let anything happen to you—not without a fight.''

"There's nothing anybody can do about it," she told him. "It's just the way it is."

Hank liked the sound of that even less. "Give me an address and I'll explain the situation to whoever's bothering you."

"It's not like that," Katy said.

"So what is it like?"

He wouldn't have thought it possible, but a half hour later he left with a story even stranger than the one he'd brought with him.

The day was starting to catch up on him by the time he reached Tony's store on Flood Street, just a few blocks south of Gracie. He normally slept from midmorning until around four, catching his six to seven hours and then having breakfast when most people were thinking about dinner. It was almost three-thirty now and he could feel it. A dryness behind his eyes. Bad taste in his mouth. Everything had an edge, especially his own nerves.

He was too old to be pulling all-nighters, he thought as he closed the door behind him.

A 45 by The Animals was spinning on the turntable— "Don't Let Me Be Misunderstood." The state-of-the-art sound system made you think the band was still together and playing in the store. Tony could as easily have been playing some classic Glenn Gould piano, Lester Young sax, Moth's favorite—Boxcar Willie—or something by local punk-folksinger Annabel Blue. It was that kind of a place. The store had no name, only a cardboard sign in the window reading, "USED RECORDS, TAPES." All they dealt in was vinyl, cassettes, and 8-tracks. No CDs. You didn't want to start Tony on an analog-versus-digital argument. Most of the off-the-street trade was DJs, buying and selling 12-inches. The real business was done by mail order, shipping product all over the world.

Tony looked up when Hank came in, a grin splitting his face. He always reminded Hank of a ventriloquist's

dummy, exaggerated puppet features peppered with
freckles and topped by a shock of curly red hair combed
up and back in an impressive ducktail. There wasn't
much meat to him—he was too lean, narrow-hipped, and
long-limbed—but he was stronger than he looked and a
stand-up guy. He and Hank went way back to juvie. The
only reason Tony wasn't doing time these days was because Hank had put up the money for the store, pretty
much forcing Tony to go legit. Music was his one passion
and having the taste of what he had, he wasn't willing to
risk losing it all for some quick money that was all too
likely to put him back inside. Not the first time out,
maybe, or even the second or third, but sooner or later.

"You look like shit," Tony said.

"Haven't slept yet."

"You want to crash in back for a few hours?"

"Not yet," Hank said. "Maybe later. Anything new?"

Tony smiled. "If what you're really asking is, 'Where
are the tapes?' " he said, "I haven't got them duped yet.
I told you they wouldn't be ready till Friday."

Whenever Hank found some choice vinyl, he left it
with Tony; in exchange, he got a tape of whatever it was
he'd brought in. Earlier in the week he'd come across
some classic 'Trane on their original pressings, including
a mint copy of the 1957 Prestige issue of *Traneing In.*

"Maybe I just came by for your company," he said.

"Maybe you just came by to get your messages."

"That, too."

"No one called," Tony told him. "But Marty dropped
by. Wanted to know if you could do some background
checks for a case he's working on."

Martin Caine had an office down around Kelly Street
and walked up a few times a week to check the blues bin
for new stock. Hank occasionally did some investigative
work for him.

"Is he in a hurry?" Hank asked.

Tony shook his head. "He said call him early next
week—which would be Tuesday, I guess, Monday being
a holiday."

"Okay."

When Hank dug a business card out of his pocket, Tony pushed the phone across the counter to him.

"Hot date?" he asked.

· Hank smiled. "You know something I don't?"

He punched in Lily's number and listened to the phone ring on the other end of the line.

8.

There was one thing Moth knew for sure about Hank: He didn't lie.

It made no difference how crazy the story he'd told was, Hank was telling it as it had happened. Moth didn't need the extra proof of the new scar on Hank's shoulder to verify it. But Hank needed something. Moth had seen it in his eyes when he went off for his run this morning, an uncertainty, like Hank didn't trust himself anymore. Didn't trust his own senses.

Which was what brought Moth to Jimmy's Billiards, a prewar pool hall that was still situated above a pawn shop at the corner of Vine and Palm, right in the heart of the Zone. It was just going on noon, but the place was already half-full with the usual crowd, working the tables, nursing drafts on the benches that lined the walls, placing bets, making deals. Moth slid onto a stool at the bar and Jimmy came over with a glass of beer, the head foaming over the sides. He put it down in front of Moth.

Jimmy wasn't the kind of person you brought home for Sunday dinner, not unless your father was a bookie, your mother a cocktail waitress, granny a stripper. He was deceptively overweight—what looked like fat was all muscle. Round-faced, double-chinned, and hairy. His forearms bristled with thick black hair, more of it pushing up through the V of his open shirt. By noon he already had a five-o'clock shadow.

Rumor had it he was a fence, a bookie, a gunrunner,

you name it. Moth knew none of it was true. What Jimmy did was take a cut from those who were and used his place as an office.

"You want a cigar?" Jimmy asked around the fat Cuban he was chewing.

Jimmy's cigar was always unlit, always the same length. For all Moth knew, it was always the same one, but he didn't want to go to where that thought could take him. He shook a cigarette out of his pack and lit up.

"Nah," he said. "I'll stick with these."

Jimmy leaned his large forearms on the bar. "So what's up?"

"I want you to tell me again about that dog-headed man who came in here."

Jimmy nodded. He looked past Moth's shoulder, out across the tables, gaze fixing on something that lay on the other side of the beer poster on the far wall.

"That was something," he said.

This was what he needed for Hank, Moth thought as Jimmy retold a story Moth had only half paid attention to before. Validation. It wasn't only Jack who believed in these kinds of things. Ordinary joes had seen them, too.

9.

Lily arrived early at the Cyberbean Café and took her café au lait and a cranberry muffin over to a small corner table by the window. Outside, the traffic had settled into a post-rush-hour trickle and there was little to hold her interest. She'd already read today's papers, as well as this week's edition of *In the City,* which someone had left behind on her table, so to kill time, she amused herself by taking mental snapshots of the café's patrons, her gaze moving from table to table.

Closest to hand, two Goths who reminded her of the raggedy girls who'd rescued her the other night were sitting with a long-haired flannel-and-jeans type who seemed almost asleep. At the table beyond theirs, three yuppie women chatting animatedly over their coffee with a younger punk woman with short-cropped hair and wearing more earrings and facial jewelry than some of the street vendors outside had on their carts. Near the door was a biker in his leathers and greasy jeans, sitting with a pretty, well-dressed young woman who looked as though she'd come directly from her office job to have a coffee with him. The rest were the usual hodgepodge of students, artist types, and hangers-on, each making their own fashion statements, or lack thereof.

Somehow she missed Joey's entrance. She blinked with surprise when he seemed to materialize beside her table, a mug of plain black coffee in hand.

"Okay if I join you?" he asked.

She nodded. Now that he was here, she was at a bit of a loss as to why she'd agreed to see him. Why, if she'd had his number, she might well have called him if he hadn't picked up the phone first.

"You seem surprised to see me," he said.

"I guess I am. I was surprised you called. But then I was trying to find you, too, so I guess I understand."

"Find me how?"

"My friend Rory—Rory Crowther."

She could hear her voice go up on the last syllable, making a question of it. It was an affectation that always irritated her when she heard others do it and it irritated her more now that she was doing it herself, but Joey only nodded.

"You know him?" she asked.

"We're not friends or anything, but I've run into him. Is he still writing?"

Lily nodded. Wasn't that usually the way, she thought. People always remembered bylines before photo credits.

"Anyway," she went on, "he was telling me about a mutual friend of ours who might know you, so I was thinking of giving him a call, see if he had your number. . . ."

Her voice trailed off.

"Look," he said. "I've got to tell you something. My name's not Joey. It's Hank."

That was going to take some adjusting to, she thought. But it did suit him better.

"Hank," she found herself repeating, testing the name on her tongue.

He nodded. "Hank Walker. I've got this bad habit of not handing out my name the way—" He smiled. "You know. Some people do a business card."

"For safety's sake?" she asked. It made sense, seeing how he was involved in an illegal activity.

"For privacy."

"Oh." She took a sip of her café au lait. "So why are you telling me now?"

"Just to keep things straight between us." He gave her a disarming smile. "In case we decide we want to get to know each other better."

Lily knew a momentary discomfort, not entirely sure what he was leading up to. She took another sip of her coffee and looked around the café.

"It's funny," she said, trying to keep the conversation light, "but people look more interesting today than I remember them being when I was growing up."

Hank raised an eyebrow.

"You know," she said. "There isn't one look anymore, one tribe. Instead the tribes are smaller, more diverse, and the lines blur between them. I'm sure there are still cliques, but they don't seem so obvious anymore and I like that."

"We live in different worlds," Hank said. "Where I come from it's the same as it's always been: There's us and there's them and that's about as complicated as it gets. We look after ourselves, same as everybody else. We just have a smaller resource base. But that's okay. Means there's less to screw up."

"Isn't that kind of insular? There are so many things going on in the world, so many problems. . . ."

"I've given up trying to save the world," Hank said. "All I do now is try to save my small part of it—make sure my family's taken care of."

"Do you have a big family?"

Hank smiled. "Yeah, but it's not the kind you think. It's more like a crew, people looking out for each other, caring for each other—not because nobody else will, but because we want to." He smiled. "Us and them."

"I guess I'd be a 'them.' "

He shrugged.

"But you stopped to help me."

"That's one of my failings. Sticking my nose in where it doesn't belong."

It was an obvious contradiction to what he'd said a moment ago, but Lily didn't call him on it. She'd learned a long time ago that there was nothing cut-and-dried about the way people did what they did, or how they justified it.

"I didn't see anything in the paper about the man who died," she said.

"I don't read the papers, but it doesn't surprise me. Lots of stuff doesn't make the papers, but it still has a huge impact on people's lives."

Lily nodded in agreement. A grandparent dying in their sleep. A new child born into a family. A daughter coming out to her parents. They weren't big news stories, but they still changed the lives of the people who experienced them. Like what had happened to them the other night.

She regarded him for a long moment, trying to understand what had brought him here to see her, what kind of a person he really was. Usually a good judge of character, she couldn't get a take on him at all. The only thing she was relatively sure of was that he didn't mean her any harm.

"Why did you want to see me?" she asked.

"A woman like you has to ask that?"

He said it easily, not like a come-on.

"No, really," she said.

"Really?"

She nodded.

"I have no idea." He looked past her, out the window for a moment, then met her gaze. "This thing we experienced . . . on the one hand, it seems like a dream, like it never really happened. On the other, I can't get it out of my mind. I've listened to Jack's stories for years, but they were always just stories, something to fill up the empty space between nightfall and dawn. Something to take our minds off of the hard times, you know, if only for awhile. But now, knowing those animal people are real . . ."

His voice trailed off.

"It changes everything," Lily said.

"Yeah. And what I can't figure out is, is it good or bad or . . ."

"Just different."

"You've got it."

Only Lily could tell there was more to it, because whatever was haunting the back of his eyes made a trail of uneasy paw prints up her own spine.

"Or more than different," she added.

"You feel it, too?" Hank asked. "It's like we've, I don't know, stumbled onto a secret and there's no backing out of it now. It's just going to keep pulling us deeper and deeper into foreign territory."

Lily nodded. That was exactly how it felt to her.

"So what can we do?" she asked.

"That's the thing, isn't it? We're on unfamiliar ground. I was thinking we could just let it slide, but I feel like a junkie, needing a fix. Not to get high, just not to feel sick, you know? To be well. I keep scaring up strange stories wherever I turn, like I've stepped around a corner and I'm someplace else. Everything looks the same, but it's different now. Changed. And instead of backing off, I want to go deeper—I *need* to know more."

"Like where did they come from?" Lily said. "Those girls from the other night. Where are they now?"

"And what else is out there?"

All around them, the patrons of the café went about their business, but the murmur of their conversations, silverware tinkling against cutlery, the music from the overhead sound system, seemed separate from the two of them sitting here at their table, as though they were cocooned and unmoored—drifting farther and farther from familiar territory.

Suddenly Lily wanted to get out of the place. But she didn't want to be alone.

"Do you want to go someplace and have some dinner?" she asked.

"I don't know. I don't think I'm in the mood for restaurants or crowds right now. Even this place is way too busy."

Again, he was on the same wavelength.

"We could go back to my place," she said, surprising herself. "Have some soup or something."

He didn't say anything.

"Look," she said. "It's just something to eat in a quiet place."

He gave a slow nod. "Soup and some quiet would be good."

10.

It was closing in on midnight and Rory was about to go online when his phone rang. Turning the volume of the radio down, he picked up on the second ring and said hello.

"You weren't sleeping?" Lily asked.

"You know me, Kit. I'm the original night owl. I was just about to go online."

"Oh. Well, I'll let you get to it, then."

Rory sighed. "But what I'm doing now, and it's way more interesting, is talking to you."

"Oh."

"So what's up?"

Lily hesitated. "I just wanted to talk to you about the other night. . . ."

When her voice trailed off, Rory gave her a couple of moments before jumping in.

"I told you," he said. "I'm okay with it. You can talk about it when you're ready, or not at all. We don't have a problem with it."

"But I do want to talk about it. I mean, that's why I'm calling."

Rory couldn't remember Lily ever sounding this unsure of herself. He wished they were talking face-to-face so he could better gauge how she was doing, then realized that was probably why she was doing this over the phone.

"I'm listening," he said.

She laughed, a nervous sound. "I don't know where to begin."

Rory didn't press, thinking it was better if she did this at her own pace.

"Remember the cabbie I told you about?" she said after a moment of dead air.

"Sure."

"He called me today and we got together at the Cyberbean. And then later he came back to my place for soup."

"So . . . do you like him?" Rory asked.

"It's not like that—or at least it's not like that yet. Who knows? His name's not Joey, by the way. It's Hank Walker."

The name rang a bell, but it took Rory a moment to place it.

"I know him," he said. "He's what? Medium height, short brown hair, brown eyes. Sort of tough-looking, but not mean."

"That's him. Where do you know him from?"

"He does some work for Marty Caine."

"Who?"

"You know, the lawyer I was doing all that research for last winter, the original 'Mr. No Comment.' Walker's done investigative work for him from time to time— background checks, legwork stuff. Sort of what I did, except he did it on the streets while I used the libraries."

"So what do you think of him?"

Rory had to smile. No, she wasn't interested in him. Right.

"He wasn't exactly the sort of person you got to know," he said. "He didn't really mix with the other people in the office, but he was good at what he did, so it wasn't like Marty was going to complain."

He looked across the room, remembering. He'd made some comment to Marty about Walker's standoffishness one day and Marty had said, "I'll tell you what's important, Rory. Hank doesn't play the middle ground. If you're his friend, he'll stand by you no matter what comes up; if you're not, if you threaten somebody he cares about, he'll take you down and he won't care what happens to himself in the process. And that's why he's so good at this kind of work. I can only get him to take a job on if he believes in the defendant, but when he does, he gives it a hundred and ten percent. Now tell me, whose side would you rather he was on?"

"So he's driving a cab now," Rory found himself saying.

"I get the sense he does a lot of things," Lily said.

"Only you didn't call me to talk about him."

"No. But he's involved. I guess it started with those stories Jack was telling me."

Rory smiled. "Now we're talking real characters. I keep telling Christy he should get together with him. I mean, you have to wonder. Where does he get that stuff?"

"Well," Lily said. "I think I know."

Rory was quiet for a long moment when Lily had finished her story. What he wanted to say was, Be careful, Kit.

Walker moves in a rough crowd. You don't want to get caught up in it. But that wasn't what she needed to hear right now.

And then there was this other stuff, right out of stories that Christy or Jack would tell.

"I believe you, Kit," he said instead.

"Really?"

"Why would you lie?"

"I wouldn't. It's just . . . I don't know if I'd believe myself. But I was there and I saw what happened."

"I can see why you needed time before talking about it."

"I know. It's all so weird. What do you think the girl meant with that business about the cuckoo?"

"Beats me," Rory told her. "It sort of sounds like a folk song, but I don't see the connection." He paused for a moment, thinking he heard someone running down the hallway outside his apartment. "You know, the way you described those women they could almost be our crow girls."

"You mean those tomboys who live on your street?"

Rory chuckled. "Sure, if they were older and feral instead of just mischievous kids. I think I heard one of them running down the outside hall a moment ago—Lord knows what she was up to."

"Why do you call them crow girls?"

"I don't. I think Annie started it and now she's got me doing it, too. It's got to do with the way they're always messing around in the trees outside and getting into everything—like the crow girls in Jack's stories."

Lily was quiet for a moment. "The girls that rescued us were like birds," she said. "I mean, they had a birdish feel about them, and then a friend of Hank's told him they must be the crow girls, the ones in Jack's stories."

Rory could see where she was going.

"They weren't the twins, Kit," he said. "How could they be? The twins are just kids."

"Of course it wouldn't be them," she replied. "It's just odd."

Not a fraction as odd as her story had been, Rory thought, but he let it go. Instead, he got her talking about other things, sticking to more conventional topics until Lily finally said good-bye.

"Thanks for listening," she said. "And for not, you know, blowing me off."

"I'd never do that."

"But it's a crazy story."

"Well, it sure stretches the way we think things are," Rory said, being diplomatic.

"I wish you could have been there."

"Me, too. You take care, Kit. Get some sleep."

"I'll try. Thanks again."

He cradled the phone and sat back in his chair, staring at the contact sheets pinned to the corkboard above his computer. He'd circled the shots he liked the best with an orange grease pencil. It was terrific work, but then Lily's photos usually were. She was so grounded. Had a little bit of trouble with self-esteem, it was true, but she dealt with it in the same matter-of-fact way she dealt with everything. It wasn't that she couldn't see the whimsical side of things. It was just that she'd always known the difference between what was real and what wasn't.

At least until now.

Jack's stories had started it—that much was obvious. But where was the jump from enjoying his stories to thinking you'd stepped into one? And where did Hank Walker come into all of this?

Rory hadn't lied to Lily. He did believe—not necessarily that it had happened the way she'd said it had, but that *she* believed it had happened that way. Only where did he go with it now? What did you do when one of your best friends turned the corner and stepped from fact into fiction?

After awhile, he turned back to his computer and logged on. He had eight messages waiting for him, but it was the last one that caught his immediate attention.

```
Sender: dgavin@tama.com
Date: Sat, 31 Aug 1996 00:37:52 -0500
From:  'Donna  Gavin'  <dgavin@tama.-
com>
Organization: Tamarack Publishing
To: rcrowther@cybercare.com
Subject: Do we have a problem here?
```

Hi Rory,

I hope you don't mind me contacting
you like this--I got your email address and phone number from Sass. I
tried phoning, but your line's been
busy for ages, so I'm sending you
this instead.

It's about Lily.

I just got the strangest phone call
from her and I need to talk to somebody about it. I'm going to be out of
town at a conference until Tuesday,
but if you could email and let me
know the best time for me to call
you, I'd really appreciate it.

I don't want to worry you, but something _really_ weird is going on with
Lily.

Donna

No kidding, Rory thought.

He hit "Reply," composed a quick response to
Donna's message, and sent it. He tried going through the
rest of his messages, but he couldn't concentrate. Finally
he shut his computer down and sat staring at the blank
screen.

There was no one except for Donna that he could talk to about this—at least not without betraying Lily's trust, and he wasn't about to do that. At least not yet. If he decided she was putting herself into danger, then all bets were off, but for now all he could do was wait.

11.

If there was any one place Hank might call home, it was that broad empty slab of concrete he'd cleared off in the Tombs. Big cleanup one spring, maintenance since then. Once the Tombs regulars figured out it was his space, they pretty much left it alone. No one had any use for it anyway, except for Hank.

That was where Moth found him, closing in on four A.M. that night. Hank sat cross-legged in the middle of that flat stretch of pavement, not doing anything except maybe thinking.

"Pretty night," Moth said, claiming a piece of the pavement beside him.

Hank nodded.

"That dog of yours was watching me as I came in. If I hadn't checked out, I think he'd have taken a piece of me."

"He's nobody's dog," Hank said. "He's just what he is."

"Like all of us."

"Like all of us," Hank agreed.

Moth let a piece of the quietness lie between them for awhile.

"You okay?" he asked after awhile.

"I don't know. Used to be I knew where everything stood, but now I'm not so sure."

"Because of these animal people?"

Hank nodded. "Them, and Jack's stories." He turned to look at Moth, his face ghostly in the starlight. "Feels like something's coming down, just like in those stories of his.''

"Doesn't have to touch you."

"But that's just it," Hank said. "It already has. Thing is, I don't know where it's taking me."

He sounded tired, Moth thought.

"You get any sleep today?" he asked.

"Crashed in Tony's back room for a few hours."

"Talk to Jack?"

"Couldn't find him." Hank hesitated for a moment, then added, "But I talked to Lily. The woman from the other night."

Moth waited.

"She feels the same. Drawn in, but doesn't know to what or where. Feels like she's just waiting."

"Waiting for what?"

Hank shrugged. "Just something. I don't know what."

Moth leaned back on his elbows and stared up at the night sky. It was quiet here. You couldn't hear the traffic from either Williamson or Yoors, light as it would be at this time of night. Couldn't hear the bikers either, and they were usually still partying. Listening to what Hank had to say, thinking of Jack and the story he'd gotten from Jimmy, he felt himself slipping somewhere else, too, into a version of the city where that kind of thing could happen. Was happening.

Hell, he was already there.

"Went by Jimmy's today," he said without looking away from the stars. "Got him to tell me that story again—the one about the dog-headed guy."

"I remember you passing that on," Hank said. "What about it?"

"Just wanted to remind you that you're not alone."

Hank gave a slow nod. "We had a good laugh about it that night. I mean, Jimmy of all people."

"But we're not laughing now."

"Not much," Hank said. He went somewhere inside his head, came back. "Jack tells the other side of that story—about the game and all."

"Yeah, but Jimmy says it took three hours, not three days."

"That's because Jack tells a better story."

Moth didn't have to turn to see the smile. He could hear it in Hank's voice.

"I won't argue that," Moth said. "But then Jack's not just passing along something strange. He's got other reasons for telling his stories. You know that thing he says, how when we understand each other's stories, we understand everything a little better—even ourselves."

Hank nodded.

"Guess we're going to have try to understand his a little better," Moth said.

The quiet lay down between them again, easy as an old dog.

"Maybe not just his," Hank said after awhile. "I was talking to Katy today."

Moth didn't say anything. He waited, content to let the night sky slip down into his eyes and fill him. Big sky like that, it did wonders for the soul. Put everything into perspective. How serious could your problems ever be when you were this small in the overall scheme of things?

After awhile, Hank lay down on the pavement beside him and started to talk.

Hearing him out, Moth realized that he'd never really known the meaning of "strange" until now. Above him, the sky seemed so enormous that it swallowed the very idea of the two of them lying here, looking up.

Moth turned to look at Hank. "So . . . do you believe her?"

"I don't know. But something's on her mind and it's hurting pretty seriously." Hank met Moth's gaze and even the poor light couldn't hide the trouble in his eyes. "Is this the way it works?" he asked. "They just line up on you, one after the other? You accept one impossible thing, so then you have to accept them all? You believe in ghosts, so now you've got to believe in aliens? Animal people are walking around among us, so Elvis is, too?"

Moth nodded. He understood perfectly. Where *were* you supposed to draw the line?

"So where do you go from here?" he asked.

Hank didn't hesitate. "Wherever it takes me," he said.

~ 2 ~

A PIECE OF NOWHERE

*They say that history repeats itself, but I have
an embellishment on that. History repeats
itself, but at an accelerated pace.*
   —DWIGHT YOAKAM,
      FROM AN INTERVIEW IN *NEW COUNTRY*
      (NOVEMBER 1995)

*The room's all fogged up, thick with a gray cloud
of cigarette and cigar smoke. Only thing that cuts
through are the lights above the tables, the click of
the balls as they hit each other, the thump when they
drop into a pocket. Jimmy's Billiards has been
around pretty much forever and it hasn't changed
over the years. It's still the same one-up above that
pawn shop at the corner of Vine and Palm,
scratched wooden floors, plaster walls and ceiling
dingy with smoke stains, beer on tap and only one
brand, bags of chips, smokes sold in packs, single
Cuban cigars, some of Jimmy's hooch if he knows
you. You want anything else, you're in the wrong
place.*

*Mostly we all know each other here. Sharks show
up, they can play by themselves or sit and watch.
We don't take too kindly to anybody trying to make
a fast buck off of us, got little enough as it is.*

*But the game tonight's different. The slip of a girl
and the tall man she's playing, they've been in before, played a few racks with most of us, but never
like this. She's never played like this.*

He's looking like a riverboat gambler, flat-out

handsome as always, black jeans, boots, and jacket, black flat-brimmed hat just like mine sitting on the bench by the table, white shirt, bolo tie. She's wearing black combat boots, black leggings coming down from under an oversized black sweater that's got so many pulls and loose bits of wool coming off it looks like it's made of feathers. A raggedy girl to his long cool. But they could be family, looking at them. Cousins, maybe. Something similar in the cut of their features. Maybe he's got that dark gray hair, hint of red in it, while hers is blue-black with those two bands of white running back from her temples, but they've got the same too-dark eyes with just a hint of yellow in them. Same dark skin, too. You could take them for Indians, or light-skinned blacks, but I know better. They're first people, like me. Got a trouble between them that goes way back.

Nobody was paying much attention when Cody won the coin toss. He broke the rack and starting putting away balls, ran them for over an hour until he finally missed an easy corner shot on a five ball. He shrugged and smiled at Margaret when she stepped up to the table, but I could tell he wasn't pleased. Something in his eyes, the way the skin on his face shivered for a moment, looking like fur, gone before anybody else could notice it.

Margaret, she's been going through racks ever since—three days now. Nobody's seen playing like this before. Talk's gone dead. The other tables are empty and Jimmy's cut the lights above them. Everybody just drinking their beer, smoking, and watching. Going home to sleep, going to work, but always coming back, shaking their heads when they see she's still at the table, sinking those balls.

First they were waiting for her to miss. Now they're just wondering how long she can stand there at the table, bright-eyed and smiling, playing like she just got up. I think of telling them, she can stand there forever and she's never going to miss, but I hold my peace because I'm curious, too. Not about how long she can keep it up, but what she's up to.

Corbœ and canid. The trouble between our families goes all the way back to the first day. We're talking the long ago, spirit time, not the way you count years. We've never had much use for calendars— not the way you do. The cycles of the sun, the moon, the seasons are all we've ever needed, same way we always had territories instead of "owning" the land. Property's something you came up with. Raven says it's because you think in terms of boxes. Every-thing's got to fit in one—you even live in them.

Territory's a different thing. It's not permanent. We mark out what we need when we're mating, when we're feeding the kids, then let it go. Don't build anything permanent on it, don't leave much of a mark at all. Some raggedy nest, maybe, feathers, scat, nothing the rain and time won't wash away. And we never keep it just to ourselves, you know, saying that flower can't grow here, sparrow can't feed, the sun can't shine here, the wind can't blow, fox can't walk through, spider can't make its web. Makes no sense to us. Oh, maybe some of us are living in boxes now, but mostly we live how we al-ways did, follow the old ways, walk in the world, tall but leaving only footprints, living on spirit time.

People, they don't know what to make of us. Most of you think we never were, or if we were at one time, we're not anymore. But we're still here, old spirits all around you, only you're not paying atten-tion to us. When you do happen to stumble upon us, you think you're seeing a ghost, or a faerie, or some little alien come down from the stars, going to stick a needle in you, steal you away in a silver saucer. You don't want to believe we could be real. Puts too much responsibility on you. Makes you uneasy, re-

membering what you're doing to our cousins.

But we don't get involved with judgments or ret-
ribution. I don't say this to put you at your ease.
You either live a life of kindness or you don't. The
payback comes when you finish your business in this
world and cross over to the next. Good people have
nothing to worry about. Everybody else, well, you'll
be getting yours. You didn't borrow that Old Tes-
tament "eye for an eye" from us the way you did
so many other stories. One of your people happened
on a glimpse into the Mystery that started it all.
Everybody's got to pay her due and let me tell you,
nothing gets by her.

But I was telling you about Cody. Maybe you
know him better as Dogface, Old Man Coyote,
though mostly he doesn't look so old; always in
somebody's business, making it his own. Truth is, I
like him more than I don't, which says about as
much about my good nature as it does about his
charm. And he is charming—a good-looking, dark-
haired man with eyes the color of a moth's dark
wings, as drawn to trouble as to a flame.

First day we're walking around, furred and feath-
ered and scaled, taking it all in, that sweet mystery
of being alive, here and now, living in Zen time.
Corbœ, we saw it happen, sun born, moon called up
from the sea, stars scattered across a darkness
blacker than our wings. We were siblings then,
slipped up out of the before from in between the
stars to take in the show. We're sitting there in the
forever trees, watching the darkness catch fire—
"It's like fireworks," Zia says, and none of us have
seem them yet, but we understand. The lights settle
down and then we're watching the long ago take
shape, hill by river by forest by sea. We're watching
our brothers and sisters sit up and blink, look
around themselves, already forgetting everything ex-
cept for what they can see in front of their noses.

And everybody's got their own skin, fits them well because they're born to it, no complaints. All except for Cody.

Oh, Cody.

He's walking among the brothers and sisters while they're not quite awake yet. Steals the bobcat's bushy tail, the hare's courage, the ant's independence, the dolphin's legs, the turtle's fine-pointed ears. Takes this and that and a bit from everybody and then he sees us sitting up there in the trees, watching him.

Oh, Cody.

Who're we going to tell? Why would we even care?

But that's where it starts. Cody, scheming, scheming. Always has to put one over on the corbœ. Sees any kind of a blackbird and it starts up a meanness in him.

Because we know.

Doesn't matter that we'd never tell, that there's no one to tell.

It's enough that we know.

Margaret starts in on a new rack and sinks five balls off the break. She steps back from the table and downs a shot of Jimmy's hooch, then calm as you please, sinks the rest of the balls, works the table so fast that balls are leaving smoke trails behind as they drop into the pockets. Somebody sets up a new rack, but she pauses again. This time it's to give Cody a considering look.

Feels like they've been at it for weeks, or she has, sinking rack after rack. Cody, all he's been doing is standing by the table, getting quieter and quieter, so still the air feels thick around him. He takes that look she gives him, then reaches into his pocket and tosses a small black pebble onto the pool table. Paying off his debt with a piece of magic. A little chunk

*of long ago, old time, weathered and smoothed. It
sits there on the green felt, sucking light into itself.*

"You know," Margaret says. She looks at that
pebble, but leaves it lie. "There's not one of us cares
about what you did. You ever hear of a corbœ could
leave some pretty thing just lying around without
sidling up and putting it in her pocket? Maybe you
invented borrowing, but we took to it like it was
ours."

Cody's heard this before. Heard it more times
than he can remember, I'd guess.

"So give it a rest," she tells him.

Cody doesn't say a word. Just looks at her, then
he snaps his cue in two, tosses the pieces onto the
table. Picks up his hat and walks out. I see something in his eyes as he leaves, something in the shadows under that low brim. The desert's in there and
the timberlands. All the lonely, wild places where he
roams—not because anyone makes him, but because
he claims he wants to.

I think of what Margaret said and suddenly I flash
on what this is all about. It's not that we saw him,
there in the long ago, taking a piece of this, a piece
of that for himself. It's that he thinks we don't care.
It's that no matter what he does to get our attention—outrageous, helpful, mean—he thinks we don't
care.

I turn to Margaret, see her putting away her cue.
She turns to me before I can say anything.

"I know, Jack," she says.

Then she heads for the door. I stop long enough
to pocket the pebble before I follow her out into the
night. I hear the crowd start to stir as I walk toward
the stairs.

"Christ," someone says. "Pull me a beer,
Jimmy."

Jimmy doesn't move. I catch a look in his eyes
and know that he's seen past our skin. Maybe not

*Margaret's or mine, but for a moment there, he saw
Cody's wild face, the long snout and whiskers, and
it turns something around inside him, you know, the
way the crow girls can make you see things differently, just by being who they are. It changes him.
Reminds him how long the world's been here before
ever he was born into it. Reminds him that somebody
was walking it in that long ago, and they're still
here, walking it now.*

"Hey, Jimmy," *the guy who wanted the beer repeats.*

"I hear you," *Jimmy says, but he stands a moment longer, looking out the door, before he finally
goes and pulls the draft.*

*I could use a beer myself, but I keep on walking.
By the time I hit the street, they're both gone.*

*I take out the pebble and look at it again. Smooth,
old. A little piece of enchantment that doesn't do
anything. It just is. I figure I'll give it to Raven.
Maybe he'll put it in that magic pot of his, unless
he's gone and lost it again. He used to collect pieces
of the first day in that pot, started up doing that a
long time now. Don't know what he ever did with
them all. Could be, the way things are, he's got no
use for them anymore. But I've got no use for them
either. Once I started remembering on my own, I
didn't need a piece of nowhere to get to the place
where history was hiding in my head.*

*But that makes me think. Maybe there's more to
my considering I should give this black pebble of
Cody's to Raven than something I'm only doing out
of habit. Maybe it'll bring him back from whatever
place it is that he's gone.*

3

THE HOUSE ON STANTON STREET

*Ultimately you understand there is order in the
universe, even if there is no order in your
immediate circumstances.*

    —JANE SIBERRY, FROM AN INTERVIEW IN
      THE OTTAWA CITIZEN, WEDNESDAY,
      AUGUST 23, 1995

1.

Newford, Labor Day Weekend, 1996

Like its neighbors, the Rookery was set back from Stanton Street, separated from the public thoroughfare by an expanse of dutifully tended lawn, unruly flower beds, and the line of hundred-year oaks that marched along either side of the street, two once-tidy rows of manicured shade trees, enormous now, and more or less gone feral. The houses stood surprisingly close to each other, barely a footpath apart at times, tall Victorian structures built of red and brown brick with delicate ironwork and wood trim, gabled and dormered, hip- and mansard-roofed, some with balconies, some with small towers, all sporting large front porches. As if to make up for their cozy proximity to one another, their properties ran the full length of the block between Stanton Street and the carriage lane in back, with room enough for sprawling gardens and coach houses—those curious, outdated relics from an older time, most of which had been turned into garages or extra apartments.

Behind the Rookery, the lawn grew in patches, too

much of it shaded by an immense elm that easily rivaled
the oaks lining the street in both its stately height and the
untamed spread of its branches. Ferns, lilies of the valley,
and trilliums grew thick in the spring shade. Dead man's
fingers and other fungi dotted the lawn in the fall. In
summer, the heavy blossoms of the rosebushes crowded
the granite of the walls separating the Rookery's backyard from those of its neighbors, while the coach house
was so overgrown with ivy that it disappeared behind a
shimmering veil of green. Between the coach house and
the lane in back was a small vegetable and herb garden.

There were no bird-feeders hanging from the lower
branches of the elm or the posts of the back porch. The
only songbirds making their home here were a small par-
liament of bohemian crows and one bad-tempered raven
that seemed more than capable of scavenging their own
meals. The boisterous flock ruled the backyard, certainly,
and most of the neighborhood with a corvine charm that
those not so enamored with their presence would describe
as noisy and bullying.

Mostly, Rory enjoyed their good-tempered shenani-
gans, but that might only be because he considered them
to be the most normal inhabitants of the property—bar-
ring himself, of course.

Or perhaps it was because of the crow lodged in his
surname: Crowther.

Rory had the ground-floor apartment, twelve hundred
square feet of high-ceilinged rooms that were austere
when he first went to view them nine years ago, but were
now so completely filled with the furniture and clutter he
had brought into them that the original floor plan was
almost unrecognizable. His office was a junkyard of paper, books, and magazines, but the spare bedroom that
served as a workshop where he made his jewelry was the
worst: a confusing jumble of supplies and finished work
haphazardly stored in ever-ascending stacks of boxes and
containers set precariously against the walls, leaving nav-

igable only a narrow corridor running between the door and the area around his worktable.

Upstairs on the second floor, there were two apartments, one untenanted at the moment, the other rented by the most remarkable, self-contained woman Rory had ever met. Her name was Annabel Blue—Annie to her friends. How familiar that might ring against the inner ear would depend entirely on how closely one followed the Newford alternative music scene, music that was truly an alternative to the charts as opposed to alternative acts who appended the adjective to their résumé simply for its rather dubious street credibility. She had her own record company that she ran out of the apartment, Uneasy Records ("Because my music makes for uneasy listening, instead of easy," she explained to him once), storing boxes of the as-yet-unsold cassettes and CDs in the basement.

Annie stood only an inch under Rory's five-ten, long-limbed and raw-boned, a striking woman with expressive eyes so dark they seemed to swallow light. Her coal-black hair had been cut short and dyed a startling blonde this past summer, at the same time as three more earrings and a nose ring joined the seven earrings that already climbed up the lobes and outer ridges of her ears. Two of them she'd bought from Rory: a simple dangling crow's feather, cast in silver, and a small stud in the shape of a torii—a Shinto shrine-gate symbol. She had a bracelet tattooed on her right wrist and another on her left ankle, intricate Celtic ribbonwork, starkly delineated with black and red pigments. Her wardrobe ran to faded jeans and clunky black workboots, T-shirts with the arms torn off in the summer, baggy sweaters and men's sports jackets in the winter.

Rory had never heard music so loud, never realized so much energy could come from one battered acoustic guitar and a human throat the way Annie could draw it out. She could be tender, too, but that was a less common side of her music. Her repertoire dealt mostly with environmental issues—sometimes overtly political, other times she slid the issues into what might at first be taken for songs dealing with interpersonal relationships. He often played her CDs when he was working.

He was mildly infatuated with her, though he wasn't certain whether it was her outlandishness that attracted him or merely the insufficiency of his own love life. Lily insisted it was both.

But Annie was almost normal compared to Lucius.

Lucius Portsmouth owned the building and shared the top-floor apartment with a woman named Chloë Graine. Rory wasn't quite sure about Chloë's relationship to his landlord. Lover, nurse, confidante? Possibly all three, though the first required a stretch of the imagination that put too much of a strain upon Rory's credulity.

Mostly it was the size difference between the two. Lucius was huge. He had to weigh at least five hundred pounds, an enormous man with skin the color of the midnight sky, round-faced, dark-eyed, a black Buddha who had never—in the nine years Rory rented from him—left his apartment, spending his days and evenings sitting by the front window of their apartment, watching the sky. He had no hair, not even eyebrows, though Rory couldn't swear the condition was inclusive of all body hair. Truth was, he wasn't sure he wanted to know. When Lucius walked across the room—a rare occurrence that took place twice a day—the entire house seemed to shift and groan under the strain and anyone in the building knew that the mountain was moving to Muhammad once more.

Chloë was taller than Rory and of normal weight, though she appeared wraithlike in the company of her roommate, her brown skin pale against the deep ebony of his. She had a Roman nose and high cheekbones, a long neck, slender hands, and a thick black fountain of hair falling to her shoulders in a torrent that could easily have serviced two women. Her eyes were birdlike and large, wide-set, their gaze forever darting about, never settling on any one thing for more than a moment.

The difference between the two was more than physical. Lucius, for all his immense presence, seemed to merge into his surroundings, absorbed by the wallpaper, the carpet, the sofa, like a chameleon. He had a calm that was almost supernatural, an air about him as though he lived in this world only by sufferance, his gaze and attention forever focused on something only he could perceive. Chloë, in contrast, was entirely present, so down-to-earth and *here* that the intensity of her attention could be as disconcerting as Lucius's indifference. When not seeing after Lucius's needs, she spent long hours perched on the peak of the roof, a gangly, wingless bird whose sharp gaze missed nothing that went on below; not so much a scarecrow as a welcoming crow, for the resident flock inevitably gathered about her, like courtiers to a lady, dreams to a dreamer.

Rory had never spoken to his landlord and only met him the once, when he first rented his apartment—if "met" was a term that could be used when one party entirely ignored the other. His only communication with Lucius was through Chloë, who was always the one to knock on his door or phone down to ask him to handle some small repair, deal with a delivery man, see to the rental of an apartment. For these favors he received modest rebates on his rent checks, welcome additions to an income that was often stretched to its very limit by the end of the month. He and Chloë got along well enough, but there was still something too off-center about her for him to exchange more than small talk.

The coach house in back wasn't free of eccentrics either. The upper of the two small apartments was rented to Brandon Cole, a young black saxophone player who had a steady gig at the Rhatigan over on Palm Street—sat in with the house band one night after Saxophone Joe disappeared and he'd been playing with them ever since. He had the tall rangy stature and handsome good looks of a Maasai warrior, but he didn't have time for the women who came by the band's dressing room between sets or after a show. He was too focused on his music, music you had to dig deep to understand, part Coltrane, part Coleman, mostly himself. Late nights, early afternoons, he'd be sitting on the top of the stairs leading up into his apartment, hands folded on his lap, composing solos in his head. He didn't need the instrument, just closed his eyes and he was there, wherever "there" was; he was gone to that place the music came from, communicating with it. Sometimes Rory thought he could hear a faint echo of a sax coming from the top of the stairs, but all he would see was Brandon, hands empty, gaze as faraway as Lucius's, but taking in a different view.

The Aunts had the apartment downstairs. Eloisa and Mercedes. They weren't Rory's aunts; they weren't anyone's aunts, so far as he knew, but that was the way he thought of them. Their given names were somewhat exotic, but they were plain women with strong features and tall bodies. He guessed them to be in their sixties, spinsters, perhaps, or widows. With their dark complexions, their thick gray hair tied back in loose buns, those long black cotton dresses, Rory could easily picture them in Rome, Madrid, Istanbul, gossips meeting in a Mediterranean village market square, or sitting together on a back stoop, heads leaning together. He couldn't tell them apart, but he didn't think they were twins. For all he knew, they might not even be sisters. No one had ever told him their surnames.

They had two passions: gardening and watercolors. They began their gardening before the last frost had left the ground, filling their windowsills with trays of small sprouting plants. Whenever Rory tried to help out, they would let him turn the soil with a spade, weed, trim, and the like, then they'd do it all over again to their own satisfaction. Finally he took the hint and left them to their devices. After the first snowfall, they were still harvesting kale and a few herbs.

The rest of the time they would paint and they could

keep to it all day, in wicker chairs under the elm in summer, by the worktable in their apartment in the winter, the cast-iron stove behind them casting off a cozy heat. Sometimes they worked on the same piece, other times each chose her own subject. Their work was highly detailed, with the same technical proficiency of a botany textbook. Rory had no idea what became of the paintings when they were done. He'd been inside their apartment dozens of times, to fix a faucet, clean the stovepipe, gout the bathroom walls, but had never seen anything of the stacks of watercolor paper with the completed paintings on them—they were not on the walls, certainly—and no one ever seemed to come to take them away. Where could they all go? Sometimes, he wondered if he only imagined them painting, the long hours filled with the quiet murmur of their voices, heads bent over the easels—the way he was sure he only imagined he could hear Brandon's sax when there was no instrument at hand.

The house lent itself to flights of the imagination. "There's no such thing as fiction," Annie told him once. "If you can imagine something, then it's happened." So he wondered, but he didn't worry. They were characters, all of them. Peculiar, certainly, more so than most one would meet in the routine of day-to-day living, but there was nothing truly inexplicable about any of them.

He couldn't say the same thing about Maida and Zia, the neighborhood tomboys who claimed to live in the branches of the old elm tree behind the house.

2.

Kerry Madan tramped down Stanton Street, the leather soles of her boots scuffling on the pavement, her knapsack heavy on her back, the valise in her hand heavier still. It was quieter here, away from the traffic on Lee Street, but the quiet made her uneasy. There was something claustrophobic about walking under this long row of enormous oaks. The trees were too big, their dense canopy almost completely blocking the sky. They cast deep shadows against the tall houses and the shrubbery collected against their porches and brick walls, throwing off her sense of time. It no longer felt like the tail end of the day. It was too much like late evening now, a time when anyone could be out and about, watching her, waiting in the shadows for her to step too close. Anyone, or anything.

She couldn't remember the last time she'd been outside like this—at night, by herself. Her anxiety took her past the usual dangers of a big city until her imagination went into high gear and she was inventing other threats, nameless things, creatures with hungry eyes and too many teeth. It didn't feel safe here, not even close. In the few moments she'd been walking under the oaks she'd gone from feeling brave and free to wondering if it hadn't been a huge mistake to so completely cut her ties with the past.

Her pace faltered. She'd given up checking the numbers of the houses, more concerned now with what might be hiding in the bunched lilacs and cedars that crowded against the porches than finding number thirty-seven.

Stop it, she told herself.

This was what she'd wanted—*insisted* on. To be on her own. To make her own way in the world—*out* in the world, not cloistered away from it like a nun, or someone who couldn't take care of herself.

Only maybe I can't, she thought. It was so easy in the other world to look into this one and think, I can do that. I can live there. I can be normal. But she didn't even know what normal was. The outer trappings were easy to figure out, but not what went on inside normal people's heads, how they coped. That was more alien to her than her world would ever be to them.

Stop it, she told herself again.

She was tired and wished she'd taken a cab now instead of trying to make it from the airport on her own. At the time it had seemed like a good idea—she wouldn't always be able to afford cabs so why not familiarize herself with public transport from the start? The first bus had been easy. She'd been congratulating herself on how sensible she was being until she went and got all confused transferring to the subway system. The next thing she knew, she'd lost her way and then been forced to ask for directions so often that she now had no idea how she'd finally managed to get here. This very scary here.

Something caught her attention, a strange, undefined sound that stopped her in her tracks and had her peering fearfully up into the branches above her. Her pulse jumped into overtime as she realized that the monsters weren't hiding in the shrubbery, but ready to pounce on her from above. They were . . .

Only birds.

She gave a quick nervous laugh and shifted her valise from one hand to the other.

Blackbirds, perched on various branches. A half dozen or so.

The momentary rush of adrenaline faded, leaving behind a shivery, weak feeling.

Crows, or ravens? She didn't really know the difference. There was some sort of a rhyme about them, wasn't there? Something to do with luck and sorrow and marriages, but she couldn't call it to mind.

Her gaze dropped from the birds and settled on the front porch post closest to the walk that started at her feet. There were numbers there, two small brass plates attached to the white wood, but they didn't really register and her gaze moved on. There were no shrubs, only a well-kept lawn and flower beds stuffed with a riot of blooms running the length of the porch on either side of the walk. She squinted, deliberately blurring her vision to turn them into one of Monet's later paintings and immediately felt calmer. Smiling, she returned her attention to the brass numbers attached to the post. Thirty-seven.

This was it.

She hesitated a moment longer, gaze lingering now on

the brass plaque above the door that read, "the Rookery." The building was bigger than she'd thought it would be, a tall old Victorian house, a little forbidding for all the ironwork curlicues and gingerbread trim—though maybe that was only the light. She wasn't so sure. The whole street struck her as gloomy, though she knew Katy would like it. The street, the house, the trees. Katy always liked—

She cut herself off, determined not to let that tangled skein of memory unravel again. Squaring her shoulders, she started up the walk. As she drew near the flower beds she spotted a few cheerful geraniums growing among the jungle of cosmos, purple coneflowers, and golden glows. The smell of them was comforting, reminding her of another garden—a safe garden, if not a happy one. Lulled by their familiar scent, she was unprepared for the front door suddenly being flung open. She paused on the first step leading up to the porch, pulse drumming, hard-gained composure fled once more.

An odd-looking girl stood grinning down at her from the patch of light that spilled out from the hall beyond the doorway. She was small in height and slight in build, a skinny childlike figure with coffee-colored skin and sharp features set in a triangular-shaped face. Her eyes were large, bird-bright and dark, her hair an unruly lawn of blue-black spikes. Though the evening was cooling, she was barefoot, dressed only in black leggings and an oversized flannel shirt with the arms cut off.

"Are you Kerry?" she asked.

Her voice held laughter, an amusement that Kerry didn't feel was so much directed at her as simply bubbling over.

"Well, *are* you?" the girl repeated.

Kerry nodded. "Sorry. You caught me by surprise. I—" She started over again. "You must be Chloë."

Because who else would know her name?

The girl called back over her shoulder. "Did you hear that? She thinks I'm Chloë."

Again the laughter, bright and innocent. A child's laughter. But when she came bouncing down the stairs to join Kerry on the bottom step, Kerry realized she was much older than she'd first thought. Tiny, not even Kerry's five-one, truly child-sized, but the eyes looking up into her own were ageless.

"I'm not nearly solemn enough to be Chloë," she said.

"I'm sorry. I've never met—"

A slender hand reached out to touch Kerry's hair. "It's so red. Is it on fire? It doesn't feel hot at all."

"No, it's just—"

"I like you," she told Kerry. "You're funny and you're almost my size. We'll have such fun, you wait and see."

"I—"

A man's voice came from inside the house. "Maida. Don't be rude."

"I'm not, I don't, I never would!"

With that the girl went cartwheeling across the lawn and sprang up into the lower branches of the oak, startling the birds there so that they erupted from their perches in a cloud of black wings and hoarse croaks.

The man came out onto the porch, a creaking board announcing his step. Maida hadn't made a sound on that board, she realized, but then the girl must have next to no weight at all from the size of her.

"I'm sorry," he said. "Maida can be so . . . impetuous. But she's really quite harmless."

What an odd way to describe someone, Kerry thought. Impetuous. She tried the word on, wondering how it would feel to have someone describe her that way.

"My name's Rory," the man continued. "Chloë asked me to show you in to your apartment and give you the keys. I guess I'm sort of the super here," he added with a smile. "Helps with the rent."

He didn't look at all like Kerry's image of a building superintendent. The casual jeans and white T-shirt, maybe, but not the bright red high-tops or the earrings, one for each ear. His hair was a light brown, cut very short. A head taller than Kerry, he had the look of a runner or a dancer—in shape, but not pumped up. Not so much handsome as striking; clean-shaven and some-how . . . safe.

He offered his hand when he reached Kerry's step. She hesitated a moment, then shook.

"Are you all right?" he asked.

She nodded. "Yes. I'm just trying to catch my breath."

"Maida has that effect on people."

"Does she live here? In the building, I mean."

"You'd almost think so, she's over so often. But, no. She must live in one of the houses on the street, but I've never been able to figure out which. She says she lives in a tree."

Kerry turned to look up into the oak. For a moment she thought she saw not one, but two spike-haired girls looking down at her, but then she blinked, or they scram-bled higher, out of sight, and were gone.

"Does Maida have a sister?" she asked.

Rory nodded. "Sort of. Her name's Zia. The other peo-ple in the house call them the crow girls—since they're always in those trees, I guess."

Kerry remembered the blackbirds that had startled her earlier. Had there been a crow girl among them?

"Mind you," Rory went on, "while the pair of them look like identical twins, they say they're not even sisters. I'm not sure I believe them."

Kerry looked at him. Why not? she wanted to ask, but let the question lay unspoken on her tongue. There seemed to be hidden currents eddying here and she wasn't ready for them. Not yet. Maybe not ever. All she wanted was for things to be normal and you didn't find normal by stirring up secrets. Even she knew that much.

She settled on offering up, "Well, they certainly seem at home in a tree."

Rory smiled. "Come on," he said, taking her valise. "Your apartment's up here on the second floor. 2A."

Kerry gave the tree a last look, then followed Rory into the building. She immediately liked the way it smelled. Clean and woody. There was an open door in the hallway through which she could see a fairly messy living room. Rory's apartment, she supposed.

"Is that your place?" she asked.

He looked at her over his shoulder and nodded. "Any time you need something looked after you can call down—when you get your phone installed, that is. I'll give you my number. Or just knock. I'm usually around."

"Superintendenting."

Rory laughed. "Not really. I work out of the apartment—writing and making jewelry."

He continued up the stairs and she followed, thinking he didn't look like a writer or a jeweler either. She liked to guess at people's occupations, but she was never much good at it.

Rory unlocked one of the two doors on the second floor and handed her the key.

"Here you go," he said, switching on the overhead and stepping aside. "I hope you like it."

"Oh, I'm sure I'll . . ."

Her voice trailed off as she stepped through the door. Except for an upright piano set against one wall, the apartment was empty. Bare plaster walls and a polished wooden floor. Not even curtains on the windows.

"What's wrong?" Rory asked.

"There's . . ." She turned to look at him, that feeling of panic rising up in her chest again. "Where's the furniture?"

"Chloë told you it was furnished?"

"No, I just . . ."

Assumed. How could she have been so stupid? You had to fend for yourself in this world, see to your own comforts. It wasn't only cooking and cleaning up after yourself and trying to feel as though you weren't entirely alien. You were expected to have belongings. Furniture.

Pots and pans. A phone. All the things that normal people acquired over the years.

Rory hefted her valise. "Is this everything you've got?"

Kerry nodded. That and the clothes packed in her knapsack. She had to work at not crying, but she couldn't stop the tears from welling up in her eyes. How could she be so useless?

"I thought the rest of it was still in transit," Rory said.

All she could do was shake her head. The puzzled look in his eyes made her feel worse. He must think she was such an idiot.

"Well, look," he told her as he set her valise down on the floor. "It's not the end of the world. We can set you up with some stuff until you get out and buy what you need. There's plenty of stores open on Sunday."

The idea of having to go shopping made her feel literally sick to her stomach.

"I've got an extra futon," Rory was saying, "and I'm sure we can round up a set of dishes and a kettle—whatever you need to get you through the night. Do you drink tea?"

She managed a nod.

"We'll brew up a pot. Have you eaten?"

She nodded again, lying.

"Well, we'll rustle up some breakfast things—for tomorrow morning." He gave her a reassuring smile. "It's going to be okay."

"I . . ." She swallowed hard and had to start again. "I've never had my . . . my own apartment before."

She cringed inwardly, imagining what he had to be thinking. Here she was, all of twenty-four, and so helpless. But all he did was give her that reassuring smile again.

"We've all got to start somewhere," he said. "I think you picked a good place to see what it's like."

Kerry couldn't help it, she had to ask. "Why are you being so nice?"

"Hey, we're neighbors now. And speaking of neighbors, let me go knock on Annie's door to see if she can give us a hand."

"Please, I don't want to impose on everybody's evening."

It was Saturday night and she was familiar enough with how this world worked to know that normal people were out having fun on a Saturday night. Unless they got stuck having to give someone the keys to their apartment.

"You don't understand," Rory said. "She hasn't got a gig tonight and she'll be bored silly, just looking for something different to do."

"But—"

"And she'd never forgive me if I didn't ask her to help out. She's been dying to meet you ever since she heard there was somebody moving in."

Kerry's heart sank, but she managed to put on a brave face.

"Great," she said.

Just great. Perfect. More opportunities for her to prove what an idiot she was.

But Rory was still smiling and that helped put her at her ease. She found she liked the way he smiled. It wasn't just with his mouth but with his whole face. Nobody she knew ever did that.

"Don't be so hard on yourself," Rory said. "Everybody has to be the new kid on the block at some point or other. You'll get the hang of things quickly enough."

"I wish."

"You will. Trust me."

Kerry took another steadying breath and decided she would.

3.

Now this was a swank apartment, Ray thought as the woman from Homefinders let him in to see the place. But then everything was swank on Stanton Street. Not like it had been in the old days, when all these stately houses had been single-family homes that took serious money to live in, but the landlords in this part of town hadn't let the buildings get run down like some of the places in Crowsea or north of Grasso Street. The walls were smooth as fine parchment, the wooden floors gleamed. With the right furnishings, this would be a beautiful apartment. Ray didn't have any furnishings, but that wasn't really a problem. He didn't plan to be living here for that long.

"As you can see," Ms. Teal said, "it's a big, bright room, even with the oaks out front. And in the winter you'll get even more light."

She was an odd-shaped woman. Like her namesake, she had a duck's plump body on short thin legs, long slender neck, a small head with dark, close-set eyes, and a slightly protruding jaw with an overbite to match. He put her in her late forties, but she already had the blue-gray hair of a much older woman, albeit cut fashionably short. He kept waiting for her to quack.

"The kitchen and bathroom are new," she went on, looking down at her clipboard, which held the listing, "and the wiring was completely replaced three years ago."

Ray walked around the room as she spoke, stopping in front of the large window overlooking the street. Was it fate, or happy coincidence, that had him look outside at just that moment? It didn't matter. Standing on the sidewalk across the street, directly in front of number thirty-seven, was a young, red-haired woman, knapsack on her back, a small suitcase in her hand. He had no doubt that this was who he'd been sent to find—the timing was perfect. She was in the right place. She was obviously arriving for a long stay.

Frowning, he watched her go up the walk to the house. Of course, he hadn't been told was *what* she was. But he should have guessed.

"Shit."

"Mr. Nardene?" Ms. Teal said.

Turning to her, Ray gave her a winning smile which made the tight pucker of her lips relax.

"I said I'll take it," he told her. "Do you have the paperwork with you?"

"Yes, of course. If you'd like—"

"Here's three months' rent," Ray said, pulling the bills from his wallet. "Where do I sign?

It seemed to take her forever to fill out the paperwork, separate the copies, write out a receipt, and finally leave him with the keys. He closed the door behind her and returned to the window, taking a cellular phone from the inside pocket of his sports jacket. There was only one ring before the connection was made.

"You didn't tell me she's family," he said.

"It didn't seem important."

"Not to you."

"Look, it's not like she knows or anything. And the blood goes way back. It's so thin in her I'm surprised she even has your red hair."

"She could get hurt," Ray said.

"That's the cost of being alive."

"You know what I mean. If Raven catches her—"

"Raven wouldn't do anything unless he felt she was acting with intent. And I told you. She doesn't *know* anything."

"Then how's she supposed to find it?"

"Let me worry about that."

"And even if she does, what makes you think she'll give it up to you?"

"Hello? Are you listening? I said it's my problem. I just want you to watch her. If you get a chance, make friends, not waves."

Ray killed the connection and stowed the phone back in his pocket.

He didn't like it. He never liked getting caught up in

Cody's plans. It was always going to work out. It was always going to be different this time. And it never was. Nine times out of ten, Cody sticking his finger in only made things worse. But here Ray was anyway, going along with it because that was Cody's gift. Even when you knew he was going to screw up, and probably take you down with him, you still couldn't help but want to stand by him, to be part of his action.

Ray stroked a long narrow chin, gaze locked on what he could see of the house across the street through the gaps and holes of the oak canopy in between.

Cody never learned, he thought. But then, neither did he, or he wouldn't be here, would he?

4.

It was a slow Saturday night. Hank had Eddie's usual pickup scheduled, a two A.M. run out to the casino on the Kickaha Reservation, north of the city, and that was about it. He could have been busier—Moth had asked him to pick up a shooter at the airport—but because of what had happened the other night when he'd met Lily, he'd let Terry make the run. There was always somebody bringing in outside talent. He'd never really cared when they were only killing each other—so far as he was concerned, there were too many damn crews working this city as it was—but he was having second thoughts about his involvement with them now.

The pros usually didn't let their action bleed over into the lives of citizens. They did their job, in and out, low profile. Some low-life drug dealer went down. A capo didn't live to make retirement. Some pedophile missed a session with his therapist because he was found floating facedown in the lake. Who really cared? But when they started in on an innocent like Lily, just for the sake of meanness, it was time to reconsider where he stood with this kind of thing.

He didn't want to think about it right now. Just as he didn't want to be studying anybody he happened to pass by and find himself trying to figure out if they were human or something out of one of Jack's stories. What he wanted to do was call Lily, but she was out of town for the weekend, taking stills for a video shoot in Arizona. The video was for some country band whose name he'd forgotten as soon as she'd told him, which had irritated Moth to no end.

"Did you at least ask her to get me an autograph?" he'd said.

"What if it's a band you hate?"

"Well, I could've sold it then. There's always an angle, kid."

There always was an angle.

Lily was making an effort to keep in touch, left a message for him with Tony and everything. So what was her angle? Take that a step further, what was his? He knew he was interested in her, and not just because of what they'd experienced together, but the two were getting tangled up in his head and even doubling his tai chi exercises and run this morning hadn't been enough to sort it all out.

Neither was driving around tonight, waiting for something to come up and fill his time.

He stopped for a red light at the corner of Kelly and Flood. Glancing across the intersection and over, he saw a light on in Marty's second-floor office in the old Sovereign Building. Working late again.

Well, there was something he could do, Hank thought.

When the light changed, he made the left onto Flood and parked a half block down in the first available space. He walked back and pressed the buzzer beside the small tag that read, "The Law Offices of Martin Caine."

Marty's tinny voice came almost immediately from the small speaker above the buzzers. "That better be on rye."

"It's Hank."

"I thought you were Mac. Hang on. I'll buzz you up."

Sean MacManus ran an all-night diner around the corner on Kelly Street. Lately, according to Marty, he'd taken to serving what he figured you really wanted instead of what you'd ordered, which could make for interesting, if frustrating, meals.

"So why do you give him your business?" Hank had asked.

"He's close, he's fast, and he delivers off-hours. Who else is open, the times I want to eat?"

Hank pulled the door open when the buzzer went and let himself into the foyer. The floor was still damp in spots and there was a faint trace of ammonia in the air; there was no sign of the cleaners. The elevator door stood open, but he took the stairs, doubling back to the front of the building when he reached the second floor. Marty's door was open.

"Tuesday would have been early enough," he said when Hank came in.

Hank shrugged. "I was in the area and had some time on my hands."

Marty waved him to a chair beside the desk and leaned back, hands behind his head. He was dressed casually— jeans, cotton shirt open at the neck, running shoes. He needed a haircut and a shave, but that wasn't unusual. Neither were the stacks of files that crowded his desk.

Hank had to guess, but he didn't think any of the uptown lawyers had an office like this: battered government-surplus desk, chairs, and file cabinets. Linoleum on the floors. Plaster cracking on the walls and ceiling. The only decorative touches were a framed diploma on one wall and a faded Matisse poster advertising a show at the Newford Art Gallery that had closed a good five years ago. But then those same uptown lawyers made on one case what Marty might take home in a year.

"Do you want me to call in an order to Mac?" he asked Hank. "Maybe he hasn't left yet."

"That's okay. I already ate. Besides, I'm not feeling that adventurous tonight."

"Ha ha."

"So what've you got?"

Marty leaned forward and pulled a file from one of the stacks on his desk and opened it.

"Her name's Sandy Dunlop," he said as he flipped through the papers. "A lap dancer at Pussy's. The D.A.'s prosecutor says she shot and killed her boyfriend with malice aforethought, so we're looking at murder one unless I can knock some holes in his argument. Thing is, the boyfriend beat the crap out of her for years, pimped her out of the club. A real sweetheart."

"So one day she's had enough and ups and shoots him," Hank said.

"I'd love to have a moment of passion to work with, but it's not that simple. The prosecutor agrees Ellis—this is the victim, Ronnie Ellis—is a scumbag, but he's got papers proving she bought the gun three weeks ago. She was working the night he was shot, so she'd have had to make a special trip home on her break, shoot him, then come back and finish working before she gets off for the night and can come home and 'discover' the body. He's got opportunity, motive, and—since she can't account for her time during her break—a lack of alibi. And her prints are all over the murder weapon."

"Who's the prosecutor?"

Marty sighed. "Bloom."

"Beautiful."

Eric Bloom was the son of a Fundamentalist preacher who'd gone into law, specifically the D.A.'s office, to clean up the city. His father saw to the safety of its citizens' souls, while he saw to their physical safety with a special interest in shutting down anybody even remotely connected to the sex trades. If he didn't think they were guilty, he'd still want to put them away, simply on principle.

"So what does she say?" Hank asked.

"Ellis made her buy the gun. She was doing a trick in some guy's car during her break. She doesn't know who killed Ellis, but she's happy he's dead—or she was, until the D.A.'s office hung a murder rap on her."

The downstairs buzzer went off and Marty pressed the appropriate button on his intercom, asking who it was.

"It's Mac—who'd you think it would be, this time of night?"

Marty buzzed him in.

"She have a sheet?" Hank asked.

Marty nodded. "But nothing violent. A couple of solicitation charges. A couple more fraud—she bounced a few checks and did some time in county for the last one."

They heard the elevator door open down the hall and put their discussion on hold when Mac came bustling in. Balding, still wearing a grease-stained apron over his expansive paunch, he gave Hank a wave and set a brown paper bag on Marty's desk. Marty unwrapped the sandwich before Mac could leave.

"See?" Mac said. "You got your rye—just like you asked." He gave Hank a what-do-you-do-with-a-guy-like-this look. "You happy now?"

"This is tuna salad. I ordered ham and cheese."

"You know the kind of cholesterol there is in cheese?"

"But there's none in the mayo?"

Mac shrugged. "I was out of ham. So sue me." He winked at Hank. "Big shot lawyer, they're all the same—am I right? Nothing's good enough for them."

Hank had to laugh.

"See?" Mac said, turning back to Marty. "That's what you need. A sense of humor—am I right?"

"You should've been a lawyer," Marty said as he paid. "I don't know how you stay in business."

"You want something?" Mac asked Hank.

Hank shook his head. "So what did you want me to do?" he asked when Mac had left.

"Finding the trick she was with during her break would be nice."

"Do we have a name?"

Marty laughed. "No. But we've got a description."

He shuffled through the papers in the file and passed one over. Hank glanced over it, then got the joke.

"That tattoo on his dick should make him real easy to find," he said.

Marty popped the lid on his coffee, grimacing after he took a sip. "No sugar—as usual."

"But even if I find him," Hank said, "you can't make him testify. He'd be incriminating himself."

Marty waved that off. "We just need confirmation on where Sandy was during her break. We don't have to get into what they were doing at the time."

"But if Bloom gets him on the stand . . ."

"It doesn't have to go that far. All I'm looking for now is a hole in his case so that he'll actively pursue some other options. As things stand, they've got their case, so nobody's digging any deeper."

"Okay."

"There's also her girlfriend," Marty said. "Chrissy Flanders."

"You've got an address for her?"

Marty nodded. "Except she's gone missing, too. She worked at Pussy's with Sandy, same shift. Maybe she can help us narrow the time frame. Sandy doesn't have a car and even with public transport or a cab, it'd be a tight run to the apartment she shared with Ellis. Any way we can narrow the time frame will help."

"I'll do what I can. How much of a rush is there on this?"

"We're entering a plea Friday. Be nice if we could defuse Bloom's case before that—make him rethink his options."

"Bloom's going to change his mind?"

"Hey, miracles happen. One more thing," Marty added. "There's this guy." He pulled a photograph from the file. "Sandy only knew him as 'the Frenchman,' but she managed to I.D. him from the mug books." He passed the photo over. "His name's Philippe Couteau. Works out of New Orleans. Been booked a few times,

but no convictions. Apparently it's a family thing—
they've been involved with organized crime for a few
generations now. Couteau's the oldest of three brothers.
Very heavy dude.

"According to Sandy, he and Ellis had just had a fairly
serious disagreement about a drug deal Ellis screwed up.
Cops are looking for him, too, but I know they're only
going through the motions. Far as they're concerned, the
case is solved and it's now in the hands of the D.A.'s
office. Which is why finding the trick she was with that
night is so important."

Hank was only half-listening. The cold eyes looking
back at him from the mug shot were very familiar.

"Hello?" Marty said.

Hank looked up. "I know where you can find Couteau," he said. "He was in the Zone the other night. I
watched a girl stick a knife in his back."

Marty gave him a sharp look. "You're saying he's
dead?"

Hank nodded.

"Jesus." Marty pushed his hair back. "Do I even want
to know how you were involved?"

"It wasn't like that. Thing is, he's dead. So why didn't
the cops I.D. him when they brought his body in?"

"I'll find out."

Hank slowly put the photo back on the desk.

5.

Annie's apartment was as Spartan as Rory's was cluttered. Where you could barely see Rory's floor, the wide
expanse of pine floorboards in Annie's living room was
like a small town square, glowing in the buttery light cast
from a lamp that stood on a small table near the window
seat. There was a Morris chair beside the lamp, a battered
sofa along one wall, a structure made of wooden crates
along another that served as a bookcase and held her CDs

and stereo, a small Persian carpet by the sofa, and that was about it. Only one picture hung on the walls, a small black-and-white photograph of Ahmad Jamal sitting at his piano, looking out at the viewer from a narrow black wooden frame.

Compared to the rest of the apartment, the living room was decidedly opulent. Her bedroom had only the bed and a chest of drawers, with no pictures on the walls at all. In the spare bedroom, which served as a home studio since she'd had it soundproofed, was a four-track on a wooden crate, a stool, a guitar amplifier, two mikes in their stands, and her guitars: a vintage Janossy six-string and her stage guitar, a Takomine, both on stands. Small speakers stood on plastic milk crates in two corners of the room.

"Don't have much use for most stuff," she told Rory once when he asked why her furnishings were so sparse. Then she smiled. "You know. Some people travel light; I live light."

Rory always felt cramped in his own apartment after a visit to Annie's. He'd step into the chaos that was his home and invariably make a serious vow to finally get started on the big tidying up he'd been promising himself he'd do for years. But just as invariably, something more pressing would come up and the task would be put aside until another day and eventually forgotten until his next visit. Like now. As soon as he and Annie crossed the hall and went into her apartment, he immediately thought of the mess and clutter of his own.

"Kerry's a sweet girl," Annie said.

Rory agreed. Kerry *was* sweet, one of those genuinely nice people that he hardly ever seemed to run into anymore. He liked how she'd confessed to feeling hopelessly lost ever since she'd gotten off the plane, where most people would have put up some kind of front and tried to bluff their way through what they didn't know. Feeling out of kilter the way she did was nothing to be ashamed of—he'd felt the same way when he'd first moved into

the city and had told her as much. It was hard to sort
everything out in a place this big, especially when you
didn't know anyone. She'd seemed grateful for that—and
for all of their help.

Between the three of them, they'd dragged an old and
remarkably unmusty futon up from the basement and set
it up in her bedroom. Then Rory and Annie had scav-
enged about in their own places for the various things
Kerry would need to get her through the night. Towels,
soap, bedding. Some pots and pans, a plate, a mug, a pair
of old Coke glasses, eating utensils. Bread, marmalade,
butter, cheese, tea, milk, and sugar. Rory gave up a spare
club chair that had been hidden under a stack of cardboard box flats in his back room. Annie donated a half
roll of Droste chocolates, a real concession since they
were her favorites and it was her last roll. Two hours
later, realizing that Kerry must be tired after her long trip,
they'd said their good-byes and left her to finish settling
in on her own.

"That takes some nerve," Annie said, closing the door
behind them. "Just packing up and moving halfway
across the country like she did."

Rory nodded in agreement. He made himself comfortable on the sofa while Annie disappeared into the kitchen,
returning a moment later with a couple of bottles of beer,
condensation beading on the brown glass. She put a
Walkabouts CD on the player, the volume low, then
joined Rory on the sofa, her long legs splayed out on the
orange crate that served as a coffee table.

"Best unknown band in North America," she said as
Carla Torgerson, one of the group's two vocalists,
launched into a version of a Nick Cave song. "More's
the pity. I wonder if Kerry ever got a chance to catch
them in concert."

"Southern California's a long way from Seattle."

"But still."

"But still," Rory agreed. "They could have been playing down her way." He took a swallow of beer. "Though

somehow I doubt she went out much." He looked across the room at the informal portrait of Jamal. "Talking to her was like meeting someone who's just arrived from a foreign country or left a convent or something."

Annie smiled. "Mmm. Innocent *and* sweet."

Rory gave her a sidelong glance.

"Just your type," she added.

"Jesus, Annie."

"I'm joking already. You have *got* to lighten up."

"Ha ha."

"But she is attractive," Annie went on.

Rory gave a slow nod.

"And when was the last time you went out on a date?"

"What are you, keeping tabs on me now?"

"Not me," Annie said. "Though the crow girls probably do."

Rory smiled. "I think they keep tabs on everybody." He took a swig of his beer. "The thing that gets me is that, after all these years, I still haven't figured out where they live. It's got to be somewhere in the area, but I'll be damned if I know where."

"Why not simply accept that they live in a tree?"

"You don't believe that."

"Why not?"

"Because it's . . ."

He'd been about to say "impossible," but the word got swallowed by the sudden eerie sensation that flooded him. *After all these years,* he repeated to himself. He'd been living here almost a decade and it had only occurred to him now that he'd always thought of the crow girls as a couple of neighborhood tomboys. Kids. Barely teen-agers—fourteen years old at the most. But they'd looked like that when he first met them and in nine years they hadn't changed. They *still* looked like the rambunctious twins they'd been the morning he'd moved in, appearing out of nowhere at his door, wanting to know who he was, and where had he come from, and how long did he plan to live here, and did he like to climb trees. . . .

"This is so weird," he said slowly. "Do you know what I just realized?"

Annie was looking at him with obvious amusement. "No. But it must have been some really deep thought because your face has gotten all scrunched up and way serious."

"It's the twins—the crow girls. They . . ."

His voice trailed off again, but this time it was because of the sound of music coming from Kerry's apartment across the hall. Piano music. Some classical piece. He vaguely recognized it, but it was nothing he could put a name to. He and Annie looked at each other.

"Rachmaninoff," Annie said.

Rory forgot about the crow girls and their unchanging looks.

"Annie," he began.

But she had a faraway look in her eyes. She was listening, only not to him.

"No one's played that piano since Paul died," she said. "He used to play that piece all the time—remember?"

Rory didn't—classical music all sounded the same to him—but he nodded anyway, to let her know he was listening.

Annie sighed and a sorrow settled over her like a cloak, the way it always did when she thought of Paul. Rory wasn't quite sure what their relationship had been—more than friends, not quite lovers. An affection that went deeper than blood ties, certainly. She'd been devastated when he died—the whole house had gone into mourning—but she'd taken it the worst.

Rory had liked Paul, too, though he hadn't been nearly as close to him as Annie. Paul had always been a little too intense for him—a man on a mission, though Rory had never quite figured out what that mission was. He'd died in his sleep, which had seemed odd to Rory, considering Paul seemed to be in better physical shape than ninety percent of the people he knew, always exercising, eating right, the whole nine yards. But the coroner's report had stated that he'd died of natural causes. Go figure.

"You still miss him, don't you?" Rory said.

"I'll always miss him."

Rory nodded. He waited a moment, then came back to what had bothered him when they first heard the sound of the piano.

"Kerry can't be playing that," he said.

Annie blinked, coming back from wherever it was that her memories had taken her.

"I hear the piano," she said. "Don't you?"

"Sure. It's just that . . . I was joking with her earlier, when we were waiting in the hall for you to answer your door, about how the apartment wasn't completely unfurnished. There was at least the piano.

" 'Doesn't do me any good,' she says. 'I can't play.' "

"Well," Annie said, "I guess she was putting you on because she plays beautifully."

"I suppose. . . ."

But it didn't seem right. What possible motivation could she have for lying about something so inconsequential?

The music stopped abruptly in midbar. After a moment Rory realized that both he and Annie were holding their breath, waiting for the music to take up where it had left off. He leaned forward, listening with his whole body, then finally let out a sigh when only silence responded. Annie took a sip from her beer.

"You're still strangers," she said, as though reading his mind. "Maybe it's just something she didn't want to talk about. Maybe something about a piano brings back painful memories—I mean, look at how suddenly she stopped."

"Sure."

Annie shook her head. "Don't read more into it than there is. I'm sure there are all kinds of things you wouldn't want to talk about with a stranger, stuff you wouldn't even talk about with me."

Rory gave her a puzzled look. "Like what?"

"How would I know? What I do know is that we've all got our hidden currents, no matter how wide and friendly the river seems. Start casting deep enough and who knows what you'll dredge up."

Rory had to smile. "Now isn't that a lovely image."

"You know what I mean."

"Yeah, I guess I do. I was just . . . surprised."

Their conversation lagged then. Rory understood what Annie had been getting at, but the logic of her argument hadn't done much to quell the disappointment he was feeling. It wasn't as though he'd had any great plans to hit on Kerry or anything, but he had liked her and the lie seemed so out of character—

Then he really had to laugh at himself. Right there was the hole in his own logic. What did he really know about her character? He'd put together a little picture in his mind of who Kerry was—pretty, sweet, innocent, and honest—and the lie had poked a hole in it. That was the real problem. Not anything Kerry had done.

Annie was probably right. Undoubtedly seeing the piano had woken a bad memory for her and rather than get into it, she'd simply denied she could play, denied any past that included a piano. It wasn't so much that she'd lied about it. She was simply trying to avoid having to deal with it. End of story.

He looked over at Annie to see her finishing her beer. She set the empty bottle down on the floor beside the sofa and raised her eyebrows.

"You want another?" she asked.

Rory held up his bottle to show he still had a third left. "I'm okay with this."

"So you were talking about the crow girls," Annie went on.

"The crow girls. Right."

It took him a moment to pick up the threads of their earlier conversation. The strangeness of his observation, once he'd considered it again, hit him as strongly as it had the first time. How could he not have noticed it before?

"They don't change," he said. "They look exactly the same now as when I first met them."

Annie laughed. "And you've changed?"

"What do you mean?"

"You don't look any different from when I first met you either."

Rory knew what she meant. Some people aged well—or settled into their looks at an early age—and he was one of them. He looked about the same now as he had when he left high school.

"But that's different," he said. "Adults don't always change that much over a few years, but kids do."

Annie gave him an odd look. "How old do you think they look?"

"Fourteen, tops."

"Really? They look to be in their late teens, early twenties to me and they don't seem to change. I think of them as being more like the Aunts, or Lucius—"

"Instead of yourself," Rory finished, "who likes to reinvent herself every six months or so."

"Keeps me interesting."

Rory had to laugh. "The last thing you could be is boring."

Annie put a palm against her chest and affected a suitably humble expression.

"One tries," she said.

"So . . . late teens," Rory said.

"At least."

He regarded her for a long moment, just to reassure himself that she wasn't putting him on. There was humor in Annie's eyes, but no more than usual.

"I'm going to have to think about this," he said.

And give the girls a serious once-over, the next time he saw them, because now he was remembering Lily's story and it was simply too close, too much of a coincidence. How could there be two pairs of raggedy wild girls in the city? Where that fell apart, though, was that Lily claimed the girls she'd seen had killed the man attacking her.

He gave Annie a thoughtful look. "Do you think they could be dangerous?" "Who? The crow girls?"

He nodded.

"Push the right button," Annie said, "and anybody can be dangerous. Why do you ask?"

Rory shrugged. "I don't know. I'm still trying to get around them not being fourteen anymore and I never noticed." Finishing the last swallow of beer in his bottle, he stood up. "I'm going to call it a night. You up for doing some running around with Kerry tomorrow?"

"You're bailing?"

"No. I just thought it would be fun if we all went."

"Okay. But not too early."

"Gotcha."

"And Rory?"

He paused by the door.

"Don't always be thinking so much—you'll wear your brain out. Try letting things just happen once in awhile without looking for hidden meanings."

"Yes, ma'am."

"Asshole," she said as he shut the door.

Rory started for the stairs, but paused outside Kerry's door. He wasn't sure what he was listening for. Maybe the piano. Maybe just to hear that there was really someone in there.

Don't think so much, he thought, repeating Annie's advice. Maybe she had a point there.

He started to turn away, then sensed he wasn't alone in the hallway anymore. Smelling a familiar scent of anise, he knew who it was. His gaze lifted past the stairs leading to the third floor to find Chloë leaning on the rail, looking down at him. Her dark frizzy hair was a halo of tiny curls around her face, lending her an odd look in the hall's low light. For a moment she was like a disembodied face, watching him from the heart of a tree. Or an animal, caught in a car's high beams.

"Everything all right with the new tenant?" she asked.

Rory nodded. "Except she was expecting the apartment to be furnished."

"Why would she think that?"

"I've no idea. Annie and I are going to help her get some stuff tomorrow."

"That's nice," Chloë said. "I think she'll need some friends to get her through these first few days on her own."

"On her own?"

Chloë shrugged. "You know. Big city, she doesn't know anybody, that sort of thing. It always takes some adjustment. And all things considered, she might need a little more time than you or I might in the same situation."

"Is there something special about Kerry?" he found himself asking.

Chloë regarded him for a long moment, an unreadable expression in those midnight eyes of hers.

"Everybody's special," she told him.

Rory nodded, waiting for more, but all Chloë did was lean on the railing and look down at him.

And everybody's a philosopher tonight, Rory thought as he finally turned away and continued on down to his own apartment.

6.

A mild panic took hold of Kerry as the door closed behind Rory and Annie.

No, she wanted to cry out after them. I've changed my mind. I don't want to be alone.

She forced herself to calm down. What was the problem? She'd been alone before. Except it hadn't been the same. In her old world there was always someone on call.

Someone to ease the panic with a pill, or even a kind word. She still had pills, to help her sleep. The small orange plastic container was at the bottom of her knapsack with a cotton ball stuffed inside to keep the pills from rattling against each other, a childproof cap she had trouble opening, typed instructions on a label glued to the side. Though she knew it was only her imagination, she could smell the faint medicinal smell of the pills from where she stood.

She'd never liked taking pills—not after the incident with the aspirin. Kind words worked better; being held, better still. That kind of medicine hadn't always been available in her old world, and here, it wasn't really available at all. It wasn't the kind of thing you asked of strangers and even if it was, she didn't know how to ask, what to say. If I start crying for no reason, could you just hold me? If I start shaking for no reason . . . if I get so scared I can't seem to breathe . . .

She stared at the door for a moment longer before she finally made herself turn away. You can do it on your own, she told herself. Without pills or kind words. Just take it one day at a time, one moment at a time.

The ghosts of past failures wanted to argue with her, but she wouldn't let them. Instead she kept busy, hanging her two dresses and one jacket in the closet, folding the rest of her clothes and placing them on the shelf above, using the stool from the piano to stand on so that she could reach. Setting her valise at the back of the closet, she closed the door and glanced at the futon lying under the window. Rory had made up the bed for her, but she wasn't ready to lie down yet. Taking the pillow, she went back into the living room and put it on the club chair, then pulled the chair over to the window seat.

Now that she'd turned off the overhead in the bedroom, there wasn't much illumination in the apartment. What there was came from the light above the stove, a dim glow that seeped out the kitchen door. It was just enough to see by.

For a few minutes she sat in the chair and looked past the vague image of her reflection on the windowpane, out into what she could see of the dark backyard of the house. The huge elm took up most of her view. There was a whole dangerous world out there, she thought, but she was safe from it for now. And there'd be good things out there, too. There had to be.

Before a mood could take hold, she hoisted up her knapsack and began to take a few things out of it. A dozen paperbacks were put in alphabetical order on one side of the window seat. Two slim hardcovers joined them, set together on one side of the smaller books. In front of them she placed a small brass candlestick, unwrapped a candle, and put it in place. It would be nice to light it, she thought, but she didn't have any matches. On the other side of the window seat she put two small plush toys. Dog, so worn and battered it was hard to make out his canine shape anymore, but she knew who he was. And Cowslip, a faded yellow monkey in a tiny crocheted pink wool dress. Neither was taller than the length of her hand. Last she brought out a small framed black-and-white photograph.

She stared at the older woman in the picture, memory filling in the colors that the camera hadn't captured: the dark red hair, hardly touched by the grays of age. Blue eyes, like cornflowers in a grainfield. And the dress, also blue, but faded from the sun and a hundred washes. The weatherworn yellows of the porch on which she sat. The field of wildflowers that could only be glimpsed in the photograph, but ran on for miles in her mind's eye, if not in the reality of when the picture had been taken. The soft brown tint of the woman's complexion was missing, too, but Kerry had only to look into a mirror to find it.

She'd inherited her grandmother's looks, a genetic blueprint that had somehow bypassed her mother. But then she'd inherited Nettie's spirit as well—an old-fashioned, sweet-natured simplicity that had also skipped a generation. It wasn't that Nettie had lacked in either intelligence or wit. She'd simply considered a preoccupation with looks and social standing a poor substitute for looking after the well-being of others and the land that sustained them. She'd preferred creative expression to small talk and the disguised spite that masqueraded as gossip. The thing that Kerry remembered most about her was how she seemed connected to something deep and mysterious. And wonderful.

"We've got an old blood," Kerry remembered her saying once. It had been one of the last times she'd been able to stay with her grandmother—"the senile old fool," as Kerry's mother called her. "We've been walking this land for a long time. You can see it in our eyes and our skin."

"You mean like Indian blood?" Kerry had asked, intrigued.

"Sure, we can call it that."

"What's it do?"

Nettie smiled. "I remember telling your mother the same thing, for all that the coloring passed her by. 'What's it good for?' she wanted to know.

"'What's it good for?' I said. 'It's not good or bad, it just is.'

"She looked at me and shook her head. 'I don't want it,' she told me and I remember thinking, that's a good thing because who knows what you'd do with it." Her grandmother had regarded Kerry for a long moment then and asked, "Do you have any idea what I'm talking about, sweetheart?"

Kerry, eleven years old at the time, could only shake her head. "Sort of, I guess, but . . . no," she'd had to admit. "Not really."

"That's okay. We've got plenty of time."

Only there hadn't been. Kerry's parents had moved to Long Beach that August, taking her with them, of course, and she'd never seen her grandmother again. They hadn't even come back for the funeral.

Kerry sighed and set the photograph up in the middle

of the window seat. Nettie, she'd later come to realize, had been a true eccentric. Artist, regional writer, environmentalist—all things that her daughter, Kerry's mother, couldn't or wouldn't understand. Kerry knew that her life would have been so different if she'd been brought up by her grandmother. In her grandmother's world, she would have been normal.

"I've got to hand it to you," a too-familiar voice suddenly said, startling her out of her reverie.

It came from somewhere near the piano, but Kerry refused to turn and look. Please, she thought, trying to still the rapid tattoo of her pulse. Just go away.

"I didn't think you had it in you, but you proved me wrong. This feels like a good place—a nice old building, lots of history, and close to some pretty funky parts of town. More like the kind of place I'd pick."

Kerry sat with a stiff back and looked out at the shadowy bulk of the elm tree on the other side of the windowpane. That was real, she told herself. The elm. This house. The chair underneath her. The voice wasn't. She was only hearing it again because she'd been thinking about Nettie, about what-might-have-beens. This was only another what-might-have-been.

"Please, Kerry. Don't tune me out. Don't let them win."

The initial cheeriness was gone from the voice now. A sadness had crept into it, a familiar wistfulness that tore at Kerry's heart. She swallowed thickly, wanting to turn now, but not daring to. She'd worked too hard to give in at this point.

"They're the ones that lied to you," the voice tried. "Not me. I'd never lie to you. Why won't you believe me anymore?"

Because you're impossible, Kerry wanted to say, but answering was part of believing and she didn't dare believe. Think of something else, she told herself. Think of—

She heard movement. The rustle of cloth, a creak on

the floorboards. She held her breath. The cover for the keys was lifted and then there was the sound of the piano. Rachmaninoff. One of the *Études-Tableaux*. She listened to the familiar music, nodding her head in time, until she realized what she was doing.

"Don't!" she cried then.

The music stopped in midbar.

"Just . . . just leave me alone," Kerry said.

The voice made no reply. The only sound in the room was Kerry's own breathing and the last echo of the unfinished music, hushed and fading. She couldn't stop herself. She had to turn. But there was no one by the piano now.

When would it stop? she asked as she faced the window once more. She burrowed deeper into the corner of the chair and clutched the pillow. When would it finally stop?

She had to take one of her pills before she was finally able to go to bed and actually fall sleep.

7.

The county jail was an imposing squat stone structure overlooking the Kickaha River just north of where Lee Street crossed MacNeil in Upper Foxville. Seventy years ago it had been on the outskirts of the city proper, but through the postwar years it had slowly been enfolded into the city until eventually it was surrounded by thriving factories and tenements. There was talk at one point of closing it down, relocating someplace where it wouldn't be in such close proximity to law-abiding, taxpaying citizens. But those same citizens fought the millions in tax dollars that the move would cost and over time the neighborhood degenerated.

Now the jail stood on the western border of the Tombs, an old horror of a building, still set apart from the surrounding architecture by its tall stone walls, topped with barbed wire. These days it was differentiated more because it was the only legally occupied building in a no-man's-land of squatters and transients, rather than by the character of its inmates.

"That is one ugly building," Anita said as she pulled the cab up near the curb on the far side of the street from the gatehouse. When Hank didn't respond, she turned to where he sat on the passenger's side. "Bringing back memories?"

Hank nodded. "But they're old ones."

He was turned out in a white shirt and tie, dark blue suit, hair combed back, carrying a briefcase that held a copy of Sandy Dunlop's file. Anybody that might have known him from the old days would have had trouble recognizing him.

Anita looked out the window again. "Do you want me to wait for you?"

"I don't know how long this'll take," Hank said. "I'll call if I need a ride."

Marty had phoned ahead so they were expecting him at the gate. One of the guards took him across the yard and handed him off to another at the front door. A familiar empty feeling settled in the pit of his stomach as the massive door closed behind him, but his face remained impassive. This was temporary, he told himself. Anytime he wanted, he could step out of here.

He was walked through a metal detector, someone went through his briefcase, and then he was left waiting in a small room furnished with only a wooden table and two chairs. There was an ashtray on the table, aluminum painted a sickly pink and so small he doubted it would hold more than three butts at a time. He laid the briefcase in front of him on the table and sat down, patient, using the time to distance himself from the familiar weight of the building as it pressed in on him.

A few minutes later the door opened and a guard brought Sandy Dunlop into the room.

"Thank you, officer," Hank said.

The guard gave him a friendly nod, then left. He was no more an officer than Hank was, but it didn't hurt to stroke the ego. The way Hank saw it, nobody became a prison guard or a traffic warden because it was a calling. They were in it because it was the only way they could feel empowered.

Sandy stood behind her chair, hands on the back, looking at him. She had a bruise under her left eye that looked about three, maybe four days old. Without makeup, her features were plain, almost washed out. Her blonde hair was showing dark roots and hung limply to her shoulders. The assets that had got her the job at Pussy's weren't evident, hidden under baggy trousers and an oversized sweatshirt. Hank knew the drill. When you were the new kid on the block, you didn't want to attract the wrong kind of attention from your cellmates. You went for tough first, fought if you had to, and you packaged yourself in something unappealing so that maybe no one would get the wrong idea in the first place.

"So how're they treating you?" Hank asked.

"I don't know you," she said.

"I work for Marty." Hank stood up and offered his hand. "I'm Joey Bennett."

She didn't shake, but she sat down. Hank took a pack of cigarettes out of his jacket and slid them across the table to her. She hesitated a long beat, then took one, nodding her thanks when Hank lit it for her. Taking a long drag, she gave him a crooked smile and pushed the pack back toward him.

"Keep them," he said.

"Thanks." She regarded him through a veil of smoke. "So what do you do for Marty?"

"Find things."

She nodded, tipped the end of her cigarette into the ashtray. "What're you looking for today?"

"What've you got?" he said.

Again the crooked smile. Another drag on the cigarette. "More trouble than I know what to do with," she said.

She was good at tough. If Marty could get her off, maybe she'd come through this okay.

"Why don't you walk me through what happened," he said.

"I've been through this, like, a million times already."

"But not with me. Humor me. I'm here to help."

She studied him for a long moment. "Okay. Where do you want me to start?"

"How about the last time you saw Ronnie."

Without thinking, she lifted a hand, touched the bruise under her eye.

"Ronnie do that?"

"Any bad thing that ever happened to me in the last two years came from that sorry piece of shit."

"He can't do anything to you anymore."

She made a small motion with her hand, trailing smoke. "What do you call being here?"

Hank nodded. "So the last time you saw him?"

"I was getting ready to go to work—you know where I work?"

"Strip joint."

"Yeah, except I was working the tables." She took out another cigarette, lit it from the butt of the first. "Anyway . . ."

Her story played out pretty much the way Marty had told it. There was more detail, more commentary on all the "assholes" in her life, from Ellis through to the D.A.'s prosecutor—"Talk about being uptight. That man desperately needs a night of serious hard-core"—but essentially, it was the same.

"How come you're not taking notes?" she wanted to know at one point.

Hank tapped his temple. "I am. You just can't see them."

She gave him a quizzical look, then shrugged and went on with her story, smoking, talking, looking at the table mostly, or just over his shoulder. Only occasionally would she meet his gaze. But as he listened to her talk,

Hank came to the same conclusion Marty had. She hadn't done it. She wasn't a Pollyanna, not by a long shot, but she hadn't killed Ellis. That left only one real suspect— so far as they knew. Philippe Couteau. Trouble was, he was dead, too.

"So this guy you were with during your break," he said. "He wasn't a regular?"

"I don't pay a whole lot of attention to their faces, but I think I would've remembered the tattoo."

"Think any of the other girls would know him?"

"You'd have to ask them."

"What about your friend Chrissy. Any idea why she took off? Where she might be?"

She shook her head. Lit another smoke.

"People come and go in my business," she said. "You know how it is. It's not like we keep a list of people to send Christmas cards to or anything."

Hank nodded. He knew how it was all too well.

"What can you tell me about Philippe Couteau?" he asked.

"The Frenchman?"

Hank nodded.

"Cold. I never saw anybody as cold as him."

"Ronnie was having problems with him?"

She gave him her crooked smile. "Christ, haven't you been listening? Ronnie had problems with everybody."

"So it could have been anyone?"

She shrugged. "Could've been. But it was all small-change crap. Piss you off at the time, but not the kind of thing you'd kill somebody over."

Hank took in the bruise below her eye, thought about the casual way she'd referred to Ellis beating her when she'd been telling her story earlier. It wasn't what he'd call small-time, but he held his peace, let her speak.

"It's funny, you know. Ronnie was like my Prince Charming when I first met him. This guy I was seeing, Louie, he was beating the crap out of me in the parking lot of a diner and Ronnie just stepped in and took care of him for me. Put Louie in the hospital.'' She shook her head, remembering. ''They had to sew him back together, like, fifty stitches—something like that.''

She lit another cigarette, chain-smoking, stubbed out the one that was done. The ashtray was overflowing now with five butts stuffed into it.

''Ronnie treated me like I was gold, you know? I could do no wrong. He moved in with me and it was like a fairy tale.''

Hank wondered which fairy tale it was that had Prince Charming pimping his girlfriend.

''So where did it go wrong?'' he asked.

She shrugged. ''Who knows? He had one hell of a temper, I'll tell you that, but he always made up after. You could tell he was truly sorry. He'd bring flowers, sometimes. Maybe we'd do a few lines. Things'd be good.'' She sighed. ''For awhile anyway.''

Hank wanted to get back to Couteau, but he knew from experience that sometimes you learned more just letting a person talk.

''Thing is, I loved Ronnie. I think maybe I still do. So what does that make me?''

''Confused?''

''I guess. I think about the way he treated me and I'm not sorry he's dead, you know? But then I keep expecting him to walk in the door and say, 'Okay, babe. Everything's been fixed.' And then we're walking out of here and everything *is* okay.''

She was staring at the ashtray as she spoke. Tipping the end of her cigarette against one of the butts, she watched the ash fall onto the table.

''You must think I'm such a loser,'' she said, not looking up.

''I don't judge people by who they've been,'' Hank told her. ''Only by who they are.''

Her gaze lifted. ''You're a lot like Marty, aren't you?''

''How so?''

''You really listen to what someone's saying. It's not

like the cops, or that guy from the D.A.'s office—you know they're just trying to catch you up in something. You and Marty make it seem like you're really interested.''

Hank shrugged. "Some people think a person hasn't got any money, or maybe they're sick or too old, and all of a sudden it's like they're invisible. They don't want to know them—don't even want to know they exist. Me, I figure if someone's taking the time to talk to me, I should take the time to listen.''

"Like some bum off the street comes up to you— you're going to stop and listen to him.''

"Some of my best friends are what other people call bums.''

She sat back, making it obvious that she was taking in the suit and tie. "Yeah. Right.''

Hank looked at her for a long moment. "There's something I heard Nicholas Payton say once. You have to be humble enough to understand and accept information from people who know something you don't. The way I see it, everybody's an expert in something.''

"Who's this Payton guy?''

"A trumpet player.''

"Yeah, well, he's a chump.''

Hank let it pass. It didn't matter what she thought of him or Payton.

"Let's get back to Couteau,'' he said. "What happened between him and Ronnie?''

"Ronnie owed him money for some dope he'd been fronted. Not the Frenchman himself, but some guy he works for. Ronnie didn't have it. The Frenchman said he'd be back.''

"When was this?''

She blew out a stream of smoke. "Tuesday—no, Monday. He came by the club because Ronnie was with me, checking out one of the new girls. She does this thing with snakes, you know? Really classy.''

Hank nodded encouragingly.

"The Frenchman doesn't look at Selma—the girl with the snakes. Doesn't check any of us out. Like I said, cold. Talks to Ronnie like I'm not even there, then he just walks out."

"Did you see him again?"

"Nah. Ronnie got the money together and paid him off."

"Who'd he owe the money to?" Hank asked. "Who was the Frenchman working for?"

"How would I know?"

Hank shrugged. "I figured a girl in your position— she'd hear things."

"Nobody ever told me squat." She sighed. "Did Marty say if they're going to set bail?"

Like they'd let her out on bail with a murder one charge hanging over her head.

"What we're working on," he said, "is getting them to drop the charges."

"No shit?"

Hank nodded. The hope in her eyes made him wish he could take her out with him when he left.

"But to do that," he said, "we've got to find the guy you were with on your break."

And the hope was gone, just like that. Replaced with the same flat gaze she'd had when she first came into the room.

"Guess I'll be here awhile then."

"Hang tough," Hank told her. "We're working on it."

"Whatever."

Her depression was contagious. It followed Hank back outside, across the yard, beyond the walls. He felt no relief when the gate closed behind him and he was out on the street, the weight of the building gone, being inside returned to something he remembered instead of someplace he was.

Loosening his tie, he started down Lee Street, heading downtown. He started to make a list of tattoo parlors in his head as he walked, then went looking for a phone

book to fill it out. It was a long shot, but the tattoo
Sandy's trick had sported was unusual enough that, if
he'd had it done in the city, someone was going to remember.

8.

Considering how long it had taken her to finally get to
bed the night before, Kerry awoke feeling surprisingly
rested. There was no residue of jet lag from her trip, none
of the usual morning fogginess that followed taking a
sleeping pill, and no bad dreams. Or at least none she
could remember. Forgotten, too, was last night's visitor
by the piano. Instead her heart was light, her mind un-
cluttered with worry. Pushing back the sheets, she sat up,
eager to meet the day.

And it was going to be a good day, she decided. Everything pointed to it. The unfamiliar sense of well-being.
The sunlight, tinted green by the leaves of the elm,
streaming into the room where it woke a honey glow
from the wooden floors and made the light-colored walls
gleam. The clean smell of the room, as though the futon
and pillow were stuffed with lemon balm. There was still
no furniture, but she found herself reveling in the feeling
of space that the lack of furniture gave the room.

Leaving the bed unmade, she washed and put some
water in the saucepan that was serving as her kettle. She
got dressed while she waited for it to boil. White T-shirt,
blue jeans, Birkenstock sandals. When the water started
to boil, she made herself a mug of tea and took it into
the living room, but the view from the window wasn't
enough to satisfy her. She had to be outside on a morning
like this. So she took her tea downstairs to the front
porch, walking quietly on the wooden stairs and easing
the front door open so as not to wake anyone in the house
who might still be sleeping.

There was a wooden two-seater swing at the far end

"It was on the window seat in your living room."

"I know that. I meant . . ."

Kerry sighed. It was hard to be angry with the picture of innocence that Maida presented as she came down the length of the porch with that same easy stride of Zia's and sat down beside Kerry on the bench. Pulling her legs up under her, Maida faced Kerry and put the picture on her lap.

Kerry was used to a lack of privacy—she hadn't had a choice in the matter for years. But that didn't mean she'd ever liked it or had to put up with it now. She had to remember to lock her door.

"You shouldn't go into other people's apartments without being invited first," she said.

Maida regarded her with obvious bafflement. "Why not?"

"Because it's not polite. You have to respect people's privacy."

This was so weird. Kerry felt as though she was explaining the basics of common courtesy to a child, except the gaze that met her own wasn't a child's gaze. It wasn't even the gaze of the young woman that Kerry assumed Maida was—seventeen, maybe eighteen—but that of someone far older. An eerie feeling went whispering up Kerry's spine.

"We know her," Zia said, leaning forward to study the picture.

Kerry glanced at her in surprise.

"Remember?" Zia went on, her attention turned to Maida now. "She lived in the yellow house with all the flowers around it. You could swim in those flowers, there were so many. She was always drawing pictures of them and writing in that little book of hers."

Maida's face lit up. "I *do* remember her now. She'd have those oatmeal cookies that she'd share with us—the ones with all the nuts and bits of dried fruit in them."

Zia nodded. "She called them field food."

"And she had a nettle in her name—remember?"

"I do, I do," Zia said. "And she made houses for bees so that they'd give her honey."

Maida licked her lips. "Mmm. Honey for the tea and she never minded when you took a dollop on your finger."

Kerry could remember those cookies and the honeyed tea, but how could either Maida or Zia have tasted them? They couldn't have been more than five or six when Nettie died. Yet here they were, talking about the yellow house and the fields of wildflowers surrounding it as though it was familiar terrain. They knew that she'd kept bees. They knew about the cookies and how Nettie called them field food because she always took a few with her when she went hiking. They knew about her sketches and the notes she was always taking that were later turned into essays.

"Why did we ever stop visiting her?" Zia said.

Maida frowned in thought. "Because Ray told us to?"

"No, Ray wouldn't be so veryvery rude. Cody's the rude one."

"But handsome."

"Oh, veryvery."

"But then . . ."

A sudden stillness settled over Zia. "I remember now," she said, her voice soft. "It's because she died."

"And she wasn't supposed to die," Maida said, subdued now as well. "That's what was so sad."

Tears swelled in Kerry's eyes. The confusion she'd been feeling as she listened to their conversation succumbed to a familiar sadness made strange by being able to share it with others who'd known and cared for her grandmother—no matter how impossible that seemed.

"How do you know her?" Zia asked.

First Kerry had to swallow. "She . . . she was my grandmother."

"So that's why you have fire here," Maida said, reaching out to stroke Kerry's messy tangle of hair.

Her hand moved on, a finger gently touching the corner

of Kerry's eye, the tip glistening when she took it away. She licked the tear from her fingertip, then put an arm around Kerry's shoulders.

"Don't be sad," she said. "Nettie's gone back into forever now. Raven says it's a good place to go."

Kerry looked back and forth between them. "I don't understand any of this," she said. "How could you have known my grandmother? Who are these people—Raven and Ray and Cody?"

"We know everybody," Zia said.

Maida nodded in agreement. "Because we've been around forever."

Kerry was beginning to think that maybe they really did live in a tree. Maybe they were faeries, the little earth spirits that Nettie used to tell her about. But if that was true, then maybe it was also true that—

"Man, is this a beautiful day or what?"

Kerry hadn't even heard the screen door open this time. She lifted her gaze to find Rory joining them on the porch and just like that, everything changed. Mysterious, wonderful things, seeming so plausible, so *possible* a moment ago, returned to their proper place as only a part of stories and fanciful imaginations, and the real world clicked back into place. The odd conversation she'd been having with Maida and Zia felt more like something she'd dreamt once than anything she might actually have experienced.

Rory smiled at her, though there was an odd look in his eyes when his gaze settled on Maida and Zia, as though at that moment he was seeing them for the first time. The way he studied them started to bring back her own fey feelings, but then he shrugged and it went away once more.

"So," he said. "You still up for a little shopping today?"

Maida perked right up, happy as a puppy who'd just heard the phrase "go for a walk."

"Shopping?" Zia said. "Oh, can we come?"

"Not a chance," Rory told her.

"Why not?" Kerry asked.

"Because they shoplift," he said. "I almost got arrested the last time they came with me."

Kerry gave Maida and Zia a worried look, but neither of the girls seemed the least bit embarrassed by the revelation.

"It's only borrowing," Maida said.

Rory laughed. "Borrowing is when you ask permission first—and then return whatever it is you've borrowed." He looked at Kerry, adding, "They're incorrigible. They'll stick whatever they want in their pockets and we're not just talking gum and candy bars here. The time we almost got busted they were lugging this huge disco ball out of a junk shop."

"We wanted to hang it in our tree," Zia said.

"But why would you do that?" Kerry asked.

Zia shrugged. "We thought it would look pretty."

"And we knew it would drive all the 'pies crazy with jealousy," Maida added.

"No, I meant why would you steal things?"

"Don't ask us," Zia said.

Maida nodded. "You're the ones who invented property."

Kerry was beginning to understand why Rory had called them impetuous last night. They really were like small forces of nature, impossible to restrain.

"Okay," she said. "And what are pies?" she added, not sure she even wanted to know how whatever they were could be jealous of a disco ball hanging in a big elm tree.

"Duh," Maida told her. "They're things you eat."

"They meant magpies," Rory explained. "They have some kind of rivalry with the magpies, whoever they are."

"So it's like . . . gangs?" Kerry asked. She looked at the girls. "The magpies are who they are the same way you're the crow girls?"

They both seemed to find this immensely amusing.

"We're a gang," Maida said.

Zia nodded enthusiastically. "I love being a gang."

"Who's up for breakfast?" Rory asked.

Kerry gave him a grateful look. She was beginning to feel very off-balance and really needed something normal to focus upon.

"What're we having?" Maida wanted to know.

Rory opened his arms expansively. "Whatever you want."

"Peaches and bacon!" Zia cried.

Maida bounced to her feet. "Biscuits and jelly beans!"

Forget normal, Kerry thought.

"Actually," Rory said, "I have all of that, but who'd have thought it could be put together as a meal?" He gave Kerry a smile. "And what about you?"

"Some more tea would be nice," she said. "And maybe some toast."

"Let's see what we can do."

The girls disappeared into the house, letting the screen door bang shut behind them. Kerry took a deep breath and let it out slowly, then looked up to find Rory smiling at her.

"They take some getting used to," he said.

Kerry nodded. "I'll say," she said as she followed him inside at a slower pace, her tea mug in one hand, Nettie's photograph in the other.

9.

Moth had a sixth sense for finding things. The only rule, if something like this could be said to have rules, was he had to have a certain familiarity with whatever it was he was trying to find. But if he had that familiarity, all he had to do was follow wherever it was that his feet would take him and sooner or later he'd find the thing he was looking for. Which was how, after first stopping by Jack's school bus, he found himself on the grounds of Butler University,

down where the common runs up against the riverbank,
saying hello to Jack and Katy.

They were fishing, neither of them showing much enthusiasm. Jack went about it with the same languid air he
did everything, leaning back on one arm, smoking his
pipe. It was as though he were at some private fishing
hole, way back up in the hills north of the city, instead
of near a bike path on the common with a constant parade
of in-line skaters, strollers, and joggers streaming by,
everyone out to take in a piece of a sunny Sunday morning. He looked lazy as some old blackbird in that flat-
brimmed black hat and duster, but his eyes were alert,
sharp gaze missing nothing.

Beside him, Katy was a splash of bright color against
the browning vegetation and Jack's Johnny Cash impression: bright red hair, yellow T-shirt, purple leggings,
green baseball cap. But where Jack was obviously at ease
in the role of fisherman, she seemed to only be going
through the motions, so withdrawn into herself that she
was drifting into invisibility. Most people glancing at
them wouldn't even see her, regardless of the bright palette of her wardrobe.

"Catching anything?" Moth asked as he sat down on
the grass beside Katy.

She glanced at him, gave him a small smile, looked
away.

"You know fish," Jack said. "They can be tricky little
buggers. Today they're demanding more incentive that
we've got to give."

Moth leaned back on his elbows and shook out a cigarette, got it lit.

"Never tried it myself," he said.

"I'd recommend fishing," Jack told him. "It's a good
way to waste time while feeling productive."

"Well, I do like eating them."

Jack nodded. "I'd say they taste better when you catch
them yourself, but who am I kidding? Doesn't matter who
caught them, so long as they're fresh."

There was nothing fancy about their gear. They each had a long stick with a length of fishing line tied to the end. Probably nothing more than a baited hook and small weight in the water.

"I've been wondering," Moth said.

The grass at the very edge of the riverbank was uncut, leaving a narrow strip of wild country between the water and the trimmed lawn of the common, two feet, no more than four feet at its widest. Closer to the water, the long grass gave way to reeds and cattails with a rose madder blush of joe-pye weed a little north of where they were sitting. Moth smoked his cigarette. Katy leaned forward and plucked a stem of grass. She stuck it between her teeth, the seeded end dangling.

"Wondering's healthy," Jack said. "Broadens the mind. Opens you up to all sorts of stray thoughts and possibilities."

"My wondering was a little more specific than that."

Jack glanced at him. "I'm listening."

"Those stories of yours," Moth said. "You know how you're always talking about how that guy Cody shows up somewhere and then the trouble starts?"

Jack nodded.

"So what I'm wondering is if maybe Cody's showed up here recently."

"That's pretty specific all right."

Jack pulled his line out of the water, checked the worm hanging on the end, then let it drop back into the water. The old nail he was using for a weight made a small splash as it broke the surface. Moth thought Jack might be evading the question, that no answer was the most answer he was going to get. He saw that Katy had sat up straighter and was looking at Jack, waiting, the same as he was. Jack turned to them, something dark sitting in the back of his eyes.

"You don't want to get involved with Cody," he said finally. "He's hard on people."

"Trouble is, I think maybe Hank already is."

"That business in the Zone the other night?"

Moth nodded. "You've been talking to Hank?"

"Nah. Katy told me about it. The crow girls told me some more." He drew on his pipe, exhaled a wreath of blue-gray smoke. "I doubt Cody had anything to do with it. He doesn't run with the cuckoos."

Moth gave him a blank look.

"We're the same as you," Jack said. "Some of us get along, some of us don't. But the thing between us and the cuckoos isn't the same as the trouble we have with Cody. It's more a killing feud—lot of pain stored up in it. Old pain."

"But what are they?"

Jack shrugged. "Meaner than most. If they were human, you'd call them sociopaths. Got voices sweet as honey and some of them are so pretty you'd think you were looking on a piece of heaven if you came upon one, but they've got no sense of right or wrong. There's just them and then everybody else. We try to ignore them unless they get in our face."

"So the other night—"

"Hank's friend was just in the wrong place at the wrong time. It happens, Moth. You know that. Happens with your people the same as mine. Random meanness and there's no accounting for it. The crow girls took care of it."

"Maybe," Moth said. "But what if it doesn't stop there? Hank feels like he's waiting for something to happen."

Jack let a long moment slide by before he spoke again. "I know what he means."

He looked out across the river, gaze on the ivy-covered buildings of the university on the far side of the common, the trees that crowded close to them in places. Or maybe he was looking farther away than that, gaze taking him somewhere else entirely, someplace only he could see.

"Raven's been living here for a long time now," he said after a moment. "Going deeper and deeper into himself—or wherever it is that he goes. Last time we had trouble with Cody, we couldn't even rouse Raven. We had to take care of it ourselves. Cody wasn't ready for it then, but he'll be ready now. The way it feels is we're due for something, so everybody's waiting."

Moth was hoping for more, some clearer explanation of who Raven and Cody really were, what they might get up to, how Hank could be involved, but Jack had fallen silent again. This time Moth let the questions lie, playing it Hank's way, ready to listen, seeing what not talking called up. He lit another cigarette, patient.

"But you know," Jack went on, "the crow girls have taken a liking to Hank, so it could go one of two ways. They could look out for him, or they could drag him deeper into whatever's going to play out this time around." The dark gaze returned from whatever it had been seeing to meet Moth's. "Because Cody's definitely in town. Nobody's seen him, but I can smell him at night, walking the streets, checking out how things lie."

"What does he want?"

"The same thing he always wants, to set things right. And the same thing'll happen that always happens, he'll screw it up."

"I don't get it."

Jack sighed. "Let me put it this way and don't take offense. The real reason we don't get along with Cody is he made you. Stirred in that big pot with that big bushy tail of his and out you came, swarming over everything like bugs. Now I'm not saying you're all bad—just the world was a better place before you came along.

"Anyway, Raven took the pot away from him, but it was too late now. Cody had the taste of it. Knew he'd made a mistake and wanted to make it right, so he stole that pot again, stirred it up, and this time he woke up death." He fixed Moth with those dark eyes of his. "Every time he gets that pot, he screws things up. Doesn't mean to, but as sure as the sun rises, you can count on it."

"So this time—"

"Like I said, he'll be hoping to fix things right. He means well. But what'll he do with it? Who knows. All I can tell you is that if history's any kind of a guideline, it'll be nothing good."

"It's like the grail, isn't it?" Katy said. "This pot you keep talking about."

"That's a story that grew out of it," Jack said, "but it's older that that, older than Cerridwen's cauldron, too." He smiled. "And Cody sure as hell isn't some questing knight."

Moth sat there thinking, remembering all those stories Jack had told of this pot, cauldron, whatever it was. Cody and Raven. Now these cuckoos. And then there was the whole business with Katy that they hadn't even gotten into today. It was hard considering it all to be here and now, real, instead of just another piece of some story. But then he thought of Hank, what had happened to him, the old bullet scar on his shoulder that hadn't been there the day before. Like it or not, things had changed. The world had expanded beyond what he'd always known it to be. All of a sudden there was too much unfamiliar territory.

"Is there anything we can do?" he asked.

Jack shrugged. "Just tell Hank to walk carefully. He gets into this, it might take him so deep he'll never get back out again."

Moth realized he didn't have Hank's patience. "Any chance you could spell things out a little more clearly?"

"If I knew any more than I do, I'd tell you," Jack said. "You're not blood, but you're family. I hear anything, I'll tell you."

Conversation fell off then. Jack smoked his pipe. Katy settled back into that place she'd been when Moth first arrived, leaning into invisibility. Moth sighed. He had more questions now than before he'd found Jack and Katy sitting here, fishing.

After awhile he got ready to go. Before he left, he reached out to touch Katy's shoulder, half-expecting his fingers to go right through her, but they stopped at the fabric of her T-shirt and he could feel the shoulder underneath, solid as his own hand.

"The thing Hank told you," he said. "That goes for all of us."

She covered his hand for a moment, but didn't speak. Didn't have to. Moth understood.

"Anytime," he said.

She took her hand away and he stood up.

"Hope you catch something," he said before he left. "We could have us a fish fry."

Jack smiled. "They've got stores that sell fish, you know."

"Well, now," Moth told him. "The way I feel about it is, the best fish are those that someone else catches for you."

He could still hear Jack chuckling as he walked away.

10.

Kerry was tired by the time they finally stopped for a late lunch, but she hadn't lost her good spirits. This was kind of a record for her, she realized as they waited just inside the front door of the Rusty Lion to be seated. She actually had stiff cheeks from smiling so much.

The restaurant was busier than she'd expected for a Sunday afternoon.

"But that's just it," Annie said when she commented upon it. "It's because it's Sunday. Everybody's hanging and this is one of the places to be."

So it seemed, Kerry thought. Most of the tables she could see from where they stood were occupied, the crowd pretty much proportionately divided between upscale and bohemian, but with a complete lack of segregation. Lower Crowsea in microcosm. She supposed she and her companions fit into the bohemian category. A musician, a writer/jeweler, and a . . . well, what was she?

For the moment it didn't matter. It was enough to be here, enjoying the English pub decor, the happy murmur of voices, the smell of good food.

When was the last time she'd gone this long feeling happy? She couldn't remember anymore. When she was a child, she supposed, before her family had moved out to the coast, before all the trouble began. For the past decade, a good day was one without an incident, never mind feeling happy, so she relished the gift she'd been given today and didn't really want to consider it too closely for fear of jinxing it.

She knew the way she was feeling was due in part to Annie and Rory being such good company, but she felt she could take some credit for it as well. Moving here was an excellent start to reclaiming some normality in her life. She had no past here, certainly not in the city itself. However she presented herself to people, that's who she was. They could have no expectations. There was no walking on eggs around her because who knew what might set her off. She and her new friends could get to know each other by what they said and did, not by reputation. She could be anybody she wanted to be and who knew? Maybe she could even convince herself that she was somebody else.

"So let's see," Rory said when they finally got a table. He retrieved a wrinkled piece of paper from his pocket and smoothed it out on top of his menu. "Looks like all we have left to get is some groceries."

So far they'd managed to track down a kitchen table with three mismatched chairs, a beautiful antique wooden chest for the bedroom to keep clothes in, a small bookcase that desperately needed repainting—"Who'd this belong to before?" Annie had asked in the junk shop when they'd unearthed the lime-green grotesquerie behind a stack of landscape paintings. "A clown?"—some fruit crates she could use as end tables, a portable cassette player–radio, and a small hooked rug, all for under two hundred dollars.

"I can't believe we got all of this stuff so cheaply,"
Kerry said.

Granted, they'd rummaged around in more antique and
junk shops than she'd ever seen in one area, little say
been in, but still. She'd seen the price on the chest before
Annie had dragged the shop owner to the back of his
dusty store to talk about it, and it alone had been over a
hundred dollars. At least it had been until Annie had
started bargaining.

"Get used to it when you shop with Annie," Rory told
her. "People seem to fall over themselves trying to give
her a bargain."

Annie grinned. "What can I say? My fame precedes
me."

"That would be infamy," Rory said. "It's not the
same thing at all."

"What kind of music do you play?" Kerry asked Annie.

"I'll give you a copy of my latest as a housewarming
present and you can decide for yourself."

"Oh, no," Kerry said. "You guys have already been
way too generous with—"

"Curtains," Annie said, interrupting. "We still need
to get curtains, too. Or at least some lace. And a plant.
Every house needs a plant."

Rory dutifully made additions to the list.

"If we're going to do this," Annie said, "we're going
to do it right."

"Yes, but—"

Annie wagged a finger back and forth in front of Kerry.
"I don't want to hear it."

"She can be a bit of a control freak," Rory explained
in a stage whisper. "Just play along and then do what
you want later. Trust me, it's way easier."

"I heard that," Annie said.

Rory smiled. "You were supposed to. Someone's got
to keep you honest."

"Fair enough," Annie said. "But control freak? Isn't

that a bit extreme? It makes me sound so domineering.''

"You do like to be in charge.''

"But that's just my nature. You can't change a person's nature. Next you'll be wanting to reform the crow girls.''

"Good luck to anyone who wants to try.''

"Don't change the subject,'' Annie said. She turned her attention across the table to Kerry. "You don't think I'm a control freak, do you?''

The waiter chose that moment to arrive, so Kerry only shook her head.

She was enjoying the easy banter between the two of them. It was so refreshing to be in a situation where you didn't have to be careful of everything you said. An unhappy memory popped into her mind, the stiff posture of the woman sitting across the desk from her, the expressionless face, except for the eyes that seemed to weigh and judge every nuance of word and countenance. She could hear the sandpaper voice as though the woman were sitting at the table with them right now.

And just what do you mean when you say 'normal'?

Don't think about that kind of thing, she told herself and tried to concentrate on the moment at hand.

"Can I get you something from the bar?'' the waiter was asking.

Annie looked up and gave him a bright smile. "Actually,'' she said, "I have a question about your meat entrées.''

"Sure. What do you want to know?''

Kerry immediately took a liking to their waiter. He was young—barely twenty, she guessed. A nice-looking young man with bright, cheerful eyes, dark hair pulled back into a small ponytail, trim physique. He was so friendly that she couldn't understand why Annie proceeded to give him a hard time.

"Where do you get the meat from?'' Annie asked.

The waiter appeared as confused as Kerry felt.

"The meat?'' he said.

Annie nodded. "You know. The chicken, the ham."
She glanced down at the menu. "The beef and lamb."

"I'm not sure I understand."

"Were the animals raised to provide you with their
meat, or did you just find it?"

"Find it?"

Kerry felt so sorry for the waiter. She looked at Rory,
but all he did was shrug as if to say he'd been here before.

Annie was nodding. "Sure. Like, is it roadkill or something?"

"I can assure you," the waiter said, "that all the meat
we serve is government approved."

"Oh." She actually seemed disappointed, Kerry
thought. "I guess I'll have a Caesar salad then, with the
bacon bits on the side."

That made Kerry remember how at breakfast Maida—
or was it Zia?—had eaten all the peaches on her plate
but only sniffed at the bacon she'd asked for. "I just like
the smell," she'd explained. "Not the taste." It made no
more sense than Annie's asking for bacon bits on the side.
What was she going to do? Smell them like Zia had?

It obviously made no sense to the waiter either. He
hesitated for a long moment, but quickly recovered.

"And for you?" he asked Kerry as he wrote Annie's
order on his pad.

Kerry ordered a grilled cheese and ham—which made
Annie pull a face—and Rory had the special of the day,
a seafood pasta. After they ordered their drinks, Annie
excused herself to go to the washroom. Kerry watched
Annie's receding back as she wound her way through the
tables before turning to Rory.

"What was all that about?" she asked.

"It's just Annie," he said. "You never know what
she's going to do. I've pretty much given up trying to
ever figure her out."

"But all those questions she was asking. It was so
weird."

Rory nodded.

A thought suddenly occurred to Kerry. "I wonder what she'd have done if the waiter had said that they did serve roadkill."

"Probably have ordered something."

Kerry started to laugh, but then she saw that Rory wasn't smiling.

"You're not serious, are you?" she asked Rory now.

"I don't know. Lord knows I love the woman, but sometimes she gets strange."

"I feel sorry for the waiter."

"It can get embarrassing. I was with her once when she told this bag lady to thoroughly crinkle the tinfoil she was using to line her hat with, because if the surface could catch any sort of a complete reflection, it would transfer it directly into her brain. The poor woman was terrified—I mean, we're talking about someone who wasn't all there in the first place."

Kerry shivered at the casual expression. She found herself asking that question all the time. Am I all here?

"When I asked her why she'd done it," Rory went on, "she said, 'Because for her, it's true.'" He sighed and leaned forward a little. "Actually, you're going to find that most of the people living in the Rookery are a bit strange. It's not that they're particularly dangerous or anything—though I know Brandon can look a little fierce. I guess it's just that you're going to find they're different from most folks you might know."

Want to bet? Kerry felt like asking, but all she said was, "Who's Brandon?"

"He lives in the coach house out back—second floor. The Aunts live under him. Lucius and Chloë live up on the third floor of the house."

"So they're a couple?"

"I don't even want to think about it."

"What do you mean?"

Rory shrugged. "You'll see. But since Paul died, that's about it—if you include the three of us."

"Paul used to live in my apartment?" Kerry asked.

"Yeah. He and Annie were pretty tight—best friends kind of tight."

"She must miss him."

Rory nodded. "Everybody misses him—he was a great guy—but Annie and Brandon miss him the most." He paused for a moment. "Anyway, you'll probably meet them all in the next week or so." He grinned, adding, "Though, of course, you've already met the crow girls."

"Who live in a tree."

Kerry smiled as she spoke, only now a part of the conversation she'd had with them earlier in the morning returned to her—not so much the actual words as the strange, off-kilter feeling the words had generated. She felt a touch of dizziness and had to take a quick breath, let it out slowly. Rory didn't seem to notice.

"Who might as well live in a tree," he agreed.

There was an odd note in his voice. More hidden currents, Kerry decided.

"Who might as well live in a tree?" Annie asked, slipping back into her seat.

"Maida and Zia," Rory said. "The banes of my existence."

Annie laughed. "You shouldn't let them get to you. The only reason they tease you as much as they do is because you let them get away with it." She turned her attention to Kerry before he could reply. "So do you still have to register for your classes, or did you set that up before you came?"

"How did you know I was going back to school?"

"Chloë told me."

"Oh." That made sense. "I should go upstairs and introduce myself to her. We've only spoken on the phone so far."

"How do you even know her?" Rory asked.

"She was a friend of my grandmother's." Again she got that twinge. Something in the conversation she'd had with Zia and Maida. She took another steadying breath and made herself ignore it. "When I decided to move back here, she was the only person I could think of to call who might know where I could find a place to live. I guess I was just lucky that there was an apartment available right at the same time.''

Rory looked surprised. "You used to live here?"

"Not in the city. Up north, in the hills. In a little town called Hazard."

"One of the old mining towns," Annie said.

Kerry nodded. "We moved to Long Beach when I was just a kid so I never really knew the city."

"What're you taking at Butler?" Rory asked.

"Art history. I . . . I've always been interested in art. I used to try to draw like my grandmother always did, but I was never much good at it and . . ." She shrugged. "I guess my parents didn't much like the idea, so I never really followed through on it."

Annie gave her a sympathetic nod. "So they've come around?"

"No," Kerry said. "They're dead now so I can finally do what I want to do." She put her hand to her mouth as soon as the words came out of her mouth. "Oh, God. That sounds so horrible."

There was a moment of awkward silence, before Rory said, "You can choose your friends, but not your family. Sometimes we don't get much luck with the draw."

Annie nodded. "Blood doesn't always tell."

"I guess."

Kerry was grateful for their support, but it didn't seem to be enough to prevent the day's good spirit from draining away. She wanted to be alone. She didn't want to have to try to make more conversation. She didn't even want to eat anymore. All she wanted to do was crawl away somewhere and—

"Okay," a voice said suddenly, making her start.

Their waiter was back, cheerful once more. She hadn't even noticed his approach.

"Grilled cheese and ham for the quiet lady," he said, placing her order in front of her. "Pasta special for the gentleman. And for you,'' he added, placing Annie's salad on the table with a flourish, ''one Caesar, bacon bits on the side.'' He winked at Kerry. ''Enjoy your meal.''

''Isn't he sweet?'' Annie said as the waiter retreated.

Kerry and Rory exchanged glances, then they both had to laugh and the awkwardness of a moment ago was gone.

Much later in the afternoon, laden with shopping bags, the three of them trudged down Stanton Street toward the Rookery. It was cooler under the shade of the oaks, but still warmer than Kerry had been expecting for early September in Newford—not that she really knew what to expect, she'd been away from the very idea of seasons for so long. She was looking forward to experiencing them again—things like actual snow and leaves falling and everything—but not so much that she didn't appreciate the perfect weather that had been with them all day. Clear skies, sun warm, the air filled with the promise of the colder weather that wasn't with them yet. She could smell the coming change.

''I'll bet the deliverymen have already been,'' Annie said, ''and we'll have to lug all that stuff upstairs by ourselves.''

''Oh, you don't have to do that,'' Kerry said. ''I don't want to be any more of a—''

''Bother,'' Rory said, finishing the sentence for her. ''We know. And you're not.''

''It's just that . . .'' Kerry looked from one to the other. ''You guys have been so great today.''

''Greatness is one of our specialties,'' Annie told her. ''Along with humility and a patient sufferance for those not quite so great as us.''

Rory's eyebrows rose in a question. ''Humility?''

''If it's not a word, it should be,'' Annie said. ''And look. I was right. The porch is full of furniture with not a deliveryman in sight.''

Kerry's gaze followed the direction Annie indicated with a bob of her head, but before it could reach the porch, something made her look up through a small gap in the heavy foliage above them to the roof of their building. What she saw made her stop in her tracks.

"Oh, my God," she said.

"What's the matter?" Rory asked.

His obvious worry was mirrored in Annie's features. Kerry pointed toward the roof of their building that could no longer be seen because they'd taken a few steps beyond the gap.

"Up . . . up on the roof of the house," she said. "There's a woman sitting on the peak."

Rory relaxed. "That'd be Chloë," he said. "She likes to sit up there," he added in response to Kerry's confused look.

"Reminds her of the long ago," Annie said.

Kerry looked back and forth between them, trying to see the joke.

"But isn't it dangerous?" she asked.

"Apparently not," Rory said.

"And if she ever started to slip," Annie added, "all she'd have to do is fly away."

Now it was Rory who looked puzzled. He regarded Annie thoughtfully, then shrugged and started walking again.

"Sure," he said. "Why not? Everybody's bird-crazy in this house."

"What did you mean about long ago?" Kerry asked as she fell into step beside Annie.

Annie gave her a teasing look. "You know. When we were all animals."

Kerry still didn't get it and it was obvious Rory didn't either, though the phrase seemed to mean something to him because it took him deep into thought again until he saw or felt her looking at him. That earned her a wry smile, as if to say, I'm as much in the dark here as you.

Annie punched her lightly on the arm. "Oh, don't take everything so seriously."

"I'm not. I mean, I won't."

"Look at this," Rory said as they joined him on the porch. "Notice how when there's work to be done, the crow girls are never to be found?"

"You really think it would go quicker if they were here to help?" Annie asked.

Rory nodded. "You're right. What was I thinking?" He hefted a corner of the table to test its weight. "So who's going to give me a hand with this?"

"You hold the door," Annie told Kerry as she put the bags she was carrying down on the wicker bench. "We'll get this and the chest up first and then come back for all the smaller stuff."

11.

When had the number of tattoo parlors in town doubled? Hank wondered as he read down the list he'd copied from the yellow pages. He recognized some of the old names. Al's Tattoo Parlor, an old biker hangout on Gracie. The Tattoo Garden, down in the Market. The Buzz, over on Williamson Street where Terry's sister, Paris, worked. But there were as many he'd never heard of before. Zola's in the Zone. Silverland. Needles and Pins. Most of the newer ones also offering body piercing.

Tattoos had never been Hank's scene, not even when he was inside. Tattoos, like jewelry, got in the way of being invisible. They attracted too much notice, made people remember you.

For a long time he hadn't really understood the compulsion to take needle and ink to the skin and make a mark. Then he met Paris Lee. If you saw her in a long-sleeved shirt and jeans, her black hair hanging down in a curtain over her neck, you'd never know that most of her body was covered with tattoos.

"It's my diary," she'd explained. "Every mark I've had drawn on my skin connects me to where and who I've been—so I never forget who I am and how I got here." There was no humor to the smile she offered him. "And you know what the real beauty of it is?"

Hank had shaken his head.

"Nobody can take it away."

Nobody could understand the diary either because the images all referred to her own personal mythology; even their positioning had a symbolic meaning. But what other people understood wasn't important. What was important was that she did. That she was able to read the complex story that was related in the bewildering pattern that ran across her torso and limbs. Some of the images were there to remind her of the things that were worth living for. The others stood as mute witness to a long dark time when a needle entering her skin wasn't adding to the story, but searching for a vein, offering only oblivion.

So Hank learned to understand the need to leave a mark, if only on your own skin. But he didn't want his to be anybody's canvas—not even his own.

Al's Tattoo Parlor was closest to the gym where he'd stopped off to change into more casual clothes, so he started there. The Al who'd given the place its name was long gone, victim of a turf war in the early seventies. The outside of the building looked like a concrete bunker, one window boarded up, the other holding a sun-faded display of tattoos. There was a sour smell inside, an unpleasant mix of body odor, machine oil, and old cigarette smoke. The half-dozen bikers hanging out were old and fat or wasted-thin, all of them out of shape, none of them able to muster much more than tired sneers at his entrance. The young turks had their own hangouts now.

The man behind the counter was tall and lean as barbed wire and unlike the rest of them, he was still dangerous. He wore his dark hair slicked back in a ducktail. A cigarette hung from his lips, smoke curling up the side of

his face. His name was Bruno and he'd done time with
Moth, back in the sixties. A real wizard with a needle,
inside or on the street. He recognized Hank and gave him
a nod.

"Got a weird question for you," Hank said.

"Shoot."

"You do penises?"

One of the fat bikers snickered. He broke off when
Bruno turned to look at him.

"I'm guessing this is someone you're looking for?"
Bruno said, returning his attention to Hank.

Hank nodded.

"Ellie might have done some, but that was back when
Al was running the place. Don't touch 'em myself."

That brought another snicker from where the bikers
were lounging. Bruno didn't even bother looking at them
this time.

"I don't suppose you keep records?" Hank asked.

Bruno gave him a thin smile. "What do you think?"

"It was worth a shot."

"What was the tattoo?"

"A cobra—goes the full length, circles around."

"Cute."

Hank shrugged.

"You might try some of those new places. They do
cock-rings, the whole shot."

"Thanks. I will."

Hank got as far as the door when one of the bikers
called out to him. He turned, leaned against the doorjamb.
It was the one who'd snickered earlier.

"That dog of yours," the biker said. "The one you
run with."

"He's not mine."

"Whatever. I was just wondering, what kind of a dog
is it?"

"Tombs-mutt."

"I was thinking it might be part bear."

"That, too."

''Ugly son of a bitch, ain't it? Surprised nobody's taken a shot at it.''

Hank knew he was just trying to save face from the way Bruno'd shut him up earlier, so he didn't take the implied threat too seriously.

''You going to be the one?'' he asked, keeping his voice mild.

The biker shrugged.

''Well,'' Hank said. ''Just remember this: I know your face.''

Before the biker could respond, Hank nodded to Bruno and stepped outside. A bus was going by, leaving a cloud of diesel fumes in its wake, but it still smelled better than it had inside. He waited a moment, but no one came out. That suited him fine. He didn't need the extra grief.

He didn't get to the Buzz until two fruitless hours later. It was clean inside and air-conditioned. Spot lighting, black-and-white checkered floor, the monochrome coloring extending to the walls and ceiling. Paris was standing at the counter, talking to a customer, a striking woman, willowy and tall, with an amazing psychedelic tattoo on her shoulder. Paris blew him a kiss when she saw him come in, then returned to her conversation. The woman was looking into getting her clitoris pierced and wanted to know if it would hurt.

Jesus, Hank thought as he took a seat on the black leather couch by the window. What do you think?

Paris suited the place perfectly, as monochrome as the decor, black jeans and combat boots, a white short-sleeved shirt, her hair like black jet against her pale skin. Black lipstick, dark eye shadow above her almond-shaped eyes. The only color in the room came from her forearms and the other woman's shoulder, a kaleidoscope of swirling patterns that seemed all the more intense because of what surrounded them.

There were tattoo magazines scattered on the coffee table beside him, but Hank didn't pay any more attention to them than he did to the conversation between Paris and her customer. He went into no-time while he waited, that place where the idea of linear time held no meaning. He could sit like that for hours, aware of everything around him, but only on an animal level. The world spun on around him while he sat patient, timeless, spidered in the center of a meditative mandala, one of his own making. He didn't need a tattoo to remember who and why he was. He simply was. Only today who he was missed Lily and that he didn't understand at all. He barely knew the woman, didn't know her angle, didn't know if she even had an angle. But there she was in his thoughts anyway, a warm presence, a small ache, a piece of happiness all the more precious because of the landscapes he'd been walking today. County jail. Seedy streets. Tattoo parlors.

He came out of it the moment Paris sat down on the couch beside him. She gave him a quick kiss on the cheek, then leaned back to look at him.

"There's something different about you today," she said. "Did you get laid or something?"

Hank smiled. "Just deep in thought."

"Yeah, right. The only guy I know who thinks less than you is Moth. I think you're in love."

"You think?" he asked, keeping his voice light.

She shrugged. "Who knows? But I hope she's good for you." Before he could admit to or deny her observation, she was already plunging on. "So what are you doing here on a Sunday afternoon? Coming to take me for a coffee?"

"You want a coffee?"

"Nah. I've had so many already today I feel like the store was named after me." She grinned and made a buzzing sound. "What's up?"

As he began to explain, she put a hand in front of her mouth, but wasn't able to stop the giggle.

"Now what?" he said.

It took her a moment to be able to speak.

"Nothing," she managed finally, humor still dancing in her eyes. "It's just that when you first started talking I thought you meant *you* wanted this tattoo."

He smiled. "What if I did?"

"Then I'd be glad you came to me—keep it in the family, you know?"

She went off on a tangent then and it was another ten minutes before he could finish telling her what he wanted to know.

"A cobra, hmm? That's better than a torpedo, I guess. How's this guy hung?"

"How would I know?"

She was back to giggling again. "I'd think it'd be one of the first things you'd have to ask—to be able to identify him properly, I mean." She tilted her head, studying him for a moment. "How *are* you going to identify him?"

Paris always did this to him.

"I was hoping to get a name."

"This is too funny. I can just see you going around asking about this guy's dick. Have you talked to Bruno yet?"

Hank nodded, which set her off again. But finally she calmed down enough to actually try to help him.

"Nobody's had it done here," she said. "At least not that I've heard of, and that's the kind of thing that gets talked about, especially if the guy"—she gave him another wicked little smile—"can pull it off."

Hank groaned.

"Okay, okay. I'm being serious already. How about if I ask around for you?"

"That'd be great." He thought of something then. "Got a pen?"

When she dug a black marker out of her back pocket and passed it over to him, he sketched Katy's tattoo on the back of one of the magazines on the coffee table:

"Ever seen something like this?" he asked. "Or know what it means?"

"Hello?" she said. "I was born in North America, Hank, not China. And besides, that looks Japanese."

Hank smiled. "I know. And you've never been to France either. I'm asking you because of your so-called expertise as a tattoo artist, sweetheart."

She stuck out her tongue. Picking up the magazine, she tore off the section of the page with the ideograph and stuck it in her pocket.

"I'll ask Rudy for you. He's into that kind of stuff, you know, Akido and Zen and the lot."

"Thanks."

She grabbed his arm and made him sit down when he tried to get up.

"Uh-uh," she said. "Not so fast. Now I want to know all about her."

Hank pretended ignorance. "Her?"

She nodded. "Come on. 'Fess up. Where'd you meet, what's she like? You're not getting out of here until you tell all, so you might as well start now."

So he told her about Lily, because Paris had always known his heart better than he did himself. Better than Moth, better than anyone. It wasn't why they were family, but it was why they were friends.

12.

After they got Kerry settled in with all of her new acquisitions, Annie went across the hall to practice and

Rory returned to his own apartment. For awhile he sat at his workbench, trying to finish up an earring order he had for Tender Hearts, a boutique over on Quinlan that regularly carried his jewelry. Through the cold-air return vent he could hear the faint sound of Annie running over a chord progression on her guitar, augmenting the syncopated pattern with brief flourishes of melody.

A new song, Rory decided, since it didn't sound familiar. He kept expecting her to retreat into her soundproofed studio to put it down on tape, but the music simply went on as though she'd fallen into a meditative trance and forgotten what her hands were doing.

He got about half the order done, his heart not really into the job. It was dull, mindless work—repeating a design that had been fun the first couple of times he'd made it, but only bored him now. Finally he shut off the light above the worktable and went into his study to finish the article for *Spin*.

It was quiet upstairs now. Annie had either fallen asleep or she'd finally gone into her studio. There was no piano playing in Kerry's apartment and the rest of the house was still as well, though, except for Lucius's twice-daily migrations across his apartment when the whole house would creak and moan, the top floor was always quiet.

The article didn't need much work—a paragraph tightened here, a few explanatory lines to add there, rewrite the intro to refer to a couple of Lily's photos. When it was done he made a stab at a short story he'd promised Alan Grant for *The Crowsea Review,* a literary journal Alan had published during his college years and was in the process of reviving.

He didn't get far with the story. Fiction never came as easily for him as did nonfiction—mostly, he supposed, because it seemed to engage the same part of his mind that was so easily distracted by puzzles such as the one presented by the crow girls not seeming to have aged a day in all the time he'd known them. More confusing,

Annie said she thought they were in their twenties while to him they were impossibly forever fourteen. Which then begged the question, if they looked different for different people, who was to say they weren't the switchblade-wielding women who'd appeared out of nowhere the other night and rescued Lily and Hank Walker?

He tried to concentrate on the story, but his gaze kept lifting from his computer screen to settle on the trunk of the elm tree that he could see from the window of his study. Maybe Maida and Zia really did live in that bloody tree. They certainly spent enough time in it. He half-expected to see them come swinging down from its branches and cross the lawn to peer back into the window at him.

Finally he gave up on making any sort of worthwhile addition to the story tonight. He saved the file—though he didn't know why he bothered since he hadn't added more than a couple of lines to it in all the time he'd been sitting here and he knew he'd be rewriting them the next time he opened the file. Frowning, he shut off the computer, then decided he was being too hard on himself. The evening wasn't a total loss. He'd gotten the article done and another dozen earrings ready to take in to Tender Hearts. The story would come. In its own time, it was true, but it would come.

Fetching himself a beer from the fridge, he walked out onto the front porch with it. The evening was well settled into night now, the street quiet, the light from the street lamps casting pronounced shadows. He sat down on the wicker bench and stretched out his legs. The crow girls were so much on his mind that when someone settled down on the bench beside him, he was surprised to see it was Annie, not one of them. He offered her some of his beer.

She took a long swallow then handed it back. "Thanks."

"Were you working on a new song?" he asked.

"I wish."

"What I heard didn't sound familiar."

Annie made a tossing gesture with her hand. "No, it was new, it just wasn't working out. There's something about Kerry that I want to capture, but I can't get a handle on it." She turned to look at him. "She's got an innocent quality about her, a sweetness, and that's fine, but there's something really interesting running under that. Something with a real edge. And that's what I want to capture with a lyric—the tension between the two."

"You think she's tense?"

"Hello? Where were you all day? She hides them well, but she's got deep worries, that one. Mysteries banging around inside her."

"Like the business with the piano."

"No." She drew the word out. "Well, maybe that's part of it, but it's more than her pretending she can't play. Which reminds me: I'm proud of you."

"What for?"

"You didn't ask her about the piano once."

"For this you're proud?"

"Well, you know how you can get."

He aimed a frown at her that got lost in the dark. "What's that supposed to mean?" he asked, looking out onto the street again.

"Sometimes you don't want to let a thing go."

"Some people consider tenaciousness an admirable character trait."

Annie nodded. "And some people just think it's pig-eyed stubborn." When he glanced over at her, she smiled, adding, "Go figure."

All Rory could do was shake his head. Annie was impossible about some things.

"Listen," she said suddenly.

For a moment he didn't know what she was referring to, then he heard it, too, a slow flap of wings from somewhere up above.

"Crow girl," she said. "Coming home to roost."

Remembering how she'd been teasing Kerry earlier

that afternoon, Rory added, "Or maybe it's Chloë."

Annie seemed to give this a moment of serious consideration, then shook her head. "Nope. Definitely a crow. A raven would sound different." She glanced at him. "Bigger wings."

Rory turned to look at her, searching for the smile, but not finding it.

"So what're you saying?" he asked. "That Chloë's a raven?"

Finally Annie laughed, letting him know she was only making mischief again. "Sure," she said. "Why not? We can't all be crow girls, hiding our wings under our skin."

Only now it was Rory who couldn't take it as a joke. Instead he found himself remembering something Lily had said to him on the phone the other night.

The girls that rescued us were like birds. . . .

"You know Jack," he began.

"Everybody knows Jack, don't they?"

"What do you think of those stories he tells?"

"You're not looking for the flip response here, are you?" Annie said, her voice going serious.

Rory shook his head. "Are his crow girls our crow girls?"

"What you're really asking is, are the stories he tells true."

"I suppose."

"They're true for him—I know," she added before he could say anything, "that sounds like I'm being flippant again, but I'm not. You must know this from your own writing—Jack's a storyteller; he tells the truth with lies. So the details aren't necessarily true, but what he's talking about is."

"So when he's laying on some tall tale about animal people and things like that, he's just being metaphorical."

"I wouldn't go so far."

"But—"

"Look," Annie said. "What if time's not linear, the way people think it is? What if the past, present, and future are all going on at the same time, only they're separated by—oh, I don't know—a kind of gauze or something. And maybe there are people who can see through that gauze.''

Rory smiled. ''That would explain ghosts and fortune-telling,'' he said, going along with her.

''And maybe it also explains how someone like Jack can tell stories about the long ago as if they were right now—as if they were still happening. He's seeing through the gauze.''

Sure, why not? Rory thought. But first you had to buy into the idea of time all happening at the same time and that took a far greater leap of faith than he was able to muster. What Lily had told him was strange enough.

''So do you believe this?'' he asked.

She shrugged. ''I don't know. I do know that the gardens of the first lands are still lying there, right under the skin of the world—pulsing the way our heartbeat drums under our own skin. And I believe that there's a connectedness between everything that gives some people a deep and abiding affinity to a certain kind of place or creature.''

''Like totems?''

''Maybe. Or maybe something even more personal—something that's impossible to articulate with the vocabulary we have at that moment.''

''This is too weird.''

Annie shrugged. ''What can I say? It's getting late, the stars are out. Once the sun sets, I tend to embrace whatever wild spirits are running around in the darkness, talking away to each other. I leave the logic of streets and pavement and cars and tall buildings behind and buy into the old magics that they're whispering about. Sometimes those little mysteries and bits of wisdom stick to the bones of my head and I carry them right out into the sunlight again. They're like Jack's stories, true and not true, all at the same time. They don't exactly shape my life, but they certainly color it.'' She glanced at him. ''I wouldn't like to live in a world where everything's as cut-and-dried as most people think it is.''

''I don't think you ever have to be afraid of that,'' Rory told her.

She shook her head. ''It's much easier to forget. It's much easier to buy into linear time and what you see is what you get. That's one of the things that makes Jack's stories so important—at least for me. They remind me of who I am. Of what else is out there.''

They seemed to be having two conversations, Rory thought, and one of them went down into that place that Annie had described a few moments ago, the place where you needed a special vocabulary to understand what was being said. He didn't have those words. He didn't even have a dictionary to look them up in.

This had happened before. They'd be talking, and it could be about the most mundane thing—a new CD, the weather, a person walking down the street ahead of them—and he'd suddenly get the impression that there was another conversation taking place on the periphery of the one they were having, that she was telling him something that he was too obtuse, or maybe simply too naive, to properly understand.

And now it was happening again. The difference, this time, was that what had set off this feeling in him was something that was already inexplicable by itself.

''They've never gotten any older,'' he said. ''The crow girls, I mean. In all the time I've known them. I've never really thought about it, but this morning I was paying attention to it. They're, like, thirteen, fourteen. No older.''

Annie didn't say anything.

''But you see them different,'' he said. ''Maybe everybody sees them different.''

''Maybe they do.''

''But how's that possible?''

''Take a look around you,'' Annie said. ''When you

really look at the world you have to wonder how any of it's possible.''

''I'm not talking about that sort of thing.''

''I know,'' she said. ''So what did you want to know about them?''

Everything, Rory thought, but he settled for, ''How do they fit with those stories of Jack's? Was it his stories that got you to call them the crow girls, or are they actually the ones in his stories?''

''I can't remember who first came up with that name for them,'' Annie said. ''It was a long time ago.''

''Okay. Then how about this: Are they ordinary girls, or something more than that? Something . . .'' He hesitated over the word. ''Supernatural.''

Annie sighed. ''You're going to think I'm being way unhelpful,'' she said, ''but I think that's the kind of thing that each of us has to decide for ourselves.''

He waited for her to elaborate, but she fell silent.

''You're right,'' he said after a few moments. ''That doesn't help me at all.''

Annie shifted her position on the bench. She turned to face him, knees pulled up to her chin.

''Everybody in the Rookery is a bit different—a bit strange,'' she said. ''But that's never bothered you before.''

''Maida and Zia don't live in the house with us.''

''No, they live—''

''In a tree in our backyard.'' Rory sighed. ''Unless that's another metaphor that I'm not picking up on.''

Annie smiled. ''You'd have to ask them.''

Like he hadn't a hundred times before, but the crow girls were adept at turning aside questions they didn't feel like answering.

''That's never done me any good,'' he said.

''So why the intense interest now?'' Annie wanted to know.

He didn't feel he could discuss Lily's experience from

the other night. It was for Lily to decide who could know about it.

"I just find it eerie," he said. "Especially how, if I don't concentrate, it slips away on me. I mean, this business is seriously strange, but if I don't keep it in my mind, it takes on a dreamlike quality. It would be so easy to forget."

"That's the problem with mystery and magic—they're hard to sustain."

"You know this from experience?" Rory had to ask.

Annie smiled. "Why do you think I listen to Jack's stories as much as I do?"

"But—"

"Let me give you a piece of advice: Try to approach things without preconceived ideas, without supposing you already know everything there is to know about them. Get that trick down and you'll be surprised at what's really all around you."

Later, Annie went back upstairs. Rory sat awhile longer, watching the street, hoping Maida or Zia would drop down from one of the oaks so he could ask one of them what it all meant, ask them before the sun stole away the stars and the dark and the questions rolling around inside his head that were so hard to hold on to. But no one joined him on the porch and all he could do was try to figure out what Annie had meant about not approaching things with preconceived ideas.

He understood the philosophy when it came to the arts—a painting, a book, a piece of music—and even in regard to meeting new people, or presupposing what someone he already knew was going to say or do in a given situation. But Annie seemed to mean it in a more global sense. She was offering up her own version of Plato's rejection of scientific rationalization: Matter wasn't fundamental because material objects were merely imperfect copies of abstract and eternal ideas. Although in her version, the world wasn't so much defined by argument as by remaining mentally open to any possibility.

She seemed to be saying that, if he looked out at the oak trees lining the street without expecting to see oak trees, he might see something else. That the cab cruising slowly by might really be . . . what? A wooden streetcar driven by monkeys? A turtle on wheels? His hand was really a paw, a candelabra, a cluster of sausages tied up with twine?

He lifted his gaze to the dense foliage of the oaks.

Or maybe that the crow girls were really birds and that was why they lived in a tree?

In his present mood, anything seemed possible, and the whole business was making him light-headed. Finally he went back inside to his apartment.

The phone rang just as he was putting his empty beer bottle into the case under the sink. He had a moment's panic at the sound—a telephone call this late at night almost always meant bad news. Then he remembered that he'd told Donna she could call him anytime before one A.M. He caught it on the third ring, just before the answering machine would take it.

"Donna?" he said.

"Hi, Rory. I hope you don't mind me calling so late, but I only just got back to my hotel room."

He glanced at the kitchen clock and was surprised to see that it was almost one-thirty.

"That's okay," he told her. "I was still up. How's your conference going?"

"The same way these things always go. There are a few bright people you want to talk to, but you never get much of a chance. Mostly you're stuck listening to people who think 'innovative' is putting a new spin on the same-old, same-old instead of actually pushing the boundaries, but what else is new?"

"So why do you go?"

"Tamarack's not so big that we can afford to miss opportunities like this to promote our books. I mean, we get lost at the ABA. Our booth's always off in some sad little dark corner—you know, wherever Stephen King or Danielle Steele aren't doing a signing."

Rory laughed.

"I know, I know," she went on. "I'm making it sound horrible and it's not really. I love working the booth. It's just the schmoozing later on in the evening that wears on me—the dinners and parties. But you must know what it's like. Lily says you've spoken at a few writers' conferences yourself."

"Except I like the schmoozing."

"You would," Donna said with a smile in her voice.

Although he'd only met her on a few occasions when she was back in the city visiting Lily, Donna didn't feel like a stranger to him. Lily talked about her so much that sometimes Rory felt that he'd grown up with the pair of them. Donna had obviously heard just as much about him.

"So what's happening with Lily?" Donna asked. "Have you talked to her lately?"

"Not since I emailed you. She's down in Arizona, shooting stills for some country band's video."

"I'm worried about her. I mean, really worried."

Rory had been, too, but now he wasn't so sure. With this business relating to the crow girls still so fresh in his mind, he wasn't quite ready to dismiss Lily's experience as something she'd only imagined. But he was no more ready to tell Donna that than he'd been to relate Lily's adventure to Annie.

"I was, too," he said. "But I think it was maybe an overreaction to the stress of what happened. She probably wasn't hurt as badly as she thought she'd been. I saw her the next day and she looked fine. No bruises, nothing."

"She says some kind of punk angels cured her."

"Yeah, well . . . things happen awfully fast in a situation like that. Sometimes it's hard to pinpoint what really happened and what we think happened."

"Being attacked as she was isn't a laughing matter."

"I'm not laughing," Rory said. "I got mugged a couple of years ago and I know just how weird and scary it is.''

There was a long moment of silence.

''So you think she's okay?'' Donna asked. ''Even with all this talk about angels and miracle healings?''

''The experience is going to change her,'' Rory told her. ''There's no getting away from that. I was a bundle of nerves for weeks after it happened to me. But you deal with it. Lily's a strong person. She'll get past this.''

''I hope so. Thing that strikes me as weird, though, is that she's *not* a bundle of nerves. She's so calm about the whole thing.''

That had occurred to Rory as well, but it wasn't something he'd felt he could ask Lily about. If she'd found some way to help her deal with what had to have been a very scary experience, who was he to burst her bubble?

''Everybody deals with things differently,'' he said.

''I guess.'' There was another pause from Donna's end of the line. ''What about this cabdriver who was with her—do you know anything about him?''

''His name's Hank. I used to work with him. He always seemed okay.''

''I feel like I'm being a mother hen.''

''You're just being a good friend,'' Rory said. ''Worrying comes with the territory.''

''Thanks for saying that. You're a good friend, too. I feel better knowing you're close by in case . . . you know, things get any weirder.''

''That's not going to happen,'' Rory said.

But later, after he'd hung up, he wasn't so sure that was something he could swear to with any real conviction.

13.

''Is it always this slow on a Sunday?'' Hank asked as Paris locked up.

Except for the woman who'd been there when he first arrived, and a couple of punky-looking girls who came in later to check out the flashes on the wall and the ring-bound portfolios of samples on the counter, they'd had the store to themselves for the past hour. The Buzz wasn't exactly buzzing with business this afternoon.

Paris shrugged. "Later in the day, yeah. But we had a busy morning."

"You should close earlier."

"I don't mind. It gives me a chance to catch up on paperwork and stuff." She tucked her arm into the crook of his as they set off for the junkyard. "So when do I get to meet Lily?"

"It's not like you're thinking."

"Who says I'm thinking anything?"

"You're never not thinking something," Hank said.

She gave his arm a squeeze. "Okay. What I'm thinking is, this could be good, so don't blow it like you did with Emma."

"Emma's the one who called it off."

"Only because you never let her behind the wall," Paris said.

Hank didn't want to get into that.

"Lily's too uptown for me," he said. "I helped her out of a jam and she's grateful and interested and everything, but it'll wear off fast once she sees that this is all there is to me."

Paris shook her head. "Boy, are you not with the program or what."

"What's that supposed to mean?"

"Nothing. But you might be surprised at how many woman are interested in a decent guy—for his own sake. Not all of us are looking for a moneyman, or some big shot who knows all the right people. You should try to be a little more trusting."

"It's hard."

"I know it's hard. This is Paris you're talking to, Hank. The original hard-luck story. But you've got to take part in the world, or what's the point of being in it?" She smiled at him. "Some bright guy I know told me that one time when I was really messed up."

It had taken Hank and her brother a week to find her, holed up in a squat, crouched in a nest of rags and newspapers in a corner, scabs and collapsed veins covering her inner arms. She hadn't even been able to focus on either him or Terry, but he'd held her and talked to her anyway, just talked and talked while Terry brought the cab around and drove them back to the junkyard. It took her a long time to get through the nightmare of going clean, even longer to really want it.

"I remember," he said.

"Don't get me wrong," Paris said. "I know where you're coming from. The people who can't deal with who or what we were are never going to be part of our lives. But if they mean anything to us, we've got to give them a chance. We've got to let them know who we were, who we are now, and let them decide for themselves if they want to deal themselves in."

Hank had to smile, hearing his own words offered back to him.

"I'll keep it in mind," he said.

She squeezed his arm again. "I know I'm being an interfering little busybody, but then, that's who I am."

"I won't argue that."

She punched him lightly with her free hand. "The thing is," she said, "I'd like to see you happy instead of just making do."

When they got to the junkyard they had dinner with Moth and Benny. Later, Hank took the cab out, dropping Paris off at a girlfriend's over on the east side before tending to the business that Moth had set up for the night. He was busier than he'd been last night, but he still had time to think about Sandy Dunlop's problem.

The tattoo had been a dead end, but he'd pretty much expected it to be. He could've gotten lucky—he might

still, if Paris had any luck when she asked around for
him—but that didn't seem to be the way this was playing
out. So maybe it was time to work on it from the other
end. Philippe Couteau hadn't been in town just to assault
Lily or hassle a small-time dope dealer.

Closing in on six that morning, he found himself heading for Eddie's club by way of Lily's part of town. A
storm had gusted in a little after midnight, leaving the
street littered with leaves and branches, thrown down
from the canopy of oaks overhead. It made a nice change
from the usual Styrofoam and litter that the cab's headlights picked out. He wondered how Lily was doing down
in Arizona. Maybe Paris was right. Instead of deciding
beforehand how it was going to work out, he should let
events take their course, stay open to the possibilities for
a change. So she was uptown. Didn't mean she wasn't
human.

He had a cut taken from one of Oscar Peterson's *Verve
Songbooks*—the '52 sessions—playing on the tape ma-
chine. That old Cole Porter standard "Night and Day."
Ray Brown on bass. Barney Kessel on guitar. He thought
Lily'd like it. Maybe he'd get Tony to run off a dub for
her.

Hank remembered reading somewhere that Peterson
had recorded those sessions in such a simple straightforward style to make the music more understandable to
people who weren't necessarily into jazz. Maybe so,
Hank thought, but you'd still have to be deaf to miss what
Kellaway had called the "will to swing" that was the
backbone of every Peterson trio. Lily would get it.

By six, he pulled up in front of the club and Bobby
"Hands" Lido, one of Eddie's bodyguards, was walking
Eddie out to the cab. Hands was built in a square, head
set squat on his shoulders, arms the size of a normal
man's thighs, hands like shovels. The story went that he
once took three shots in the chest and still got those hands
on the shooter and broke his neck. Looking at him today,
Hank found himself wondering if maybe the story was

true. He touched his shoulder where a small bullet scar puckered his skin. Maybe Hands had himself a visit from a couple of switchblade-carrying punk angels, too.

Eddie Prio was from the old school. He was in his sixties—Moth's age—and looked ten years younger. Still dark-haired, still in good shape. A sharp dresser—you never saw him out of a tailored suit, tie knotted just right, shoes shined so they'd hold a reflection. He rewarded loyalty and came down hard on anyone who tried to screw him.

He and Moth went way back. He'd fronted Moth the cash for his first gypsy cab and gave Moth his business right from the start, a way of letting people know Moth could be trusted. It was a favor for a favor. Moth had been on the farm with one of Eddie's cousins and stepped in to help when he got in the line of fire between the blacks and the Aryan Brotherhood. The AB wasn't so organized in those days, but hatred and racism didn't need a tag to be kept alive.

"Yeah, but why's he still giving you his business?" Terry had asked when he first came on board with the junkyard crew.

"You don't fix what isn't broken," Moth had told him.

Hands opened the back door of the cab, closed it behind Eddie, not stepping back until he heard the click of the lock being engaged. He tapped the roof of the cab and Hank pulled away.

Eddie settled back into the seat, his briefcase beside him. "I like the city after it's rained," he said. "Especially this time of day."

Hank nodded in agreement.

"You have a good night?" Eddie asked.

"Busy for a change. How was the club?"

"We've got a hardware salesmen's convention in town this week. I don't know where they get the money, but they sure like to spend it."

Hank smiled. They drove along for a few blocks in silence, then Hank glanced in the rearview mirror.

"So, Eddie," he said. "You know anything about a guy named Philippe Couteau—works out of New Orleans?"

"What do you want to know about him for?"

Hank shrugged. "His name came up in something I'm working on for Marty. He's defending this lap dancer from Pussy's."

"The one who popped her boyfriend pimp?"

Hank nodded.

"If Couteau's involved, you don't want to be."

"I've seen his sheet. There's not much there."

Eddie gave him a humorless smile. "That's because witnesses have a habit of dying before anything gets to trial. Thing is, these guys hurt people for fun—you know what I'm saying? You don't have to pay them to drop somebody. All you've got to do is point 'em in the right direction and hope the body count doesn't get out of hand."

"You're talking about him and his brothers?"

"I don't know how many of them there are," Eddie said. "There's a whole family of them—father, the three brothers, cousins, uncles, and aunts. You seen this one you're asking about?"

Hank nodded.

"Well, they all look pretty much the same. Except for their sex, it's hard to tell 'em apart."

"I hear they're connected," Hank said.

Eddie laughed. "Yeah, everybody's connected now, you listen to the press. Like it means anything. It's not like the old days. I don't know which is worse, the families or the crews working out of the projects."

"Couteau was collecting from Ronnie Ellis—the dancer's boyfriend. I'm trying to figure out what kind of business he could have with a small-time loser like Ellis."

"You think Couteau popped him?"

"I don't think it was the dancer," Hank said.

He looked in the mirror again to see Eddie's lips pursed in thought.

"Who's the prosecutor?" Eddie asked.

"Bloom."

Eddie shook his head. "Too bad. He won't back off on her. He's got too much of a hard-on for anyone in the sex trade."

"But if I could get him looking a little more seriously into Couteau's connection with Ellis—"

"A word to the wise, Hank," Eddie said, breaking in. "You don't want to get connected to trouble in their minds. If they come looking for you, nobody's going to be able to help you."

"They're that bad?"

"Worse," Eddie said. Then he dropped his gaze from the mirror and turned to look out the window.

Hank frowned. This was getting more complicated now. He'd seen Couteau buy it, but there was no body to I.D. And if the whole family looked the same, then maybe it hadn't been Philippe who'd died in the alley, but one of his brothers or cousins. Which meant there could be more than one of them in the city. Doing what? He had a Couteau connected to Ronnie Ellis who maybe was, maybe wasn't, the same person who'd assaulted Lily. The thing that was making him nervous now was, what if the attack on her hadn't been random?

Probably the only ones who knew the answers to any of this were those two girls from the alley. Trouble was, he had no idea how to go about finding them.

14.

Kerry gave a last scrub along the joint where the bookcase's middle shelf met the side of the unit, then dropped the steel wool onto the newspapers that were covering the floor and sat up. She stretched her back and admired her handiwork with pride. Instead of covering over the garish paint on her new bookcase, Rory had suggested she strip it.

"I think it's butternut under all that crap," he said. "It'll look really nice once you get it cleaned up and rub some oil into it."

It did look nice. The wood had a lovely grain and a soft yellowy-brown color and she was the one who'd made it look like this, all by herself. She'd never done anything like it before.

Her living room was a bit of a mess at the moment. Newspapers covered the floor around where she was sitting and there seemed to be bits of paint everywhere— long curling pieces that she'd peeled off with a scraper, hundreds of tiny flecks and dried paint dust. But the room felt homey all the same, all her new acquisitions helping to fill it out and make it seem cozier. She now had two plants on the window seat with her books and stuffed animals—a small climbing ivy and another green leafy plant that she'd already forgotten the name of—the hooked rug on the floor in front of it by her chair. In the kitchen she had a real table with chairs. Her new clothes chest was standing in her bedroom, the lid open so that it could air out a bit. The cassette player was on the floor beside the outlet near the kitchen door, silent now.

It was like a real home now, furnished and everything. Maybe she wasn't doing so badly after all. Maybe she really could make a place for herself in this world.

If only the past would leave her alone.

Don't think about that, she told herself.

She'd been playing the cassette Annie had given her and got up now to turn it over. It was funny listening to a professional recording made by someone she actually knew. She'd never heard music like this before. In her old world, it was all sweet soft voices and mushy strings so that no one would get upset. They were intent on people not getting upset there. Annie's music seemed to ask just the opposite of its listeners. It wanted you to question everything. It insisted that you not take anything for granted.

That would be a good way to live, Kerry thought. To be brave and true. To stand up for yourself and for anybody else not strong enough to be able to do it for themselves. It seemed to come so naturally to Annie. Did she ever have doubts? And if she did, how did she overcome them? Was it something you could learn?

Probably not. You probably had to be born brave.

Kerry didn't think she'd ever been brave. She could endure, but that wasn't the same thing at all.

She sighed and set about cleaning up the mess she'd made. The paint peels and chips into the garbage, newspapers refolded so that they could go into the recycling bin, scraper and steel wool returned to the bag they'd come in so that she could give them back to Rory in the morning. Tomorrow she'd ask him if he had any linseed oil she could borrow, but for now she placed the bookcase against the wall.

The tape machine was set at such a low volume that when she went into the kitchen to make herself a cup of herbal tea, she could no longer make out the words. But she didn't want to turn it up any louder in case she bothered somebody with it. She finished making her tea and returned to the living room, stopping the tape and rewinding it so that she could listen to it properly tomorrow. Turning off the lights, she sat in her chair and looked out the window, sipping her tea.

She was so tired she thought she might be able to get to sleep without having to take a pill. Unless her night visitor returned. That was what was really keeping her up. Just thinking about it made her chest go tight. But by ten o'clock, she'd finished her tea and the ghosts had left her alone.

Leaving her cup on the window seat, she went into the bedroom and undressed in the dark. She loved the firmness of the futon, the way you could turn over on it with-

out making a bedspring creak, because there was no box
spring underneath, only the floor.

"Thank you for a perfect day," she said.

If she'd been asked whom she was addressing, she
wouldn't have been able to say. Perhaps she was only
speaking to the night.

She fell asleep more quickly than usual. Sometime
later, drifting deep in the shoals of early morning with
the dawn not even a promise on the horizon, she stirred
at the light touch of a hand on her arm.

"You're grinding your teeth again," a voice said.

Not at all alarmed, she burrowed her face deeper into
her pillow.

"You're not real," she mumbled. "You were never
. . . real. . . ."

As she fell back asleep, she thought she heard someone
weeping softly. In the morning, she remembered it only
vaguely, like a dream.

15.

Closing in on three that same morning, Ray was in the
lane that ran behind the Rookery—a tall, red-haired figure, standing so still he was almost invisible unless one
knew to look for him. His gaze was fixed on what he
could see of the dark bulk of the house through the
boughs of the elm, a small frown furrowing the V between his red eyebrows. He didn't hear the other man
approach. He wouldn't have seen him either, the newcomer's black duster and flat-brimmed hat letting him
meld with the shadows, but Ray knew he was there all
the same.

"Hey, Jack," he said without turning. "Long time no
see."

"A little out of your usual territory," Jack said, stepping closer.

Ray shrugged. "You know how we are. I like the high

country, but the whole world's our territory.''

Jack made a noncommittal sound low in his throat.

"You don't seem too happy to see me,'' Ray said.

"You're scouting for Cody and Cody means trouble, so why would I be happy to see you?''

Ray shrugged. "Cody keeps things interesting.''

"Chinese think 'interesting' is a curse,'' Jack said.

"Yeah, but I'm not Chinese. I thrive in interesting times.''

Finally Jack smiled. "Got an answer for everything, don't you? Some things never change.''

Ray turned to look at him. "You've changed,'' he said finally. "You're fat with stories.''

Ray knew that would make Jack smile again, as if that tall fence post of a figure could ever be considered overweight. He caught the flash of white teeth under the brim of Jack's hat, then went back to studying the Rookery. Jack did his whisper-walk and stepped up right beside him. They stood quietly together then, watching the house, aware of the night around them and everything in it, but distanced at the same time, as if they were one step outside the world, just beyond peripheral vision.

"Cody's not here to cause trouble,'' Ray said after a time.

"I know that. But trouble happens all the same whenever he's around.''

Ray shook his head. "That's the way it used to be, Jack. But I've talked to Cody and he's really thought it through this time.''

"You believe that,'' Jack said, "and I've got a bridge to sell you.''

Ray didn't blame him. He'd been just as skeptical when Cody first approached him a few weeks ago.

"Look,'' he said. "Every time it's gone wrong was because Cody was trying to fine-tune that first mistake. This time he's going back and changing everything to the way it was before. He's going to clean the slate of all of this''—Ray lifted a hand, indicating the city around them—"and take us right back into the long ago, like nothing was ever changed."

Jack was so long in replying that Ray had to turn to make sure that the presence he still sensed was actually there. He found Jack's dark gaze studying him from under the brim of his hat.

"That what you want?" Jack asked finally.

"You don't?"

Jack shook his head. "Oh, I'll admit the idea has some immediate appeal, when I think about all the ways they've found to screw things up, but I've made too many friends to be able to turn my back on them just like that." He snapped his fingers. "Now I know some of them are no better than cuckoos, mean for the sake of meanness, but the thing is, most of them're more like Cody than maybe he'd like to admit. You know what I mean? They mean well, even while they're making things worse."

"I suppose."

"And besides," Jack added, "I'd think you'd be the last one to want to turn back the clock like that."

"What's that supposed to mean?"

"You think I don't know who that is, moved into the crow house?"

"Some cousin," Ray said with a shrug, pretending an unconcern he couldn't quite pull off.

Jack nodded. "Family of yours . . . and family of mine, too."

So that was how Cody got her into the roost, Ray thought. She was carrying blood from both sides of the argument. No wonder Cody was using her.

"So?" he said, keeping his voice casual.

Jack studied him. "You really don't know, do you?"

Ray sighed. He hated riddles.

"Know what?" he asked.

Jack stepped up to him. "Come on," he said, taking Ray by the arm and pulling him down the lane. "Take a walk with me."

"What for?"

"I want to tell you a story," Jack told him. "But it's a long one. I figured maybe we could find ourselves a diner and you could buy me a coffee—just to keep my whistle wet."

Ray hesitated a moment. He looked back at the Rookery and thought maybe there was someone looking out at them from the one second-story window that had a clear sight line through a hole in the elm's boughs. He didn't see so much as sense a flash of red hair. There was something about the person it belonged to that was both familiar and not.

"Everybody knows how you like to ramble the woods around Hazard," Jack was saying. "How you're kind enough to help some of those hill girls ease their loneliness."

Now the window was empty. Ray turned and let Jack lead him away, down the lane to where the shadows pooled thick. Hazard, he thought, and his thoughts went sliding back to the old mining town.

"What're you getting at?" he said.

"Well," Jack said, "her name was Edna Bean, a widow living by herself in a yellow farmhouse outside of town. Had herself a little girl she named Annette, but most folks called her Nettie, and she was more than a cousin to either of us."

Ray stopped walking. He started to pull away, but Jack's grip was stronger than he expected and he couldn't shake it.

"If what you're telling me is that Nettie's my—"

"Listen to the story," Jack said. "Maybe you'll learn something you didn't know."

"Look, Jack. I don't need to hear some story—they always turn out the same. The humans die and we carry on. If you've got something to tell me—"

Jack cut him off. "They all turn out the same, do they? I didn't know this one had all played out yet."

Ray didn't have the patience for this.

"Just tell me straight," he said. "That girl living in

the crow house . . . what's her connection to me? How close are we related?''

Jack gave him a mild look. ''How close. That's going to make that big of a difference to you? I didn't know family was a thing you could measure like that.''

Ray had to pull in a steadying breath. It was worse than he'd thought. Damn Cody with that handsome lying smile of his. This time he'd gone too far.

''I've got to go,'' he told Jack.

What he needed right now was to have Cody standing here in front of him, not Jack. He needed to be taking what was owed to him out of coyote skin.

''Maybe you should hear me out first,'' Jack said.

Ray shook his head. ''I appreciate what you're saying, but I've got a previous appointment I didn't know I had, so I'll just be saying—''

''I've been carrying this story for you for a long time,'' Jack told him, cutting him off again, voice firm. ''The least you can do is have the courtesy to take it from me.''

''Maybe some other time. Right now I need to—''

''Besides, I really could use that coffee. How about you?''

Ray met Jack's gaze and knew he had to let it go for now. Jack had a gift that could take the air out of anything—even this. Even Cody playing games with him, games that ran too deep.

''Okay,'' he said. ''We'll have that coffee. I'll listen to your story. I'll do that much. But then—''

''Then maybe you'll think about what you've learned and who knows what you'll find yourself wanting to do?''

Ray had to smile. ''Maybe,'' he said.

This time when Jack gave his arm another tug, he went along.

16.

It was Anita who found Katy, curled up in the backseat of the junked canary-yellow Volvo that she had to pass on her way to the VW bus she was summering in herself. She returned to where Moth was sitting out with the dogs and brought him back to see, picking her way easily through the rows of rusting vehicles and other metal trash that were stacked fifteen feet high in places. Moth followed at a slower pace, Ranger and Judith ambling along on either side of him. He didn't know these back rows as well as Anita or the dogs—not at night.

"So that's where she's been squatting," he said when they reached the Volvo.

He'd often wondered what kind of person would've bought a car so flashy and bright when it was new, but he wasn't surprised to find Katy claiming it. When the mood was on her, the girl could live on color, the flashier the better.

Anita shook her head. "I'd have known if she was staying here on a regular basis."

That was true, Moth thought. Hell, he'd have known, too. But he still didn't see what the big deal was. So she was crashing in one of his old cars. Better here, where she was safe, than out in the jungle of the Tombs.

"I don't have a problem with this," he said. He turned away from the small figure to look at Anita. "Why the concern?"

"You don't get it, do you?"

Moth took the time to light a smoke. "What am I not getting?"

"Look at her," Anita said. "She's got the look of an old cat that's crawled off to die."

Or turning invisible for real, Moth thought, having a closer look. She wasn't a real distinct shape, lying there on the backseat, and it had nothing to do with stillness or the bad light. It was more like she was slipping away, withdrawing from the world to someplace they couldn't follow.

"You've got to talk to her," Anita said.

"Me?"

Anita smiled. "Kids like you, Moth, damned if I know why. Maybe it's because you never grew up."

"Yeah, I'm a regular Peter Pan. Look at me fly."

"Just talk to her," Anita said.

She was gone before he could argue.

Moth sighed. Ranger trailed after her, but Judith settled down in the dirt by his feet, tongue lolling.

"You ever get the feeling you're not really in charge anymore?" he asked the dog.

All she did was give him a steady look in response.

Well, what were you expecting? he asked himself. That she was going to talk? The world hadn't gotten that weird yet.

He took a drag from his cigarette, lit another from its butt before he ground it under his heel. Judith lifted her head sharply when he tapped a knuckle on the window of the Volvo.

"Hey there, sleeping beauty," he said when Katy turned around to look at him.

Those eyes, Moth thought. You'd swear she had a summer sky stashed away behind them.

"You mind some company?" he asked.

She shook her head, so he cracked open the front door and stretched out along the front seat, back resting against the passenger door. The ashtray was gone, so he flicked ashes out the window behind him.

"Nice place you've got here," he said.

"I didn't think you'd mind."

"Help yourself. I told you before—you want something, all you've got to do is ask. We look out for each other."

"I won't be here long."

Moth pretended indifference. He leaned his head back

and blew smoke out the window behind him.

"Going on a trip?" he asked.

She shrugged. "Just going away. Back to wherever it is I came from. I can't stay here anymore."

"Why not?"

"I don't belong."

"Everybody gets to feel like that, one time or another. It's a hard thing to have to live with, but it's fixable."

She made no reply. Moth gave her the space to talk or not. There was no hurry. That was the thing people forgot in their rush to fix this and set that right, as though problems—especially problems of the heart or spirit—were like cars, you just needed to find the right part to replace. Didn't work that way.

He finished his cigarette and dropped the butt on the ground outside his window where it would burn out in the dirt.

"I always thought Jack was just being nice," she said after awhile, "but now I know he was telling the truth."

"About what?"

"Me not being able to die."

Moth wanted to take this slow, talk it out, no histrionics, but she didn't give him a chance.

"I've figured out why I can't die," she told him in a flat, empty voice. "It's because I'm already dead. Or maybe I was never really alive."

"Bullshit."

She gave him a wistful look that made his old jaded heart want to weep.

"I wish it was," she said, then she turned away again, face against the seat, back to him, hands tucked into her armpits, knees pulled up tight.

Moth started to argue, then thought better of it. He went back to his trailer and chased down a blanket, brought it back and laid it over her. She didn't move, didn't give any indication she knew he'd gone, or come back. When he returned to his trailer again, Anita was sitting on a lawn chair, waiting for him.

"How'd it go?" she asked.

Moth stared away into the darkness beyond the junk-yard. Judith picked up on his mood and moved in close against his leg, whined. That was the problem with a dog—you couldn't explain a problem to her. You just had to be there for her. Moth went down on one knee and laid a hand on her shoulder, felt it tremble. He looked over to Anita.

"It didn't go at all," he said.

"What can we do?"

"Damned if I know. Maybe Hank'll come up with something."

Moth showed up at Hank's stretch of concrete in the Tombs when Hank was in the middle of his push-ups. The day had begun overcast, a heavy cloud cover settling in so low it seemed to sit on your shoulders, but it didn't smell like rain. There was a sense of something else in the air, something Moth couldn't quite put his finger on. An expectation that ran deeper than weather, he decided.

He sat down, cross-legged, waiting for Hank to finish. Fishing out a cigarette from his battered pack, he lit up, blowing the smoke away from Hank. Across the pavement he could see the big mongrel dog that followed Hank around in the Tombs chowing down on whatever it was Hank had brought him today.

"That is one seriously ugly dog, kid," he said.

Hank only grunted in response.

"It'd probably feed on small children if you weren't providing for it."

"Or. Old men. Who. Talk. Too much."

Moth took the hint. He smoked his cigarette and waited until Hank reached his hundred-count before he spoke again.

"Anita found Katy sleeping in that old Volvo at the back of the yard," he told Hank. "Looking like an old cat that's crawled off to die, is the way she put it."

Hank sat up and reached for his shirt, wiping his face on it.

"You talked to Katy," he said, not making a question of it.

Moth nodded. "Sounds like she's pretty much packing it in all right."

Hank got that look in his eye, the one he always got when the situation seemed hopeless but he was determined to do something about it all the same.

"We have to help her," he said.

"You got the time?" Moth asked.

He regretted the words as soon as he spoke them. Hank was grown up now. He knew what he was doing, how much time he had, if it was stretched too thin or not.

"You don't think I should've taken on this job with Marty, do you?" Hank said.

Moth shrugged. "The way I heard it, she popped her old man. Pretty much cut-and-dried."

"Maybe."

They hadn't had much of a chance to talk about it over dinner last night, so Hank took the time now to fill him in on the previous day, detailing his interview with Sandy Dunlop, how he'd gone chasing through the tattoo parlors and body-piercing joints—"I would've loved to have seen Bruno's face when you asked him that," Moth couldn't resist saying. He finished up with the talk he'd had with Eddie this morning.

"So do you think she did it?" Moth asked.

Hank shook his head. "No. But don't ask me why. I wouldn't trust her with anything that wasn't nailed down tight, but I didn't see a killing instinct."

"People do a lot of things you don't expect. She bought the gun. And she had cause."

"It's Couteau that bothers me."

"You sure we're talking about the same guy you saw get dropped?"

"I wouldn't forget that face." Hank sighed, looked away over the empty lot, the abandoned buildings beyond it. "There's some kind of connection here, but I just can't put my finger on it."

"Where, exactly, are you going with this?" Moth asked.

"I can't see that far yet. I've got to dig a little deeper first."

"Maybe this photographer—"

"Lily."

"Maybe she's working on something the Couteaus don't like."

Hank nodded. "Could be. I'll ask her."

" 'Course you could just drop the whole business," Moth said. "Eddie wouldn't give advice he didn't mean. If he says they're out of our league, I'd believe him."

"I've made promises," Hank said.

"To who? The lap dancer? To Lily?"

Hank shook his head. "To myself. I'm not going to let Sandy Dunlop take the fall for something she didn't do and if the Couteaus are gunning after Lily, she's got no one standing between her and them except for me."

Moth sighed. He took the time to light up another cigarette, blew out a stream of smoke the same cool gray of the cloud cover. There was too much going on here—too much that strayed from odd all the way over into seriously weird. He could feel a storm coming and all he wanted to do was get them all under cover. His family. Let the world deal with its own problems. But maybe it was too late. Maybe the storm was already catching up to them.

It sure looked that way, when you counted up the score. If he believed Jack, and he half did. If Katy was really what she said she was, and he was starting to lean toward accepting that as well. If he believed his own gut feelings, and they'd never let him down before.

But were they in the eye of the storm, or still watching its approach? Maybe they had time to retreat, get under cover and pull the boundaries of their small patch of the world in behind them. He knew what Hank would say, but he had to try anyway.

"You're set on this," he said.

Hank nodded. No hesitation.

"Who's the skinny guy in that book, used to tilt at windmills?" Moth asked.

"Don Quixote."

"Take a lesson from what happened to him to see how the world treats idealists."

"I can't let it go," Hank said. "Guess you taught me too well."

Moth ground his cigarette out on the pavement. "Only you weren't listening. I told you to keep it in the family."

"I can't do that."

"That's your problem in a nutshell," Moth told him.

But he didn't really mean it. Truth was, he admired Hank's generosity of spirit. He only had to think about how Hank had been there for Terry and Paris, took them off the street when no one else gave a damn. And it wasn't just them. Hank had a habit of stepping into what wasn't his business and doing the right thing. A lot of people owed their life, or a second shot at making something of themselves, to Hank. That kind of selfless charity wasn't something Moth had ever been much good at mustering in himself, except when it came to family. When he was being honest with himself, he saw it for the failing it was.

"But first we've got to deal with Katy's problems," Hank said.

Only when they headed over to where the Volvo sat rusting in the back of the junkyard, Katy was gone. Anita hadn't seen her go, and she'd been keeping an eye on the car. They checked Jack's bus, but she wasn't there and neither was Jack. So then everybody got into looking for her. The whole crew. Benny, Terry, Paris, the dogs. But it was no good. And not even Moth's sixth sense at finding things could help them track her down.

It was as though she had stepped right out of the world.

And when you knew her history—if what she'd told Hank had been true—maybe that was just what had happened.

17.

Tucson, AZ

Lily found herself with more free time over the weekend than she might have liked, but since the video production company was paying for the shoot, she couldn't really complain. It was like being paid to take a holiday. In somebody's oven, it was true, but a holiday all the same.

The shoot was in an airplane graveyard in the south part of the city. It reminded her of the junkyard near Jack's bus in Newford, only on a much larger scale. Here rusting cars, stacked two or three high, had been replaced by row upon row of rusting aircraft—a drowsing elephants' graveyard of helicopters, transport planes, and fighters, suddenly invaded by a film crew with their lights and gear, and of course their subjects: the latest Nashville chart-toppers. The director had the band members playing in the open bay doors of junked transports, line-dancing on their wings, gear all set up under the old propellers of others, marching with guitars over their shoulders down the rows of out-of-commission helicopters and fighters. Lily's job was to keep a photographic journal of the proceedings.

It was fun at first, dealing with the desert and the towering saguaro cacti, the big sky and the wonderful light as it played upon the hulking metal shapes. The band were all photogenic—pretty boys in cowboy hats, tight jeans, and pointy-toed cowboy boots. The lead singer wore a Nudie suit, but he didn't have either the grit of a Buck Owens or the good-natured party attitude of a Marty Stuart to pull it off. Shooting them got old fast. The film crew was much more interesting—probably because they all looked like individuals rather than inter-changeable mannequins pulled off some Nashville assembly line.

The single for which they were filming the video was played over and over again, a slick, catchy song that sounded more pop than country to Lily's ears, but then that was what it was all about these days. New Country. Young Country. It was all just Boomer pop with the addition of a steel guitar or fiddle, so far as she was concerned. When it came to country, her tastes ran more to that high lonesome sound that had come down to the cities from the Appalachians, or music that had its roots in the border music of Texas and Mexico.

But they weren't paying her for her taste in music and she was enough of a professional to get the shots the director was looking for, candid and casual, but with the band still looking good. Some of them were going to be used in the video—short flashes juxtaposed against the action sequences; some for promo. Most would gather dust in the director's file cabinets.

The most interesting subject on the shoot, the one her viewfinder kept returning to, was a tall young woman in a black tank top, raggedy blue jeans, and cowboy boots as pointy as the band's, only hers were scuffed and well worn. Her blue-black hair was long and tangled, with two bands of white running back from her temples. She was deeply tanned, or naturally dark-skinned, it was hard to tell which. Her eyes were so dark they were almost black, but with a faint hint of yellow in them, and she liked jewelry. She was wearing a half-dozen earrings, a charm necklace that had to have thirty or forty silver charms dangling from it, rings on the pinkies and ring fingers of both hands, a fistful of bracelets that jangled when she moved her arms.

After awhile, Lily got the idea that the woman wasn't really involved in the shoot. It was more as though she'd simply wandered onto the set when no one was paying attention. And they still weren't. Perhaps she was a local,

Hispanic, or from the Tohono O'Odham Reservation west of the city. By the end of the first day, everybody was feeling wilted by the heat, except for her. She looked as casual and fresh as she'd been when Lily first noticed her.

Putting away her cameras and gear, Lily went over to where the woman stood, leaning up against the shiny bulk of some junked plane, thumbs hooked in the belt loops of her jeans.

"So what's your secret?" she asked.

The woman looked startled, as much, it seemed, from the fact that she'd been approached as by the question.

"I'm Lily, by the way," she added, offering her hand.

"Margaret."

Her handshake was firm, her skin dry, almost rough.

"It's just so hot," Lily went on, "but it doesn't seem to bother you at all."

Margaret smiled. "If you think this is hot, don't come visiting in the summer."

I was right, Lily thought. She was local and probably not supposed to be on the set. Not that Lily cared. Security wasn't her responsibility and Margaret didn't give the impression that she was about to cause any trouble, though she did look as though she could deal with any that might come her way.

"So you're from around here?" she asked.

"I never really think of myself as being from anywhere specific," Margaret said. "But I've been most places and this is a place I always come back to."

"Why's that?"

Margaret cocked her head like a bird and grinned. "What are you up to tonight?"

"I don't know. We're finished here for the day so I guess we'll all be going back to the motel. I've no idea what anybody else is planning to do, but I'm going to have a long cold shower."

"Let me show you around a little tonight."

Lily hesitated for a moment, then thought, why not?

She was tired, but not that tired. Her only other options were staying in her motel room by herself or hanging out with the others from the shoot, which was too much like joining the band's admiration society.

"Sure," she said. "But I have to have that shower first. Do you know where we're staying?"

Margaret nodded. "Do you have a car?"

"No, I came down with the crew."

"Well, let me drive you back. I don't want to rush you, but before we do anything else, we *have* to do the sunset and that doesn't give us much time."

"Do the sunset?"

"You'll see."

Lily glanced over to where the others were packing up. Well, in for a penny, she thought. They wouldn't miss her, except maybe for the bass player, who'd been making it clear that he could show her a good time, all she had to do was say the word. Yuck. She turned back to Margaret.

"Okay," she said. "Let's do it."

"This is so unbelievable," Lily said later.

Now she understood what doing the sunset meant. They'd driven west of the city to a lookout on Gates Pass Road, parked Margaret's Jeep, and climbed the red dirt hills to a vantage point from which they could see the hills on all sides, dotted with scrub, towering saguaro, and other, smaller cacti. Staghorn, aptly named. Teddy-bear cholla which wasn't nearly as endearing as *its* name—get too close and the thorns seemed to jump right off the plant at you. The city was a distant grid of lights and squares to the east. And in the west, the sunset.

It was like nothing Lily had ever seen before. She didn't even bother to try to capture it on film. Instead, she wiped the dust from her glasses and then, like Margaret, she lay back on the wide flat stone that Margaret had led them to and simply let the rich palette of color swell inside her, holding it in memory where it could live forever, unchanged, untouched by the whim of how film was developed, the printer's colors.

They weren't alone. The parking lot by the lookout had been filled with cars and the hillside was dotted with other climbers, tourists and locals, all taking in the sight. There'd been laughter and talking while she and Margaret climbed to their vantage point, but when the sun finally floated down to the horizon, a hush fell over them all as though everyone held a collective breath.

Lily glanced at her companion. "This'd be worth living here for—all by itself."

"I knew you'd like it," Margaret said. "You've got an artist's eye."

"I don't think you have to be an artist to appreciate this," Lily told her.

"No," Margaret agreed. "You just have to be alive."

From the lookout, they drove to a small Mexican restaurant on Fourth Avenue called La Indita. It looked like nothing special inside—booths and some tables, set up no differently than a hundred other greasy spoons Lily had been in—but Margaret led the way through the front part of the restaurant to a patio in back overhung with vines. Lily's stomach grumbled as they passed the kitchen and its hot spicy smells. Happily, a waiter followed them outside, bringing water, a basket of tortilla chips, and a small bowl of salsa to their table as soon as they sat down. Margaret ordered Mexican beers for both of them while Lily sampled the salsa.

"Hot," she managed after having some water.

"But good?"

"Mmm."

On the wall in front of them was a stylized terra-cotta sun with small birds perched on its beams. From the birds' studied looks, Lily decided they were waiting for her to drop a tortilla chip on the flagstones underfoot. When she obliged, small brown shapes winging down to pluck the morsels up, she looked up to find Margaret smiling at her.

"I guess that just encourages them, doesn't it?" Lily said, returning the smile with a rueful one of her own.

Margaret shrugged. "Even the little cousins need to eat."

Though she wasn't exactly sure what Margaret meant, Lily liked the sound of it. Little cousins. She crumpled another tortilla chip and tossed the broken pieces onto the flagstones for the birds, licking the salt and crumbs from her own palm.

It had cooled down with the sunset and Lily was glad she'd brought along a jacket. The change in temperature didn't seem to faze Margaret at all. She was still in her tank top, unconcerned, boots propped up on one of the table's spare chairs.

Lily found herself studying Margaret when she could do it without being too obvious. She loved the character in her companion's features, the fluid shift of expressions across them, the dark wells of her eyes. She tried to place her nationality, but couldn't. Margaret spoke fluent Spanish to the waiter, sounding like a native, but her English had a cowboy drawl that appeared entirely unaffected.

And she certainly knew the city—better than Lily knew her own.

When they left the restaurant, they drove all over in the Jeep, stopping at places Lily could never have found for herself, all of them with great atmosphere. Clubs, roadhouses, cafés. A biker bar. A little cantina with a Mexican band playing. A dance club playing jungle and trance so loud it was almost impossible to think, little say talk. There was someone Margaret knew wherever they went and it quickly became obvious that she was equally at home with a wide spectrum of people, blending into any crowd like a chameleon.

Around two-thirty in the morning, they finally ended up back downtown, close to where they'd had dinner, drinking espresso in a bohemian café that was part of a

place called the Hotel Congress. The building was old
and worn, not all slicked up like the motel where Lily
was staying, and she immediately fell in love with it.
Next time she came to Tucson, she decided, she'd stay
here, even if the rooms were as small as Margaret told
her they were. She couldn't resist taking a few pictures
of the foyer with its mix of art deco design and South-
western art, Margaret posing for her good-naturedly. In
the café itself she kept expecting to turn around and see
Leonard Cohen or William Burroughs sitting at the next
table.

"So what do you think so far?" Margaret asked.

"So far? I've had the best time. But I'm running out
of steam, so don't tell me there's more."

"There's always more, but we can leave some for another night, except . . . you're only in town for a day or
two, right?"

Lily nodded. "If Kenny gets everything he wants tomorrow, we're flying out around noon on Monday."

"That's not nearly enough time."

Lily had to laugh. "What are you? A one-woman tour-
ist board?"

"I just like to have fun."

"Well, you'll have to let me return the favor if you
ever come to Newford."

"Oh, I love Newford."

"When were you there?" Lily asked, surprised.

Margaret shrugged. "I go there all the time."

"And do you know as many interesting nightspots
there?"

"More."

That figured, Lily thought.

Lily was sure she'd be far too tired to go out again with
Margaret on Sunday night—she couldn't have gotten
more than five hours' sleep before she had to get up to
make it to the shoot the next morning—but the other
woman's enthusiasm and good humor were too infectious

to ignore. Once she made sure that her part in the shoot was finished, Margaret drove her back to the motel so that she could shower and change, and they were off again.

This time they watched the sunset from a hiking trail in the foothills of the Rincon Mountains, then went rambling through the city, following an even more eclectic program than they had the night before. They ate in what seemed to be the backyard of someone's house, an incredibly savory vegetable stew with flatbread and homemade beer. Went dancing in a club so small only six people could press onto the dance floor at a time. Stopped by a foundry where a sculptor friend of Margaret's was working on enormous statues of hawks. He had the wing of one completed and it was easily the length of a car.

Around one in the morning, they finally ended up on a ranch somewhere west of the city in the Catalina Foothills. A bonfire was blazing, casting shadows to dance with the revelers around it. There was live music: electric guitars, bass, drums, accordion, fiddle. There was chanting and singing, dancing around the fire, and copious amounts of wine and beer consumed. Though there were a few Anglos such as herself, most of the people were dark-skinned and raven-haired. Lily couldn't quite place them any more than she could Margaret.

"They're crows," Margaret told her when Lily asked in a break between songs.

Lily hadn't realized that the Crow lived this far south. She'd always thought of them being from around the Yellowstone and Platte Rivers.

"So you're all Native Americans," she said.

Margaret laughed. "Oh, very native. But I'm not a crow myself. I'm a 'pie."

"You mean a Paiute?" Lily said.

That made sense, because she knew they lived in the Southwest.

"No, I mean a magpie," Margaret told her.

Lily gave her a confused look. "What kind of tribe is—"

But then the band started another tune and talking became impossible again. Margaret swirled her out onto the tramped-down dirt in front of the band so that they could form a line with the other dancers and Lily lost her train of thought as she concentrated on following the somewhat complicated shuffling dance step that the music seemed to require.

At some point she was vaguely aware of being asleep on her feet. The next thing she knew, she was waking up on a sofa, a blanket with a Navajo weave tucked around her. She blinked with confusion and sat up. Her glasses were on a table beside the sofa, but when she put them on she was still looking around an unfamiliar living room. A mild panic ran through her until she remembered the party the night before. Margaret appeared in the doorway, a mug of coffee in her hand, as she swung her feet to the floor.

"So you're finally up," Margaret said.

She sat down beside Lily and handed her the coffee.

"Thanks," Lily said and took a sip.

"I thought you were going to sleep the whole day."

"What time is it?"

"Almost eleven."

Lily woke up completely. "Oh, my God. I'm going to miss my flight."

"Don't panic," Margaret told her. "We'll pick up your stuff from the motel and I'll get you there on time. We'll just make all the lights be green."

"Yeah, right."

But they didn't hit a red light, not from the ranch to the motel, nor from the motel to the airport. By the time Margaret parked her Jeep and they'd carried Lily's luggage and camera equipment into the terminal, they still had another fifteen minutes until boarding time.

"I'm surprised I don't have a hangover," Lily said after she'd checked in and they were walking toward her departure gate. She liked the small size of the Tucson airport—it seemed to have been built on a human scale, especially compared to the vast labyrinth that was the Newford International Airport.

"I've never believed in them myself," Margaret told her.

Lily had to smile. "Do things ever not work out in your favor?"

"Oh, sure. If I'm not paying attention."

"So that's the trick."

Margaret nodded. "Anyone can do it. You have to be in the moment—instead of thinking about what's happened, or what might happen—and you have to know what you want. It's simple, really."

"Simple."

"Most things are. People just make them complicated. 'Course, you have to know your limitations. There's no point in trying to move a mountain, or changing winter into summer. But that sort of makes it more interesting, too, don't you think?"

"I suppose. Except—"

"Don't look," Margaret said suddenly and walked Lily into the cluster of people waiting to go through security.

But of course Lily had to. When she saw who Margaret was trying to avoid, she quickly ducked her head, her pulse drumming far too fast, her chest tightening until she thought she might not be able to breathe. Walking past them was the man she'd seen die in a Newford alley, the man who'd attacked her and shot Hank, before he was killed himself. It wasn't possible.

"I don't think he saw us," Margaret said. "But you'd better board quickly."

"He . . . he's supposed to be dead. . . ."

She knew she wasn't making any sense, but Margaret only nodded, as though she knew.

"He is," Margaret said. "That's Gerrard, one of his brothers."

It took a long moment for that to sink in. Lily forced herself to take a steadying breath. She caught Margaret's arm.

"How could you know?" she asked.

"Word gets around."

"No," Lily said, shaking her head. "This is something different. What's going on here? Who are you?"

"A friend."

But then Lily knew. "You're like those girls from the other night, aren't you? In Newford. The ones who killed—"

There was an announcement over the P.A.

"That's your flight," Margaret said. "You'd better go. I'll head him off if it looks like he's going to board your flight."

She started to pull away, but Lily kept her hold on Margaret's arm.

"What's going on?" she said.

Margaret loosened the grip of Lily's fingers, not roughly, but with an economy of effort that told Lily she was far stronger than she looked.

"Nobody knows," Margaret told her. "But anyone who's earned the enmity of the cuckoos is automatically our friend."

"But—"

"Since they seem to be so interested in you, we thought it'd be better if I came down here to look out for you in case one of them followed you."

Lily felt as though she'd stepped through Alice's looking glass, from the world that made sense into one where nothing did.

"So you do know those girls who—"

Margaret gave her a push toward her gate. "It's too late to talk now. He's coming back."

"But—"

"I'll be in Newford soon. If I see you there, I'll try to explain more."

"But—"

"Go."

Lily let herself get caught up in the flow of people hurrying through security. She found herself beside Sharon Clark, the makeup woman from the video shoot, who immediately started enthusing about this gallery she'd been in this morning where she'd gotten the sweetest earrings. . . .

Lily looked back to see Margaret confronting the tall and dangerous man she'd referred to as a cuckoo. She hadn't meant he was a lunatic, Lily realized, because now the words of the raggedy girl who'd rescued her in that Newford alley returned to her.

> *The cuckoo is a pretty bird, he sings as he flies,*
> *He sucks little bird's eggs, and then he just dies.*

She meant animal people. They were all animal people. When Margaret said "crows" and "magpies" and "cuckoos," they weren't tribes. It was who they were. Just like in Jack's stories.

And then, as though to confirm that they had pulled her into some other world where all the rules were changed, she saw Margaret produce a switchblade, the knife dropping into her hand from her sleeve as smoothly as the raggedy girl's had back in Newford, the blade jumping from its handle. The cuckoo moved to one side and disappeared. No. He didn't quite disappear. It was as though he'd stepped around an invisible wall, out of sight. Margaret followed behind him. And they were gone. Just like that.

Gone, and no one had noticed. No one was paying any attention. . . .

Lily's shortness of breath returned. Vertigo made her sway and she would have fallen except Sharon took her by the arm.

"Lily?" she was saying. "Lily, are you all right?"

"I . . . I . . ."

None of this could be real, Lily thought. And straight

on the heels of that came, why was it happening to her? What did these horrible cuckoo men want from her?

"Lily?"

Finally she managed to focus on Sharon's worried features. She swallowed hard. Made herself breathe.

"I . . . I'm okay," she said. "Thanks. I just had a little . . . dizzy spell, that's all."

"Does it happen a lot?" Sharon asked. She kept a hand on Lily's arm as they continued toward security, steadying her.

"No. It must just have been . . . all this heat."

It was the first thing that came to mind and seemed lame to her, but Sharon nodded with understanding.

"My mother-in-law's like that," she said. "She went to Las Vegas for Christmas one year, and of course she's got to go see the countryside, like there's any kind of countryside in Nevada. Anyway, the next thing we know we're getting this call from the state police because . . ."

Lily kept smiling, but tuned her out. She stole a last glance at the hallway before it was her turn to go through the metal detector, but there were only other travelers going by, carry-ons slung over their shoulders, pulling suitcases with narrow straps. Margaret and the cuckoo were still gone. It was as though they'd never been.

Lily turned suddenly to Sharon, interrupting her story.

"There was a woman seeing me off," she said. "Dark-haired, wearing a jean vest and a baseball cap, lots of jewelry. Looked sort of Native American. Did you see where she went?"

Sharon gave her a puzzled look. "I didn't see anybody with you."

Lily gave a slow nod. That explained why there hadn't been a great outcry when two people simply vanished from the hall of the airport.

"I must have lost track of her in the crowd," she said.

If you could call the dozen or so people who'd been waiting to go through security a crowd.

"Are you *sure* you're all right?" Sharon asked.

Lily nodded and gave her a bright smile. "So you were telling me about your mother."

"My mother-in-law," Sharon said, happy to be derailed back into her story. "Well, it turns out the rental had no spare tire, so . . ."

Not everybody can see them, Lily thought. Was that why the cuckoo had attacked her in Newford, why the one here had followed her into the airport? That didn't seem to make a great deal of sense—why should they care if she could see them or not? It wasn't as though she'd seen them doing anything. But what else could it be?

And then she thought of Margaret, gone to wherever on the heels of the cuckoo. She hoped the bird girl was able to hold her own as Lily had thought she was when she'd first seen her.

~ 4 ~

IN A FIELD OF GRACE

Tell me, baby, have you seen a crow girl like me
Now shifting, now lifting away on that breeze
Does it make your heart long for those black shiny
*   wings*
To rise up in the sky, to give life to your dreams
— MARYANN HARRIS,
FROM "*CROW GIRLS*"

1.

Hazard, Summer, 1940

I followed the crow girls up north that summer, an old
jackdaw winging in their giddy wake. They don't slow
down for much, but I kept pace. I only look like I'm too
used up to be any good. And I can look better, need be.
We tend to settle into a skin, get used to it, we've worn
it so long. I could work up something as slick as Cody
any day of the week if you gave me a reason, but I had
no need of handsomeness that trip. The crow girls were
meeting some northern cousins for a hooley in the woods
and I was only tagging along. I can fly strong, steady as
the girls, but once they get to considering a party, just
thinking about how they can carry on wears me right out.

My joining them was only an excuse to visit those
piney wood hills.

Everybody's got a true home—maybe not where
they're living, but where their heart lives. Mine's in a
meadow, deep in a hidden hollow of these old hills, hemlocks growing up one side of the hill, birch and cedar

and pine walking up the other, creek easing its way down the middle, the water icy cold even at this time of year, like it's still underground, like it never seeped up between the rocks and started on its way down to the river. The meadow's yellow-green with thick grass, starred with constellations of wildflowers, and smells like summer: heady and sleepy and unworried. Bees humming, june bugs whirring, the wind soughing through the trees and grass, a few clouds trailing through a sky so blue it's like to swallow you whole. There's an old rock, right up near the top of that hollow, smooth on the sun side, mossy on the shade. I find that rock and stretch out, sun pouring down on me like honey, and you know I'm home.

Why don't I stay, I love it so much?

It's complicated. Place like that makes you forget. You fill up on the beauty and you stop remembering yourself, who you are, what skin you're supposed to be wearing, that you've even got a choice. You disappear into something bigger than yourself and that's okay, but I've been there, done that. Lots of us take that route, but I worked so hard to get back to remembering, I'm not ready to lose myself again—not so soon. And if I lose myself, I lose the stories, and I've spent too long collecting them this time out.

But I'm eager to see the place all the same, just like anyone's eager to get home. You know you're going back out the door, the next day, the next week, but that doesn't keep you from settling in, recharging the soul, catching up on all the local gossip.

This time, everybody's talking about the fox girl. Not full-blooded canid, but she's got as much of Ray in her as she does from her mother's side of the family. The human side. She's a skinny, raw-boned girl, eleven, maybe, no older than twelve. Got a long, narrow, heart-shaped face and the red hair from her father's side. Goes tumbling through these woods like a nettle, curious about everything, into everything, gets so close that all the bits and pieces she sticks her nose into cling to her when she goes. Twigs and burrs and seeds. A wild girl.

I'm not looking for her, though I'm curious. I circle above the meadow, drifting down from the blue in long lazy circles. The crow girls have already meet up with their cousins and you can hear their hooley from two hills away. Me, I get settled into my hollow, soaking up the sun and beauty, not scared of losing myself because the girls have promised to come by and pick me up on the way home.

So I'm lazing there, catching up on the gossip. Like I said, I'm not looking for her, and this wild fox girl, she's not looking for me, but we meet up all the same. Me sitting up suddenly, sleepy from the sun. Her bursting out of the forest at a run, stopping dead in her tracks when she sees me there on that rock. I think maybe this is her place, too. Her rock. Her heart home. Maybe that's why I don't change my skin and fly away, why she doesn't bolt back the way she came. We know each other and we've never met.

"Hey there," she says, bold as brass, not scared, not even nervous.

"Hey, yourself."

"What's your name?"

"Jack."

"Everybody calls me Nettie on account of that's my name. Not the name I was born into, my mammy says, but the one I grew into."

"Makes sense to me," I tell her. "You live around here?"

She waves her hand vaguely off to the other side of the hemlocks. "Me and my mammy have a house back in yonder."

"And your father?"

"I don't have no pappy on account of he's a no-good bum who run off on my mammy, 'cept she don't seem to mind much."

I didn't know then that Ray's been through these hills, stopped and tarried a spell with a good-looking widow

and nine months later she's got herself a girl-child to raise
by herself. Maybe I should have guessed, but fox blood
all smells pretty much the same to me and it's not like
Ray's got a monopoly on sowing wild oats. All those fox
men have a taste for honey.

But I take a liking to this raw-boned child. Maybe it's
only a whim, or maybe even then I could see she was
more like me than a fox, collecting stories like Margaret
collects trinkets, keeping them not to have them, but to
pass them on. And I'm thinking it's a shame she's got
the blood and doesn't know what to do with it except run
wild through the woods. Leaving her on her own like this
no better than a cuckoo, dropping its eggs in a corbæ's
nest.

"Maybe I'll be your pappy," I tell her.

She gives this a moment's consideration.

"You gonna run off on me like the last one did?" she
asks.

"Probably," I tell her. I'm not going to start off with
lying to her. "But I'll always come back."

"I don't need a pappy," she says then. "But I do need
a husband. I hear they're useful."

I have to laugh.

"What's so funny?" she wants to know.

"You're just too young to be thinking about courting."

"Jenny-May's only a couple of years older'n me and
she's got two kids."

It's enough to make you weep. Too many of them get
old fast and die young in these hills. If the mines don't
take them, the travails of their life do. You try farming
these hills, or breathing when your lungs have an inch of
coal dust coating them.

"That doesn't make it right," I tell her.

"Now you sound like my mammy. The way she sees
it, everything's got a wrong and a right."

"And you don't agree?"

She shrugs. "Things just is, is all."

You could take that for cynicism, but I see it for the innocence it is.

"If you could have anything," I say, "what would it be?"

She doesn't even have to think about it. "Only one thing I'd want and that'd be to fly."

"Fly?"

She grins. "Like the crow girls."

"How do you know about them?"

"I've seen 'em. They meet with the wild crow boys in our woods most every year. I've seen 'em dancing and laughing up yonder, happy as can be. And I've seen 'em flying."

Foxes don't fly, I think, but how do I tell her that?

"I could be a red crow," she goes on, grubby fingers reaching up to touch her hair, red as Ray's tail. "On account of my hair."

"All the crows I know are black," I tell her, "except for a white crow I saw once, and that's no color at all."

"What crow was that?" she wants to know.

"The white crow that showed the Kickaha how to grow corn," I say, and then I tell her the story.

She lies on her back in the grass as I talk, wriggling like a worm on the end of a hook, but I know she's listening because every time I stop for a moment, she goes still and cocks her head in my direction. I'm betting she could give it back to me, word for word, if I asked. When I'm done she lies there looking up into the blue. There's someone circling high above. A hawk. No relation.

"Is that a true story?" she asks after awhile.

"True as I remember it."

She sits up, smiles shyly at me. "I never knew corn had a story."

"Everything's got a story. Take that milkweed you're about to knock down with your knee."

She moves back and gives it a wary look. "What about it?"

So I tell her its story, tell her the june bug's, whirring in the high grass just out of sight, the lacewing's, and the one that belongs to the cedar—not the ones growing up the side of the hollow here, but an older stand that were thick in the middle of one of Cody's mischiefs.

"Do you know any more?" she asks when I'm done with that last one.

But the sun's lowering, and the shadows of the trees are creeping across the meadow. The first bats are sailing down out of the woods. In the distance, we can still hear the crows' hooley. It's louder now, the sound carrying farther on the gray shoulders of the dusk.

"I know hundreds," I tell her, "but let's save them for another time."

"I want to know them all."

I have to smile. "Even I don't know them all, but I'll tell you the ones I know and you could learn some yourself, too, and then tell them to me. Because that's what we storytellers do." Her little chest swells a bit when I include her with that "we."

"What do *we* do?" she asks, savoring the word when she uses it.

"Share our stories with each other."

She's eager, but doubtful, too. I can tell.

"I don't even know where to start learning stories," she says.

"You've just got to pay attention. You have to practice listening and learning to hold them all in your head. It's hard to do and it takes time, but you could start with writing some down. Can you get yourself a pencil and some paper?"

"Oh, sure."

"Well, you take them out with you, the next time you go rambling, and sit down, maybe draw some old weed or wildflower, listen close while you're doing it, maybe you'll hear some no-account gossip about what the rabbits have been up to this week, or those bees that never stop humming. Or maybe you'll get a piece of its story and you can add that to the page.''

She looks a little disappointed. "That's not the same.''

"That's how all the stories start,'' I tell her. "With some little thing.''

"But why do I got to learn how to draw?''

"You don't. But it's a good way to learn how to pay attention. To really *see* what you're looking at, instead of what you expect to see.''

The doubt is still there, but the eagerness is stronger.

"So are you gonna be here tomorrow?'' she asks.

I nod.

Turns out I'm there for most of the summer.

The crow girls think it's too funny when they come by to collect me a few days later and I'm not ready to go.

"Are you going back to sleep?'' Maida asks, which is what we call it when we lose ourselves, when we forget we're people and spend all of our time in our animal skins.

"Naw,'' Zia says before I can answer. "He's found himself a puppy and he's going to teach her how to fly.''

"I didn't know puppies could fly.''

"They can't. But don't tell Jack. He'd be ever so disappointed.''

They both erupt into giggles and I can't help laughing with them. But they wait with me, black-winged, perched on the stone, for when Nettie comes tramping through the field that morning and I can tell right away that they like her, too. The crow girls wear their hearts on their sleeves. You know when they're happy, you know when they're sad.

"Be careful,'' Zia whispers in my ear. "That one's going to break your heart.''

"It's not that kind of thing,'' I tell her.

"Not now. But she's not always going to be some skinny little fox child, too young for an old jackdaw.''

I give Maida a look to see what she thinks, but she

doesn't have anything to add right away. She sits there, filled with quiet, dark gaze fixed on that wild fox girl making her way through the tall grass.

"She could fly," she says finally and then the two of them rise on black wings that shine blue in the sunlight.

Nettie comes running up, shades her eyes as she watches them go.

"I never saw anything so pretty," she says. "Jenny-May's pappy plumb hates crows—like most folks do around here—but I don't."

"Me, neither," I tell her.

She's carrying the sketchbook we made the second day we got together. Brown wrapping paper, torn up neatly, folded together into a book, the spine held together with twine stitching. She keeps her stubby pencil behind her ear, sharpened to a fine point with the little penknife I gave her.

I remember the look on her face when I pulled that penknife out of my pocket and told her it was hers to keep.

"Nobody's ever give me something this good before," she said, turning it over and over in her hands.

She's got a knack for drawing. I saw that in her, same as I saw the empty places waiting to be filled with stories. Next summer, I'll bring her a proper paint box, but for now she's using berry juice, red dirt, coffee grounds, and the like to add some color to her sketches.

"Lookit this," she says, scrambling up to sit beside me.

I take the sketchbook on my lap and look at the page she wants to show me, every corner of it crammed with pencil drawings and faded colors that look almost misty against the brown paper background. A sparrow. Queen Anne's lace. Joe-pye weed. A hickory leaf. Ground beetle. Pinecone. Her own hand, the outline traced, but she's filled in the detail—creases, scab on a knuckle, dirt under the nails and all. At the bottom of the page she's written in a child's scrawl: "What I seen teday."

"You get much schooling?" I ask her.

She grins. "Only what I can't avoid."

I've brought her a book today—bought it for her in a pawnshop over in Tyson. It's bigger than Hazard by a couple of thousand people, lying south, about halfway to the city. The book's a field guide to wildflowers, full of pictures, but lots of words, too. Latin names, common names, stories about how they got those names and such. She's so delighted with such a simple thing it makes me want to give her something every time I see her, but I won't.

"I can't read that good," she tells me.

"Lots of stories in books," I say. "They're like the woods. You can learn a lot from them."

"Yeah?"

"It's the truth. And the beauty is, you can go into that little library in the basement of the town hall in Hazard and they'll let you borrow any one you want. All you got to do is go in and ask."

She gives me a suspicious look. "What're you really trying to tell me?"

"Maybe you shouldn't be avoiding your schooling."

She weighs the field guide in her hand, then gives me one of those sudden grins of hers.

"Maybe I won't," she says.

2.

Summer, 1941

The next summer she's a year older and I'm looking about sixteen, trying to even the gap so that her mammy won't be so worried when she sees her daughter spending so much time with me. The crow girls laugh when they see me, no more handsome than the Jack they've always known. Only younger.

"Jack's going courting," Zia says. "All he needs is a bow tie and some flowers."

Maida pokes her in the shoulder with a stiff finger. "Don't tease him," she says. "Jack's our friend." But she's giggling, too.

"Not like he wants to be friends with her. Jack's in love."

"Is that true?" Maida asks.

I shake my head. "No. Not like you're thinking."

That sets them off again. Why? I don't know. The crow girls have a whole other way of deciding what's funny and what's not.

"But she's in love with you," Maida says when she catches her breath.

She's not joking now.

"Maybe she thinks she is," I say, "but she'll grow out of it."

Zia shakes her head. "That girl's too stubborn to grow out of anything she sets her mind to."

"Then she's just going to have to live with the disappointment," I say.

There's a long moment of silence, the two of them looking at me, serious.

"No," Maida says. "You are."

As I'm walking down the dirt road that leads out of Hazard to the Bean farm, I find myself wondering if Nettie'll recognize me, but I needn't have worried. She comes running down the windy path from the farmhouse and gives me a hug, then grabs my hand and tugs me back up to the house to meet her mammy.

Edna Bean is a well-favored woman and it's easy to see why some fox came tapping on her window late one night. She has the look of corbæ blood, our dark hair and eyes, but her skin's brown from the weather and the only place I guess she ever flew was in her dreams. Her build is slight, but there's nothing weak about her. These hill women get born strong and only grow stronger. She watches our approach, not exactly suspicious, but not exactly welcoming either; wondering about me, the way they do in the hills when a stranger comes to their door

Back in the woods, I can hear the crow girls giggling.

"I'm guessing from the way the girl's carrying on that you'd be Jack," Nettie's mammy says to me after giving me a slow once-over.

"Yes, ma'am. Pleased to meet you."

"Summering in Hazard, are you?"

"Yes, ma'am, if I can find some work."

A crooked smile touches her lips and I know then where Nettie gets that grin of hers.

"Looking for work," she says and lets her voice trail off.

"Yes, ma'am."

"Well, you're sure enough polite—I'll give you that much."

Nettie's shifting her weight from foot to foot, impatient to be done with the talk and go rambling through the woods. But her mammy's not done yet. She's still eyeing me, trying to get my measure. I do my best to look harmless.

"So you're the one who got her to work at her schooling," she says.

"I couldn't say, ma'am. All we did was talk one afternoon about how learning's a good thing."

She cocks her head, corbælike. "You think learning can feed you?"

"Depends on what you're hungry for, ma'am."

The crooked smile widens into that familiar grin of Nettie's.

"You'll do," Edna says. "Tell you what, Jack. You'll eat with us and you can sleep in the barn. All I ask is that you help out around with the chores some."

"Yes, ma'am."

"And maybe keep my Nettie here company. I figure you're a good influence, seeing's how she came home with straight A's last year."

"That must've made you proud," I say.

"She doesn't need to do good at school to make me proud," Edna tells me. "But I figure schooling's the only thing that's going to get her out of these hills on her own terms."

What makes you think she wants to leave? I think, but I keep it to myself. Edna's laboring under the same misconception that's snared too many parents before her. She wants to make sure her child doesn't repeat the mistakes she made herself, but I doubt she's got to worry on that account. Any mistakes Nettie makes, they'll be her own, and whatever else they'll be, they'll be interesting.

"And one more thing, Jack," Edna says.

"Yes, ma'am?"

"Call me Edna. I hear you call me 'ma'am' and I keep looking around to see where my mammy is and her dead seven years now, God rest her soul. It's disconcerting. Save your respect for those who've earned it."

"I figure you've earned it," I say.

"Nobody likes an apple-polisher," she tells me, but she smiles.

Saturday nights they have the barn dances and pretty much everybody shows up at one of those old granges, high on a hill like the cows need a view, the farmhouse tucked down in some little hollow out of the wind. Inside, there's music and singing and dancing, a long table along one wall with pies and cakes and cookies, coffee and tea, pop, juice. There's no never mind on the old wooden dance floor, old folks, young folks, all taking a turn together. Outside, there's drinking and a few fights, nothing too serious, and a lot of spooning in the hayfields, or maybe the back of someone's wagon.

The night Nettie insists we all go to the grange there's a full moon, the stars are hanging high and bright, and the air's brisk, more like an autumn night than one in late June. Look hard and you can see Venus, Mars. Sometimes a little streak of light as a meteorite comes zipping from space to hit the air and burn up. Falling stars to wish upon. I don't make a wish, but maybe I should have.

The music's already playing when we arrive—a pickup band, Edna tells me. Two fiddles, five-string banjo, wash-tub bass, and steel-bodied resonator guitar. People danc-ing, congregating around the laden food tables, laughing, gossiping, sneaking out for a drink or a kiss. I'm sur-prised to see Ray there, flirting with a sweet young thing on the far side of the barn, but I guess I shouldn't be. He does get around. Then I see the way Edna's looking at him and I know for sure who it was sired that wild fox child of hers.

Ray doesn't even look in our direction and I think, that's hard. But Edna makes a quick recovery. She smiles brightly, cheeks flushing pretty, and it's like he's not there for her any more than she is for him.

"Let's you and me dance," Nettie says, tugging at my hand as the band finishes one tune and starts right into another.

I shake my head. "I can't dance."

"Sure you can," she says, still pulling at my hand.

"I'm saying I can't."

I reclaim my hand, then wish I'd left well enough be. Wish I'd gone out on the boards with her and made a fool of myself, because the hurt in her eyes is something I don't ever want to see again. It jumps into my chest, cuts too quick and deep. She puts away her own hurt like her mammy did hers, got the same flush on her cheeks, the same too-bright smile, but I can't forget it. And then it's too late because some handsome young man is step-ping up, dark hair slicked back, his smile offering her everything I can't. The next thing I know the two of them are out there dancing and I'm standing there beside her mammy, watching them go.

"His name's Randall Miller," she tells me. "Cuts a fine figure, don't you think?"

Not so fine as Ray does, I'm thinking, but I've learned my lesson and keep my mouth shut.

"The Beans and Millers, we go back a long way," Edna's saying. "My husband was a Miller, third or fourth cousin of Randall's father, I suppose."

"That a fact."

"Nettie, she'll probably marry a Miller, too, if she doesn't get away from these hills."

I look at her. "Nettie'll do whatever she sets her mind to."

She sighs. Her gaze darts across the barn to where Ray's managed to talk his sweet young thing into going for a walk. We catch the back-end of them, heading out the door. That young woman on his arm, leaning close to her newfound fox man, has a figure to make you catch your breath.

"You're going to lose her, you don't watch out," Edna says.

"I never had her to lose."

"You think that, maybe you're not so smart as I took you to be."

"You don't want your daughter running off with some no-account hobo boy," I tell her.

"No," she says. "I surely don't. Is that what you are, Jack?"

"I don't know what I am," I say.

Her gaze drifts over to the barn door before settling on me again.

"Maybe," she says. "But do you know what you want?"

"I don't know that either," I lie.

We don't talk much after that, just watch Nettie and Randall Miller dance away pretty much the whole night. I make my own way home, before the dance is over, jackdaw wings lifting me up above the grange and off to that meadow in the hollow where I first met the fox girl. It's just as pretty at night, prettier maybe, but I don't see much of it. I don't see much of anything at all.

* * *

Nettie finds me the next morning, sleeping in the long grass.

"You should've give it a try," she says, sitting down beside me. "The dancing, I mean. It was some fun."

"I got that impression," I tell her.

She has this little leather satchel that holds her sketch-book and pencils and the paint box I gave her when I first got here this summer, carries it with her pretty much everywhere she goes. When she pulls out an apple and offers it to me, I shake my head. She takes a big bite and gives it a thorough chew, like working her jaws is helping her think.

"Guess you don't much like me," she says finally.

"What makes you think that?"

She shrugs. "You never try to kiss me."

"We're not that kind of friends," I tell her.

"Randall tried to kiss me last night."

"He seems like a nice boy."

She throws that apple at my head and I only barely manage to duck out of its way. The way she's glaring at me, I hope she doesn't have any more tucked away in her satchel.

"You don't know nothing about feelings, do you?" she says.

I know she's looking for a father she's never going to have, not with Ray having sired her. I wouldn't be much better. And I sure as hell don't plan to start courting her like some spoony-eyed Miller boy.

"You're too young and I'm too old," I tell her. "That's just the way it is."

She glares at me some more, but I can see her lower lip start to quiver. I want to give her a hug and ease the pain, but I know we've got to stop this notion she has, right now, before it gets out of hand. So I do the thing I do best; I do nothing.

"I hate you," she says.

I watch her stalk off across the field. I see the hurt in the set of her shoulders and I know what she's feeling because she's put a piece of that pain in my chest with her parting words.

I'm hoping we can get past this and still be friends, and I'm right about that. Things settle down to how they were before, pretty much.

I figure she'll grow out of this notion of us being sweethearts, and I couldn't be more wrong about that.

3.

Summer, 1946

The high school in Tyşon's not much by big-city standards, but it's got all the trimmings it needs: library, gym, auditorium. It sits on a wooded lot on the edge of town, a big old brick and wood building, all those shiny yellow school buses parked in a line outside at the end of the day, waiting to take kids back to Hazard and the other small towns nearby.

Come Nettie's graduation day, we're sitting in the auditorium, all in a row with Edna—me and the crow girls, Margaret, Alberta, Crazy Crow, Jolene, and Bear, and some of the others. Over the years a lot of them got to know Nettie, got to love her as much as I do, so we're all here to cheer her on. Usually you get the crow girls and Jolene together and you've got nothing but trouble, but they're on their best behavior for Nettie's sake, wearing dresses even, hair combed, only giggling a little bit. You can't expect miracles.

Edna's past wondering about us, me living in the barn every summer, all these friends of her daughter's who don't seem to have homes except for the woods. I think she liked Crazy Crow best, seeing how he's got that coyote blood mixed up with the crow. Edna, she's got a fondness for those canids. Without it, there never would have been a Nettie and we wouldn't be here with Edna now, hooting and hollering and clapping our hands, when

Nettie goes up to get her diploma and the principal announces how she's won this scholarship to Butler University.

Edna takes my hand and gives it a squeeze.

"This is your doing, Jack," she says. "Lord, but I'm grateful."

"I'm not stealing your girl's thunder," I tell her. "She's earned this on her own."

"You know what I mean."

I suppose I do. But Nettie was hungry to learn. All I did was point her in a direction or two.

There's a party at the Bean farm later that day, a regular hooley with wild crow boys coming down out of the wooded hills and everybody having themselves a fine old time. At one point Maida and Zia are doing a two-step along the peak of the barn and when Jolene tries to join in, the three of them fall off on the far side of the roof, out of sight. Everybody laughs, except for Edna, who lets out a sharp gasp.

"Don't you worry about those girls," Crazy Crow reassures her. "They never get into something so deep that they can't pull themselves out."

"But the roof's so high. . . ."

Her voice trails off when the girls come round the side of the barn, poking at each other and giggling.

When it starts on getting dark, Bear and Nettie put together a huge bonfire in the middle of the farmyard and we all pull up chairs and stumps to sit around it, except for Maida, Zia, and the wild crow boys, who start up to dancing again with Jolene, going round and round the fire, feet stomping in time to some strange tune Alberta's pulling from a fiddle, who knows where she got it, fiddle and tune both.

A long time later, Edna's gone in to bed and there's stories being told around the coals of the fire, songs being sung. Nettie comes walking up to where I'm sitting on the porch of the farmhouse. I'm looking off across the field of wildflowers that sides the house, thinking of what seems like a long ago time when this fox child was just a skinny little thing running wild. Now she's a young lady. Still has the hills in her, the accent and the turn of phrase that make the big-city folk laugh, but she's gained something else from these wild woodlands and fields that can't be born into a body or taught: the grace of learning how to listen, and learning how to speak. I see the studies she does of weeds and flowers and such, I read the essays she writes, and I know these hills have found themselves a voice in her.

I think I'm proudest of her for that. These days she tells me stories, like I still tell them to her, and she's not shy about it anymore. We're meeting on common ground, like equals, the way I always wanted it to be but she never felt she was up to before.

"Hey, Jack," she says as she comes up and sits beside me on the bench. "You okay?"

I nod. "I'm just admiring the starlight on that field of flowers."

"You're missing the stories."

I glance at the bonfire. Crazy Crow's telling one of his, that long rambling account of the year he and Raven wintered in Africa and found Cody teaching people how to make fire.

"I've heard them all before," I say.

She smiles and gives me a light poke in the ribs with her elbow. "Wasn't it you who told me that you can never hear a story too many times?"

"That's true. A good story's like a good song. It doesn't age."

She doesn't say anything, just listens like I taught her to listen to the wild, and like the wild, I find myself filling up the quiet that lies between us with words. What I'm thinking is: Sometimes the love you have for someone can spur you on to great and wonderful things, takes all that potential you've got resting inside you and lets it blossom and grow. But sometimes a love can hold you back. Nettie, she's had both with me, and now it's time for her to get on with her life and stop wishing for what's never going to be.

Corbæ and human, even a human with fox blood running strong in her, can't ever pair up for too long. It doesn't work because how do you reconcile a life that stretches back to when the medicine lands woke up out of the long ago to make this world and a life that's as brief in comparison as a candle flickering in the wind? It's why Ray doesn't stick around, it's why the crow girls wear their hearts on their sleeves and will share them, from time to time, but they don't ever give them away.

And it's not like I haven't tried before. But it hurts too much and I'm too old to carry that pain again. Except this hurts, too. Maybe more. Who am I kidding? This calls up an ache that goes bone deep and settles in the marrow. But it's got to be done. She needs a chance at a real life with her own kind.

So that's what I'm thinking, but what I say is, "You've got a lot of good friends here. See you don't forget them when you're living in that big city."

She always had insight as a child. Now she's a young woman and that insight's only grown sharper. She gives me a look and I know she can see straight through me. I'm like an open book to her.

She knows I'm not telling her to remember anything; I'm saying good-bye.

"I will always love you, Jack," she says.

Maida warned me of this years ago. Zia, too. But that doesn't make it any easier to bear.

I'm carrying a big hurt when I leave the farm next morning, early, before daylight, jackdaw wings carrying me south, over Newford, over the lake, all the way down to Mexico. But distance doesn't ease the pain. Nor do the years.

And one day I just have to see her again.

4.

Late summer, 1971

I hear about how Nettie is doing from the crow girls, from Jolene and Crazy Crow and all, never tire of it, not the smallest details that come my way. And I collect the stories that spring up like trod-on grass where she's walked.

It's not just the hills around Hazard that gossip about her now. She's on a world stage—maybe not in a big way, like someone making the *New York Times* bestseller list, which she doesn't, but her books are being read in a lot of places that never heard of the Kickaha Hills or those hollows and high lonesome ridges around Hazard until she wrote about them. So people talk. People write about her.

I have the books. The catalogues for a couple of her art shows. But it's not enough. One day I know I have to see her. I don't plan on entering her life again, I just want to look at her one more time.

'Course nothing works out the way you expect when it comes to Nettie Bean. Must be the fox blood in her.

Edna took ill, the winter of '49, and never did live to see Nettie graduate from college. Didn't see her graduate and didn't see how she moved back to the farm and settled in like she'd never been off studying for all those years. Nettie just had enough of cities, missed her woods and her hills too much to put the farm up for sale when her mammy died.

Her returning would have broken Edna's heart. Edna wouldn't have seen Nettie's happiness, only how she was trapping herself the same way her mammy had in her time.

But the farm was no trap for Nettie. By the time she moved back home, she'd been having essays and articles published in naturalist journals, was selling her paintings, even had a book sold and coming out in the fall. She wasn't rich, but she could cover her living expenses and the land taxes. And maybe she wasn't making a lot of friends in the towns roundabout, fighting for closure of the mines and to stop the clear-cutting and all, but she was still happier than Edna had ever been on that land.

Because Edna hadn't been close to it the way her daughter was. They were neither of them farmers, though they grew their own greens and such, kept chickens for the eggs, a cow for milk. Edna had rented out her hay-fields, done washing and mending, whatever she could to make ends meet. That farm was like a big ball and chain, holding her down. For Nettie it was a piece of freedom.

She was old by hill standards—almost twenty-four—when she finally married Randall Miller in '53, and the marriage lasted long enough to produce one child the next year, a daughter. She was baptized Lilah, after Randall's paternal grandmother, and was a dark-haired, sullen girl as different from the wild fox child Nettie had been as honey is from vinegar. Lilah took an immediate dislike to her mother, wouldn't suckle, couldn't even abide Net-tie holding her. I can't explain it. Nettie might have carried her for nine months, but it was like Lilah was someone else's child. If she had any of the blood in her, no one could smell it, which, if you know anything about genetics, makes no sense either.

The marriage didn't last much beyond Lilah's first year, though from all accounts, it was never any great shakes in the first place. Nettie kept her name, kept at her work, and plain ignored any attempt on Randall's part to give up either just to fit the picture he had in his head of what a wife was supposed to be. It took a couple of years before he finally gave up trying to fit that round peg she was into the square hole he imagined for her.

He didn't divorce her at first. What he wanted was that land, the Millers having lost all their own through mis-management and plain bad luck over the years. So instead of having the marriage annulled, he tried to have Nettie institutionalized for incompetence, claiming she was a danger to herself and those around her. Like father, like daughter, I suppose, since Lilah took to that idea in her own time like a duck does to water.

Nettie didn't have many friends round there by that time—not human ones. There wasn't a whole lot of understanding or support for her fights with the mining companies and the loggers. Truth was, even before she got into all of that, folks thought she was a little too strange, even by hill standards. So Randall might have had his way, except Alberta got wind of what was happening and she went and had a talk with Chloë, who sent this lawyer to the county seat, where the competency hearing was being held. To hear Alberta tell the story, it took maybe all of five minutes for that lawyer to straighten things out. He handled the divorce, too, when Randall filed the papers a few weeks later.

I would have been there for her myself, stood by her through that hard time, but by the time word got to me, it was all over. Nettie kept her name and the family farm; Randall kept the daughter and moved back into Hazard where the two of them lived up above the work bays of his garage in that small apartment he'd had before he got married. Maybe no one can explain why Lilah took that sudden dislike to her mother, pretty much from the moment she was born, but it's not hard to see why she never gave it up. Randall harbored a grudge against Nettie till the day he died and it stands to reason that his daughter never heard a kind word in relation to her mother.

Lilah eventually married Stephen Madan, a real estate agent who made himself a tidy bundle when he parceled and sold off his own family farm before his father was cold in the grave. Of course she poisoned him against Nettie, too, but with a man like that, it wouldn't have taken much.

Lilah was a puzzle to me, but in some ways, Randall puzzled me more. I never could figure how a man who'd loved Nettie as much as I know he once did could bring so much hurt into her life.

But then sometimes I wonder if, in my own way, I was no better than him.

I love those piney wood hills around Hazard any time of the year, but I think I love summer the best. It's late in the season when I fly up, the August fields awash with milkweed, goldenrod, and great purple sweeps of joe-pye weed. I ride a warm updraft, circle the hollow where I first met a wild fox girl. When I'm sure there's no one nearby, I glide down out of the blue to the old piece of granite that's still resting in a field of tall grass and wild-flowers and settle down on its rough stone surface.

It's not changed much. The forest has crept a little closer, the trees are taller. Still old growth. Crickets cheep like high-pitched squeaky wheels and the air's full of bees, humming and buzzing from one purple blossom to the next. This time of year, the creek's almost dry but I can still trace the route it takes down the hollow, follow-ing a thin trickle of water that gleams like a silver ribbon in the bright sun.

It's a drowsy kind of a day and I've had me a long flight. I nod off after awhile and the next thing I know it's late afternoon and I'm looking up at a red-haired woman with eyes so blue you'd think they'd swallowed a piece of the sky above us.

"Well, look what the crows dug up," she says.

She's standing there, hands on her hips, smiling. Not a wild fox child anymore, but the fox is still there, and I don't doubt she's only part-tamed. She'd be forty-two, but looks ten years younger, and whatever I told myself when I flew up here today, I can't pretend that the real reason wasn't to see her.

"How're you doing, Nettie?" I say.

"I've been better." She sits down and talks like it hasn't been twenty-five years since we last saw each other. "I slept funny last night and woke with a crick in my neck."

She's still carrying that old leather satchel of hers—it's a wonder it's still all of a piece. Reaching in, she takes out some oatmeal cookies wrapped up in a piece of checked cotton cloth.

"Care for some field food?" she asks.

"Thanks."

The cookies are good and go well with the tea we share out of the canteen she's carrying on her belt. It's sweetened with honey from her own hives, she tells me.

"You're doing well for yourself," I say after awhile. "I hear about you all the time—read your books."

"I don't hear about you at all."

I shrug. "Yeah, well, I don't do much of anything. Collect my stories, tell 'em when and where I can. They've still got my picture in the dictionary, right there beside the word 'footloose.' "

"I could've sworn it was beside 'feckless,' " she says, but she smiles—same crooked smile her mother had.

I figure I deserve that. I never got the words out the last time. I told myself I didn't need to, that she'd understand, maybe not right away, but at some point, only the truth was, I just didn't have the courage. I won't let that happen again.

"I can understand your being mad," I begin, but she cuts me off.

"I'm not mad, Jack. I was never really mad. I just missed you. You took yourself out of my life—for my own good, I'm sure is what you were thinking—but you never asked me if that's what I wanted. You never stopped to think how I'd feel."

"I thought I knew how you felt."

"That I was head over heels, crazy in love with you from the first time we met?"

"Something like that. But it wasn't right. You were just a child."

"And later? When I grew up?"

"I could see too much hurt coming out of it," I say.

She gives me a steady look. "And whose feelings were you sparing? Mine or your own?"

"Some of both," I admit.

"You figured it'd be like the way it worked out with Ray and my mother," she says.

"How'd you know about that?"

She shrugs. "I think Jolene told me."

"So maybe now you understand."

"I don't understand at all," she says. "What's wrong with taking what good you can when it comes? Might as well. Life's short enough. Sooner or later, we all die anyway, so why not take our happinesses where we can?"

"My people don't die," I say. "Not unless somebody kills us and even then I'm not so sure. I think some of us—like the crow girls and Raven—are going to be here right until that last day when they finally close the curtains and start sweeping down the stage."

She just looks at me.

"What did you think we were?" I ask.

"I don't know. Some kind of spirits, I guess. I never thought about it all that much."

"Most of us have been here since the first days," I tell her. "But the corbæ, we were here before there even was a 'here.'"

"How . . . ?" she starts to say, but then she just shakes her head.

She looks out across the field and I can almost see her thinking, working out what it all means. I lie back on the grass and look up into the blue so like her eyes. I hear a couple of crows argue in the distance and I wonder if the crow girls are visiting, or if it's just those cousins of theirs squabbling. Closer at hand, the crickets are still cheeping. They put me in mind of a piece Nettie wrote about them for some magazine or other. I remember all the little pen and ink illustrations she did to accompany it and I can't help but smile. She was drawing crickets from the first time she took pencil to hand.

"What's it like?" she finally asks. "This living forever."

I shrug. "Everybody takes to it a little different. The crow girls, they live each day like they just got here, like it's still the long ago. Zen time. Every day is now and forever. Some of the rooks and jays, they get deep into expressing themselves, take their music and their art and keep walking it deeper and deeper into the place that everything comes from—you know, trying to walk it all the way back to those dreaming places that sleep under the forever trees."

Nettie nods, remembering that story, I guess.

"Others, they like to wander—like Crazy Crow. And then you've got Raven. He's carried the weight of history for so long that he's just stepped out of time. Nothing touches him there. No responsibilities, no worries."

"And how about you, Jack?" she asks. "How do you handle it?"

I sit back up to look at her, resting my weight on my elbows. "I tell the stories. First I told them to remember them because a long time ago, I got like Raven and stepped out of time, didn't know my history, didn't care anymore. Forgot everything. Just wandered around and let things happen to me. That could still be me, except I ran into the crow girls one day and . . . well, I've told you how it is. You see them, and things change for you. You start looking for meaning again. Start wanting to make a difference."

I've never talked about this to anyone before. I guess I should have started a long time ago—started with that wild fox child Nettie once was so that she'd understand.

"And now," I say, lying back on the grass. "Now I tell the stories so that maybe we don't have to keep making the same mistakes over and over again."

It's like old times, biding here by our rock in this hollow, passing the time with pieces of quiet and conversation, the sun starting to slide behind the trees. We don't talk for a time, just watch the shadows grow, wait to see what the twilight brings.

"Come back to the house with me," Nettie says after awhile. "Let me make you some dinner."

I know I should leave, follow the road away from her again, but I can't. I've had this taste of her company now, and after all these years, it's too little.

"Sure," I find myself saying.

She tucks her arm in mine and we go ambling back through the woods, following a familiar route that takes us out above the wildflower field that sides the old yellow farmhouse the Beans have lived in for a half-dozen generations.

I don't want to pretend it was all her doing, that I had no hand in what happened that night. I'm just as guilty as she is for how we end up together in that big four-poster bed of hers on the second floor, except she doesn't feel guilty and that's the problem.

"I'm not a child anymore," she says. "You think I don't know that was the issue? Of course I was too young for you back then. But I'm a grown woman now."

I shake my head. "That's only partly it."

She sits up against the headboard, a sheet covering her breasts.

"Goddamn it, Jack," she says. "I'm a woman, you're a man, and we love each other, so what's the problem?"

I realize then that she still doesn't get it. Everything we talked about in the hollow this afternoon, and later, sitting together in front of the fire downstairs, sipping coffees laced with whiskey . . . none of it ever really sank in. Corbæ is just a word to her. She's seen us in more than one skin, the crow girls, Jolene, Crazy Crow, and all. She knows we live in the woods and wild, that we're older than she can ever begin to imagine. But none of it's registered where it counts—in her heart, where belief doesn't just happen, but settles down into the bones and can't be denied.

"I'm not a man," I tell her. "I'm a corbæ. A jack-daw."

"You're a jackass."

"Maybe so, because this should never have happened."

She always had a temper and I can see it smoldering now, a storm cloud on the horizon of those blue-sky eyes.

"Are you telling me you don't love me?" she asks.

"Not even close."

"So you're telling me you didn't enjoy yourself?"

"That's not the point."

"So what is the point?" she asks, her voice gone dangerously soft.

"The point is, I do love you, but I can't stay—it's not in my nature any more than it was in yours to give up your art and the hills for Randall Miller."

"I didn't hear anyone asking for some lifetime commitment here, Jack."

I won't get pulled into that.

"So my being here in your bed makes me no better than Ray," I say. "Here for a few hours, then gone again by morning. You deserve better than that, just as your mammy deserved better than what he gave her."

"I don't think my mammy ever regretted that night. I know I sure don't because otherwise I wouldn't ever have been born."

"I'm not explaining this right."

"That's an understatement if I ever heard one." She shakes her head. "I've been waiting my whole life for what we had here tonight, Jack, for what I thought this was the start of, and now you're making me wonder what the hell was wrong with me for doing that."

"That's what I'm trying to tell you," I say. "It's not right. Bad enough you've got the fox blood in you, making you restless in human company. But then you've had this yearning for something that's never going to happen between you and me and that's not only making you restless, it's pushing you right out of any hope you could have for a normal life."

"I've told you before," she says with a hardness in her voice. "Don't you go deciding what's best for me. I can make my own decisions on that count."

"And if you're making a mistake?"

"Then it's my mistake to make."

I sigh. "I can't stand back in good conscience and let you do that," I say. "I love you too much."

"I don't think you ever loved me at all."

I look at her, see she believes it, like she won't believe what I am, like she won't believe the fox blood in her or that there's such a thing as corbæ in this world with her.

"I think you better go," she says.

I want to make things right, but I don't even know where to begin. And she's not about to give me the time to work it out.

"Just get out of here," she tells me. "I ever see you creeping around here again and I'll take the shotgun to you."

Those blue eyes of hers are brimming with tears, but she's keeping them in check. The mad she's got for me is that much stronger.

"I mean it, Jack."

Maybe it's better this way, I find myself thinking as I get up from the bed. Maybe it's better that she sends me away, that she hates me instead of loves me. Maybe she'll be able to get on with her life.

But I've got feelings, too. I've heard some say that that's all we are, pure feelings. I'm sad, but I'm hurting, too. No one likes being misunderstood. So I do a stupid thing. For the first time in all those years we've known each other, I shift skin in front of her. One moment she's got what she thinks is a man standing naked at the side of her bed, and the next she's got herself a black-winged jackdaw. I make one circle of the room, then I fly right out the window, tearing through the screen like it was tissue paper, and the night swallows me.

But not before I see the look on her face. Not before I see that she finally understands what I've been trying to tell her. In that one moment, she believes—not with her head, but right down into the marrow of her bones.

I leave her crying, crying with the same hurt that's burning in my own chest, but I leave her scared, too. Leave her staring at the window where this *thing* she's taken to her bed turns out to be everything it said it was. Leave her with her world changed forever.

I leave her with something else, too, but it'll take a few months before it starts to showing and nine months all told to come to term, but I don't know that then. I don't hear about that till a long time later.

5.

Newford, Winter, 1973

I'm passing through Newford one winter and stop in to see Chloë and the others at the house on Stanton Street. Annie and Brandon don't live there yet. Nor does Rory. Margaret's living in what'll be Brandon's apartment, but she's out of town. I just ran into her a couple of weeks ago in Texas. Paul's still alive, but he's out of town, too. Nadine's living across the hall and we pass a few words, me coming in as she's going out the front door. The Aunts smile and nod hello, but they don't have time for me—too busy making up their plans for next year's garden, their kitchen table covered with watercolor sketches and scraps of paper scribbled with dense notes.

A couple of students are renting what'll be Rory's apartment and I meet them briefly. Dawn and Salinda. Neither of them's hit twenty yet, a pair of shy doe-eyed girls, talk in whispers, but they're friendly. "Alberta's kin," Chloë tells me and I nod. It's easy to see the deer blood in them.

We go up to her place and there's Raven, sitting by

the window like an enormous black Buddha, looking at who knows what. He doesn't register my presence— Chloë's either, so far as I can tell. It makes my heart ache to see him like this.

"Is he ever coming back?" I ask.

Chloë shrugs. "It's hard to tell, not knowing where he's gone."

The crow girls troop in as soon as Chloë has tea and biscuits on the table, but they get bored quick and I can tell they want to go looking for something a little more exciting than the slow talk that's stretching out at Chloë's table.

"We have to go," Zia says.

Maida nods. "We're working on a surprise for Margaret for when she gets back home."

"Do you know where we can get a thousand spiders?" Zia asks.

They've each had two cups of tea with more honey than tea in each cup, biscuits lathered with jam.

"What's going to happen to all those spiders after you've finished your trick?" Chloë asks in a patient voice. I can remember a time she'd be out helping them round up those spiders, but that was before Raven went away. "You can't let them go—they'd freeze outside."

The crow girls look at each other, then back at us.

"Puh-*leeze*," Maida says.

Zia rolls her eyes. "We meant plastic spiders."

Chloë and I sit there for a long time after they're gone, drinking tea, switching over to whiskey in the late afternoon.

"You hear about Nettie?" she asks after awhile.

I'm filling my pipe, tamping the tobacco down until it's just right, and look up. "I don't want to hear about her."

But she just goes on like I didn't say a thing. "She had herself a little girl about a year and a half ago now. Red-haired like her grandfather Ray, but there's corbæ blood in her, too. Jackdaw, I'd say."

All I can do is stare at her with my mouth hanging open.

She was supposed to have twins is what Chloë tells me. All the signs pointed to it and there was no doubt in anybody's mind—at least not among our people—but when her time came, just the one baby girl was born, six pounds, seven ounces, blue-eyed like her mother, with that red fox hair and a healthy set of lungs. Sweetest child you ever saw, by all accounts. The name on her birth certificate was Kerry Jacqueline Bean. Father, unknown.

It was different this time, from how it had been with Lilah. Nettie loved this daughter and the child took right to her, but Nettie couldn't shake the understanding that there was supposed to be two of them, that she'd *known,* the way a mother knows, that she was carrying twins. She went a little crazy, trying to find the missing child— said she could hear her crying at night, outside in the woods, crying for her mammy. Came to the point where Social Services was ready to take away the daughter that wasn't lost, but then Lilah stepped in.

Lilah was married to her real estate man by now, that Stephen Madan fellow, and they adopted Kerry. Considering what his kind was doing to Nettie's beloved hills, clear-cutting the old timber stands, parceling up the family farms, and selling the lots off for housing developments, I'd have guessed Lilah married him just to spite her mother, but Chloë says there's a real affection between them. Like attracts like, I'm thinking.

I don't know why Lilah wants to raise her half sister like Kerry was her own daughter. It just makes no sense to me.

"I'd say it's her way of putting a claim on that Bean land," Chloë says. "We fixed it last time so that neither she nor that no-good father of hers could get their hands on it. This time we had a hard time just keeping Nettie out of an institution. She was in a bad way, running around the woods night and day, looking for this child that never got herself born. Best we could do was let Lilah and her new beau adopt Kerry and be the girl's trustees if anything should happen to Nettie before Kerry comes of age. It was that, or let the government raise her.''

I can't believe what I'm hearing. ''You think Lilah was the better choice?''

''I don't see there was much else we could do, one way or another. You ask Paul what it's like to grow up in an orphanage in those hills.''

Paul got himself lost once, fell asleep like we've all done from time to time, except he fell asleep in the skin of a little boy and the state raised him, up there around Hazard. Life's hard enough in the hills as it is; without kin it can be pure hell, because then you've got nothing. You've got nobody.

''I'm going up there to talk to Nettie,'' I say. ''See if I can't fix things somehow.''

Chloë shakes her head. ''You'll do no such thing.''

Now I really can't believe what I'm hearing.

''I'm that girl's daddy,'' I say. ''And if Nettie—''

''Nettie's just starting to do fine,'' Chloë says, cutting me off. ''She's finally laid off searching for that unborn child and is putting her life back in order again. She's even got visiting rights. They're making out that she's Kerry's grandmother—not that the girl's old enough to know much more than that she loves Nettie, heart and soul. If you go up there now, you'll just set her off again.''

I want to argue, but I know she's right. I can't even pretend to myself that I'd get any kind of a welcome. It's so clear in my mind, it could almost be yesterday, the night she ran me off. I can still see that look in her eye, hear the hard promise in her voice as she shut me out of her life.

I ever see you creeping around here again and I'll take the shotgun to you. I mean it, Jack.

And then I had to do that damn-fool thing and shift

skins, right there in front of her. If she thinks of me at all now, she'll be thinking of some monster. That might even be half the reason she let her child go. She wouldn't want to be raising the offspring of that monster. Bad enough she ever welcomed it into her bed.

"What can I do?" I ask, hating the helplessness I hear in my voice.

"Same thing we always do," Chloë says. "We carry on."

"I don't know that I can do that again."

Chloë looks at the far side of the room where Raven sits staring vacantly out the window.

"There's your other choice," she says.

~ 5 ~

TARNISHED MIRRORS

I would say that I'm madly polishing this unbelievably tarnished mirror and hoping something shines forth.
—LOREENA MCKENNITT,
FROM AN INTERVIEW IN *NETWORK*
(APRIL/MAY 1994)

1.

Newford, Labor Day, 1996

If Lily had hated the flight back to Newford, she hated the walk from the terminal to where she'd parked her car even more. It was a long hike in the relative dark—three lots over, with too much space between the lampposts so far as she was concerned. Hundreds of vehicles, row on shiny row of them, but not many people. If there was trouble, if that cuckoo rose up from behind some car, who was going to help her? Though maybe the worst thing, what kept her nerves jangling raw and too bright, was that he didn't even have to be hiding. The way he and Margaret had stepped into thin air back there in the Tucson airport . . . didn't that mean they could probably step right out of it again, too? So you couldn't know where they might be, waiting for you. No place was safe.

She hadn't been too scared in the plane. It was a full flight and hopefully too public for anyone to consider assaulting her while they were in the air, though she couldn't entirely dismiss her fear. How badly did these cuckoos want her? The airport seemed safe as well. Brightly lit, too many people milling about, too many uniformed men and women. Police, airport security. But out here in the parking lot, weighted down with her backpack and dragging the wheeled hard-shell case that held her camera equipment, she felt far more vulnerable. Her hands were shaking so much by the time she reached her car that she could barely get the key into the lock of the trunk.

Stowing away her luggage, she shut the trunk and leaned on it for a moment, gaze darting nervously about. If only she'd arranged for someone to meet her at the terminal. Rory. Or Hank. Maybe she should have taken up Sharon's offer of a lift and come back to get her car tomorrow. Right now she'd readily welcome the woman's barrage of conversation if it meant she didn't have to be alone.

She was sure she was overreacting, but the fear wouldn't go away. The memory of the cuckoo's assault in the alleyway a few days ago had stopped slipping and sliding away from her, and the strange calm following the incident fled. Now the attack sat foremost in her mind, firmly ensconced, reminding her of just how frail she was. When the cuckoo had attacked her, she hadn't been able to do a thing to stop his assault. She'd survived that night by luck, pure and simple. She couldn't count on a Hank to show up out of nowhere, on crow girls to drop from the sky.

Straightening, she moved around to the driver's side of the car, carefully peering into the backseat before she unlocked the door. When she got inside, she immediately locked all the doors, then pressed her head against the top of the steering wheel, weak with relief at having gained this much safety. Now all she had to do was drive home.

I can't live like this, she thought, finally sitting up to fit the key into the ignition.

But then who could? Nobody chose to be a victim. Nobody chose to be assaulted in an alleyway, stalked in an airport. . . .

Starting the car, she pulled out of her spot and drove toward the exit. She had another bad moment when she had to open her window to pay the attendant, searching the lanes between the parked cars and the faces of the other drivers as she waited her turn in the line of exiting cars. The parking lot attendant gave her an odd look when she handed her money over—God, I must look like a wreck, she thought—but she managed to get through the transaction and leave the airport without incident.

Once she was on the parkway, she drove in the right lane and far too slowly, constantly checking her rearview mirror and the cars that passed her, expecting someone to be following her, to run her off the road, to pull up beside her and point a gun at her face. When she finally reached her exit and got off the parkway, she had to pull over to the side of the road and park—just to unclench her hands from the wheel for a few moments and try to ease the knotted muscles in her neck and shoulders. But simply sitting there felt too vulnerable and a heartbeat later she pulled out once more, cutting off a vehicle because she hadn't thought to check if the road was clear. The blast of the other driver's horn startled her so badly she almost lost control of the car and she had to pull over again.

The drive from the airport to her house was a familiar one. On an evening such as this, with little traffic, the trip would normally take about forty minutes. Tonight it was closer to an hour and a half before she was finally turning onto McKennitt Street. She knew one moment's relief at being so close to home, back in familiar territory, before she realized she'd be alone in her apartment.

She almost kept on driving right past her house, but she didn't know where to go. Rory's perhaps. Or somewhere busy with people, crowded. What stopped her was the squat bulk of Hank's cab parked at the curb in front of the house and Hank himself, sitting there on her steps, easily recognizable in the yellow wash of the porch light.

Pulling into her lane, she shut off the car's engine and let relief wash over her.

And then she felt stupid.

How could she have let herself get so carried away? What had she been thinking?

The immediacy of her fear vanished as though someone had thrown a switch inside her head. It left her giddy with relief, if still a little unsteady on her feet as she got out of the car and walked over to where Hank was standing by the steps. She could tell he wasn't entirely sure of his welcome—showing up here unannounced and all, she supposed—but she'd soon put his mind to rest on that score. She didn't think she'd ever been so happy to see anyone as she was to see him at this moment.

She gave him a hug that obviously startled him, but then he enfolded her in his arms.

"You must be a mind reader," she said into his shoulder. "I can't tell you how much I didn't want to be alone right now."

"Bad day?"

She stepped back and shook her head. "Weird day."

Taking his hand, she sat down on the steps with him. She liked the feel of his hand. It was calloused and the skin had the rough texture of someone who wasn't afraid of physical work; obviously a strong hand, but capable of great gentleness.

"So what are you doing here?" she asked. "Not that I'm complaining or anything."

He shrugged. "Just thought I'd drop by to see you. I wasn't sure when you were getting home—I only knew it was sometime tonight—so I thought I'd wait around for awhile."

"That's so sweet."

He smiled. "I've been called a lot of things before, but never sweet."

"I'll bet you say that to all the girls."

His smile faltered.

"I was only joking," she said, giving his fingers a squeeze.

"I know. It's not you. It just reminded me of this friend of mine who's gone missing. We've spent the whole day looking for her, but it's like she's stepped right out of the world."

The ground seemed to shift underfoot for Lily. She still felt safe, sitting here with Hank, but what he'd said cut too close to what she'd hoped she'd left behind in the Tucson airport.

"What's her name?" she asked.

"Katy. Maybe you know her. She hangs around with Jack a lot."

"Red-haired, kind of punky-looking?"

"That's her. She's a good kid, but she's got some strange ideas."

"Strange how?"

"Well, for one thing," Hank said, "she doesn't think she was ever born."

"Maybe you should run that by me again," Lily said when he didn't elaborate.

Hank sighed. "It gets weird."

"The way things are working these days," she told him, "weird is beginning to be normal."

He looked up. "Did something happen to you in Tucson?"

"You first."

She thought he might argue the point—it was a guy thing, she'd decided a long time ago, wanting to hold on to all the facts before they shared what they knew—but Hank didn't seem to be like that. Another point in his favor.

"Fair enough," he said. "I went by the bus a few days ago, looking for Jack—I can't even remember why anymore. Anyway, he's not there, but Katy is. We get to talking and that's when she tells me . . ."

* * *

"You sure she said cuckoo—not Couteau?" Hank asked.

She'd just finished telling Hank about Margaret, how she seemed invisible to the other people on the video shoot, the odd things she'd said that only made sense in retrospect, how she'd headed off a second confrontation with the man they'd both seen die in a Newford alley— "Except she said this guy was the other one's brother"— how the two of them had vanished from the middle of the Tucson airport and nobody had even noticed.

"Pretty sure," she said. "Why?"

He told her about the case he was working on for Marty Caine. "The girl—Sandy—IDed this Philippe Couteau guy from a mug shot the cops had and I swear he's identical to the man we saw killed."

"So there's . . . more than one of them?"

"Three brothers, at least." He went on to tell her what he'd learned about the Couteaus from the files Marty had, and later from talking to Eddie Prio. "So the big question is, what do they want from you? The guy in the alley—he didn't say anything?"

Lily shook her head. "He just tried to take my camera bag."

"And you're not working on something, some story that they don't want public?"

"The closest I've come to the drug trade in the last little while is taking some photos of junkie musicians for an article Rory did for *Spin*. And that was after the business in the alley. I've never heard of the Couteaus before. Or cuckoos either, for that matter. Or at least, not in this context."

"Well, judging from what happened to you in Tucson, they're going to keep coming after you and until we figure out why—what they want—it's going to be hard to stop them."

"That makes me feel a lot better."

He pressed her hand. "Sorry. I didn't mean to put it like that."

"But it's true, isn't it?"

He nodded. "Is there somewhere else you could stay—somewhere with a lot of people around and they wouldn't think to look?"

"I don't know. Rory's got a spare room and there's always someone in the house. Or I could go to a hotel. But for how long? I can't live my life in fear."

"No one should have to live like that." There was a grimness in Hank's voice that made her look at him, worried. "No one."

They ran out of words for awhile, sat there in the yellow pool cast by the porch light and looked out at the shadowed lawn, Hank's cab, the street beyond. That was what was oddest about all of this, Lily thought. Everything still seemed so normal. The world went on, oblivious to what was happening to them, to what they'd found when they'd inadvertently peeled back a layer of reality to find something else waiting for them underneath.

"What's happening to us?" Lily said. "How can we live our whole lives in one world, never encountering any of this stuff, and now suddenly we can't get away from it?"

"I guess we just weren't paying the right kind of attention before," Hank said. "Though you were already out looking for it—pumping Jack for stories and all."

"Like that takes any work."

That earned her a smile.

"Though even with these cuckoos after me," Lily went on, "I still think I'd rather know than not. And I wouldn't have wanted to miss out on meeting Margaret. Or you, for that matter."

She wondered how he'd take that, but where she'd been half-expecting him to duck the issue, he surprised her.

"I know what you mean," he said. "I've been thinking it'd be worth going through a lot more than this to have had the chance to get to know you."

He wasn't exactly blushing, but she thought he was

about as close to it as you could get without actually
getting a flush on.

"Don't get me wrong," he added quickly. "I'm not
trying to pressure you or anything. It's just . . . you
know. . . ."

His voice trailed off and she had to smile. Big tough
guy. She was liking him more and more all the time.

"Why are we dancing around like this?" she asked.
"What's wrong with people liking each other, straight
off, and talking about it?"

"Maybe because we're not very good at it?"

"Why don't we make a deal with each other?" she
said. "We'll take it as it comes—slow or fast or not at
all—and try not to hold each other to any expectations
of how we think it might or ought to go."

"Deal," he said and offered to shake on it.

Lily laughed. She put a hand behind his neck and
pulled him in for a kiss instead. It was a momentary impulse that got serious real fast.

"Wow," she said when they finally came up for air.
"That was nice."

"Except now you're going to think I'm so easy,"
Hank said.

Lily smiled and shook her head. "No expectations—
remember."

"I'll try."

"Mmm. Still, let's change the subject before I get to
expecting something else."

"I can't think of anything else."

"Me, neither," Lily said. She stood up. "So why don't
you help me get my stuff upstairs."

Walking over to the car and opening its trunk gave her
time to reconsider what they seemed to be getting into
here. Warning bells weren't going off. In fact, it felt so
right, she found that a little more scary than if she had
been having second thoughts.

"You're stronger than you look," Hank said, dragging
her camera case out of the trunk.

"How so?"

"Lugging this thing around."

Lily pointed to the bottom of the case. "It's got wheels."

"Yeah, but you had to lift it into here."

She grabbed her knapsack and closed the trunk. "This is true. And I have to schlep it up and down my stairs five or six times a week, so you can see why I'm so happy to have you here tonight. Who says only musicians need roadies?"

"Not you, obviously."

She held the front door for him. "Oh, come on. Don't try to kid me. You guys always like to show off how strong you are."

"Says who?"

"I don't know," she said as she led the way upstairs to her apartment. "Maybe all those teen magazines I read when I was a kid."

"Is that what they talk about in them?"

"Wouldn't you like to know."

She adjusted the strap of her knapsack, which was starting to slip, and fit her key in the lock.

"You'll have to excuse the mess," she said as she swung the door open and reached for the light. "But I left in a hurry and . . ."

Her voice trailed off as the light came on. Her living room looked as though someone had been running around in it with a small front-end loader. Sofa and chairs overturned, cushions pulled out. Books and CDs strewn from the shelves. All the drawers had been pulled out of her sideboard and were lying on the floor, their contents scattered around them.

She felt as though someone had punched her in the chest. All the air vacated her lungs, leaving her dizzy and weak. She had to lean against the doorjamb to keep her balance.

"Lily?" Hank said from behind her. He stepped

around her and took in the disorder. "Jesus, it really is a mess."

"This . . . it's not . . ."

He gave her a concerned look. Moving past her, he righted a chair and replaced the cushions in it, then came back and walked her over to it.

"Put your head between your legs," he said. "And take slow breaths."

She did as he said and the dizziness eased up. But when she sat back up she still felt sick. Hank gave her knee a squeeze and rose to his feet.

"Wait," she said, trying to get up as well as he moved toward the hall leading to her bedroom and office.

He waved her back and walked cautiously through the clutter. Lily started to protest, then realized what he was doing. Whoever had done this might still be in here. She pulled her legs up onto the chair and hugged her knees, staring down the hall as he checked the rooms.

It only took him a few moments, but it seemed more like forever before he returned to where she was waiting.

"It's okay," he said. "Whoever did this is long gone. But they really tore the place apart."

"Why? Who could've done a thing like this?"

Hank shrugged. "Could've been anybody, but considering what happened to you in Tucson, I'd guess we're looking at one or more of the Couteaus."

"I don't understand."

Lily could feel the panic welling up inside her. Getting beaten up last week had been horrible, but for some reason this new violation felt even more personal. It was as though someone were trying to tell her that no place was safe for her. Not anymore.

"Maybe you'd better call the cops," Hank said.

Lily shot him a surprised look.

"What about you?" she asked, remembering his reaction a few days ago to her suggestion that they bring in the police.

"This is different," he said. "We're not reporting a

murder now. It's not like they're going to pull us in when it's your own place that got trashed.''

Lily lowered her legs to the floor and started to look around for the phone. She still felt shaky, but having something to do helped to ease the feeling of helplessness that had pretty much knocked her off her feet when she first saw what had been done to her apartment.

''You're sure?'' she asked when she finally found the phone under another one of the chairs. It had been pulled from the wall, but the jack was still intact. When she stuck it back into the outlet and picked up the receiver, she got a dial tone. She looked at him before she started to dial. ''Do you want to go before they get here?''

He shook his head. ''I'm not leaving you alone unless you tell me that's what you want.''

''I want you to stay,'' she told him.

''Okay.'' He nodded to the phone. ''Give them a call and then let's see if you can figure out what's missing.''

The police answered her call far more quickly than she'd expected. They were knocking on her door only a few minutes after she dialed 9-1-1 and proved to be sympathetic to her plight, but apologetic when they told her there wasn't much they could do. They simply didn't have much manpower for cases such as this, where vandalism appeared to be the primary motive. So far as Lily could tell, nothing had been taken. All her camera equipment, lights, and the like were still here. As was her computer. Her darkroom had been trashed, but the enlarger hadn't been taken.

One of the police officers took her statement and asked her to drop by the precinct tomorrow with a list of whatever had been stolen. While he was with them, his partner looked around outside with a flashlight, and then they were gone, answering another call from their dispatcher.

Lily slowly closed the door behind them.

''Well, that makes me feel like my tax dollars are being put to good use,'' she said.

"Don't blame them," Hank told her. "Unless they catch somebody in the act of creeping a place, it's pretty hard for them to do much more than take a statement these days. You ever seen the stats on this sort of thing?"

She shook her head.

"There's been an epidemic this past year and it's only getting worse."

"Now I feel really safe." She hesitated before adding, "Maybe we should've told them about the cuckoos."

"And told them what?"

Lily knew he was right. They'd been through this before the police came. What were they supposed to say? That a few nights ago they'd been rescued by two bird girls from a guy who'd shot Hank and beaten her so badly she should be in the hospital, except they had no bruises or wounds to show for it, because the same girls had magically healed them, and oh yes, the corpse seemed to have disappeared as well. And earlier tonight the same man, or some guy that looked exactly like him, had been following her around the Tucson airport, but suddenly vanished into thin air.

"Let's see if we can get this place cleaned up a little," Hank said.

She nodded, grateful again that he was here. She didn't know what she'd do if she'd had to deal with all of this on her own.

"You know," Hank said later after they'd finished straightening out the living room and had moved to the kitchen, "it's not you they're after. It's something you've got—or they think you've got."

She glumly surveyed her usually tidy kitchen. Cans and boxed foods had been pulled from all the cupboards. There were dry goods tossed everywhere, their packaging torn, the contents strewn about the floor and counters and table like the debris from some sudden summer storm. Flour and sugar and loose tea. Rice, coffee, pasta, cornstarch. It would all have to be thrown out.

It stank in here, too, even with the windows open. Meat

from the freezer was thrown onto the floor on top of the rest of the mess, rotting where it lay. The chicken was the worst. Pools of melted ice cream, once-frozen spaghetti sauce, milk from the fridge. Rancid butter, jam and condiment jars opened, their contents dumped out.

The vandals had obviously struck only hours after she'd left for the airport, so this mess had been stewing for days. The smell was enough to make her sick all over again.

"What could they possibly think I have?" Lily asked.

Hank had found her garbage bags and was beginning to fill one with the spoiled food.

"If we knew that," he said, "we'd probably be a long way toward figuring out just what the hell this is all about."

2.

Cody was still lying low so it took Ray awhile to track him down once he'd parted company with Jack in Lower Crowsea earlier that day.

It was almost noon before he finally spied the long white Lincoln Continental parked out front of Cecil's All-Nite on Williamson north of the Tombs, a twenty-four-hour diner that used to be on the highway before the strip malls caught up with it and made it part of the city. He pulled his rented Ford Escort in beside Cody's long white and killed the engine. From where he sat, he could see Cody sitting in a booth with his back to the door, his bristly hair pulled back into a dark gray braid, skin so dark it looked like he spent his days sleeping in the hot summer sun.

If it hadn't taken Ray so long to find Cody, things might have worked out differently. Maybe they could have talked things out. Maybe Ray would just have yelled at him. But by now he'd had too much time to brood and the immediacy of his anger had banked into hot coals sitting deep in his chest. The heat wouldn't let him think straight. Jack had been wrong. Even hearing the whole story, he only had one message for Cody.

He slid his lanky frame out of the car and walked into the diner. The woman at the cash register looked up as he came in and started to speak. Her voice died in her throat at the look in his dark eyes. He moved down the aisle between the booths and tables, not trying to hide his approach, but already in hunter's mode, leather boots not even raising a whisper from the linoleum underfoot.

When he reached Cody's table, he grabbed Cody's hair and slammed his face down onto the table. A half cup of coffee and the remains of Cody's late breakfast when skidding across the table, some of it falling on the floor, some on the opposite seat. The customers at the nearest table scrambled away. Ray jerked Cody's head back, fist cocked, but then he froze. The long barrel of a pearl-handled .45 was pointing at his stomach.

Ray released his grip on Cody's hair and stepped back.

Cody's nose was broken, blood running in small rivulets from his nostrils, down his chin, dropping onto the tabletop, his lap, the front of his white shirt. There was no expression in his eyes, but he was smiling. The .45 never wavered as his free hand found a napkin and wiped the blood from his face.

"Thing is, Ray, I like you," he said. His voice was muffled, like he had a bad cold, but his tone of voice was as though they were having a normal conversation, as though his nose wasn't pushed to one side and spewing blood. "Which is why you're not dead. Yet." He grabbed hold of his nose and forced it back into shape, giving no indication of how much just touching it must have hurt. "You want to tell me what this is all about?"

Ray hesitated.

"I'm not asking," Cody told him.

He motioned Ray into the opposite seat with the barrel of the .45. When Ray had brushed off the vinyl and sat down, the gun disappeared back into its shoulder holster. Cody looked around the restaurant.

"Show's over, folks," he said.

Nervously, the two men who'd been sitting at the table nearby returned to their seats. At the counter and other tables, the customers turned away. The woman at the register had a phone in her hand. When Cody's gaze lit on her, she slowly cradled the receiver and stepped away to fuss with a coffeepot. A murmur of conversation arose once more, but everyone was studiously ignoring them.

"I'm waiting," Cody said, turning back to Ray.

"You didn't tell me she's my granddaughter."

"You didn't ask."

Ray gripped the edges of the table, knuckles going white.

"Don't do anything stupid," Cody told him.

"Why'd you involve her in this?"

"Because she's perfect. You know how rare a canid-corbæ breed is?"

Ray had to take a steadying breath. "We're talking about my family."

"Oh, like you've ever paid any attention to her before this morning."

"I didn't know she even existed before this morning."

Cody wiped the last drip of blood from under his nose. Wadding up the bloodied napkin, he tossed it onto the table and settled back in his seat. Ray waited—there was nothing else he could do—as Cody pulled out a pack of cigarettes, shook one free, lit up.

"Who told you about this anyway?" Cody asked.

"Jack."

Cody laughed. "That old fart tell you anything else interesting?"

"That you've called the cuckoos in on this."

"And that's a problem? We've got no beef with them. Only the corbæ need to worry about them and I don't see you sprouting black feathers all of a sudden."

Ray could only shake his head. Bringing in cuckoos

was like asking a school of piranha to help you find a
ring you dropped in the river while you and your friends
were still standing around in the water, looking for it
yourself.

"She's got corbæ blood," he said.

Cody took a long drag and blew a stream of smoke up
to the ceiling. He was oblivious to the surreptitious
glances they were still getting from the diner's other customers.

"You have to learn to relax," he said. "Relax and trust
me. Your little girl's not in any danger."

All Ray could do was shake his head. "Do you have
any idea what could happen to all of us if they get hold
of Raven's pot?"

"It's not going to happen."

"How you figure that?"

Cody flicked his cigarette toward the ashtray. Most of
the ash went on the tabletop.

"Because I've got everything under control," he said.

"Like you have every other time? Or is this going to
be the exception?"

Cody shook his head, put on a sad look. "This isn't
like you, Ray. Since when did you get so negative?"

Ray stood up.

"I don't remember saying we were finished with our
conversation," Cody told him.

"So shoot me."

"Did you ever think that maybe I was trying to help
her?" Cody said as Ray started to walk away.

Ray paused and looked around, but Cody was still facing the other side of the booth, cigarette smoke trailing
up along his cheek. Ray moved back until he was standing beside the table.

"Help her how?" he asked.

Cody turned to look at him. "The Morgans never liked
her people."

So Jack was right about that, too, Ray thought. Cody
had brought in more than one family of cuckoos. The

Couteaus were bad enough, but the Morgans had a long-
time grudge against the corbæ, Jack in particular, which
made it even more dangerous for his granddaughter, seeing how she was also Jack's daughter.

"*We're* her people," he said. "She's almost full-
blooded."

"I mean her human people."

"What's that got to do with—"

Cody cut him off. "Plus she's got more corbæ than
canid in her. Lot of strikes against her—do you see where
I'm going with this?"

Ray shook his head.

"Pay attention, Ray. Now I don't know why Chloë's
brought your little girl into the middle of all this, but the
only way to keep her safe is to let the Morgans know
she's on our side. That she's working for us."

Ray sighed. Cody was the master of justification and
like any explanation he ever made, this had a certain ring
of truth about it. The problem was, he wasn't prepared
to believe Cody anymore.

"Tell them she's out of this," he said.

Cody made a helpless gesture with his hands. "You
know I can't do that. When it comes to them, you're
either on their side or you're expendable. And considering the serious strikes your girl's got going against her—
I'm talking about how they see things, now—she doesn't
even have to get in the way. They'll do her for the fun
of it."

"Then you better figure out a way to convince them
otherwise," Ray told him.

"I thought we were friends."

"You don't have any friends," Ray said. "Only people you use. Funny. It took a corbæ to help me figure
that out."

He walked away from the table again, half-expecting
a bullet in the back, but Cody let him go. Ray didn't
know whether to feel relieved or not. He was still alive,
but maybe the only reason he was still alive was that

Cody couldn't be bothered to kill him. In the grand scheme of how Cody looked at the world, maybe Ray wasn't enough of a threat.

Or maybe he was going to let his new allies do the job for him.

Ray didn't plan to stick around and find out. Soon as he got on the road, he was going to pick up his grand-daughter and get them both as far away from this place as he could, as fast as he could. Considering the large population of corbæ living here, and with at least two families of cuckoos now on its streets, the city was about to turn into a war zone.

3.

"Did you know you talk in your sleep?"

Kerry woke bleary-eyed to find one of the crow girls sitting cross-legged on the floor by the head of her futon, the girl's dark birdlike eyes peering down at her with great interest. Maida or Zia? Kerry still couldn't tell them apart and being woken from such a deep sleep didn't help. Her head was full of a fog that was only slowly clearing.

"Which one are you?" she asked.

"Maida, silly. Your friend—remember?"

The crow girl's good humor brimmed over with such infectiousness that Kerry automatically found herself grinning back at her.

"Does that mean Zia's not my friend?" she joked.

Maida shrugged. "I don't know. I just saw you first, that's all."

Kerry sat up to put her head level with her uninvited guest's, feeling more awake now. She liked these girls, though that didn't mean she wanted them to have free run of her apartment. Only how did you explain the idea of privacy to someone who had no concept of it?

"What are you doing here?" she asked.

"Waiting for you to wake up. You are such a sleepy-head. It's almost ten. Everybody else has been up for hours and they're all busybusybusy."

"I guess I needed to sleep in."

Maida immediately looked unhappy. "Did I wake you? I didn't mean to wake you. I was just sitting here being ever so quiet."

"You didn't wake me," Kerry assured her.

"Rory says we're not supposed to wake people unless it's an emergency, like if we really need some jelly beans and he's gone and hidden them and we can't find them no matter how hard we look."

"That's what Rory calls an emergency?"

"No. But we do."

Kerry had to laugh.

"I need some tea," she said and pushed aside the comforter so that she could get up. "How about you?"

"Will it be sweet?"

"As sweet as you like it."

"I like it very sweet," Maida said, trailing after her into the kitchen. "I like it more sugar than tea."

"Have a sweet tooth, do you? Maybe I should just give you a cup of sugar and not bother with the tea."

Maida got up on one of the kitchen chairs and perched there like a bird, sitting on her heels.

"That would be good," she said.

Kerry filled her saucepan and put it on the stove. From a cupboard above the sink she brought down two tins and two mugs. She took a tea bag out of one tin and placed it in her own cup. Glancing at Maida, who was watching her with an expectant expression, she filled the other mug from the sugar tin and brought it over to the table. Maida lifted it to her mouth and licked some of the sugar out.

"Mmm," she said. "Just the way I like it. Not too hot and not too cold."

"Are you hungry?" Kerry asked, going back to the cupboard to get some bread.

"No."

"Well, I'm having toast."

"I'll just watch and have my very delicious tea," Maida told her.

Kerry turned from the counter to find the crow girl regarding her guilelessly, as though there wasn't anything in the least odd about licking sugar from a mug and calling it tea. Kerry could only shake her head.

"I feel like Alice after she fell down the rabbit hole," she said.

"Who's Alice?" Maida wanted to know. "She must have been very small. To fall down a rabbit hole, I mean."

"It didn't happen for real. It's just a story from a book."

"But still . . . she'd have to have been small."

"Sometimes she was small," Kerry told her, "and sometimes she was big. As big as a house. She had all sorts of adventures—playing croquet with a pack of cards, meeting a talking tortoise." She had to stop and think about that for a moment. "Or was that in the other book?"

"I know some tortoise people," Maida said. "I could introduce you to Sleepy Joe—he lives right here in town. One time Zia got into a face-pulling contest with a tortoise boy that went on for days and days and days."

Kerry's water was boiling. She took it from the stove, turned off the burner, and poured the hot water over her tea bag.

"What do you mean by tortoise people?" she asked as she returned the saucepan to the top of the stove. When Maida didn't answer, she looked around to find the crow girl regarding her with confusion.

"That's just what he is," Maida said. "You know, the way Zia and I are crows."

"Oh, I get it."

They had a friend who pretended to be a tortoise. For a moment there, Kerry had thought she was being serious.

Turning back to the counter, she took out a couple of slices of bread and put them in the toaster.

"You sure you don't want some toast to go with your . . . um, tea?" she asked.

"I'm sure. This is very filling."

Kerry didn't doubt that a whole cup of sugar would be very filling.

"So what was I saying in my sleep?" she asked as she joined Maida at the table.

Maida shrugged. "Nothing much. I thought you were telling me not to give you some sort of a pill and I told you I didn't have any to give, but then I figured out you were talking to someone in your dreams."

A dream from her old world. She was having them almost every night. She'd probably always have them.

"What sort of pill was it?" Maida asked. "In your dream, I mean."

"Something to make me feel normal."

"They have pills that can do that?"

"It depends on how you define 'normal,' " Kerry told her.

"Sometimes we wonder what it's like to feel normal," Maida said. "You know, like all the people you see out on the streets or sitting in their little boxy homes."

Kerry gave her a curious glance. Were the crow girls supposed to be on some sort of medication? That might explain how they looked to be almost Kerry's own age, but acted so young.

"But then," Maida went on, "we see how boring they are and we're happy to be the way we are."

Was that how she should approach her own life? Kerry wondered. Stop trying to fit and just see where the hallucinations took her?

"You know what else you do?" Maida said.

Kerry shook her head.

"Sometimes you grind your teeth."

That called up a partial memory. Hadn't she dreamt that someone had told her to stop doing that . . . was it last night? It was. And the more she thought about it, the more she was sure she'd dreamt it, not this morning, but much earlier than that, just when she was falling asleep.

Kerry frowned. "How long were you sitting by my bed?"

"Oh, hours and hours."

Kerry looked at her, troubled. The issue of her privacy lay between them again. She'd been enjoying Maida's company so much that she'd forgotten the need to address this bad habit of the twins. She didn't like the idea of anyone, even when they were as sweet as the crow girls, wandering about her apartment whenever they felt like it. Going through her things, few though they were. Sitting beside her bed and watching her sleep.

"You shouldn't do that," she said. "It's not right to sneak into people's houses uninvited and spy on them."

"Why not?"

It was yesterday morning all over again. The question appeared to spring from an innocence so profound, Kerry didn't know how she could even begin to explain.

She settled on, "It's just not polite. Would you like it if people did that to you?"

"People do it all the time," Maida said. "They're always poking about in our nests or cutting down our trees."

Kerry sighed. "You're not a real bird."

She felt like her therapist back in Long Beach as soon as the words came out, could almost hear the woman's tight voice. *These things you're seeing, Kerry, you do understand that they're not real, don't you?* Her therapist hadn't been big on self-discovery, preferring to tell Kerry what she was supposed to be thinking and feeling.

"I know *that*," Maida said.

"Good," Kerry told her. The toast popped up and she went to get it. Returning to the table, she went on, "Play-acting can be fun, but if you—"

"I'm a corbæ."

The interruption took Kerry off-guard. "A what?"

"A corbæ," Maida repeated. "We were here first," she explained patiently. "You know, long before Cody stirred you out of the pot."

Kerry shook her head. "I have no idea what you're talking about."

"But you have lots of the old blood in you."

Something froze inside Kerry and she was remembering her grandmother talking to her one day while they sat out on the porch of the old farmhouse.

We've got an old blood, she'd said. *We've been walking this land for a long time. You can see it in our eyes and our skin.*

Kerry had always thought she meant that they were descended from Indians.

"What do you mean by . . . old blood?" she asked.

"Fox from your mother, jackdaw from your father. Didn't you *know?*"

"No. I . . . what does it mean?"

Maida laughed. "It doesn't mean anything except that's who you are."

Kerry's toast lay forgotten on her plate, cold. She looked across the table at the small girl perched on the other chair and seemed to see the true foreignness of her for the first time.

"So you really . . . are a crow?" she found herself asking.

"Nonono. I already told you. I'm a corbæ and that makes me older than any old crow. But I can look like a crow when I want to."

"When you want to," Kerry repeated.

"Sure," Maida said. "And since you've got lots of old blood in you, oh ever so lots, you can probably change your skin, too." Then she started to giggle. "But what would you be? A black fox with wings? A red crow with a big bushy tail?" She couldn't control her giggles. "Oh, this is too funny."

But Kerry didn't find it funny at all. Because the more she listened to Maida prattle on, the less she could believe the girl was real. Which meant Kerry was just imagining she was here, saying all these confusing things. Imagining crow girls the way she imagined she had a—.

"What's so very wrong?" Maida asked, giggles replaced with a sudden concern.

Kerry couldn't look at her. She stared at her cold toast, trying to regain her equilibrium, but the plate and the table appeared to recede, slipping further and further away from her range of vision, the more she tried to focus on them.

"I . . . I should never have come here," she said in a small, tight voice.

She tried to hang on to now, to being here, in this place, but it was too hard.

"I should never have left. I was safe there. They were right. I can't take care of myself. I just can't. . . ."

She was dimly aware of Maida hopping up onto the table, the table teetering precariously under her weight, then the crow girl was sitting in her lap, blocking her view. She had a moment's respite from the horribly disconcerting view of the receding table. Her gaze was so close to Maida's that the crow girl's deep, dark eyes were all she could see. But she could still feel the world falling away around them, dissolving into whirling shadows. The world was falling away, and molecule by molecule, she was falling away with it.

Maida put two fingers to her lips and licked them, then put them against Kerry's brow. Light flared in Kerry's eyes, banishing the shadows, drawing all the fragments of herself and the world back together again. It happened with such a suddenness that for a moment Kerry couldn't breathe.

"Do you feel better now?" Maida asked.

Kerry could feel the crow girl's sweet breath on her face when Maida spoke. She seemed to weigh next to nothing, sitting there on her lap, hands on Kerry's shoulders now, brow furrowed, gaze peering worriedly into Kerry's eyes. Kerry couldn't imagine why she'd thought the girl was another hallucination, why she'd let herself get carried away as she had. Maida had so much physical presence it was impossible to think of her as anything but real and here.

And when she stopped to think about it, she wasn't alone in seeing and interacting with Maida—Maida and Zia, both. Rory knew they existed. As did Annie. So the girl on her lap was real. But Maida being real didn't explain how she'd been able to stop Kerry's panic attack with no more than a touch of her fingers. Kerry could still feel the light Maida had woken inside her. All the hurt and lost and scared pieces of her clustered like moths around the bright and comforting warmth of that light and were transformed so that she felt strong.

"What did you do?" she asked.

Maida slipped from her lap and skipped back to her perch on the opposite chair.

"Happy magic," she said. "You were turning all dark and coming apart so I called up a light to glue you back into place."

"Just like that."

Maida nodded. "Quickquick seemed best."

"But magic . . . ?"

"Is it the wrong word?" Maida asked.

"It's not that. It's just . . . it all seems so impossible."

"Then call it medicine."

"I don't know," Kerry said. "It doesn't feel like any medicine I ever took before." She raised a hand to her forehead. "It really does feel like a light, shining inside me. How did you put it there?"

Maida laughed. "You're so funny! I didn't put it there. Nobody can do that—not even Raven."

"But—"

"It was always there. I just made it a little brighter so that you could find it."

Kerry regarded her for a long moment. It was so strange to see the world as calmly as she did at the moment, without the edge that was usually present.

"Always?" she said.

Maida nodded.

"How can I make sure I don't lose it again?" she asked.

"You can't. But paying attention to it helps. Crazy Crow says that's a magic all in itself. Paying attention, I mean. It's like touching a piece of the long ago."

Kerry didn't think she was ever going to be able to make sense out of Maida's convoluted logic. Every time the crow girl explained something, Kerry only felt more confused. But she wanted to understand.

"What's the long ago?" she asked.

"You know, where the forever trees grow. The place we first stepped into from the medicine lands. Remember?"

Kerry shook her head. "I wasn't there."

"Oh. I forgot. Do you ever forget things?"

"Sometimes not as much as I'd like to."

"I know just what you mean," Maida said. "When your head gets all filled up with this and that, it feels like there's hardly room for anything new to come in, doesn't it?"

"I suppose."

Though that hadn't been at all what Kerry had meant.

"Sometimes," Maida said, "I scrunch my eyes and try to forget as much as I can so that everything seems new and strange again. Do you ever do that?"

Kerry shook her head.

"You should try it. It's fun." Maida paused. "But you don't ever really forget anything, you know. It's always hiding away somewhere, in some little corner, and pops out just when you're not expecting it at all. But that can be fun, too." She held out her empty mug. "Can I have more tea?"

Kerry blinked at the sudden switch in topic. Then she focused on the proffered mug. The "tea" was all gone except for a few grains of sugar left on the rim.

"You . . . um, drank it all already?" she said.

"It was only one cup."

Kerry hesitated, then went to the counter and filled the mug up with sugar again.

"Thanks," Maida said. "Your toast's gone all cold."

"I'll put some more on."

"Don't throw that away," Maida said as Kerry was about to toss out the cold toast. "We can feed it to the little cousins down the street. They're very fond of toast, you know. It doesn't matter how hard or cold it's gone."

Kerry laid the toast on the counter and put a couple of slices of fresh bread in the toaster. Pouring out her cold tea in the sink, she made herself a fresh mug.

"So these cousins," she said. "They're corbæ, too?"

"Oh, no. They're just birds."

"Are there many corbæ here?"

"Oh, ever so many. Jolene calls it the City of Crows because there's so many of us living here. There's me and Zia and Annie and—"

"Annie's a crow girl, too?"

Maida laughed. "As if. She's a jay—couldn't you tell?"

"No. I . . . what about Rory?"

"He's like you. He has the blood, but doesn't know it." Then Maida grinned. "Except I told you, so now you do know it, don't you?"

"You weren't serious, were you?"

She remembered Maida telling her she'd gotten fox blood from her mother, jackdaw from her father, but she couldn't imagine it in either of them.

"I'm always ever so very serious," Maida said, licking at her "tea." She had a white dusting of sugar in either corner of her mouth and on her lower lip. "Can't you tell?"

Kerry smiled. "Not really."

She had a sip of her own, liquid, tea. When the toast popped, she fetched it from the toaster and brought it back to the table.

"I don't understand what you mean about my parents

having had animal blood,'' she said as she buttered her toast.

''What's not to understand?''

Everything, Kerry thought.

She spread jam on her toast and took a bite.

''Well, for starters,'' she said when she'd swallowed, ''how does animal blood show itself? Or does it even show itself? I mean, I have red hair, so is that from this fox blood?''

Maida nodded.

''But my mother didn't have red hair.''

''Yes, she did. I'm remembering that particularly well.''

''You knew my mother, too?''

''Didn't I?'' Maida asked, looking as bewildered as Kerry felt.

Kerry shook her head. This was far too confusing for her.

''I don't know,'' she said.

Maida put her mug down on the table and hopped down to the floor.

''We should go ask Zia,'' she said. ''Maybe she remembers. And then we could go feed the cousins your old toast.''

Sure, Kerry thought. Why not? The day was already so off-kilter that she might as well simply give up and go with the flow.

She plucked at the oversized T-shirt she was wearing as a nightie.

''Let me finish my breakfast and get dressed first,'' she said.

Fifteen minutes later the pair of them came down the stairs, Maida in the lead, carrying the toast in a paper bag. The door to Rory's apartment was open and Kerry had the sudden urge to talk to him about all of this. Maybe he could make some sense out of it. But as soon as she paused by the door, Maida was tugging on her arm.

"Come on," she said. "They're being ever so too serious in there."

Before Kerry could ask who was being so serious, Maida had pulled her onto the porch, down the stairs, and out onto the lawn. Sticking the paper bag under her arm, Maida cupped her hands and called for Zia. With both of them looking up into the trees for the other crow girl, neither of them paid much attention to the Ford Escort that pulled up to the curb. It wasn't until the tall red-haired man got out of the car and spoke her name that Kerry turned to look at him.

"Yes?" she said.

He gave Maida a wary glance before returning his attention to her.

"Look," he said. "I know how this is going to sound, but you have to come with me."

Kerry shook her head and backed toward the house. "I don't think so."

"I don't know what they've told you, but the longer you stay here, the more danger you're in."

"You stay back," she said as he took a step toward her.

He immediately stopped moving forward and held his hands out to her, palms up, face earnest, conciliatory.

"It's not what you're thinking," he said. "I'm here to help you."

"Yeah, right."

The oddest thing about all of this, Kerry realized, was that she was dealing with the situation instead of dissolving into a panic attack, the way she'd normally react to something this stressful.

"I don't even know who you are and you expect me to—"

"That's Ray," Maida said.

Kerry turned to look at her. The crow girl seemed different. Taller, perhaps. Her features sharper. Her usual good humor swallowed by a great stillness.

"You know him?" she said.

Maida nodded. "He's your grandfather."

"My . . ."

"But don't get your hopes up," the crow girl went on. "It's not likely he's here for a family reunion. Whenever he's sniffing around, Cody's not far behind, and that only means trouble."

"You stay out of this," Ray told her.

The smile Maida gave him in return was sweet and dangerous and utterly out of keeping with what Kerry thought she knew of the girl's character.

"Or what?" Maida said, her voice deceptively soft.

At that moment Zia dropped from the trees to land on the hood of Ray's car. She, too, seemed changed. She radiated confidence and danger as she perched there, sitting on her heels.

"Mmm, what?" she asked.

There were undercurrents of tension present that Kerry couldn't begin to fathom. She sensed history lying between the crow girls and the red-haired man, not entirely based on animosity, but a lack of trust was definitely involved.

"Will somebody explain what's going on here?" she asked.

"I'm not with Cody on this one," Ray said.

That made the crow girls laugh.

"Who's Cody?" Kerry tried, but no one was paying attention to her.

Ray sighed. "I was hoping it wouldn't come to this," he said and reached under his jacket.

4.

Rory knew he should have been working on the Tender Hearts earring order, but he'd gotten sidetracked by a dream he'd had that morning of Kerry sleeping in the backseat of a junked car, a fox curled up beside her, an enormous blackbird perched on the top of the seat behind her head. The residual memory of the dream put a design combining the two animals into his head that was too fascinating to ignore, a tangle of feather and fur, sharp beak and pointy fox muzzle. He wasn't sure if he wanted it to be a pendant or a matched set of earrings. It would work either way.

He sat at his kitchen table, sketching the various possibilities, music from a CD he'd borrowed from Annie coming from the speakers atop his cupboards. The group was called Afro Celt Sound System. An apt name, he decided as he listened to its blend of African and Celtic musicians playing their traditional instruments over a bed of trance dance-music rhythms. It was during a break between cuts that he heard the sharp rapping at his door.

Speak of the devil, he thought as he got up to answer it.

It had to be Kerry because neither Annie nor the crow girls ever bothered to knock.

"I had the weirdest dream about you last night," he started to say as he opened the door to the smell of anise.

His voice trailed off when he found Chloë standing in the hall. Tall, dark-eyed, the fountain of her hair only barely contained with a black ribbon. It wasn't always easy to reconcile the schoolmistress figure she cut at such close proximity with the woman who could so often be seen perched on the peak of the house.

"Did you now," she said, a trace of amusement in her voice.

Rory flushed. "I thought you were somebody else," he told her, almost mumbling. He stood a little straighter and cleared his throat. "Do you want to come in? I've got coffee on."

He made the invitation out of habit. In the nine years he'd lived here, Chloë had never been farther into the apartment than the front hall. But she surprised him this morning.

"Coffee would be pleasant," she said.

He stood aside and she stepped by him, trailing her anise. Rory was never sure if it was a perfume, or if that was simply the way she smelled. Following her into the kitchen, he cleared some space at the table and then poured her a coffee while she sat down.

There was an embarrassing moment of silence that seemed to stretch on for far too long. Rory felt he should say something, but his mind had never been more blank than it was at the moment. He couldn't have been more surprised to have her sitting here than if it had been Brandon knocking on his door this morning. Brandon, who barely seemed to register that there was anything in the world besides music.

"So," he began and immediately regretted speaking since "so" was about as far as he could take the thought.

Chloë smiled. "Yes, this is a bit awkward, isn't it?

"Not at all," Rory said, but then gave up. "Well, a bit. We've never really talked much."

"It's not your doing. I've gotten far too spare with words in the last few years—at least so Annie says."

"I wouldn't—"

"So I'll come straight to the point and spare both of us any further inconvenience. Do you remember, I believe it was this spring, when I asked you to clean out the attic?"

Did he? Even with Annie's and Lily's help, it had still taken them the better part of two days, but what a garage sale they'd had. Better yet, Chloë had let them split the proceeds three ways. Life had been good that month.

"Sure," he said, wondering where she was going with this. He hoped she wasn't looked for a cut of the profits at this late a date.

"I've been looking for an object that I believe might have inadvertently found its way into one of the boxes you removed. A small black tin, about so large." She indicated a shape about the size of a small hardcover book. "It was filled with small black pebbles. Do you remember it?"

Rory nodded. "I've still got the pebbles—well, most of them. I tried cutting a couple to set in a bracelet, but it didn't work out."

She leaned forward, obviously interested. "What happened?"

"It was the weirdest thing. As soon as I started to cut them, they just turned to powder. But the stones are so hard you can bounce them off the sidewalk and they won't break. They don't even get marked. It doesn't make any sense. I keep meaning to bring them around to this lapidarian I know to see if she can identify them, but I never seem to get around to it. What kind of stone are they?"

"I don't believe I know the proper name."

Just that. Not, I've heard them called this or that.

"Look," Rory said. "I'm sorry about this. I had no idea you still wanted them."

"Not to worry."

"Because I still have the rest of them."

"The stones aren't my concern," she said. "It was the tin in which they were stored that I was hoping to retrieve. Do you still have it?"

Rory shook his head.

"Do you know where it might be?"

He closed his eyes, trying to picture the tin.

"It wasn't much," he said. "Old and pretty battered, right?"

She nodded. "But of great . . . sentimental value."

"Sure. I know the feeling. But I don't—no, wait a minute. I think Kit has it. Or at least she took it. She was going to use it in her camera bag to hold her film canisters."

"Kit?"

Rory laughed. "Oh, sorry. I mean, Lily—Lily Carson. I started calling her Kit for a joke one day—you know, as in Kit Carson—and it kind of stuck."

"I see."

Though it was pretty obvious to Rory that she didn't really. Or if she did, she didn't think it was all that funny.

"Do you want me to see if she's still got it?" he asked.

"If it wouldn't be too much trouble."

"No trouble at all. She's out of town for the long weekend, but I'll give her a call tomorrow."

"I would really appreciate it." She looked as if she were about to rise from the table, but she put a finger on one of his sketches, a stylistic intertwining of a fox head with the head and wings of a crow. "This is an interesting design. What made you think of it?"

"Remember I was talking about a dream when you came to the door?"

Amusement touched her lips again.

"Well, I had this dream of Kerry last night. She was sleeping in this junked-out old car, see, and there was a fox and some kind of blackbird—a crow or a raven— sort of watching over her, like protectors. Or maybe like totems. Anyway, when I woke up, I couldn't get this image out of my head so I've been playing with it ever since."

Chloë was nodding as he spoke. "Do you often dream of people you know being accompanied by some sort of animal companion?"

"Not really. But everybody's got an affinity to some animal or other, don't you think? And I guess I tend to pick up on that sometimes. Especially when I'm doing commissions. It's one of the first things I ask, because I prefer to deal with images from the natural world than with pure design. You know, birds, animals, trees, flowers." He paused and smiled. "I guess I'm going on a little."

"No," Chloë said. "I find it very interesting." But she glanced at her watch. "However, I do have a few things I must still attend to today."

"Oh, sure. I understand. I'll let you know as soon as I've talked to Lily."

"Thank you. I appreciate it."

She stood up and Rory followed her to the hallway where another awkward silence fell between them. Rory was about to just say good-bye and make his retreat when he glanced out the door. Chloë's gaze followed his.

Not quite able to believe what he was seeing—this was Stanton Street, after all, in the heart of Lower Crowsea—Rory watched a tall, red-haired stranger standing on their walk pull a handgun out from under his sports jacket. He felt Chloë tense beside him.

"Damn him for meddling," she muttered, then started for the porch.

5.

Ray hadn't wanted it to play out this way, but the presence of the crow girls left him no choice. Logic had no place in their lexicon, or if it did, it traveled its own road through their twisty thinking. There was no reasoning with them—never had been.

"Let's everybody just take it easy," he said.

From under his jacket he pulled his own .45—the one he should have put to the back of Cody's head instead of trying to settle things without weapons. His didn't have pearl handles, but the barrel was as long, and he held it as steadily as Cody had held his.

"I know this looks bad," he said, addressing Kerry, "but I swear to you, I won't hurt you. Only you have to get in the car."

There was a whisper of movement at his back and he stepped quickly to one side to where he could keep an eye on them all—crow girls and Kerry. Zia was now halfway between her perch on the hood of his rental and where he was standing, casually cleaning her nails with the point of a switchblade. She raised her eyebrows as the muzzle of his .45 swung in her direction. Maida hadn't moved, but she watched him intently, eyes narrowed to slits.

Jack was always telling him stories about how serious they could be, but Ray had never put much store in the idea before. He'd always thought of them as a couple of kids—cute, relatively harmless. But looking at them now—the economy of their stillness, their watchfulness—he found himself thinking that maybe they really were as old and dangerous as Raven.

He really didn't need this. And neither did Kerry, not if the sudden pallor of her complexion was anything to go by. She looked like she was about to faint.

"It's okay," he began, hoping to reassure her. "Really. But we don't have a whole lot of time and . . ."

His voice trailed off. From the corner of his eye he caught movement on the porch and then Chloë was there, accompanied by the young man who rented the downstairs apartment. Ray sighed. He'd really wanted to avoid any complications, but this was getting worse by the minute.

"Hey, Chloë," he said. "Brandon," he added as the tall black man came around the corner of the house. "Been awhile."

Damn crows. He hadn't heard a warning caw, but something had called them together. Annie was sitting up on the roof of the porch, now, looking down at him. It took him a moment to recognize her, with her hair cut short and dyed so blonde. He couldn't spot the Aunts, but they were probably close by, too. In the trees, maybe, wearing feathered skins. He could hear something rustling up above.

"The child has been under our protection since the day she was born," Chloë told him.

"And you've been doing a great job of it, from what I've been hearing."

That touched a nerve, he thought as Chloë frowned. Fair enough. They weren't exactly making this easy on him either.

"We all make mistakes," Chloë said. "But I've been trying to make up for mine—with better success than Cody has his, I might add."

"I told your girls here, Cody didn't send me."

"No?"

Chloë was doing all the talking. The rest of them simply watched him from their various vantage points, letting her take the lead.

"Truth is," Ray said, "we've had a falling out—over the girl. I'm not agreeable to his having put her in the line of fire." He let them chew on that for a moment, before adding, "You do know he's brought the cuckoos in on this, don't you? Three, four families—including your old friends, the Morgans."

"Shit," Chloë said.

That was better, a crack in the ladylike demeanor to make her a little more like the Chloë he'd known in the old days.

"Oh, yeah," Ray told her. "We're talking fierce times coming. You sure you want Kerry to have to deal with the hurt they can bring down?"

"We can protect her."

"What? With this bunch?"

Brandon took a step toward him and Annie slid down from the roof of the porch to land softly on the grass, knees absorbing the impact. But Chloë waved them both back.

"You'd better leave," she said.

"I'm not conning you. I'm here to help."

Chloë shook her head. "We can't take that chance."

"I'm telling you that if you don't—"

"Don't make me raise my voice," Chloë told him. "You wouldn't want to wake Raven and have him become involved."

"Raven's too far gone for anybody to wake him now," Ray said, though he didn't feel nearly as confident about that as he hoped he sounded.

He turned his attention to Kerry. She seemed to be

coming around. Her back was a little straighter and she didn't look so faint. Chin up, gaze meeting his. Trying to look determined but obviously completely in the dark as to what was going on here. No surprise there. Except for Jack, the crows always played their cards close to the vest.

"What do you say, Kerry?" he asked. "You want to take your chance in this war zone they've put you in, or will you let me take you someplace safe?"

"I'm not going anywhere with you," she said.

Well, that settled that. Outnumbered as he was, he couldn't exactly snatch her anymore. Thing to aim for now was to get out of here with his own skin intact.

"Okay," he told her. "Your choice. But if you change your mind, come see me. I'm living right across the street, second floor."

He saw Chloë's eyes widen slightly at that and would have taken pleasure in the fact that he could still slip in under their noses if it didn't also point out how totally unprepared they were for one of the cuckoos simply walking in on them. But that was their problem. He'd watch out for Kerry, even if she didn't want his help, but the crows could fend for themselves.

"We're done here, right?" he asked Chloë.

He could see she didn't like it. None of them did. Not letting him walk away. Not his living right across the street from their roost. But what were they going to do? There was no percentage in trying to take him down. Not while he was the only one standing here with a gun in hand. They had him outnumbered, but somebody was going to die along with him if they pressed the point.

"We're done," Chloë said.

"And I'm walking?"

She nodded. "No one will harm you."

Zia was the only one with a weapon in view. Shrugging, she snapped her switchblade closed, then it disappeared back up her sleeve.

"Obliged," he said to Chloë, tipping a finger against his brow.

He put the .45 away and returned to his car. The skin prickled at the nape of his neck as he walked the short distance, but he knew he could turn his back on them. Whatever else you might say about the crows, they didn't break their word.

He got in the car and started it up, pulled away. He could still see them in his rearview mirror, standing where he'd left them, watching him go. They'd be looking for him now, but that was okay. He'd work up a different skin, maybe take a note from Annie's book and dye his hair. Black, he decided. Crow-black.

He only drove as far as the corner, turned right onto Lee, then made an immediate right again onto the lane that ran behind his building. When he parked behind the house, he sat in the car for awhile, thinking. He wasn't doing so well—two strikes against him so far. First Cody, now this business at the crow's roost. For Kerry's sake he'd better not strike out when he had to go up against the cuckoos that'd be coming for her. Because that'd be it. Game over for both of them.

6.

"What was *that* all about?" Rory said as they watched the red-haired stranger drive away.

Kerry nodded in agreement with him, but no one seemed to be in much of a hurry to explain things to either of them. Brandon had already stepped around the corner of the house, vanishing as quickly as he'd appeared. Annie had her hands on the small of her back, stretching, her gaze still on the end of Stanton Street where Ray's car had turned out of sight onto Lee. The crow girls were obviously just bored, now that the excitement was over. Chloë stood on the porch with Rory, eyes narrowed, a frown on her brow.

Since she'd been the spokesperson during the confrontation with the stranger, Kerry really expected her to be the one to answer at least some of her most pressing questions. Like, who was Ray? Why did Maida say he was her grandfather? What had Chloë meant when she'd said that Kerry had been under their protection since the day she was born? Who were Cody and Raven? What were cuckoos?

But all Chloë did was turn to Rory and say, "I'd really appreciate it if you would call your friend Lily as soon as you can tomorrow morning."

Then she stepped back into the house, the screen door banging shut behind her. And that was it. No explanation—not even a hello, Kerry, nice to see you made it here safely, how was the trip.

"Are you okay?" Rory asked.

She nodded as he came down the stairs to join her. He really was the nicest man.

"I didn't go away," she found herself saying.

"Nobody was going to let him take you anywhere," Rory said.

She didn't bother to correct him. She'd meant she hadn't withdrawn into herself, curled up into a ball like a hedgehog and pulled the curtain down tight between herself and the world. That was the biggest surprise of the morning, that she could have had an experience such as this and still be standing here, completely functional.

"Can we go now?" Maida asked.

Looking at the crow girl brought back a glimmer of confusion. She and Zia were like kids again, smiling brightly at her, all the darkness fled as suddenly as the knife had up Zia's sleeve.

"To feed the cousins," Maida said, holding up the paper bag with the toast inside. "Remember?"

"Can somebody tell me what just happened here?" Kerry said.

Rory shook his head. "Damned if I know."

"It's just old business," Annie told them. "I wouldn't

worry about it. Ray talks a lot, but he's not dangerous.''

"That gun looked awfully dangerous," Rory said.

"Guns always look dangerous."

"Maida said he's my grandfather," Kerry said.

Annie shot the crow girl a sharp look, but Maida only shrugged.

"Well, he is," Zia put in.

"I've seen pictures of both my grandfathers," Kerry said. "That man didn't look like either one of them. He's not even old enough to be my grandfather."

Except, she thought, he had the red hair and dark skin. He was as red-haired and dark-skinned as she was. As Nettie had been.

"It's a complicated story," Annie said, "and not really mine to tell."

"Then who can tell me?"

Annie sighed. "I wouldn't necessarily be in such a hurry to find it out."

"Why not?"

For a moment Kerry thought she wasn't going to answer. Annie looked up into the dark canopy of the oaks above them, her gaze focused on something Kerry thought only she could see.

"Because stories are like mirrors," Annie said finally. She turned to look at Kerry. "When they've gone dark and the glass is obscured, it's maybe for a reason. Polish them and you might not want to accept the person looking back at you as yourself." She touched her chest. "We carry those stories inside us—mirrors we can look into, or show to other people. But I don't want to be your mirror. I don't want to be responsible for what you see."

"You never let on that you knew anything about her," Rory said.

"I didn't know that I did. It wasn't until Ray showed up that I realized I knew as much as I did. But it's not anything I can talk about." She looked at Kerry. "I'm sorry."

As she started to turn away, Kerry touched her arm.

"Please," she said. "I need to know."

"Then ask Jack."

"Who's Jack?"

"He's kind of a hobo storyteller," Rory said. "He lives up on the edge of the Tombs in an old school bus."

Annie nodded. "Jack tells stories—that's what he does—and your story is one he knows particularly well."

"But I've never even heard of him before. How can he know anything about me?"

"Well, Jack's like that. Stories stick to him like burrs and who knows where he gets them all from in the first place?"

This wasn't helping at all. Kerry remembered telling Maida about Lewis Carroll's Alice earlier this morning and found herself wondering if she hadn't fallen down her own rabbit hole. None of this made any sense. Nothing had made sense since the moment she'd woken up this morning to find Maida peering down at her. It was too much like she'd stepped into somebody else's life. Even the way she was dealing with things was alien. It was the way other people seemed to deal with their problems, not the way she ever had.

She took a steadying breath.

"Okay," she said. "I'll talk to this Jack. Would I find him at this school bus?"

Annie shook her head. "Let Jack find you. He'll know when the time is right. Meanwhile, why don't you go feed the little cousins with the girls? Think about other things. Let them teach you how to not let things worry you so."

"But we worry, too," Maida piped up.

Zia nodded. "We worry all the time. We're excellent worriers."

"And what do you find so worrying?" Annie asked, smiling at them.

"Just things," Zia said.

"Important things."

"Worryful things."

"Like what if we can't find something to worry about when we're in a particularly worrying mood?"

They all had to laugh and suddenly it felt like yesterday afternoon again when Kerry had found everything so refreshingly normal and stress-free.

"The crow girls to the contrary," Annie said, "worrying does nobody any good." She laid an arm across Kerry's shoulders and gave her a hug. "I don't mean to make this all seem mysterious and awful. It's just that I really believe we all need to take responsibility for what we say and do, and holding up the mirror of your history to you is not something I can comfortably do. Do you understand?"

"I suppose so . . ."

"Good." She stepped back. "Well, enough with all this excitement, already. I was in the middle of recording a demo when Ray showed up and I need to get back to it before I lose the tune completely. You guys go off and have some fun."

"Sure," Kerry said.

"You're not mad?"

Mad angry, or mad crazy? Kerry wanted to ask, but all she said was, "No, it's okay. I understand."

"I don't," Rory said, but Annie only gave him a playful punch on the shoulder and went back inside, this time using the door instead of the window above the porch that she'd come out of earlier.

Maida held up the bag of toast and gave it a shake.

"Can we go now?" she asked.

But Kerry wasn't going to be so easily dissuaded. If Chloë was going to ignore her and Annie wouldn't help, then she planned to keep looking until she found someone who could.

"Can you tell me?" she asked Maida.

The crow girl gave her an utterly guileless look. "Tell you what?"

"Well, for starters, how about why you think Ray's

my grandfather and why you think my mother had red hair.''

Maida's only response was a shrug, so Kerry turned her attention to Zia. ''Can you explain any of this to me? Maida said you'd know.''

Zia shook her head. ''Chloë thinks we already talk too much.''

''But we could make something up,'' Maida said.

''Oh, good idea,'' Zia said. ''That'd be ever so very much more interesting.''

''I need to know the truth, not something you've made up.''

''But what's true?'' Zia wanted to know. ''Sometimes even Jack gets confused. Some of those stories he tells are old and true, but some of them haven't even happened yet. He just tells them like they have.''

''He can see the future?''

Zia laughed. ''You're so funny. Time's something you made up—same as property.''

''What are you saying?''

''What are you hearing?''

Kerry sighed and knew she had to give up. For now at least.

Maida plucked at her sleeve and asked, ''Can we go for real now? You promised ever so solemnly that we would.''

Agreeing to do something wasn't quite the same as a solemn promise, at least not so far as Kerry was concerned, but she didn't have the heart to put a sad look on that sweet earnest face looking so expectantly at her.

''Of course we can,'' she said. Turning to Rory, she added, ''Do you want to come?''

''Sure, why not? I can tell you about this dream I had last night.''

They walked down to River Park on the far side of Battersfield Road, the crow girls bounding far ahead like eager puppies, unable—or perhaps simply unwilling—to contain their excitement. Kerry started to feel tired just watching them skip and dance about. She and Rory followed at a slower pace, more suited to the hot, sleepy day it had turned out to be.

Anyone seeing them might think they were a couple, Kerry found herself thinking and that made her blush. Luckily Rory was too busy describing the odd dream he'd had of her last night to notice.

When they got to the park, they found a shaded bench from which they could watch Maida and Zia skip about on the grass, tossing minuscule bits of toast into the air at the birds that came flocking around them. For some reason their antics didn't disturb the birds at all and the pair soon had a busy cloud above them, darting and swooping about, snapping up the toast. It was a playfully odd sight—two small and exuberant punky-looking girls, surrounded by a crowd of feathery courtiers. Odder still, no one seemed to be paying the least bit of attention to them except for Rory and her.

"Do you believe in magic?" Kerry asked suddenly.

Rory gave her a confused look. "What do you mean by 'magic'?"

"Well, like Maida and Zia. They're magic to me. You can almost believe them when they say that they're crows."

"They said that?"

"Well, not exactly." Kerry had to search for the word. "I think Maida said they were corbæ. Annie, too, except she's a blue jay."

"I don't know about that," Rory said. He spoke slowly, as though choosing his words with care. "But I do know that they've looked around fourteen in all the years I've known them."

"They don't look fourteen to me. They *act* like they're fourteen—or even younger."

"And Maida told you that they were really birds?"

Kerry shook her head. "It was more like they could look like certain birds. Or that they were the"—this time the word came more easily—"corbæ equivalent of certain birds. Crows, blue jays."

"Of course, this is the crow girls we're talking about," Rory said. "Who eat jelly beans for breakfast and claim to live in a tree."

"But what if they do? What if there really is something magical about them?"

Rory gave her a sharp look. "Something happened to you with them, didn't it?"

Kerry wasn't sure how to reply. To explain Maida's healing touch meant she had to drag out all the old baggage and place it here on the bench between them. She'd lose the chance for it to be the way she'd imagined it could be yesterday—that she could simply invent who she was and that was how everybody would take her. At least it wouldn't be like that with Rory anymore.

"It's kind of hard to explain," she said.

Rory nodded. "That's okay. You don't have to tell me."

"It's not that, it's just . . ."

She sighed. This was so hard. It wasn't at all the kind of thing she could talk about easily. But she liked Rory and since one part of her really did want someone else to know, maybe it should be him. He seemed to be too easygoing to weird out on her and she thought he might like her, too. He'd dreamt of her last night, hadn't he? Of her and some totem animals. A jackdaw and a fox . . .

"What did you say was in the car with me?" she asked, suddenly needing to confirm that she had it right.

"You mean in my dream?"

She nodded.

"A fox and a blackbird—I'm not sure what kind exactly. It could've been a crow, or maybe a raven."

"Or a jackdaw?"

"I guess. They're smaller, aren't they?"

But Kerry wasn't really listening. "See, this is so weird. That's what Maida said I have—fox and jackdaw blood."

"Come again?"

"She called it old blood. She seemed to think I have enough of it so that I can—how did she put it?—change my skin, too. That's when I really focused on her and realized how foreign she is—do you know what I mean?"

Rory looked to where Maida and Zia were still playing with the birds. Her gaze followed his. The girls were running up and down the lawn now, arms outstretched, trailing a ragged line of birds behind each of their hands. Sparrows, wrens, chickadees.

"See?" Kerry said, her voice soft. "Isn't that amazing?"

Rory nodded. "Mesmerizing."

"But no one's paying attention to it—except for us. I mean, wouldn't you be staring openmouthed at something like that if you were walking through the park and came across it?"

"I'm doing that now."

"It's like they can decide who can see them and who can't. Or maybe it's got something to do with this old blood business."

"But I can see them and I don't have old blood," Rory said.

"But you do. Maida said you just didn't know it."

Rory sat back against the wooden slats of their bench and closed his eyes.

"This is weird," he said.

"I know. That's why I started to lose it when Maida was talking to me about it this morning."

Rory opened his eyes, his gaze settling on her. "Lose it?"

Kerry had to take a deep breath. Let it out slowly.

"Okay," she said. "This might take a little time and maybe it'll be more than you wanted to know about me."

"Anything you want to tell me, I want to know."

He took her hand as he spoke, closed his fingers around

it. Kerry wondered if he could feel how much she was trembling.

"It's a bit weird, too," she said. "Not crow girl weird, but . . ." She ran out of words and had to shrug. "Just weird."

"The buildup's good."

Kerry would have smiled, but her chest felt too tight and she had to take another deep calming breath. Rory gave her fingers a squeeze.

"Okay," she said. "Here goes. When I was twelve, I had to have an operation. I'd gone in for a regular checkup, see, and the doctor found this lump in my side, so they admitted me immediately for exploratory surgery. . . ."

Date: _5/28/85_   **Info obtained by:** _MS_

PATIENT: **REFERRING PERSON:**

Name: _Kerry Madan_   Name: _Dr. Elizabeth Stiles_
Address: _1224 Cerrilos_   Address:
         Long Beach

Tel: Tel:
Age: _13_   Marital:____ No. of:____ Relationship: _psych md_
            Status   Children   (if physician,
                                      give specialty)

(**NOTE:** If relative called, provide name & address of physician to
contact; or if physician called, provide name & address of relative or
friend to contact:)

            Name: _Stephen Madan_
            Address: _1224 Cerrilos_
                     Long Beach
            Tel: _contact Dr. Stiles_   Relationship: _father_

DISCUSSION OF FINANCES (including rate):
            parents will cover all expenses as required

IF PT IS TO BE ADMITTED: Expected arrival time:_____
Mode of arrival:____ will be accompanied by: _alone_ ward: _2B-3_

            leg. status: _minor_
            case assigned to: _Dr. Stiles_

REASON FOR REFERRAL: _patient seemed confused throughout
testing; withdrawn, possibility of a bipolar disorder; parents report
hallucinations, destructive tendencies; recommend constant supervision_

PREVIOUS PSYCHIATRIC TREATMENT: _Peterson Clinic_
Type: Eval ( ) Therapy (✓) Other (specify) _____
when: _Tuesdays and Thursdays, 11/20/84 thru 5/26/85_
by whom: _Dr. Thomas Evans_

PHYSICAL HANDICAPS:_____ **ALLERGIES:**_____
   SUICIDAL ( ) ASSAULTIVE (✓) ESCAPE (✓)

IF FOLLOW-UP NEEDED: (give summary here; details on
separate sheet, sign your name)

IF PATIENT NOT ADMITTED: (give summary of reasons; sign
your name)

Revised - 4/22/84   F-73

7.

When I was twelve, I had to have an operation. I'd gone in for a regular checkup, see, and the doctor found this lump in my side, so they admitted me immediately for exploratory surgery. I was pretty out of it during the operation—well, I would be, wouldn't I?—and afterward in the recovery room, too, so it wasn't until the next day that anybody explained anything to me. But even then they didn't tell me everything. I didn't find out what the doctor really cut out of me until a lot later, when I was in the institution and got to sneak a look at my medical records.

They told me it wasn't cancer, like the doctor had thought at first, but a piece of fetal matter that had somehow gotten absorbed into my body while I was still in my mother's womb. Totally not dangerous and it had been successfully removed now, so I had nothing to worry about.

Well, that was true enough, but it was only part of the story. What they really took out was a tiny fossilized fetus about the size of a small crab apple—a twin my mother'd never even known she was carrying that had died in her womb and was pulled into my body during the months before my own birth. I'd been carrying my dead sister around inside me in the form of a little compacted pellet of bone and hair ever since I'd been born. Weird, huh?

I guess they didn't want to tell me the whole truth because they thought I'd freak out or something. It's not like you hear about this kind of thing every day—except maybe in the pages of a supermarket tabloid.

Anyway, that's when Katy first showed up. Not the dead, fossilized twin I'd been carrying around in me, but a real, living, breathing twelve-year-old girl who looked just like me, except she'd never been born. "I got lost," is the way she put it once.

I remember I was still in the hospital, half-asleep one morning, when I realized I wasn't alone anymore. There was a girl sitting on the side of the bed, smiling at me. I couldn't believe it. It was like looking in a mirror. She was even wearing the same dress I'd worn when I went in for the checkup that ended up putting me here. She took my hand, the one without the IV drip, and held it in between the palms of her own. Just sat there, holding my hand and smiling.

"You . . . you're me," I said.

She laughed. "No, I'm not. I'm Katy Bean."

I repeated her name, thinking it was all one word. Katybean. Like Kathleen. That made her laugh more. I liked her laugh. It wasn't at all like mine, which I think sounds kind of tight. Hers was throaty, as though it came from low down in her chest. I liked her speaking voice, too. It was husky and she seemed to shape her words with a smile so you felt good just listening to her, it didn't matter what she was talking about.

"No, it's Katy and then Bean," she said. "Like you're Kerry Madan."

"You look just like me."

"I know. We're twins."

"My grandma's name was Bean," I said. I winced as I said it, but then remembered that my mother wasn't here. She hated it when I talked about Grandma and insisted that if I had to bring her up, I could at least call her "Grandmother" because I wasn't some hillbilly.

"She was my granny, too," Katy said.

"But you . . . where did you come from?"

"I don't know exactly. From out of you, I think."

"I didn't even know I was having a baby," I said and then we both started to giggle.

We never did figure out where she got her body, but later on we decided her spirit must have been sort of riding silently along inside me since I was born, because we had exactly the same memories up until the moment of the operation. It was only after the operation that they changed, that we started making our own individual memories. I don't mean for it to sound like we were one person split in two by the operation. We had a shared history up until that point, but while the details of what we'd experienced were the same, the way we felt about them was different. For one thing, she'd always hated our parents while I didn't . . . or at least I didn't until they had me institutionalized.

But I'm getting ahead of myself again.

That morning it was just so wonderful to have this sister all of a sudden. We'd been living in Long Beach for about eight months by then, but I still didn't have any friends. People used to make fun of my accent and—well, you know how kids can be, especially when you're the new girl in the school. I don't think they even disliked me. Someone just started the teasing and it became like this horrible habit.

Anyway, we're sitting there on the bed, giggling and having a great time, when the door to the room opens and the nurse comes in. I'd turned to look at the door. When I looked back at Katy, wondering if we were going to get in trouble for fooling around too much, she wasn't there. I just burst into tears.

"What's the matter?" the nurse wanted to know.

"Where did she go? The red-haired girl. My twin sister."

She gave me an odd look and said, "Kerry, honey. There's no one in here but you and me. And so far as I know, you don't have a sister, twin or otherwise. You must've been dreaming."

That was the first clue that other people couldn't see her—not unless she wanted them to and she didn't want anybody to see her because she said that'd give them control over her. But I didn't know that then. I just knew that she'd been here and I'd found not only a friend, but a twin sister, and now she was gone. Vanished like she'd never been. Like a dream.

Maybe the nurse had been right, I started thinking.

Maybe I *had* only been dreaming. She had me halfway convinced of it, only then I saw Katy standing behind the nurse, a finger held up to her lips. She grinned when she saw she'd gotten my attention and slipped out the door.

Relief came as suddenly as my tears had earlier. She was real. I didn't know how the nurse had missed seeing her—Katy must have ducked out of sight as soon as the door opened, I supposed at the time, and then snuck around behind the nurse. I didn't know why Katy wanted her existence to be a secret either. None of that mattered. Not then.

But keeping it secret got old pretty fast.

There was a lot that was good about having Katy come into my life. I finally had someone to talk to, someone I could do things with. Sometimes, when she was in the mood, she'd give me a hand with my chores, or to clean up my room. She'd help me out with tests at school, standing beside me and whispering answers in my ear that she cribbed from the brainy kids. She had a natural talent for the piano, too, and used to do my practicing for me—only that backfired because my parents would hear this beautiful music that she was playing and then want me to play for guests they'd have over for dinner, and of course I couldn't. They thought I was being ob-stinate on purpose and that got me in trouble.

Actually Katy got me into a lot of trouble. You can't hide an invisible person's presence in a house. Maybe no one could see her, but Katy had to eat so there was always food missing. She'd borrow my clothes, then just drop them wherever she felt like it when she was done with them. There was the business with the piano. And since she hated our parents, particularly our mother, she was always leaving nasty surprises for them. Frogs in their bed. Worms in her jewelry box. Dead flies in the liquor bottles.

Do I have to tell you who got the blame? I tried to make out like our house was haunted—that a poltergeist or something had moved in—but that didn't fly. After a few months of this, they started sending me to see a psychologist and somehow he got the fact of Katy's existence out of me—or rather the fact that I believed in her existence.

I didn't mean to tell; it just slipped out. But when I look back on it, I guess I'd just had too much. She was fun—she was always fun—but she never had to deal with the punishments like I did. She never stopped to think of what'd happen to me when she was pulling one of her pranks and whenever I tried to talk to her about it—or talk her out of something, if I knew she had something planned—she'd just laugh and make a joke about it.

Once it was out, the psychologist got me talking about her—why I'd wanted a twin sister, how I felt about her now that she was getting me into trouble all the time, all sorts of things. It was sort of a relief to have someone to talk to about it, except after a few weeks of my sharing these secrets with him he started in on how he could understand the appeal and all, but maybe I was a little too old to have an invisible companion now, and didn't I think it was time to start facing my problems, and I realized he'd never believed me at all. When I got stubborn about it, insisting she was real, he talked to my parents and then Katy found out.

She was furious. We were home alone and she started shouting at me and then she went crazy, breaking windows and dishes, the TV. . . . It was so awful. I tried to stop her, but she was stronger than me and finally I just gave up and huddled in a corner while she trashed the house.

Naturally, I took the fall for what had happened. I got sent for psychiatric testing at Baumert Hospital then—that was my first visit to the institution that'd be my home for the next ten years or so. If I'd been smart, I would have gone along with them. I would have agreed that the move had been stressful and how Grandma dying made me so depressed, especially since we hadn't gone back for the funeral—"for closure" was the way they put it.

How it was hard not fitting in at school and all the other crap they had to explain my behavior, but I was still a kid and you know what it's like, you can't understand why no one will believe you when what you're saying is true. It's so unfair. That just made it easier for my parents to have me committed.

I caught on after awhile and tried to pretend that I agreed with my therapist, but it was too late by then.

It's easy to get into a psychiatric institution, but impossible to get out again if there are people who want you kept in there and they've got the money to pay an unscrupulous doctor to phony up your records so that you never show any signs of improvement. They kept me zoned out on drugs for years.

I saw Katy once at the beginning, when I came in for my two weeks of testing. Neither of us realized just how bad this was going to be for me, but we knew it was serious. Katy was so sorry and I made her give me a solemn promise not to be bad anymore, made her promise on Grandma's grave because Grandma was somebody we could both agree deserved to be loved. She also promised to come visit me as often as she could, but the next day I was committed and the drugs they put me on made me as blind to her as everybody else.

They weren't mean to me in there and it wasn't like I was a vegetable or anything, but I learned after awhile that I was never getting out—not so long as my parents were alive and were willing to pay off my doctor. Whenever I started to push at getting released, my dosage would be upped and I'd truly zone out for awhile.

Of course I wasn't aware of any of that for a long time. I just thought I really must be crazy. I mean, I felt okay and everything, but these were doctors and I wouldn't be in here if I were normal, would I? And if you think about it, no one knows what "normal" really is. Not inside themselves. Everybody has crazy thoughts from time to time, or feels weird or depressed or panicky. But for most of them it passes and they carry on. But you can't do that inside a place like that. As soon as you start to display any signs of anxiety or stress, out comes the medication.

My record said that I was a danger to myself and others and prone to violence when I was off my medication, so it's not like anyone was going to listen to me when I tried to explain that I was really all right, it was just a passing mood, not some huge trauma. They'd just up my medication and put me into a zone state. I'd spend a couple of days in seclusion, then when I'd get back out on the ward, I'd go from half-hour checks to five-minute checks—you know, when they open your door and check up on you.

Doctor's orders. Paid for by my loving parents.

I'd been in there for three years before I finally found out what was going on. My doctor had taken her annual two-week vacation and I got to see someone else while she was gone. I was used to the procedure by now. But this time the replacement therapist I got for the two weeks she was away was different from the ones I'd had before. He was a young guy and not quite the good soldier the others had been since he didn't believe in following orders when they seemed wrong.

During the first week, he decided to lower my dosage and it was like someone had unwrapped a half-dozen layers of gauze from around my brain. Not the first day, or even the third, but by the middle of the second week I was thinking and feeling things more clearly than I had in years.

And then Katy came back.

I had grounds privileges at the time, so I was outside, sitting on a bench by myself in the garden. There were other patients around and of course the ever-present nurses making sure that one of us didn't suddenly take it into our heads to run screaming for the walls or attack each other or something. It happened at times.

Katy seemed to come out of nowhere. One moment, the grounds were the same as always, patients shuffling about or staring at their feet, the nurses looking bored, the next, there she was, sauntering down the path heading right for me.

I'll admit that the first thing I felt was pure panic. I'd been in here long enough that I'd pretty much started to accept that she really was only something I'd made up. The fact that no one else noticed her didn't help. No surprise with the other patients, but the nurses were oblivious to her as well, which didn't help my peace of mind. What I wanted to do was go back inside and ask for more medication. What I did was sit there, pulse too quick, feeling a little dizzy, and wait to see what would happen next.

"Oh, Kerry," she said.

It was a voice filled with heartbreak and despair. I looked around to see if anyone was watching me before I dared speak.

"What . . . what are you doing here?" I asked.

She looked at me so sadly. "I come here all the time. You just can't see me because they fill you up with drugs."

"They say you're not real."

She sat down beside me and put her arm around my shoulders, leaned her head against mine. I couldn't move. I sat there stiffly, staring straight ahead. She felt real.

"What do you think?" she asked.

"I . . . I don't know."

She took my chin in her hand and turned my face so that I was looking at her.

"Don't let them win," she said. "If you truly don't believe I exist, I think it'll come true."

She dropped her hand and I looked straight ahead again. Megan, one of the girls on my floor, was sitting cross-legged beside the flower bed in front of us. Not close, not so she could hear. She was here because she'd tried to kill her father. She was so sweet, it was hard to believe. But then people probably said the same things about me.

"I wouldn't be here if there weren't something wrong with me," I said.

"That is such bullshit. You're here because our loving parents are paying off one of the doctors to make sure you stay locked up and out of the way."

I turned to look at her. "That's not true. I'm here because I . . . because they think I imagine things."

"Like me?"

I had to look away again. Katy took my hand, like she had in the hospital, all that long time ago. She held my fingers between her own.

"Kerry," she said softly. "Just because something seems impossible that doesn't mean it's not real."

"I don't know . . . it's all too confusing. . . ."

"It wouldn't be if you were out of this place. If *they* let you out."

"You just hate our parents," I told her. "That's why you're saying they're having me kept here."

"I've heard them talking. I've seen the checks our dear daddy writes—one to the institution and one to Dr. Elizabeth Stiles. Every month, regular as clockwork."

"But why?"

"Money."

I shook my head, not understanding. "But Daddy's rich." That wasn't entirely true. He wasn't rich by California standards. But compared to the people back home in Hazard, he was rolling in dough. "He sells all those houses, works all those deals."

"Oh, yeah. But the thing about some people is that no matter how much they have, it's never enough."

"I don't see how keeping me in here makes him any money."

Katy sighed. "They were expecting to get the farm when Granny died. That's a serious piece of real estate. The logging rights alone are worth a small fortune. But she screwed them out of it and had it deeded to one of those environmental groups she belonged to on the condition it be kept as a nature preserve. Everything else she left to you."

"Everything else of what?"

"The royalties from her books. Her paintings. Everything."

I hadn't known anything about that. "I didn't know."

"And you're never supposed to because the money goes into a trust fund managed by our dear daddy. He's sold everything else. All of it. The paintings, the sketchbooks, everything. And that's why he's rich."

"But that doesn't explain why they'd want to keep me in here."

Katy shook her head sadly. "Because everything's supposed to go to you when you turn twenty-one, except there's nothing left except for what's in the trust fund and that's what's keeping you in here. There'd have to be a reckoning when you turned twenty-one and took over your own affairs and then there'd be all hell to pay, wouldn't there? Except if you're in here, that reckoning is never going to come.

"But I won't be twenty-one for years. Why would they do this to me now?"

"So that you don't have to be around. They don't love you, Kerry, any more than they'd love me, if they thought I was real. Any more than they loved our granny."

I knew that was true. They'd always hated Grandma. But when we still lived in Hazard, they'd let me see her. Sometimes I even got to stay overnight. But then we had to move here and she died. . . .

But I couldn't accept that they didn't love me.

"They do love me," I said.

"Then why don't they ever come see you here?"

I didn't have to answer. She already knew. And now I did, too.

I kind of fell apart after that. Started crying. Katy tried to comfort me, but then a nurse approached and took me back inside, called the doctor. I tried to explain to him that I was okay, that I was just sad, but I couldn't mention

Katy, so I couldn't explain why I was sad, and in the end
he upped my dosage again and put me back in the zone
where Katy was lost to me. I lost my grounds privileges
and went back on group, but I kept my half-hour checks
and didn't have to go into seclusion like I would if Dr.
Stiles had been there.

I guess it was a few weeks later that the books came.
Two of them, both illustrated with the author's own pen
and ink and watercolor sketches. One was a collection of
nature essays called *Writing the Hills,* the other a journal
of one summer's rambling through the wooded hills outside of Hazard. It was called *Fieldsong.* The author's
name was Annette Bean. They were from Katy. She'd
inscribed each of them, "for Kerry, love Katy," and included a letter with the package that made it sound as
though she'd been one of my friends in school and that
she'd found these in a secondhand bookstore and thought
I might like them because they were set in and around
my old hometown of Hazard. I'd never had any friends
in school, but I suppose that, for all their expertise, no
one in the institution knew that.

Dr. Stiles decided they were harmless and let me have
them, which was both a blessing and a curse. I loved
having these reminders of my grandma, of getting this
peek into her mind. But they also reminded me that Katy
wasn't something I'd made up—which was probably half
the reason she sent them to me.

I guess I could go on about the time I spent there but
I think you get the picture. I did get to see Katy a few
times when I managed to not take my medication for
awhile, but I always got caught and put back on, dropped
back into the zone. One time Katy had us write letters to
myself and we hid them in one of Grandma's books so
that I could find them when I was zoned and they'd remind me that being zoned wasn't normal—that wasn't
who I am. I was the girl who wrote the letters. But they
found those letters one time.

This was a real setback, Dr. Stiles told me. She made

me tear them up in front of her in the office, though luckily she let me keep the books. They were all I had from who I was before I got trapped in here. Those and two plush toys I've had since I was a kid that I also got from my grandma—Dog and Cowslip. When things'd get really bad, I'd bundle them all up together and lie on my bed, hugging them. I'd do that for hours—at night, when I was less likely to get caught.

They were so strict with my medication after the business with the letters that I never saw Katy again. And finally I came to believe them about her, though not entirely. I believed that she'd existed once, that she *had* been real. But that she was gone now. I guess that's because the last time I saw her, she told me she was going away. They'd given me an extra dosage of my medication after Dr. Stiles made me tear up the letters and then put me back in my room.

Katy was waiting for me there.

"I'm going away," she told me, "because all I do is cause you trouble."

I didn't say anything because it was true. I didn't want her to go, but I was tired. So very tired. Of being here. Of everything. I tell myself now it was the drugs, but I'm not entirely positive about that.

"I'll miss you," she said. "But I guess it's better this way."

I think she was hoping that I'd ask her to stay, but she was already fading away on me. I hardly looked at her. Just gathered up my talismans—two books, two toys— and crawled into bed with them.

"Better this way," I mumbled.

I was in the institution for another three years and then my parents died in a car crash. I didn't feel anything when I found out, but then the medication kept me on such an even keel I hardly ever felt anything. No real downs, but no real ups either. I just was. Day to day, I was.

But when I was told that they were dead I remembered what Katy had told me. I started hoarding my pills again, taking them, but coughing them up again as soon as I could get away from the nurse's station. I'd walk real casually into the TV room and then bring them up. The TV audience was the worst of us, the catatonics and depressives, so it wasn't like they were going to tell on me.

I didn't get completely clear of the gauze, but I managed to unwrap enough of it to be able to work out a deal with Dr. Stiles. See, my trust fund would continue to pay my hospital bills for awhile—how short a while I didn't realize then—but there'd be no more extra monthly checks coming Dr. Stiles's way because my father wasn't there to write them anymore.

I remember being so scared when I went into Dr. Stiles's office that day. I thought she'd put me on megadoses, or maybe shock therapy like Megan had undergone. But Dr. Stiles just looked at me from across her desk for a long time before she finally spoke.

"Not that I'm admitting anything," she said, "but what exactly is it that you're proposing?"

By that I knew she'd already been thinking about it. The deal was, I got out and I'd sign over the trust fund to her, but the joke was on her because once I got out and saw the family lawyer, my father's debts had pretty well swallowed up all his assets and the trust fund. For all the cars and real estate and stuff they'd had, my parents had died broke. All that was left when all the bills were paid was about four thousand dollars and I kept that for myself.

Only maybe Dr. Stiles knew that as well, that there'd be no more money. She was never a stupid woman. Maybe she just wanted to be rid of the situation.

Of course, once I was out, all I wanted was to be back inside again.

The world's a funny place. When I used to look at it from inside, sometimes it was this huge, overwhelming presence, vaguely menacing and all sort of quivery. Other

times it was this perfect jewel, tiny and hand-sized, and
all I wanted to do was cup my hands around it and experience it. It was the same when I was out in it, except
I couldn't ignore it anymore and there was just too much
of it, with no respite. Inside, in my old world, you could
turn it off, but you can't do that in this world, in the real
world.

I stayed for a couple of weeks with Mindy, this girl
who'd been in Baumert with me a few years ago. She
tried to help me fit in, look for a job and stuff, but it
didn't take me long to know I couldn't stay on the coast.
She'd ask me what I wanted to do and I'd say, I want to
be like my grandma. I want to write and paint. It was
like a kid's fantasy because I didn't know much about
either. But she suggested I take some courses, or even go
back to school, and then I realized that if I was going to
do that, I wanted to do it at home. I was still thinking of
Hazard as my home, even though I'd been away from it
for half my life.

I remembered the name of a friend of my grandma's
who lived in Newford and I took a chance in calling her
up and seeing if she'd help. That was Chloë. I dialed
information and got her number and then before I could
lose my nerve, I phoned her. She was so nice. She's the
one who set me up in the apartment, got me registered at
Butler even though I don't have regular high school cre-
dentials.

And here I am.

8.

"Jesus," Rory said. "That's all so horrible. Your parents
kept you in there for *ten* years?"

Kerry nodded. Once she'd started, the old history had
gushed out of her. At first it had given her a great sense
of release, but now she was feeling embarrassed by the
shared intimacy, Rory's sympathy notwithstanding. She'd

never told anybody the whole story and while she was
gratified that someone else could finally see the injustice
of what had happened to her, at the same time it left her
feeling so pathetic. By her age, most people had done
and experienced all sorts of things. All she had to show
for her life to date was ten years locked in a zombie zone.

"I mean, you can sort of understand their wanting you
to get help with the invisible-sister business," he went
on, "but what they did to you was no way to deal with
the problem."

Kerry's heart sank. He didn't believe her either. But
then why should he be any different? Even she knew that
a sister who'd never been born couldn't be real. Not really. All that had been real was the small fossilized fetus,
and the doctors had removed that from her side twelve
years ago. But there were so many times when logic
wouldn't take hold in her, when it slipped and slid away
and instead, she saw her twin, heard her voice. . . .

I want it to be true, she thought. She folded her hands
on her lap and looked across the stretch of lawn that lay
between them and the river. That was why she couldn't
let it go. She wanted to have a sister, even if nobody else
could see her.

"You believe she was real, don't you?" Rory said.

She turned to find him looking at her. She couldn't
read his expression at all. Not wary, exactly, but worried
maybe. A dash of pity. She couldn't blame him.

"Sometimes I do, sometimes I don't," she said.
"Mostly I don't know. But there's so much that can't be
explained otherwise."

"Was that you playing the piano in your apartment the
other night?" Rory asked.

"You heard that?"

He nodded. "It was beautiful."

"Katy always played beautifully. She learned everything by ear. All she had to do was hear it once."

Rory looked uncomfortable.

"Go ahead," Kerry said. "Tell me what you're thinking."

"Well, I'm just wondering . . . is it possible that you were the one at the piano but you just don't . . . remember it?"

"You think I'm one of those multiple personalities."

"I'm no psychiatrist."

"Well, I wouldn't know, would I?" Kerry said. "I mean, if another personality was to take over, I wouldn't be aware that it was happening."

She'd seen it at Baumert with a girl named Wendy. Sometimes the personalities went flickering through her so fast it was like someone was holding a remote and surfing through the channels. Wendy never knew it was happening at all. She just lost time, like the epileptics did when they had a seizure.

"I guess not," Rory said.

Kerry sighed. "Except, I'm me when it happens. Katy manifests externally. I mean, if she exists. If I'm not just making her up."

"I didn't say—"

"You don't have to. Nothing else makes sense."

An akward silence fell between them. Kerry looked for the crow girls but they seemed to have wandered off. Unless that pale-skinned punk with the wild black hair sitting a few benches down was one of them in a new disguise. She couldn't tell if the androgynous figure was a boy or girl. Her gaze moved on.

"I guess they got bored and left," Kerry said.

Rory nodded. "They don't exactly have the longest attention spans."

He shaded his eyes as he searched the lawn for the pair, but Kerry had already stopped looking. Her attention was now on the gray stone buildings of Butler University on the far side of the river. Weird to think she'd be going there tomorrow morning. One thing she vowed. She wouldn't tell anyone anything about Baumert or Katy when she was on campus. She was going to pretend she was normal and just hope that if she pretended hard enough, it would come true.

"What happened this morning with Maida?" Rory asked.

Kerry turned back to him. She had to think for a moment before she remembered what it was that had started this whole sorry monologue of hers. This morning already felt like weeks ago. She knew she could let it slide. While Rory might not believe in Katy, he seemed like a nice guy and she didn't think he'd press her. But she figured she might as well finish it now. Closure and all, as Dr. Stiles would have put it.

"I fall to pieces really easily," she said, letting her gaze drift back to Butler U. "Anything can set me off because I'm so unsure of myself. It's like I walk this narrow balancing act between being crazy and being normal, only being normal's like a really thin wire and it's so easy to fall off."

She could feel his gaze on her but she couldn't look at him because her story was wandering back into the territory that on old maps would carry the legend "Here there be dragons."

"That's what happened to me this morning," she said. "I fell off the wire, only this time Maida was there to catch me. She licked her fingers and put them against my forehead and just like that, everything was clear."

"What do you mean?"

"I don't know how to explain it better than that. I guess, it's just that I walk around scared all the time and I don't feel that way anymore—not after this morning. What happened with that red-haired man . . . any other time and I'd have been back in bed for the rest of the week, just trying to deal with it."

"I hate it when people sell themselves short," Rory said.

"I'm not. But I know my limitations. I've lived with them for long enough. Maida did something to me. She worked a piece of magic. That's all I can call it."

"Magic."

Kerry smiled. "You're uncomfortable with the idea, aren't you?"

"You're not?"

She shook her head. "No. I find it kind of liberating, actually."

"But—"

"And it makes me feel better about Katy, too. Because while we both know that logically she can't have existed, how do you explain the things she told me that I couldn't have known otherwise? Like how my parents were paying Dr. Stiles to keep me doped up in Baumert so that they could blow my inheritance? An inheritance I didn't even know I had."

"I can't," Rory said. "But that doesn't mean it can't be explained."

Kerry licked two fingers and pressed them against the air in front of her.

"And Maida's miracle cure?" she asked.

Rory laughed, then caught himself. "Sorry. It's just that nothing the crow girls do ever makes much sense to me."

"That's because you only see things from outside of their point of reference."

He nodded slowly. "Fair enough."

"While I prefer to believe that they're magic."

"But that's only because . . ." His voice trailed off.

"It allows me the option that I'm not crazy," she finished for him.

"I wouldn't have put it quite like that."

She shrugged. "You don't have to be delicate. We all knew we were lunatics in Baumert."

"Just because you were undergoing—"

"You can't have it both ways," she said, cutting him off. "Either I'm crazy, or I'm not. And if I'm not, then Katy's real and the crow girls are magic. I have old blood, you have old blood, and we live in a house full of corbæ."

Rory shook his head. "I've lived there for nine years. Don't you think I would have seen something in all that time?"

"Depends. A lot of people live in a place and never really see it. Never pay attention at all. They're not completely disassociative, but you can't say they're completely aware either."

She could see he didn't like that, but too bad. Let somebody else be in the hot seat for once. Let somebody else have to wonder what was real and what wasn't.

"And besides," she added. "Didn't you tell me that the crow girls have looked around fourteen in all the years you've known them?"

"There's that," he agreed. "But that doesn't mean they're magic."

"No," she said. "I don't suppose it means anything at all, does it?"

And suddenly she felt very tired. Not "I have to lie down until the world stops spinning" tired, but drained all the same. She couldn't remember the last time she'd talked this much—and never with so much emotional baggage in tow.

She stood up. "We should go back. I've got a big day ahead of me tomorrow and I haven't done anything to prepare for it yet."

He quickly rose to join her. "Look, I didn't mean to seem unsympathetic. It's just . . ."

"I understand," she said. "Really I do. I wish I could be as sure of things as you are. It must be so much easier to go through life knowing that this is the way things are, this is real, this isn't, and anything that deviates from that concrete reality is simply an anomaly that you haven't found an explanation for yet."

"You make it sound so calculated and cold."

Kerry gave him a sad smile. "But the world is cold. For me the warm places are few and far between. That's why I treasure something like the crow girls so much."

She raised a hand to her brow. "They warm the lonely cold in me."

She started to walk back toward Stanton Street and he fell in step with her.

"I really don't blame you for not believing," she went on. "And you've listened with more patience to me than anyone else ever has."

Rory didn't say anything for at least half a block. Kerry listened to the sound of their footsteps on the pavement. It was so hot and still that everything seemed to be hushed, the whole city on hold. It was all slow motion and lazy, the passing cars, the other pedestrians, people sitting on their front stoops. She knew how they felt. She was used to the drier heat of California. Her shirt was damp, sticking to her back, and she wished she were wearing shorts instead of jeans, but she didn't have a pair in her minuscule wardrobe.

"Have you ever told anybody everything you've told me?" Rory asked suddenly.

She shook her head. "No. The doctors usually stopped listening the moment I brought up Katy."

"I was afraid you were going to say that."

"Don't feel guilty," she told him.

"Right."

"No, honest. You've been very kind and I really appreciate it. You and Annie both. I was sort of surprised at how brusque Chloë was this morning. She was so nice to me on the phone."

"Oh, that's just Chloë," Rory said. "She's never been one to hang out and gab. I mean, I don't know about magic, but everybody in the Rookery is seriously eccentric. I won't say Chloë's the strangest of the lot, but when you think of how she'll sit out on the roof the way she does . . ."

Kerry let him talk, happy that she'd been able to get them onto a different topic of conversation. But later, when she was alone again in her own apartment, it was hard not to feel lonely, to know that no one understood.

She made herself concentrate on her preparations for school tomorrow, stood in front of her closet and tried to decide what to wear, had a supper of cheese on toast, but the loneliness wouldn't go away. At one point, she almost went downstairs to knock on Rory's door, but she thought she'd bothered him enough for one day. The crow girls were noticeable for their absence and she felt everybody else had been a little too distant the last time she'd seen them for her to be able to approach them now.

Finally she sat in her chair and looked out at the big elm tree. She had her window wide open to let in the cooler air that had come with the fall of night. Magic was on her mind. The touch of Maida's fingers. The mystery of a house full of corbæ. She only half-understood what that meant, but it reminded her of her grandmother, so instead of worrying over meanings, she simply held on to the hope that there really was magic in the world and she wasn't crazy. Rather, she was lucky that pieces of it had come her way.

After awhile, she picked up Dog and Cowslip and cuddled the two stuffed animals against her chest.

"Katy," she found herself saying. "If you're out there, come see me."

But there was no response.

9.

Rory sat at his kitchen table, doodling intricate fur-and-feathers details onto the various jewelry designs he'd sketched earlier in the day, his mind a thousand miles away from what the pencil in his hand was doing.

First Lily, he thought, and now Kerry. What was happening to the world? Maybe all those years of watching shows like *The Twilight Zone, The Outer Limits,* and now *The X-Files* were finally taking their toll. People weren't only accepting that the impossible was possible—if not in their hometown, then *somewhere.* They were now convincing themselves that they'd experienced these kinds of things as well, complete with special effects and all. Alien abductions, Bigfoot in the piney wood hills, faeries skipping through downtown streets, goblins in the sewers. No wonder Christy's books did so well—though, of course, he was a believer, too.

It wasn't hard to tell that the millennium was approaching. What was hard was maintaining one's own equilibrium when everything else seemed unbalanced, or leaning that way.

He found himself writing words along the bottom of one his sketches: "There's no such thing as fiction. If you can imagine something, then it's happened."

It took him a moment to remember who'd told him that. Annie. Annie who'd been in fine mysterious form this morning with her cryptic comments about mirrors and Jack's stories.

And then there was the business with the crow girls.

The worst thing about all of this was that there were pieces of Kerry's story that seemed to fit into the jigsaw puzzle of what Lily had been talking about before she'd left for Tucson last week. Especially when he added in the odd behavior of the crow girls this morning. They'd seemed genuinely menacing—Zia with that switchblade in her hand—until the red-haired stranger finally drove away. So why had he been so quick to dismiss Kerry? Worse still, why did he dismiss Lily's story when he knew she'd never lie to him?

Because it made no sense, he told himself. No sense at all. The world didn't have room for imaginary twins being real, or for secret races of animal people.

But still . . .

He wondered now: On the walk home from the park, when he'd been talking to Kerry about the eccentricities of the Rookery's residents, who had he been trying to convince that their behavior was merely odd, not proof that magic existed? Kerry? Or himself?

10.

When they were finished cleaning up the kitchen, Hank began taking garbage bags down to the bin beside the house, leaving Lily upstairs to set up her computer and check her camera equipment to make sure it was all still in working order. The gear was all too specialized for him and he knew he'd only get in her way if he tried to help.

He was on his second trip to the bin when he saw a beat-up black VW bug pull in behind his cab. Shoulder muscles tightening, he stepped quickly into the shadows alongside the house. Then he had to smile and the tension left his shoulders. It was only Moth, driving one of Anita's junkers.

"Hey, kid," Moth said as Hank approached the VW. "You not answering your phone anymore?"

"Left it in the car. What's up? You find Katy?"

Moth shook his head. "Can you believe Anita actually likes these cars?" he said as he struggled to get out.

"That's because she's half your size."

"So's Terry and you don't see him driving one."

Hank laughed. He liked VWs himself. First car he'd actually owned, as opposed to boosted, had been a bug.

Moth gave the porch light a pointed look. "Think we can kill the light?" he asked. "Makes me feel too much like a target."

Hank went into the hallway to turn it off, then joined Moth on the porch steps. Moth pulled an ever-present pack of cigarettes out from where it was tucked in between his biceps and the sleeve of his T-shirt, shook a cigarette out, lit up.

"Still can't find Jack either," he said.

"Maybe they took a road trip together."

"Yeah, that's what I'm hoping, too."

But neither of them believed it.

"How'd you know I was here?" Hank asked.

Moth blew out a stream of blue-gray smoke. "Lucky guess."

"Too bad you can't use a bit of that luck to find Katy and Jack."

"That's what's got me worried," Moth told him. " 'Course the pair of 'em have always had a kind of elusive quality."

"That what you were calling me about?"

"Nah. Paris's been trying to get hold of you. Said to tell you she found your dick." Moth grinned. "And I didn't even know you'd lost it."

"Marty's going to owe me big-time for all the crap I've been taking on this."

"And to think I never thought he had much of a sense of humor."

"You've just never liked lawyers."

Moth shrugged. "What can I say? Whenever I see one, the next thing I know some judge is handing me a few years in the state pen."

"Must be tough, you always being innocent and all."

"You know the drill, kid. Inside, everybody's innocent."

"Except for the short-eyes," Hank said.

Moth's eyes went hard. "Any guy can't keep his hands off a kid deserves what he gets. We know it and they know it. Why the hell do you think they're always whining about rehab? Like therapy's going to help when the wires are that crossed. But the lawyers push for it and the judges buy into it and next thing you know the freak's out on the street, stalking kids again."

"Marty doesn't defend pedophiles."

"Never said that he did." Moth flicked his butt toward the sidewalk, where it landed in a shower of sparks. "So are you doing the run with Eddie tonight?"

Hank shook his head. "There was a little problem here," he said and explained what had happened to Lily in Arizona and how her apartment had been torn apart.

"What're they looking for?" Moth asked.

"Damned if we know."

Moth nodded, lit up another cigarette. "You like this one, don't you?"

"You're beginning to sound like Paris."

"I thought you did," Moth said. "You should bring her by the yard sometime, give us all a chance to meet her."

Hank smiled. And let her see what she was getting into. Because one thing would never change. The family was always part of the package.

"I'll do that," he said. "When all of this blows over."

"That can't come too soon for me."

"Tell me about it."

Moth took a long drag, slowly let it out. "This woman you were saying Lily met in Tucson—you think she could be the same Margaret in Jack's stories?"

As soon as Moth said it, Hank knew he had to be right. Jack's Margaret was also dark-haired with those white stripes of hair at her temples. Feisty, knew her way around.

"How'd you make the connection?" he asked.

"I'm not saying she is or she isn't," Moth said, "but it'd make sense."

"You ever meet her?"

"Nah. She'd run more with Paris's crowd. Ask her when you call her about your dick."

Hank sighed. He refused to look at Moth, but he couldn't ignore the snicker.

"Let me know when you get tired of this one," he said.

That woke a deep belly laugh from Moth.

"Oh, kid," he managed when he finally caught his breath. "If you could see your face you'd know that might never happen."

Great, Hank thought. Like he was ever going to hear

the end of this now. Marty was *really* going to owe him for this.

"Can you pick up Eddie tonight?" he asked.

"Sure. I'll just do some mix and matching with Terry, but we can work it out."

"I was thinking," Hank added. "Maybe you could ask Eddie to do me a favor."

Moth's voice was cautious. "What kind of favor?"

"Set up a meet for me with the Couteaus."

Moth shook his head. "I don't know if that's such a good idea, kid. Eddie already told us how he feels about getting involved with them."

"I'm just asking him to set it up."

"I've got a bad feeling about this."

"You two go back a long way," Hank said. "He'll do it for you where he'd just put me off."

Moth gave him a long steady look.

"What've you got planned?" he asked.

"Nothing. I just want to talk to them, get them off our backs. Find out what they're looking for."

"And if it's something you can't give?"

"I have to know what's going on," Hank said. "We're getting nowhere, stumbling around in the dark, and if we don't do something, somebody's going to get hurt."

"Somebody's already gotten hurt—or are you forgetting that one of them's dead?"

"They aren't going to know we had anything to do with that."

"You hope."

Hank sighed. "Okay. So feed me some ideas. We've already tried to stay out of it, but that didn't work. They trashed Lily's apartment and came looking for her in Tucson. Do I wait until she's dead before doing something?"

Moth didn't reply immediately. He lit up another smoke and stared at the dark houses across the street, then finally stood up.

"Okay," he said. "I'll talk to Eddie."

11.

```
Sender: dgavin@tama.com
Date: Sun, 1 Sep 1996 15:40:22 0500
From:    'Donna    Gavin'    <dga-
vin@tama.com>
Organization: Tamarack Publishing
To: lcarson2@cybercare.com
Subject: Check this out
```

Okay, now before you say anything, I
didn't tell anybody what you told me.
But I have been doing some research
into this whole 'bird people' business. (Hello? Do you feel as weird as
I do taking this seriously?)

Anyways,

You know that guy Andy Parks in Sales
that I told you about--the one who
acts like he knows _everything _and,
unfortunately, is really bright and
not in your face about it so that you
can't hate him for being so damn
smart?

I called him up earlier today and
pretended I'd been talking to a
writer who's trying to research legends and folktales and stuff about
crows that can also be people but she
couldn't find any reference material
on it, so did he have any sugges-
tions. What, like werewolves, except
they're crows? he says. So I go, I

guess except then he says, wait a
minute, isn't there some kind of Indian thing about--I hope I get this
word right--shapeshifters. Or was it
shapechangers?

Well, the upshot is he says he'll
look into it and I figure, that's
that, he's blowing me off, only he
calls me back a couple of hours later
and says the only thing he can find
on our bird people, crows in particular, is this book called _Kickaha
Wings_ which was written by a retired
Butler U. prof (!) who still lives in
Newford (!!). His name's Bramley
Dapple. I think I actually remember
him. Didn't he teach art history and
actually look a little bit like a
bird himself?

Andy doesn't have a copy of the book
himself, but he knows someone who
does. He says it's a fairly slim volume collecting a handful of Kickaha
myths dealing with shapeshifting
bird entities. Published by East Side
Press in Newford--that's still Alan
Grant's imprint, isn't it?--and illustrated in what Andy's friend calls
a Rorschach inkblot style by a Bar-
bara Nichols.

If they don't have a copy at the
library--though they really should,
considering the author's local and
all--Andy's offered to photocopy his
friend's copy for you.

```
>won't  be  back  until  late  Monday
night


Well, I hope you had a good time in
Tucson and I expect a full report.


You are being very careful, aren't
you?


Love


D.
```

A soft tap on the door of her office made Lily look up from Donna's latest email. She smiled when she saw Hank standing there.

"Everything working all right?" he asked.

She shook her head. "The computer and modem seem to be okay, but my printer won't work. All the parts look the way they're supposed to—at least I'm pretty sure they do—so it must be something internal."

The screen on her monitor had been smashed as well, but she'd hung on to her old monochrome dinosaur, storing it in the closet. They'd only knocked it over onto its side and it still worked.

"How about your developing equipment?"

"It seems to have survived," she said. "The bulb's broken on the enlarger, but it's pretty sturdy so I think it'll be okay."

"You've got insurance?"

She nodded. "Two hundred deductible. I suppose that should make me feel better, but it doesn't. It's going to take so long to get everything fixed up again. And the worst thing is, I don't even know if I want to live here anymore. This used to be my home; now it's more like some Tombs squat and I don't feel at all safe in it."

There were dents and holes in the drywall from having had computer components and the like thrown against it.

Deep gouges in the wooden floors. Lily and Hank had replaced all her files in the file cabinet, but it was going to take days to put them back in order—not to mention the weeks it would take to reorganize all her file photographs. And that was just this room. Her darkroom smelled so strongly of spilled chemicals that it was hard to stay in it for any length of time. The kitchen still reeked, even though they'd had it airing for hours now.

"We don't have to stay here," Hank said. "We could find a hotel room. Maybe you'd feel safer there."

"But all my things would still be here. If they were to come back . . ."

"I don't think they'll be back. They went through this place pretty thoroughly and didn't find what they were looking for."

He hesitated then and Lily knew what he was leaving unspoken.

"It's me they want now, isn't it?" she said.

"Hard to say," he told her. "We don't know what they're looking for."

She appreciated the way he was downplaying the danger, but they both knew that anyone who'd gone to this much trouble wasn't about to give up now. Whatever they wanted from her, the state of her apartment was proof that they wanted it badly. Sighing, she swiveled her chair so that she was facing her computer screen again.

"I got an email from a friend of mine," she said. "Here. Read it."

He came into the room and looked at the screen over her shoulder. When he'd finished, he pulled a straight-backed chair over and straddled it so that he could fold his arms across the back.

"Do you remember this Professor Dapple?" he asked.

"Not really. But it'd be worth stopping by the library in the morning to see if they have the book, wouldn't it?"

Hank nodded. "The more we know, the better off we'll be."

"Oh, I've got something to show you," Lily said. "Wait here a sec."

She went into the living room and brought back the knapsack she'd taken with her to Arizona. From the open top she took out a small soft leather pouch and passed it over to him.

"What's this?"

"Look at it. I found it in my knapsack when you were putting the garbage out."

Hank opened the pouch and shook a handful of silver jewelry onto his palm. There were three bracelets, one a smooth solid band almost an inch wide, the other two braided. A fourth was inlaid with a vibrant piece of polished turquoise holding dark red-brown veins that made an almost recognizable pattern. Half-formed pictographs. Maybe a fossilized bird track. The same turquoise was in a couple of the rings and the brooch. The earrings were spiraling silver designs.

He looked up at her. "When you say you found it . . . ?"

"I mean I didn't pack it," Lily said. "Margaret must have put it in there. She's the only one who could have."

"Because she helped you pack."

Lily nodded. "I got my camera gear together while she put everything else in the knapsack."

"So . . ." Hank looked down at the jewelry in his hand, then slid it back into the pouch. "What are you saying? You think whoever trashed your place was looking for this?"

"No. I mean, how could they? I didn't have the jewelry—I hadn't even met Margaret yet when my place got trashed, or when we first met in that alleyway."

"These must be worth a lot."

"I'd say. This woman I sat with on the plane paid a fortune for the jewelry she'd bought while she was there and none of it was nearly as nice as this."

"I don't get it."

"Me, neither." She gave him a sudden smile. "Maybe it's her hoard—you know how magpies are supposed to collect bright objects? I never saw anyone wear as much jewelry as she did. But on her it wasn't, like, overkill or anything. It worked.''

Hank hefted the pouch. ''Maybe you're supposed to wear them ... or carry the pouch around with you. For protection or something.''

''You think?''

''Well, don't talismans come up in those stories of Jack's?''

''The only one I can think of is that pot of Raven's that Cody's always stealing.''

''I remember one where someone was given a bone flute,'' Hank said. ''And there were others. Black stones that were pieces of the first land. Fetish bundles filled with seeds and animal teeth and feathers. Things like that.''

''I probably haven't had the chance to hear as many of those stories as you have.''

Hank nodded. ''I guess. But I'd keep these close by anyway—just to be on the safe side.''

''I will,'' she said as he passed the pouch back to her. She tried, unsuccessfully, to stifle a yawn.

''One more thing before you head for bed,'' Hank said. ''A friend of mine came by while I was taking that last load of garbage out and we talked about some of this.''

''I thought you were gone awhile.''

''The upshot is, he knows somebody who might be able to set up a meet for us with the Couteaus.''

Lily couldn't suppress a shiver. ''Is that such a good idea?''

''Funny. That's exactly what he said.''

''I'm serious.''

''So was he. But like I told him, the way I see it is we have a choice: We can either meet them on safe ground and see if we can work something out, or we wait for their next move.''

''There's no third option, like running away?'' Lily asked.

"Sure. But if they're determined enough, they'll find you."

"You've already asked your friend to set this up, haven't you?"

Hank nodded. "I can be patient about a lot of things, but not this. Not where there's the chance someone's going to get hurt."

How had her life drifted so far from the safe, normal existence it had been just a week or so ago?

"I don't understand," Lily said. "If you've already arranged for this, what is it that you're asking me?"

"I just need to know—are you in or out?"

"You mean do I want to come along?"

Hank nodded. "I don't have to tell you it could be dangerous. We don't know anything about these guys. But you're involved so I thought it was only fair to give you the option."

"I don't want anything to do with them."

"Okay."

Lily took a deep breath. She had to be nuts and Donna would kill her if she found out.

"But I'm in," she said.

His look of approval warmed her, but didn't make her feel any braver or more sure of her sanity.

"We won't be hearing anything until sometime in the morning at the earliest," he said. "You should probably take the opportunity to grab some rest."

For the first time since they'd discovered that her apartment had been torn apart, Lily found herself wondering again if they were going to end up sleeping together.

"You'll stay?" she asked.

"If you want me to."

It was like he was always giving her the option to gracefully back off and Lily couldn't figure out why, but she wasn't going to spend time tonight worrying at it. She looked him directly in the eye.

"I want you to," she said.

This time he leaned close and kissed her.

12.

Ray thought of Jack as he stood in the lane behind the crow house that night, wearing his new skin.

The lonesome dark.

That's what Jack called a night like this. When you were distanced from everything and everybody. Out on your own and there was nobody to care if you were happy or sad. If you lived or died.

The lonesome dark hadn't existed in the old days. That was something people invented. Like time. Parcel up the days, parcel up the seasons. Add a minute here, a day there when it doesn't quite fit. Trim the square peg so that you could slide it into the round hole. In the old days the night was as open as the day. It wasn't a better place to hide because there was nothing to hide from. You weren't outside, looking in, because there was no in.

In the lonesome dark it was easy to agree with Cody. Put everything back to the way it was before that first big mistake of his. 'Cept it wouldn't happen. Jack was right. Pretty much anything Cody touched had a way of screwing up and that was something that was never going to change.

The thing Ray needed to work out now was, how was it going to mess up this time?

There was a gathering tonight, up in the Tombs somewhere, a murder of blackbirds. Corbæ and their little cousins. Ray had been out, tracking elusive cuckoos, when he first heard the crows squawking and carrying on. So he headed back to the crow house to finish what he'd started this morning: grab Kerry and make a run for it. Except once he got there he found that they hadn't left her unguarded. Raven was inside—like he'd do much good, the state he was in—but Chloë was perched up on the roof. Neither of them seemed to pay any notice to him, but you never knew.

Everybody else was gone.

Ray'd had a lot of time to think today. What he finally came up with was that the crows had a use for Kerry the same as Cody and the cuckoos did. And that was as far as he could get. His granddaughter was so innocent—to the world and to her blood—that it made no sense. She'd spent half her life as a child, the other half cloistered away from the world like a nun, numbed with drugs instead of married to God. What did they think she could do?

Did Cody expect her to reinvent the world for him? Did the crows think she could stop Cody and the cuckoos from getting their hands on Raven's old pot? Or maybe . . .

His eyes narrowed suddenly and he studied the crow house with new interest as he considered Raven's pot. Perhaps the crows had no more idea where the pot was than Cody did.

Was that possible? Had they gone and lost the damn thing again? Set it down someplace and the next thing you knew, nobody remembered where? It wouldn't be the first time, though you'd think by now they'd start paying a little more attention to where they stored it, considering what you could do with that old shapeshifting cauldron. Maybe Raven wasn't actually enough in this world to pay much attention to where it should be, but you'd think Chloë would be keeping a close eye on it.

The way the crows were carrying on now, they'd either lost the pot and were organizing a search for it, or they were preparing an attack against the cuckoos that Cody had supposedly brought into the city as a diversion— something to keep the crows busy while he snatched the pot. But if the pot was lost . . .

He knew nothing about his granddaughter, didn't know if she had a finder's gift. Some humans had it. Not like the hawks or cuckoos did, not so focused and strong, but if she did, her corbæ and canid blood would make it all that more potent. And if she did have the gift, that would explain why Cody was so interested in her and the crows were protecting her.

It made so much sense, Ray couldn't understand why he hadn't seen it earlier. But now he was sure he'd figured it out. Why else would Cody have been so interested in Kerry? Cody couldn't use the cuckoos to help him find it because they'd just grab the pot and cut him out of the deal. And the crows didn't have that kind of tracking gift. If they did, they wouldn't keep losing the damn thing in the first place.

So if Kerry did have that gift, they'd both have a use for her.

Trouble was, that brought up the big question: What should he do with this knowledge? There had to be some way he could use it to keep Kerry safe, because if either party tried to get her to find the pot, it was going to put her right in the line of fire.

Maybe it was time to hook up with Jack again. Kerry might be his granddaughter, but she was the old jackdaw's daughter.

He gave the crow house a last thoughtful look, then set off into the night, still wearing his new skin. The height and red hair were gone, along with the long narrow face. He was crow girl–sized now, with hair and skin as dark as any corbæ. He probably wouldn't fool most crows for long, not the ones that knew him, not once they got his scent. But they'd be so busy with their gathering he figured he could slip in and take Jack aside for a few words before anyone was the wiser.

It was worth a try. At this point he didn't have anything to lose.

13.

Paris sat on an overturned pail outside Moth's trailer, a half-dozen dogs sleeping in the dirt around her. She'd pinched a pack of cigarettes from a carton in the trailer and smoked one, but the nicotine hit hadn't helped calm her nerves. All it did was put a bitter taste in her mouth that the tea she was drinking couldn't seem to wash away.

The hot day had finally cooled off but she was still in short sleeves. Holding her tattooed arms near the fire in the oil drum, she moved them back and forth so that the flickering light made them seem less like her familiar journal, more like some obscure movie filmed by a Dadaist.

She was in an odd mood, brought on as much by the proliferation of crows in the Tombs tonight as by their lack of success in finding Katy. Though she was trying to ignore them, she could still hear the birds, loud and raucous though they were at least a half-dozen blocks away. They'd been flying over the junkyard since late afternoon, heading deeper into the Tombs, singly, in pairs, in flocks of a hundred or more. It was just *too* weird.

One of the dogs lying by her foot lifted his head and suddenly they were all alert, staring down one of the narrow lanes separating the junked cars. The eerie feeling the crows had put in her made Paris twitchier than usual. She reached down and picked up a stick that was on its way to the fire, ready to use it as a makeshift billy club, then relaxed when she saw it was only Anita.

"Any luck?" she asked as the older woman drew near and settled in the lawn chair beside her.

Anita shook her head. "Wherever that girl is, she hasn't come back to that nest she made in the Volvo last night."

The word "nest" made Paris think of the crows again.

"What do you think they're doing?" she asked. "There's got to be a couple of thousand crows over there by now."

"Damned if I know." Anita's eyes seemed to hold a strange light, but it was only the fire reflecting in them. "Jack'd know. Hell, Jack's probably over there in the thick of them. We could waltz over and ask him."

"Not me," Paris told her. "All those crows are starting to give me the creeps."

"I know what you mean. It's too much like one of

Jack's stories." Anita gave her a tired smile. "You know, like they could be true."

Paris thought of what had happened to Hank.

"They are true," she said.

"Don't you start. I'm spooked enough as it is without starting to believe there's more to them than Jack passing the time around a campfire."

"We can't pretend they're not true."

Anita sighed. "You ever see one of those animal people of his?"

"No. But Hank has."

"Jesus. Are you serious?"

Paris nodded. "He saw the crow girls."

They both looked in the direction of the noisy gathering. If anything, it seemed to keep getting louder.

"Did you ever see that Hitchcock movie?" Paris asked. "You know the one where—"

Anita cut her off. "What're you trying to do, girl? Make me a complete nervous wreck?"

"Sorry," Paris said. She only managed to stay quiet for a few moments. "But still . . ."

Anita sighed again, heavier this time. "Yeah. There's some kind of trouble brewing over there all right. Let's just hope they keep it to themselves."

Only they hadn't, Paris thought. Jack and Katy were still missing, Hank was involved in . . . something, and now there were who knew how many crows gathering in the Tombs. If all of that didn't add up to something, then what did?

But this time she kept quiet. She reached down, dug her fingers into the thick fur of the dog lying closest to her. It didn't help that despite the animal's apparent disinterest, under its fur, the dog's muscles were as tense as hers.

"You staying the night?" Anita asked after awhile.

"No. I thought I'd crash at Jack's bus. You know, just in case one of them shows up."

"I'd take a couple of the dogs with me, if I were you."

Paris nodded after a moment. "I guess maybe I will."

14.

Ray had managed to get within a block of the crow's gathering without being noticed when a familiar voice suddenly called out to him from the shadowed doorway of a nearby building.

"Hey, Ray. Nice skin. What're you supposed to be—a boy or a girl?"

Cody. Just about the last person Ray was hoping to run into tonight.

"I'm through doing business with you," he said to the shadows.

For a long moment there was only silence from the doorway. Then a piece of the darkness stepped away and took Cody's tall, lean shape. Ray backed up a couple of paces. He started to reach under the ragged jean jacket he was wearing, letting his hand fall back to his side when he saw Cody was unarmed.

Cody caught the movement and smiled. He looked as handsome as ever. You'd never think he'd gotten his nose broken this morning. There was no swelling, no bruises, nothing.

"I'm disappointed," Cody said. "I thought we were friends."

"And here I thought you were just using me."

Cody's gaze went hard. "Drop the attitude, Ray," he said. "It doesn't suit you."

Ray sighed and shook his head. Turning away, he looked farther down the street, past the abandoned car that was rusting by the curb close to where they were standing. You could see the ledges and rooftops were thick with crows. Thousands of them, black-winged and dark-eyed. Not corbæ, but their little cousins—just as the small red foxes running in the woods were his. The birds had been noisy as hell for hours, setting up a racket that you couldn't believe could get any louder, except it did. They were finally quieting down now.

"Whatever happened to the good times we used to have?" he asked. "We traveled a lot of long roads together and it wasn't always this way. We weren't always planning and scheming and screwing up."

"I get tired of it, too," Cody told him. "But my conscience won't let it slide."

Ray didn't turn around. "Your conscience."

"That's right. Even this old coyote's got one. I try to let it all go, take it as it comes the way you or the crow girls do, but then I get this compulsion—I get crazy, that's the truth. Nothing tastes good, nothing looks good. Can't sleep, can't eat, and all I can think of is how all of this is my fault—this ugly mess the world's in. Only thing that keeps me going then is trying to make it right."

"But you can't. What's done is done."

"I can try, Ray. I've got to try."

How many times had they been through this before?

"You know what happens," Ray said. "It just gets worse. You can't fix what's broken. Hell, for all we know, this is the way things are supposed to be."

"You really believe that?"

Ray was quiet for a long moment, before he finally turned to look at Cody.

"No," he said. "I guess I don't."

"Don't worry," Cody told him. "I'm not trying to win you back to the cause or anything. If you want out, you're out." He smiled and touched the bridge of his nose. "No hard feelings."

"I appreciate that." Ray hesitated, then added, "And the same goes for Kerry, right?"

Cody sighed. "Sure. No problem."

Ray knew he was lying, but there was no point in pushing it. Better to let Cody think he was taking everything at face value and just be careful. That wouldn't be too hard. It never hurt to be careful around Cody.

"So what's going on here?" he asked.

"Hard to say. There's maybe a couple of dozen corbæ having themselves a powwow somewhere over there"— Cody made a casual motion with his hand in the direction of an abandoned tenement farther down the street—"but I haven't been able to get any closer because there's too many of their little cousins around. Every time I try to get a little closer, they start dive-bombing me."

"You see Jack go in there?"

"I don't know *who's* in there." Cody gave him a sharp look. "What do you want with Jack, anyway? Since when did the two of you get so tight?"

Ray shrugged. "Maybe since we realized we're kin."

"So we're back to the girl."

"Kind of hard to avoid her," Ray said, "seeing how everybody's so interested in her."

"Did you care so much for her grandmother?" Cody wanted to know. "Hell, do you even remember her?"

"That's not really the point."

"Then what would be the point? Either you've got a reason to be so concerned about the girl or you're just blowing air my way. Which is it, Ray?"

"Blood," Ray said. "It's that simple. We're kin."

"I don't remember that ever meaning so much to you before."

Ray smiled humorlessly. "I guess that's no big surprise seeing how we've already figured out you never really knew me."

He could tell Cody wanted to push it, but something held him back. That made Ray nervous. There had to be a pretty good reason for Cody's playing nice and that could only mean the trouble was more serious than he'd thought.

"Screw it," Cody said. "I'm not here to argue with you."

"Suits me."

"But let me tell you one thing," Cody added. "While you're getting so cozy with your new crow friends, think about this: Just because your granddaughter's got some crow blood in her doesn't mean they'll be welcoming you into the fold with open arms.''

''I'm not expecting them to. I just want her out of this. I don't want anybody using her—not you, not them.''

''Yeah, well, don't turn your back on them,'' Cody said.

Ray never saw him leave. One moment he was standing there on the street, the next he'd twisted the shadows around him, wrapped them around his tall body like a winding sheet, and he was gone. Ray stood for a time, the skin prickling at the nape of his neck and up his spine, waiting for he wasn't sure what. A gunshot, maybe. A knife in the back. Some kind of payback for breaking Cody's nose and walking out on him the way he had.

What he got was a pair of crow girls dropping silently out of the sky. They landed giggling on the street in front of him and immediately found places to lounge—one sitting cross-legged on the roof of the junked car, the other on its hood, legs dangling, heels kicking against the fender, which woke little clouds of rust.

''This is a much better look,'' Maida told him, looking him up and down. ''Black is so veryvery you.''

Zia nodded. ''Mmm. I could eat you all night long.''

''Nice to see the two of you again,'' Ray said, not quite sure how to take their welcome.

The last time he'd seen them, they'd been ready to cut him. Now they were greeting him like a long-lost friend. Crow girls. Who could figure them?

''So are you in disguise?'' Maida wanted to know.

''Who are you disguised for?'' Zia added.

''Because we knew you ever so right away.''

''If not even quickerly-er.''

Ray shrugged. ''I'm just trying to fit in. You know, this being the City of Crows and all.''

''You've been talking to Jolene. She always says that.''

''How is Jolene? Is she big or small?''

Ray had to smile. "Been a few years since I saw her last, but she was small then."

"We like her better small," Maida told him.

"We like it when everybody's our size."

Maida nodded. "That's why we like you now."

"I appreciate that," Ray said, which made them both giggle. "So what's going on over there?" he added, nodding toward the tenement.

"Oh, you know," Zia said, obviously bored by with the question. "Talktalktalk. They never stop."

"What're you all talking about?" he asked.

Maida shrugged. "Who knows? Nothing fun."

"Completely without fun."

Ray studied the pair of them for a moment, unsure as always if they were only being disingenuous, or if they really didn't know. Looking at them sitting there on the car, acting goofy, it was easy to forget how hard they could be, how quickly the switchblades could slip down out of their sleeves and appear in their hands. But having seen it firsthand earlier in the day, he had no trouble believing Jack's stories about them now.

"You've gone and lost Raven's pot, haven't you?" he said.

Maida shook her head. "Oh, no. Whatever made you think that?"

"We've just forgotten what it looks like," Zia said. "That's all." Then she added a "Whoops" and put her hand across her mouth.

"I kind of already figured that part out," Ray told them. "Thing I'm wondering about is, where does Kerry fit in?"

There was no immediate response. The crow girls exchanged a look Ray couldn't read. Zia glanced back at the tenement, before returning her attention to her companion. Maida merely shrugged and began to bounce a small rubber ball on the pavement.

"People are kind of upset," Zia said. The playfulness had left her voice and she seemed years older than she had moments ago. "Jack's always warning everybody about Cody, but no one pays attention. 'Either keep that pot safe, or break it,' he says, 'or there's always going to be trouble.' "

"Only no one wants to break it," Maida put in, her voice changed now, too. She caught the ball and rolled it back and forth between her palms. "It's so long ago. Oldold."

Zia nodded. "Older than Raven."

"Older than us, maybe."

"So people are mad," Zia went on, "because Raven's gone away and he's let the pot get lost again, but it's not just his to take care of, you know. It's everybody's, really."

"Only nobody want's the responsibility, so why get mad at Raven?"

"Except we're not mad at him."

"We're never mad at him," Maida agreed.

"So now Cody's back and he's brought the cuckoos with him and everything's gone dark and dangerous again—like it did when Jack went killing crazy."

"Nobody likes that most of all."

Ray wasn't surprised. You'd have to be crazy yourself to want to see those times come back again.

"Is Jack in there with the rest of them?" he asked.

"Nobody knows where Jack's gone," Maida said.

"Jack's gone away. Not like Raven, but gonegone away all the same. Looking for Katy."

Ray was getting confused. "Who's Katy?"

Zia shrugged. "Just some girl."

"Some old friend."

"Nobody important."

"Except to Jack."

This was getting way off the topic so far as Ray was concerned.

"Look," he said. "I just want to know what Kerry's got to do with it. You're planning to use her to find it, aren't you? That's why you brought her here."

Maida shook her head. "Who told you that?"

"I just figured it out."

"Nobody brought her here," Zia said. "She just called Chloë and Chloë invited her to stay at the house to be nice."

Ray smiled. "Uh-huh."

"Chloë can be very kind," Maida assured him.

"So why are you all so protective of her? Why wouldn't you let her come with me?"

"Because she didn't want to go," Zia said.

Maida nodded. "Duh."

Their answers were as pat as Cody's but he didn't think they were lying to him.

"So you're not using her to find the pot?" he said.

"No," Zia replied. "But that's a veryvery good idea."

"Veryvery," Maida agreed. She began to bounce her ball again. "Maybe she can see things that everybody else is too tired and old to see."

Zia looked over her shoulder to the tenement. "We should tell them and then maybe they'll stop all their talktalktalking."

"And we could have some fun again."

"Don't," Ray said.

They both looked at him.

"I'm not telling you," he said. "I'm asking. She could get hurt."

"We like her," Maida said. "She's so funny."

"We'd never want to see her get hurt."

"Cody wants to use her," Ray told them. "And maybe those cuckoos he's brought into this. I'm not sure how much they know. Maybe they're just using all of this as an excuse to settle some old scores. . . ."

Ray's voice trailed off. He never saw the switchblade appear in Maida's hand, never heard the *snick* as it opened. But suddenly it was there and the small plastic ball was impaled on the point of its blade.

"We don't much like cuckoos," Zia said.

Her dark eyes flickered with dangerous light and the

tense promise of violence hung in the air around them.

"Nobody does," Ray said.

The crow girls remained silent, their attention gone inward, or off someplace Ray couldn't see. On the ledges of the buildings, along the rooflines, the little cousins began to stir. Ray found himself remembering something Jack had told him once, how the crow girls dealt with living forever by moving through the days in an ever-present now. Zen time. They didn't worry about tomorrow, didn't think about the past. He also said that they didn't directly involve themselves in events. Ray didn't think either observation was true—not by what he was getting from them now.

"You remember everything, don't you?" he said. "You only pretend to forget."

Maida blinked. She stuck the ball in her mouth and pulled the point of her knife out of it, then spit the ball into her hand. The switchblade disappeared back up her sleeve.

"When we don't remember, we really don't," she said.

Ray didn't recognize her voice at all now. It held neither a giddy good humor nor a hardness, but was as matter-of-fact as Chloë's—or Raven's before he went away.

"But that doesn't mean it goes away," she added.

Zia tapped a finger against her temple and nodded. "Everything goes on living somewhere in here. Mostly we choose not to think about it."

"Because if we did," Maida explained, "we might start thinking like Cody and try to change the world."

"Maybe that'd be a good thing," Ray found himself saying. "Maybe you wouldn't screw it up."

They both shook their heads sadly.

"That's where Cody's got it wrong," Zia said. "You don't change the world by stirring up something in Raven's pot."

"Then how do you change it?"

"By being strong and true."

"See," Maida added. "That's what makes the cuckoos so bad. You can only gentle them by killing them and every death diminishes us."

Zia nodded. "We should know."

"Or ask Jack if you don't believe us."

"I believe you," Ray said. "I just never thought of it that way."

"The best change you can make is to hold up a mirror so that people can look into it and change themselves. That's the only way a person can be changed."

"By looking inside yourself," Zia said. "Even if you have to look into a mirror that's outside yourself to do it."

"And you know," Maida added. "That mirror can be a story you hear, or just somebody else's eyes. Anything that reflects back so that you can see yourself in it."

"We can't do that with the cuckoos?" Ray asked.

Maida shook her head. "You can't do it with people who never look outside themselves."

Was that what had happened to him? Ray wondered. All those years of going along with Cody until Jack held up one of his stories, bright as any mirror, and all of a sudden Ray had found himself thinking about somebody else for a change.

"So do you think Jack's right?" he had to ask. "Should we be trying to smash Raven's pot?"

Maida shrugged. "First you'd have to find it."

"And then," Zia said, "you'd have to understand it."

"And then you'd be able to decide what to do."

Zia made a helpless gesture with her hands. "So you see the problem."

Ray shook his head.

"Duh," Maida said, playfulness returning to her voice.

She tossed her ball to him and he caught it without thinking.

Zia took pity on him. "That pot's deepdeep mystery, Ray. Nobody can understand it."

"So . . . ?"

"Not even Raven," Zia said, "and he's had it forever."

"Is that where he's gone?" Ray asked. "Looking for the mystery?"

Zia shrugged. "Who knows? But if he did, he's looking in the wrong place."

"Why's that?"

She knocked a knuckle against the rusted metal of the car she was sitting on. "Because this is where the mystery lives. Out here. In the world. The only thing we carry around inside us is a reflection of it."

She jumped down to the ground, landing lightly on her feet. Maida pushed off from the hood of the car to join her.

"We should go," Zia said.

Maida nodded. "They like it when we listen to them talktalktalk."

"You won't mention Kerry?"

They shook their heads.

"But maybe we'll take a turn looking for that pot."

"If we could only remember what it looks like," Maida said.

"Try remembering how it smells," Ray told them.

Zia clapped her hands. "Oh, *good* idea."

The two of them came up on either side of him and kissed him on the cheek, one on the left, one on the right.

"I do like this new skin of yours," Maida said.

Then they were rising on black wings, soaring high above him before gliding down toward the tenement building where the other corbæ were meeting.

Ray stood by the car where they'd left him. He held the ball Maida had tossed to him, watching until they vanished, one by one, through one of the building's broken windows. Absently, he bounced the ball against the pavement, caught it, bounced it again.

For the first time he found himself wondering what it would be like to fly. Wishing he could. And that only made what had happened to his daughter all the harder to bear. He hadn't known Nettie was kin then, but he'd heard the story. Everybody had. Only now he finally understood why she'd turned to the cuckoos when no one else would—or could—help her.

She hadn't had a choice. Flying wasn't something she'd ever have been able to do, it wasn't in her blood. But she'd had to try.

15.

September 3

First thing Tuesday morning, Kerry got up early, washed and dressed, and was ready to leave for the university by eight. Her first class wasn't for another two hours but she wanted to go early to orient herself to the campus. At least that was the plan.

It looked to be another unseasonably hot day so she was wearing her coolest dress—a short-sleeved cotton flower-print, one of only two dresses she owned—and had done her hair up so that it would be off her neck. She had no idea what styles were in fashion on campus and hoped she wouldn't look too out of place. What if they were all into really trendy stuff? Tattoos and body piercings and elaborate makeup?

She'd half-expected one or both of the crow girls to show up while she was having breakfast, but the house seemed very quiet this morning. There'd only been the usual rumbling sound that, when she'd asked Rory yesterday, he'd explained away as their mysterious landlord making his way across the apartment upstairs. From the way the house creaked and groaned, it was more as though there was an elephant moving around up there. She couldn't imagine how big a person would have to be to make that sort of a noise when they simply went from their bedroom to their living room.

''Oh, he's big all right,'' Rory had told her yesterday.

"I don't know how he ever got through the doorways in the first place, little say up all those stairs to the third floor."

"But doesn't he ever go out?"

"I've never even seen him move. I've only heard him cross the apartment, twice a day. So far as I can tell he's completely catatonic the rest of the time. When you're in the room with him, his eyes don't even track your movements. Chloë acts like he communicates with her, but I'll bet she's the one who really runs this place, not him. Even if he is the landlord."

From Rory's descriptions and what she'd seen herself so far, she guessed they were all a little strange in this house. Maybe that was why she felt so comfortable here. It was almost like being back on a ward. She grinned. That'd make the crow girls the nurses doing checks.

Well, that was pushing things, maybe, but otherwise . . . A catatonic upstairs. The agoraphobia Chloë seemed to suffer. And that scene in the front yard yesterday afternoon. It wouldn't have been out of place at Baumert, except it wouldn't have gone on for as long as it had. A nurse would have been telling them to "stop acting out" almost as soon as it had begun and hustled everybody back inside. It was hard to fault them for that at Baumert. Things could get out of control very quickly. As they almost had here.

That crazy red-haired man. Ray. What had he been thinking? That she'd simply jump into the car and drive off with him? Like she'd just go along with someone she'd never seen before in her life. Except Maida had said he was her grandfather.

Her grandfather . . .

She paused in the middle of packing her knapsack and set it down by the window. Going into the bathroom, she studied her face in the mirror. She raised a hand to touch her cheek, to finger her hair. She had his dark complexion. The same fox-red hair.

Suddenly it was hard to breathe.

She remembered yesterday morning, Maida telling her that her mother was red-haired. But that wasn't true. She didn't take after her parents at all. Both of them were dark-haired and pale-skinned. Brown-eyed.

She'd had a little fantasy during those first years in Baumert. That her parents weren't really her parents. That her real parents were going to show up one day and take her away. Out of the institution. Away from the ward and all it entailed, into the loving embrace of a family unit that she'd only ever been able to experience in books, or seen in films and TV shows.

Of course it never happened. How could it? But what if it was true? What if she really *was* a displaced child who had somehow ended up with the wrong family? She'd always tried to be a good daughter, to love her parents, to believe that they wanted the best for her, but that got harder and harder to maintain until finally it was impossible to keep up the pretense. The longer they kept her institutionalized, the more she felt estranged from them, and that only made her feel more guilty and confused.

But now . . .

She had to sit down. She backed away from the mirror, found the toilet seat behind her with fumbling hands, and lowered herself onto its porcelain lid. Closing her eyes, she tried to visualize the light that Maida had called up inside her yesterday. She thought of candles, of a soft glow that grew bright and strong when you paid attention to it, pushing back the encroaching dark.

It was easier than she'd thought it would be. After a few moments, the tightness eased in her chest and she could breathe again. She leaned her elbows on her knees and cupped her chin, thinking.

"Ray," she said, trying out the name.

Could he *really* be her grandfather? Was that why he'd been so concerned about her? Was that why he'd expected her to go away with him?

It seemed so improbable—but no more improbable

than him showing up the way he had, pulling out that old-fashioned gun. Or Maida being able to cure her panic attacks with moistened fingers.

The world outside Baumert was proving to be even stranger than living on the ward had been. The difference was that there they had medical terminology to explain everything, drugs and treatments and therapy to make the strangeness go away. Out here you were on your own.

She got up and splashed some cold water on her face, patted it dry with a towel. Her first day at the university was going to have to wait. Until she got some answers, all she'd be doing was going through the motions of attending classes and interacting with her fellow students. She even knew who to ask: this storyteller named Jack that Annie'd talked about yesterday. The one who lived in a school bus on the edge of the Tombs.

According to Annie, she was supposed to wait for him to come to her, but she was tired of waiting, of reacting instead of acting. She was long past due taking up responsibility for her own life. Dealing with Dr. Stiles as she had, leaving California, coming here to attend Butler were all good steps, but they weren't enough. They didn't tell her *who* she was, where she'd really come from.

She collected her knapsack and left the apartment, hesitating in front of Annie's door. There was no sound from inside, no hint that Annie was awake. And considering how evasive Annie had been yesterday, it would probably be a waste of time to ask her even if she was awake.

So she'd ask Rory for directions, because from what he'd been saying yesterday, it sounded as though he knew this Jack as well.

"You can't possibly go up there by yourself," Rory said.

"Why not?"

"Because it's dangerous. The only people living in the Tombs are the desperate and those who just don't care anymore. You're liable to get mugged, if you don't get your throat cut first."

"I don't care. I have to go. I have to talk to him."

"Why can't it wait? Annie said he'd come to you."

Kerry sighed. "You know who you are, don't you? Who your parents are, where you came from?"

"Well, sure."

"I don't."

Rory looked confused. "But yesterday you told me—"

"I'm beginning to think it was all a lie," Kerry said, cutting him off. "The only person in my family that I resemble is my grandmother."

And a strange man who showed up yesterday who tried to make me go away with him at gunpoint, but she left that unsaid.

"And that makes me feel totally ungrounded," she added. "It's like I don't even have the basic facts of my life the way everybody else does."

"So what are you saying? That you were adopted?"

"I don't know. All I know is that Jack is supposed to have the answers, so I need to talk to him. I don't want to have to spend any longer than I already have not knowing who I am and where I come from."

"Okay," Rory said. "I can understand that. But Jack . . . he's a storyteller. He exaggerates everything and tells really tall tales. You're not necessarily going to find out anything useful by going to him."

"But Annie said—"

"Annie was being particularly cryptic yesterday—I mean, even for her."

"I still have to try," Kerry told him.

"I understand, but—"

"And if you won't give me directions, then I'm just going to have to go up there and try to find him by myself."

She turned from his door and started for the porch. For a moment she thought he was just going to let her go, but then he called after her.

"Oh, hang on, Kerry. If you're that determined, I'll take you up to see him."

She looked back at him and gave him a smile. "I'm not usually so pushy," she said, "but this is really important to me."

Rory returned her smile. "Yeah, I got that impression. Just give me a moment to get my keys."

She thought he meant his car keys, but it was his apartment keys he was fetching. They took a crowded bus north to Gracie Street, transferring once. Twenty minutes later they'd left the downtown rush hour behind and were standing at the edge of a no-man's land, looking out across Gracie Street at the abandoned buildings and overgrown lots that made up the Tombs.

"Oh, crap," Rory said. "I forgot. Chloë wanted me to call Kit first thing this morning."

"Who's Kit?"

"My friend Lily—I just call her Kit because her last name's Carson."

Kerry smiled. "I saw some phone booths back down the block."

She followed him down the street and waited while he made his call, too nervous to be by herself anywhere in this area. While she was waiting for him, she started counting all the blackbirds she could see from where she was standing. There were so many of them—as plentiful as pigeons. But unlike pigeons or gulls, they didn't seem so much interested in handouts as in looking for something.

Rory wasn't on the phone long.

"She was out," he said when he rejoined Kerry on the pavement. "I had to leave a message."

"Was it important?"

Rory shrugged. "With Chloë, who knows? So what do you think?" he added as they crossed the street to where the Tombs began in earnest.

"It's so big," Kerry said.

Which was an understatement. From what she could see of it, the Tombs went on for block after block, a desolate landscape, like the images of bombed-out cities that showed up on the news to accompany reports on the war in Bosnia and the like. Except here it was neglect that had finally left this part of the city so ravaged. It was so much more expansive than she'd thought it would be. And rougher.

There were few people to be seen from where they stood, but those she could made her glad that Rory had come with her. A trio of grizzled men sat on what was left of a stone wall, sharing a bottle despite it being barely nine o'clock. Some street toughs were lounging farther down the block, giving them the eye. Maybe even Rory's being here wouldn't be enough, she found herself thinking. She'd almost decided that perhaps they should beat a strategic retreat, maybe she should just wait for Jack to come to her, but then Rory started walking toward what looked like a junkyard and she fell quickly in step with him.

"Yeah, it's big all right," he was saying. "And it's spreading like a disease." He waved a hand to the other side of Gracie Street where many of the storefronts were boarded up. "It wasn't so long ago most of those places were still open, but now look at them."

"It's pretty depressing."

He nodded. "There's no excuse for letting things get as bad as they are now. I used to think they could still make a go of a lot of these places—I mean, there's a lot of history here and it'd be a shame to lose it. But now I just wish they'd bulldoze it all and start over again. We've already lost the history. Now we've got to cauterize the wound before it spreads anymore."

"What about the people who live here?" Kerry asked.

"Nobody lives above those abandoned stores," Rory said. "And as for the Tombs, the people squatting there will just move on. Or we could build some decent housing for them."

Before they reached the junkyard, he cut into an empty lot. They took a winding path around the mounds of rub-

ble and low walls that had once been buildings, aiming
for a bright yellow school bus that stood at the far end
of the block. Crows rose from the roof as they approached, scolding them. Three large unidentifiable dogs
lunged to their feet and began to bark. Lying on an old
beat-up sofa in front of the bus was a pretty, but tough-
looking Oriental woman in T-shirt and jeans with intricate tattoos running up and down the lengths of both
arms. She hushed the dogs, but showed no sign of welcoming them. The barking of the dogs subsided into low
growls, rumbling deep in their chests.

Kerry moved closer to Rory. The stiff-legged advance
of the dogs made her nervous. The crows still winging
overhead seemed ominous compared to the small flock
that roosted on Stanton Street—why were there so many
of them in this area anyway? But the woman scared her
most. As they were first coming up, Kerry had gotten the
sense that she'd recognized them, had maybe been waiting for them to arrive, but then her face closed down into
a mask and her dark gaze regarded them coldly.

The crows settled back on the roof of the school bus
and perched in a line along the edge of the roof. One of
the dogs returned to the couch to stand by the woman.
The other two stayed closer to Kerry and Rory, trembling
as though they were only waiting for the woman's word
to attack.

She should have listened to Annie, Kerry thought. Instead of trying to force the issue, she should have waited
for Jack to come to her. All she had to do was look at
this woman to know they weren't going to find any help
here.

She glanced at Rory. We should go, she wanted to tell
him, but he was obviously not going to let either the
woman or the dogs deter him.

"Hi there," he said.

The woman didn't answer.

"Is, um, Jack around?"

The woman sat up and swung her legs to the ground.

"Christ," she said. "You've really got some nerve coming around here."

Rory held up his hands, palms up. "Look, we're not here to cause any trouble. We just wanted to have a word with—"

"Take a hike, or I'll sic the dogs on you."

Kerry had definitely never seen this woman before, and she was pretty sure Rory hadn't either, so why was she so angry with them?

"Okay," Rory said. "We're going. Could you just tell Jack that we were looking for him? Tell him Rory and—"

"I *know* who she is. What makes you think Jack'd ever want to see her?"

Kerry found her voice. "Annie said he knows who my parents are."

"Annie."

"Annie Blue. Do you know her?"

The woman's eyes narrowed. "What's she got to do with any of this?"

Kerry turned to look at Rory, but he only shrugged as if to say, it's your call. So Kerry took a steady breath. Trying to ignore the dogs, she went on.

"It's kind of complicated," she said. "Do you know Maida, too?"

The woman's gaze went from Kerry's face to Rory's, then settled back on Kerry.

"What's Maida to you?" she asked.

"She's my friend," Kerry said.

"Your friend."

Kerry nodded.

"I don't believe this. The crow girls are your friends? Do they have any idea who *you* are?"

Kerry was getting a very bad feeling about all of this. The woman was making it out like she was some kind of monster. But she nodded again.

"Annie didn't want them to tell me. She said Jack should be the one."

The woman studied them for a long moment, then seemed to come to a decision. The hardness left her features and she sighed. The dogs relaxed and lay down in the dirt. The crows began to groom their already shiny black feathers.

"I'm Paris," she told them. "I'm a friend of Jack's."

"Could we . . . would it be all right if we talked to him?" Kerry asked.

"Jack's not here."

"Do you know where we could—"

"He's disappeared—he and Katy both."

Kerry felt as though her heart had stopped. "K-Katy?"

"I thought you were her when I first saw you coming, but when you got closer I knew you were her sister Kerry." A faint smile flickered on Paris's lips. "No offense, but Katy'd never wear a dress like that."

Kerry absently smoothed the fabric against her stomach. No, Katy never would.

"You . . . know her?" she asked in a small voice.

"Well, sure. She's been hanging around with Jack for a couple of years now and she'd come by the 'yard with him all the time."

Kerry was speechless. After all these years it was hard to accept that Katy was really and truly real. It was so much easier to go along with the party line as put down by her parents and Dr. Stiles. When you're diagnosed as delusional, it's hard to believe that something really happened, even if you thought—you were sure—you'd experienced it.

"Wait a sec," Rory said. "Are we talking about your . . ."

He let his voice trail off, but Kerry could have finished what he'd left unsaid: her imaginary sister.

"My twin sister," she said aloud.

"But I thought . . ." He shook his head. "Never mind."

Kerry returned her attention to the woman on the sofa. "Why were you so mad at us when we first got here?"

''Because Katy told Hank that you'd come to Newford to kill her.''

Kerry's eyes went wide with shock. ''To *kill* her?''

''Well, not stick a knife in her or anything that dramatic. What she said was''—Paris suddenly looked apologetic—''that you could disbelieve her into not existing. Not from far away, but if you were physically with her and you could look her in the eye and still say with conviction that she didn't exist, then she wouldn't.''

''I . . .''

Kerry didn't know what to say because she knew it was true. Not that she'd ever deliberately will Katy to not exist. It was that she desperately wanted to be normal, to live a normal life, and she couldn't do that if she kept imagining that she had a twin sister. So in a way she'd been perfectly willing to kill her off by not believing she existed.

''But you wouldn't do that, would you?'' Paris was saying. ''I mean, you look so . . .'' She shrugged. ''You know. Nice.''

''I . . . I'm not so nice,'' Kerry said.

Paris's pencil-thin eyebrows rose quizzically.

''I didn't want to believe in her,'' Kerry explained.

''But the crow girls . . .''

Kerry sighed. ''Why does my having made friends with them make such a difference?''

''Because according to Jack they've got bullshit detectors like you wouldn't believe. They'd never befriend anyone who'd . . . you know . . .''

''Kill their own sister?''

Paris gave a reluctant nod.

''I didn't want to believe in her because nobody else could see her. She'd make trouble, but I'd always get the blame.''

''But siblings do that to each other all the time,'' Paris said. ''My brother and I were always at each other's throats when we were little kids.''

''Yeah,'' Rory said. ''But you didn't spend ten years

in a mental institution because you believed he was real, did you?''

Paris looked from one to the other.

"Is this true?'' she asked Kerry.

Kerry nodded reluctantly.

"You were right,'' Paris said. "This is way too complicated. Christ, I wish Jack were here.''

"You said he disappeared?'' Rory asked.

Paris nodded. "Maybe you guys should come back to the 'yard with me,'' she said, standing up. "We could talk to the others and see if we can make any sense out of this.''

"What yard?'' Rory asked.

She pointed in the direction of the junkyard. "My family runs it.'' She gave them a faint smile. "Not the family I was born into, but the one I acquired.''

Both Kerry and Rory hesitated.

"It's okay,'' Paris said. "They're good people.''

"But if they're on Katy's side,'' Kerry began.

"I don't think this is about sides, do you?''

"No,'' Kerry had to agree. "I guess it's not.''

16.

Hank was reluctant to let Lily go off on her own the next morning.

"These guys are too unpredictable,'' he'd told her while they were having coffee and toast on her front porch. The kitchen was still too rank to think of eating in it. "We don't know what they're going to do next.''

"I don't think they'll try anything in broad daylight,'' Lily said. "And we both have stuff to do.''

"Yeah, but—''

"I won't be long,'' she said, "and then I'll come straight home and lock the door and I won't let anyone in unless they know the secret password.''

"I don't know the secret password.''

She'd grinned. "So you see how safe I'll be."

"But—"

"I won't do anything stupid, Hank. But I've got to get these color rolls developed this morning, pick up some replacement chemicals for what those guys trashed in my darkroom, and then develop all my black and whites. I promised Kenny I'd have them to him by five this afternoon."

So he'd let her convince him, but no sooner had she driven off than he began to worry. He was cursed with an overactive imagination. Most of the time he could shut it off, but that didn't work as well when he was worrying about someone else. And it didn't work at all this morning. To try to get his mind off it, he took their dirty dishes upstairs and washed them, then called Paris's apartment. She wasn't home and neither was she at the Buzz when he tried to get her there. Finally he called the junkyard.

"Anita says she was staying at Jack's last night in case anyone showed up there," Moth told him.

"So there's still no word?"

"Nothing."

Hank sighed. It was past time to stop by the house on Stanton Street where Katy had told him her sister was living. But what would he say to the woman? *I know you've disbelieved your sister out of existence. Yeah, right.*

"Did you talk to Eddie for me?" he asked.

"He wouldn't go for it."

"But—"

"It's not that he doesn't want to help us," Moth said. "But he said setting up a meet with the Couteaus is like taking a gun and sticking it in your own mouth. They don't negotiate."

"That bad."

"Worse. But Eddie wanted you to know that he's going to fix things up for you. 'Tell Hank his problems are all going away,' is how he put it."

Hank didn't like the sound of that at all.

"What do you think he meant by that?" he said.

"Beats me," Moth said. "I didn't want to ask."

Hank carried the phone over to the window and looked out at the unfamiliar view. The quiet street was as alien to him as the junkyard would be to Lily.

"How'd our lives get so complicated all of a sudden?" he said.

"By not minding our own business."

"It's not like I could've walked away from any of this."

"I suppose," Moth said, but Hank could tell from the tone of his voice that he didn't agree. "One more thing. Tony wants you to know that Marty Caine's been trying to get hold of you all morning."

"Great. More unfinished business."

"That's what happens when you fill your whole dance card, kid. Tony says he's called the store maybe a half-dozen times and sounds pissed. What'd you do? Send him a book of lawyer jokes?"

"I was heading over to Stanton Street to have a talk with Katy's sister," Hank said, "but I guess I'll stop by Marty's office on the way."

"You don't have to take any crap from him."

"Marty's not like that."

"Yeah, but you're not his pet dog either. He says jump, are you going to start asking how high?"

"Give it a rest," Hank told him.

He shifted his view from the houses across the street to the VW parked in front of Lily's building.

"Those plates on Anita's bug," he asked. "Are they legit?"

He could almost see Moth shrug. "Good as. Just don't run any red lights while you're driving it."

Perfect. Neither Moth nor Anita liked to give the government any more than they had to—neither money nor paperwork. He didn't blame them. It made life a lot easier when you didn't exist on paper. But all he needed now was to get stopped by some overzealous traffic cop having a slow day.

"I'll talk to you later," he said into the phone.

Naturally, there were no parking spaces anywhere near the Sovereign Building, so Hank had to park the VW a half-dozen blocks away and hike back to Marty's office. He stopped in at Mac's deli to buy three coffees and took them upstairs with him. During the day there was no need to be buzzed into the building, but you had to enter Marty's office by way of the front office, where his secretary, Robbie Norton, held court. Robbie was a big man, solidly built. More like a linebacker or a bodyguard than Hank's expectations of a legal secretary. He had fingers like fat sausages and it always fascinated Hank to watch how delicately they could work a computer keyboard.

Robbie looked up when Hank came in and smiled his thanks for the coffee Hank handed him.

"Marty in?" Hank asked.

Robbie nodded. "You wearing a flak vest?"

"He's that mad?"

"Let's just say that bringing him a coffee's not going to come close to smoothing this over."

"What's it all about?"

Robbie shook his head. "I'm not getting in the middle of this." He pushed the "Talk" button on the intercom and said, "Hank's here."

Marty's voice came back, holding the cool terseness he usually reserved for somebody he didn't respect. A crooked cop. A client who'd lied to him. "Send him in."

Hank glanced at Robbie, eyebrows raised.

"Good luck," Robbie said.

He really didn't need this on top of everything else that was going down, Hank thought as he opened the door to Marty's office and stepped in. Marty gave him a look that held as much sadness as it did anger.

"The good news," he said before Hank could speak, "is that Sandy's out of jail, all charges dropped."

"What's the bad news?"

Marty tossed an envelope on the desk. "Here's your money."

"That's the bad news?"

"I won't be using your services anymore," Marty said.

Hank set the two Styrofoam cups of coffee on the edge of the desk and sat down.

"There's really nothing more to discuss," Marty told him.

He was using his no-give lawyer's voice. Cold. Impersonal. Like he was talking to the press. Or to a staff sergeant at a precinct where one of his clients had "tripped in his cell" and now required stitches and a stay in the hospital.

"Bullshit," Hank said. "You want to tell me what the hell's going on here?"

"I just don't do business your way."

"Well, let's see." Hank counted the items off on his fingers. "So far I've interviewed your client and spent a day visiting every tattoo parlor in the city. Seems like pretty straightforward investigative work to me. You planning to use psychics or something now?"

"Do you think I'm stupid?"

Hank gave him a steady look. "Never thought so before, but you're doing a good job of changing my mind."

Marty returned his gaze, anger barely kept in check. Hank waited him out.

"Cute," Marty said finally. "But we both know there's no way Bloom would've backed off the way he did unless you leaned on him."

"*I* leaned on him?"

"I don't know what you dug up on him, but I know scared and he was terrified when I saw him this morning."

This made no sense at all.

"You're telling me that the D.A.'s office is dropping the charges on your client because somebody leaned on the prosecutor who's handling the case?"

"I told you, Hank. Don't play me for a mark."

But then Hank got it. He sighed. This was the work of Eddie Prio, doing a "favor." Now he knew what the message Moth had passed on meant. He wondered what other surprises Eddie had for him.

"I had nothing to do with leaning on Bloom," he said. "At least not directly."

Marty waited for him to explain.

"It's complicated," Hank said. "Remember what I told you about Couteau?"

Marty nodded.

"Well, his family's involved in some other business I'm trying to deal with so I asked Eddie Prio to set up a meet with them."

"You deal with Prio?" Marty asked.

"It's not like you're thinking. He uses the cab to transport his bank deposits from the club. I figured with his connections, he'd be able to get them to listen."

"So what happened?"

Hank shrugged. "I got the message this morning that he won't do it. Too dangerous, he says. The Couteaus don't negotiate. Then he told my partner to tell me that all my problems were going to go away."

"You didn't ask him to get involved?"

"Come on, Marty. Do I look that stupid? Setting up a meet's one thing. Dealing with Bloom the way he did would've put me deep into his pocket and I don't work that way with anybody."

Marty didn't say anything for a long moment, but then he reached across the desk and took one of the coffees.

"I should've talked to you first," he said.

"Yeah, you should have."

"It's just . . ." Marty sighed. "I never liked Bloom. And I never liked his private agenda. But you should have seen his face. The man is seriously screwed up about this. Whatever Prio's got on him, it's deep."

"If you're dirty, Eddie'd be the man to know. He's got his fingers in everything."

"But that's not the way to deal with someone like Bloom," Marty said. "It makes us no better than him."

Hank shrugged. That all depended. He wouldn't have asked Eddie to do anything on a stranger's account. But if it had been a matter of his family or Bloom, he wouldn't have hesitated.

"So what're you going to do?" Hank asked. "Set the record straight?"

"Christ, you're kidding me, right? It's too late to play innocent now. And what worries me is the D.A.'s office is going to think I'm connected to Prio. Or maybe next thing you know, he'll be calling me up for payback."

"There's worse things could happen," Hank said.

"Like what?"

"Like having Eddie pissed at you."

Marty shook his head. "I run a clean office. It's going to take more than Eddie Prio to change that. I just don't need the grief."

"I'll talk to him."

"No. If it comes up, I can deal with it."

Hank stood up. "Well, if you change your mind . . ."

"I won't." Marty pushed the envelope of money across the desk. "You're forgetting something."

Hank pocketed the envelope. "We're square?"

"We're square. Only next time, don't get my business involved with Prio."

"I've got no argument with that."

Marty called him back again as he started for the door. "This other problem you've got . . . you need any help with it?"

"No."

"But if you do?"

Hank smiled. "Trust me. I'll call."

"You're good," Robbie said when Hank stepped out of Marty's office and closed the door behind him. "I don't know many people can calm him down when he's that mad."

"Comes from clean living."

"Uh-huh."

"I'll see you, Robbie."

"Hang on there," Robbie called after him. "There was a call for you while you were talking to Marty."

Hank paused at the door and turned.

"Someone named Anita," Robbie went on. "Said you're needed at the junkyard."

Hank's pulse quickened. Now what?

"Thanks," he told Robbie.

"And she also wanted you to know that Moth—you know someone who calls himself Moth?"

Hank nodded.

"Well, she says Moth was pulling your leg. That make sense?"

Hank smiled. So the plates were legit.

"Perfect sense," Hank said. "Thanks."

"Moth," Robbie repeated as Hank left the office. "What kind of a name is that?"

17.

Lily might have put up a brave front to Hank, but she was nervous as she dropped off her film at Kiko's Kwick Print and then drove on to the library. Nervous and happy, which made for an odd mix of emotion. She couldn't stop looking for suspicious characters, or constantly checking her rearview mirror, as she followed the familiar route from her apartment to Kiko's, then back to the library in Lower Crowsea. At the same time she was positively beaming with a happy glow from how things were working out with Hank. She was sure that the goofy grin she couldn't quite erase was telling everyone exactly how she'd spent the latter part of her night. In bed, making deliriously wonderful love.

Oh, let them just be jealous, she decided.

There was a small parking lot behind the library, but

she found a space on the street and parked there instead. The lot was too secluded, too cut off from the view of the main street for her to be comfortable leaving her car there. She didn't feel entirely safe until the large oak-and-beveled-glass doors of the library had closed behind her and she was crossing the wide wooden floor of the foyer, camera bag a familiar weight as it hung from her shoulder.

She stopped by the bank of computers near the circulation desk and sat down. The library's search program took her through a half-dozen different menus before it finally came up with the information that Professor Dapple's book wasn't available.

"Excuse me," she asked the young woman at the circulation desk, "but can you tell me when you expect this book back?"

She handed over the slip of paper on which she'd written the title and author.

"Oh, it's one of the professor's books," the librarian said.

She had the faint trace of a British accent and a peaches-and-cream complexion to match. With her long brown hair done up in a loose bun and lovely large eyes, she made Lily think of those Pre-Raphaelite women immortalized by Burne-Jones and Rossetti. Her name tag read, "Ms. Pierson" and while Lily had never really spoken to her before, they'd often exchanged smiles as they each went about their business.

"Do you know him, Ms. Pierson?" Lily asked.

"Oh, please. Call me Harriet." She smiled. "Bernard makes us wear these tags with our surnames on them because, well, he's very old school. Given names would be so unprofessional."

Bernard, Lily assumed, would be the head librarian, a rather stern-looking older man she sometimes saw lurking about, keeping what she thought was far too close an eye on his staff. She wouldn't like to work for anyone who was that particular.

"And yes, I do know Professor Dapple," Harriet said. Her fingers danced across the keyboard of the computer on her side of the wooden counter. "He used to be quite the regular fixture in this branch."

"Used to be? He's not . . . ?"

"Dead? Oh, no. Though he's certainly getting on in years. No, he and Bernard had something of a falling out a few years ago. Now the professor only comes by on Bernard's day off." She smiled. "It's all so terribly political."

Lily raised her eyebrows.

"Literary circles political," Harriet explained. "They had a huge blowout one day over the literary merits of one of the professor's protégés, which subsequently carried on in the letters pages of various literary journals." She gave Lily another of her ready smiles. "I don't know why I'm telling you all of this. It must seem ever so boring."

"Not at—"

"Oh, here we are," Harriet said. She gave the screen a small frown. "That's odd. It's supposed to be kept in the Newford Room and shouldn't be out on loan." She copied a number down on Lily's slip of paper. "Let's go have a look and see if someone's made a mistake, shall we? It might well still be on the shelf where it's supposed to be."

"I appreciate all your trouble."

"It's no bother at all," Harriet said as she led the way through the main room of the library and up the stairs to the reference section. "It's lovely to be walking around in here without a huge armload of books."

The Newford Room was near the front of the building, just off the main reference room. Three of the walls were lined with floor-to-ceiling bookcases, one of them separated by two large bay windows with window seats. The fourth wall held a rotating display of local artwork that was managed by the Newford School of Art. Under the hung art was a glass cabinet displaying manuscripts and diaries by notable Newford writers. A long oak table sat in the center of the room, surrounded by high-backed wooden chairs. Four club chairs completed the furnishings, one of them occupied by a man reading a newspaper.

Harriet went straight to one section of the bookcases.

"This is so odd," she said as she ran a finger along the spines of a dozen or so of the professor's other books. "I can't imagine where it could be."

There was the sound of a newspaper being lowered, followed by a familiar voice asking, "Where what could be?"

Lily and Harriet glanced toward the club chair and Lily smiled. She hadn't seen Christy Riddell in ages, but he looked the same as always. Clothes slightly rumpled, hair a bird's nest of brown tangles, dark eyes alert and curious.

"One of the professor's books," Harriet said. "*Kick-aha Wings.*"

"Now why would you want a copy of that, Lily?" Christy asked.

"Hello, yourself," Lily said.

Harriet looked from one to the other. "You know each other? Well, yes, of course," she added before either could respond. "It's obvious that you do."

"Was it something in the book you needed?" Christy asked Lily. "Or did you just want to have a look at it?"

"A bit of both, actually."

"I'll tell you what," Harriet said. "I'll let Christy bend your ear while I go back downstairs and see if I can't get to the bottom of this little mystery."

"Put Bernard onto it," Christy said. "That should keep him out of your hair for at least a week or two."

"You're a nasty man," Harriet said, but she was smiling. She turned back to Lily. "Stop by at the desk on your way out and I'll let you know what I've found out."

"Thanks again."

"Not at all. I'll see you in a bit."

When Harriet left, Lily crossed the room to where Christy was sitting. She put her camera bag down on the floor and took the chair beside his.

"*Kickaha Wings*," Christy said. "Now there's an obscure book to be looking for. I think there were only a few hundred copies published in the first place. Where did you hear about it?"

"It's sort of an odd story."

"Then I'm your man."

This was certainly true, Lily thought. Christy's own writing was about equally divided between fairy tales that took place in the modern world and his more popular collections of urban myths, hauntings, and odd facts.

"I've gotten interested in—" She hesitated. "I suppose animal people would be the best way to put it."

"Animal people. Like shapeshifters, you mean?"

Lily nodded. "I suppose. Or beings that—oh, I don't know exactly—appear to be what we expect them to be, but that's not necessarily what they actually are. We just see them that way. But they're really animals, not people at all." She sighed. "I'm not being very clear, am I?"

"It's a confusing subject. Judging by your interest in Dapple's book, I take it you're specifically interested in the legends of the crow shapeshifters in the Kickaha Hills?"

"I'm interested in anything I can find out about these animal people. Donna tracked down the title of Professor Dapple's book for me, so I thought I'd start with it."

Christy nodded. "It's a good collection, but it only skims the surface. Most of that sort of thing is still more in the oral tradition—and not simply that of the Kickaha, though theirs is the most thoroughly documented. The problem is, the stories aren't entirely consistent. There appear to be two main schools of thought here."

"Which are?"

"Well, Jilly—have you ever met her?"

Lily shook her head. "I've just heard you talk about her."

"I should introduce you to her sometime. Anyway, she's got a friend named Bones who talks about beings that are part people, part animal. According to him, they originate in the spiritworld—which he says we can visit when we dream. In turn, the spirits visit our world and sometimes inhabit the bodies of people or animals. And sometimes they all get mixed up—people, spirits, animals—and you end up with these odd mythological sorts of creatures. You know, the kind that populate folktales?"

Lily nodded.

"So that's one take on these beings. But then there's Jack—you know him, right?"

"Sure," Lily said. "The storyteller."

"That's him. Lives in a school bus on the edge of the Tombs. He says that the animal people were here first—everybody else came later. Regular animals, people, all the trappings of the world. Where exactly these first people came from isn't so clear, but their existence makes a tidy explanation for the similarity of so much folklore throughout the world, the way certain stories keep turning up in the most unlikely of places, all courtesy of these animal people. He even claims to be one himself." Christy smiled. "Maybe that's why he calls himself Jack Daw."

"So which version is true?" Lily asked.

"I don't think they're mutually exclusive. Keep an open mind, I always say. Drives sensible people mad, I know, but what did we ever get from sensible people? Not poetry or art or music, that's for sure."

Lily wasn't so sure she agreed with that. Why couldn't an artist be both inspired and sensible?

"Anyway," Christy finished up. "I could probably be of more help if you explained what exactly it is you need to know."

"I . . ." Lily could feel her cheeks redden under his curious gaze and had to look away, across the room. "I need to know if they're real."

"The animal people."

She nodded, gaze still fixed on a painting that hung on one side of the door. It was an odd piece, an abstract, all earth colors and subdued tones. Almost monochromic, except when you really focused on it and realized the subtle gradations of color. When Christy didn't speak, she finally turned to look at him.

"Could they really exist?" she asked. "I mean, not just in stories, but for real. Could creatures like that be sharing the world with us right now?"

Christy regarded her thoughtfully for a long moment. "You've experienced something, haven't you?"

She nodded.

"And how you're hoping to rationalize it away. What you really want is for someone with some authority in the subject to tell you that this sort of thing is hopelessly romantic and impossible."

"No," Lily told him. "I think they could exist. The real problem is, if they do exist, what do they want from me?"

"I think we'd better backtrack a little bit here because I have no idea what you're talking about now."

Lily glanced at her watch. She wondered if Hank had finished his errands and was back at her apartment waiting for her. It was sweet the way he was so worried about her this morning—though she appreciated the seriousness of the situation. When she looked back at Christy he was smiling at her.

"Is it that long a story?" he asked.

"Yes and no," she said. "I'll try to give you the *Reader's Digest* version."

"That bit of rhyme about cuckoos," Christy said when she'd finished outlining the strange turn her life had taken in the last week or so. "Geordie's got a better head for that sort of thing than I do, but I'm pretty sure it's a bastardization of a traditional ballad. English, I think. And when you put the words up against each other—cuckoo, Couteau—there's a similar resonance."

Geordie was Christy's younger brother, as absorbed with traditional music as Christy was with literature and folklore.

"But what could they want from me?" Lily asked. "I'd never heard of either of them before that night. Jack's stories were what got me interested in these animal people in the first place, but he never mentioned anything about cuckoos or this family of New Orleans gangsters."

"Well, the answer's not in the professor's book," Christy said. "I know that, because I've read it. But he might know."

Lily shook her head. "I can't just go up to him, introduce myself, and then tell him all this."

"Well, if you knew him, you'd realize that you could, but if the idea makes you uncomfortable, I could go with you."

Lily still wasn't convinced.

"He'd think I was nuts," she said.

Christy laughed. "You *really* don't know him. He thrives on this sort of a puzzle."

He stood up. Folding his paper, he laid it on the table, then gave her an expectant look.

"I feel really awkward about this," she said.

"You shouldn't. Trust me."

"Yes, well that's easy for you to say because . . ."

Her voice trailed off as someone entered the room. It took her a moment to make sense of the familiarity she felt looking at the woman in the dove-gray suit who was now standing in the doorway. She cut an impressive figure, tall and sleek, fine-boned features, short-cropped ash-blonde hair, eyes a dark, penetrating gray and wide-set like a bird's. It was impossible to guess her age. She might have been from anywhere in her early twenties to her late thirties.

When Lily did place the woman, her throat went dry, her pulse jumping into overdrive. It was the newcomer's being a woman that had initially confused her. But now she—

The woman moved out of the doorway, into the room, and a man who could've been her twin stepped in behind her.

Looking at him, Lily couldn't breathe. It was Philippe Couteau. Except it couldn't be. She'd seen him die. She'd seen a small punky girl stick a knife in his side and drop him to the pavement, where he'd lain in a pool of his own blood.

And then she'd seen him alive again, in the Tucson airport, except Margaret had said he was the dead man's brother. Gerrard. Unless this was yet another of them.

The man closed the door behind him and leaned against it, arms folded across his chest.

"We are not a patient family," the woman said. Her voice held the faint hint of a French accent.

Christy took a step forward, stopping when the man straightened up from the door, one hand going under the tailored jacket of his suit. Dove-gray. Like the woman's. Like the one worn by the dead man in the alley.

"What's going on here?" Christy said.

The woman gave him a dismissive glance. "Don't speak unless you're spoken to—it'll simplify everything."

"Who do you think you—"

Lily cleared her throat. "It . . . it's them," she said.

"I like that," the woman said. " 'Them.' It's so anonymous." She gave Christy another glance. "Why don't you sit down."

Lily thought he was going to argue the point. Before she could warn him not to get them mad, the man brought his hand out from under his jacket. Christy stared at the automatic weapon the man was now holding, then backed slowly toward the chair he'd so recently vacated. Sat down. The man lowered his arm, the muzzle of his automatic pointing at the floor.

"That's better," the woman said.

She returned her attention to Lily. The full weight of

her gaze made Lily feel like a small animal mesmerized by a snake.

"Lily," the woman said.

Lily didn't know if it was a question or a statement, but she quickly nodded in response.

"My sons tell me that you've been most persistent in eluding them. It's been very annoying."

Her *sons?* Lily had an eye for plastic surgery and she'd swear this woman had never been under a surgeon's knife. She looked more like the man's younger sister than his mother.

"They . . . they scare me," Lily found herself saying.

"Yes, and well they should. They're very serious boys. Very focused."

"Look," Christy began. "I don't know what you think you—"

He broke off when the muzzle of the automatic lifted and was trained on him.

"This will go much more quickly if you will simply do as you're told," the woman said. "Sit. Hold your tongue. Do you think you can do that?"

Christy nodded.

"Good. Now, Lily. Would you please empty your bag on the table."

Definitely not a question, Lily thought.

Her hands shook as she picked up her bag and slowly brought it over to the table. Opening the top, she began to reach inside.

"Don't!" the woman said sharply.

Lily froze. Her gaze lifted to meet the woman's.

"My son gets uncomfortable when he can't see your hands," the woman explained. "Simply hold the bag above the table and empty it."

Lily did as she was told, wincing when her camera fell out and landed with a loud clunk on the oak surface. It was followed by plastic 35-millimeter film canisters, which went rolling. Some filters. The pouch of silver jewelry that Margaret had secreted in her luggage. A macro

lens and a telephoto, her flash unit—all of which made
her wince again as they banged against the tabletop. The
small address book she used to note picture subjects,
f-stops, lighting information. The small black tin that she
kept exposed films in until she got home. A couple of
pens. Her wallet. A handful of business cards—hers and
other people's.

"I swear I never took any pictures of you or your
sons," she said as she shook a last few filters, business
cards, and lint onto the tabletop.

The woman gave her an odd look. "This has never
been about photographs."

"But what else could I possibly—"

"Sit."

Lily dropped her camera bag on the table and quickly
returned to her chair. The woman stepped forward and
picked up the black tin.

"You see how simple it was to get it?" she said to
her son.

He regarded her, expressionless.

"That's it?" Lily said. She knew she should keep
quiet, but she couldn't help blurt it out. "That's what all
of this has been about? A tin that would've gone into the
garbage if I hadn't found a use for it?"

The woman held it up, turning it in the light coming
from the windows.

"Is that what you see?" the woman asked.

Lily began to nod, but it wasn't a tin the woman was
holding anymore. As though her words had been a key,
Lily's familiar tin, battered and dented, black as a coal
except for where the paint had chipped away in places,
shimmered in the woman's hands, became translucent,
changed. . . . It was now an ornately decorated clear crystal goblet or stemmed vase that didn't so much catch the
light from the window as absorb it and cast it back into
the room. Stronger. Glowing. More golden. More intense.

The goblet wasn't empty. At the bottom was a splash
of color. Lily leaned forward in her chair and her mouth

opened as she realized there was a tiny red-haired woman curled up in the bottom of the glass container. It didn't look like a sculpture. It was too lifelike. Lily could swear that the figure's hair moved as the woman turned the goblet about to get a closer look herself.

"Now what have you put in here?" the woman said.

Her dark gaze left the goblet and settled on Lily.

"N-Nothing," Lily replied. "I just used it to keep films in, that's all. I never saw that . . . that . . . What is it? It almost looks real."

"Perhaps it is," the woman said. "I must think about this."

She took Lily's camera bag and carefully placed the goblet inside, zipped it closed.

"If you are wise," she said, returning her attention to Lily, "you will make the most sincere effort you can to never cross our path again."

"*Mais*, Dominique—"

It was the first time the woman's companion had spoken. She turned on him, her voice dark with anger.

"*Ne vous permettez pas de me questionner. Si vous et vos frères n'étiez pas de telles brutes, toute cette histoire serait terminée depuis longtemps—et de façon moins désolante. Philippe serait encore vivant.*"

"*Oui, Maman,*" he said, gaze on the ground.

Dominique Couteau faced Lily once more, anger still flashing in her eyes.

"Be grateful that I decided to take a hand in this myself," she said.

Lily nodded. "Yes. I am."

"I hope we will not be meeting again," Dominique added.

She swung Lily's camera bag to her shoulder and a moment later both she and her son had left the room.

"Me, too," Lily said in a small voice, then she collapsed back into her chair, all her muscles turned to rubber.

"I could have done without that," Christy said after a few moments.

Lily nodded weakly.

"Are you okay?"

"I guess. . . ."

Lily turned to look at the door, half-expecting the man to come back and kill them.

"Did you see what happened to that old black tin of mine?" she said. "I can't believe I've just been carrying it around in my bag for the past half year or so."

Christy nodded. "It turned into a chalice." There was a haunted look in his eyes as he remembered. "It almost seemed to be made out of light."

Chalice, Lily thought. That was the perfect word to describe it.

"And in the bottom . . . ," she said. "That little woman. She looked so real."

"They weren't expecting to find her in it," Christy said.

"No kidding. Like we were?"

Christy didn't reply. When Lily turned to him he was wearing a thoughtful expression.

"I don't like her having it," he said. "It doesn't feel . . . right, somehow."

"I wasn't about to argue with her about it," Lily said.

"No. Of course not. It's just . . ."

"Did you understand what she said to her son—when she was so angry?"

Christy nodded. "She was saying that he and his brothers had been acting like thugs. That the whole business could have been handled a lot more expediently. And if it had been, Philippe wouldn't have died—Philippe being the man you saw killed in the alley, I assume."

"That's what Hank said his name was. God, talk about identical twins—or family resemblance, I guess, because she could have been their sister. And that guy with her, he looks *exactly* like his brother."

"He wanted to kill us."

Lily shivered. There was no doubt in her mind about that. He wouldn't have cared that they were in the middle of the library with people all around. All he'd wanted to do was pull the trigger.

Christy glanced at her. "I think we were very, very lucky."

"I guess you're right," Lily said. The rubbery feeling in her legs was starting to go away, but she still felt weak with relief. "Still, at least it's over now. They've got what they wanted from me." The memory of the chalice filled her mind's eye—less an exact representation of it as the feeling it had woken in her. "Except . . ."

Christy gave her an expectant look.

"How can I let them just take it away and keep it?" she said.

It was impossible to keep a clear image of that glowing chalice in her mind. The harder she tried, the further it seemed to slip away. But she couldn't forget it either. It was as though all the enchantment and mystery of the world had been bundled up into one magical object.

"How can you stop them?" Christy asked.

"I don't know. But I have to try. Is there a phone around?"

"On the ground floor. Are you going to call the police?"

Lily shook her head. "Like they're going to devote any manpower to tracking down what for all intents and purposes is just an old tin. No, I'm going to call a friend of Hank's to see if he knows where he is and then I'm going to talk to Jack again."

"If you need some help," Christy began.

"I'll ask," Lily said. "Never fear. Brave I'm not. But I don't think just talking to Jack is going to put me into any danger."

"But you'll be careful."

"Oh, I'll be very careful."

She looked at the mess of her belongings on the table.

"God," she said, thinking aloud. "How am I going to carry all of that?"

"I'll come down to the circulation desk with you," Christy said, "and see if I can't scare up a shopping bag while you're making your call."

Lily paused in the doorway as they were leaving and looked back into the room. The air still seemed to hold some of the golden glow cast off by the chalice. It even smelled like old mysteries in the room. The scent made her pulse beat more quickly—not from fear, as it had when the Couteaus had threatened them, but from awe.

There was no way she could let them keep the chalice, she thought as she joined Christy. No way at all.

Hank's friend didn't know where he was, so after saying good-bye to Christy and thanking Harriet again for her help, Lily decided to go talk to Jack on her own. She left the library carrying her camera equipment in a paper shopping bag, holding it against her chest, hands on the bottom to give it support. Shopping bags hadn't been made to safely transport precious camera equipment. She only hoped that nothing had been damaged from being dropped on the table earlier.

Her car was where she'd left it and didn't seem to have been tampered with, nor did anyone appear to be paying undue attention to either it or her, but she still had to check the backseat before she unlocked the door and put the shopping bag inside. Dominique Couteau had seemed to make it clear that she and her sons were no longer interested in her, but Lily saw no reason to take any chances. For all she knew they could read minds. And if that was the case . . .

Don't make yourself crazy, she told herself.

As she started the car, she remembered that she hadn't had a chance to get to the bank after her trip to Tucson and didn't have a penny on her in case of an emergency. Since her bank was on the way to Jack's bus, she stopped in, actually finding a parking space right out front. Maybe things were finally starting to look up for her.

There was only a small line inside and soon she was standing at a teller's window, asking to see a balance for her account. When she looked at the amount, she pushed her bankbook back toward the teller.

"There must be some mistake," she said. "I never deposited ten thousand dollars this morning."

The teller turned the book around so that he could look at it. He pointed to a line of code in front of the amount.

"It was an electronic transfer from another bank," he said.

Lily shook her head. "I don't understand. What other bank?"

"Just a moment," the teller told her, "and I'll see what I can find out."

This was too weird, Lily thought as she waited for him to get back. She watched him conferring with a dark-haired woman sitting at a desk, and then the two of them came back to the wicket.

"I have the transfer record here," the woman said. She smoothed it out on the counter between them. "It was sent to us from the Williamson Street branch of the Unity Trust."

Lily looked at the transfer record. The name under "Client" was the Newford Investment Group, Inc.

"This doesn't make any sense," she said. "I've never heard of these people before."

The woman smiled. "Well, they certainly appear to have heard of you."

Lily remembered a friend who'd once had a large amount of money simply show up in her account one day. Instead of questioning it, she'd spent the money and then had to pay it all back when it was found to be the result of a computer error. She wasn't about to repeat that mistake.

"It's so much money," she said.

The woman nodded. "I'd be happy to discuss some excellent investment opportunities that we can offer."

Lily shook her head. "Um, maybe another time. I can't deal with this right now."

"Of course. Let me give you my card."

It was easier to take the card than argue.

"I'd like to withdraw fifty dollars," Lily told the teller when the woman returned to her desk.

"If you could just fill out this withdrawal slip. . . ."

Lily returned to her car in somewhat of a daze. This was crazy. Not the same crazy that was filling the rest of her life, but definitely weird all the same. But as she'd told the woman in the bank, it wasn't something she could deal with at the moment. Not when there was that chalice to think of. And that curious figure lying in the bottom of it.

But ten thousand dollars. How many financial worries wouldn't *that* solve?

Focus, she told herself.

First she had to talk to Jack, then she could worry about large amounts of money mysteriously appearing in her bank account.

She dropped her bankbook into the shopping bag that held her camera equipment and started the car. Pulling out into the traffic, she headed north, toward the Tombs and Jack's school bus.

18.

Linear space was as much a human invention as linear time and like most corbæ, Margaret had no idea what purpose either served. It certainly couldn't be because they were faster or more convenient. The direct line between two points ignored the folds in the fabric that made up the world, the nooks and crannies that might not only provide a shortcut from one place to another, but were also the hidden resting ground of things that strayed too far out of the world to return. They were washed up like tidal hoards in these secret havens: Lost objects. Forgotten places. The tired, the unwanted, the lonely. Sad places, some, but there were happy ones, too.

They were a corbæ's dream, magpie treasure nests in which you might stumble across anything. A shiny bauble. A gold ring. A missing friend. Why anyone would develop a logic that wouldn't admit to their existence had never made any sense to her at all. But human logic often confounded her. She was very much like the crow girls in that regard, always more interested in what lay behind the obvious, the hidden lane as opposed to the well-used thoroughfare, the secret roomlike space in an old elm tree instead of the expected rooms in a house.

Tuesday afternoon found her poking about in the secret places around Jack Daw's school bus, looking for the tall storyteller. She finally found him in a curious room behind a stop sign that was rusted and almost bent in two. It had worn wooden floors, white plaster walls, and two windows. Through one window you could see the afternoon sun as it fell upon the Tombs. Through the other you were looking into a night sky, freckled with stars. The discrepancy between the two didn't seem at all remarkable to Margaret, but she was used to such places.

Jack sat on the floor, long legs splayed out in front of him. The tails of his coat pooled on either side of his figure like limp black wings.

"You look terrible," Margaret said, slouching down against the wall beside him. "Like you're all dried up."

"I lost her, Maggie."

"Lost who?"

"My girl. Katy. She's faded back into wherever it is that she first came from."

Margaret shook her head. "That's hard. You want some," she added, offering him a stick of chewing gum.

"No, thanks."

She unwrapped a piece and stuck it in her mouth, returning the rest of the package to her pocket.

"You ever tell her you're her father?" she asked.

Jack shook his head. "No. She liked me. I didn't want to screw that up."

"If you think a kid wouldn't want to meet her father, you're really out of touch."

"Even one who abandoned her the way I did? One who went along with everything people were saying about how she didn't exist, so there was no point in looking for her?"

"You just got some bad advice," Margaret said. "None of us knew."

"Nettie never gave up."

"And look where it got her."

"That had nothing to do with her chasing after Katy."

"I guess."

Margaret looked out through the window from which the sunlight came in. She didn't recognize the view, but then she didn't really know the Tombs all that well, never really liked the place. It was too used up. Sometimes you looked on a ruined structure and you could still appreciate the splendor it had lost, but that never happened to her in the Tombs.

"What about the other one?" she asked.

"Kerry."

"Are you going to tell her?"

"I think I let her life get messed up enough as it is without me bringing more trouble into it."

Margaret sighed. "I'd say you should let her make up her own mind on that, but I guess I'd be wasting my breath."

Jack didn't reply for a long time. Finally he put a hand on her knee.

"I appreciate your sitting with me," he said.

Margaret covered his hand with her own.

"Sometimes I understand Cody's wanting to change things," Jack told her then. "You know, going back and trying to make right what you screwed up the first time around."

"It never works."

"I know that. I'm just saying I understand the impulse."

"You've got too much sympathy for that mangy old dog," Margaret said. "Sometimes it seems to me that everything that ever went bad came out of something he did."

"He didn't send Nettie to the cuckoos."

"And neither did we. I'm not saying we can't make our own mistakes. I'm just saying we don't need Cody adding to them."

Jack shrugged. It was an old argument.

Margaret changed tack. "The crow girls had me looking out for a friend of yours down Tucson way."

"Who's that?"

"Lily Carson—a photographer."

Jack nodded. "Oh, sure. I know her. She's a good listener." He gave Margaret a curious look. "What's she got to do with the crow girls?"

"I thought maybe you could tell me. Lily's got the cuckoos chasing after her, though I don't think she knows it."

"The crow girls've got a thing about the cuckoos."

"And you don't?"

"I'm done killing them," Jack said.

"Maybe. That who you're hiding from, Jack?"

At first she thought he wasn't going to answer.

"Meanness comes naturally to them," he said finally. "Trouble is, they call that meanness up in us, too. Take a look at the crow girls. Sweetest kids you'd ever want to meet until you put a cuckoo in front of them and then they're all knives and hardness."

"The crow girls aren't kids," Margaret said. "They're older than any of us, except maybe Raven."

"You know what I mean."

"I guess."

"I don't like who I become when those cuckoos are around," Jack said. "That's what it boils down to. I don't want to know that person. I don't want to be that person."

Margaret waited him out.

Jack sighed. "You weren't there, Margaret. You heard about it, but you didn't see what they did to her."

He was talking about Nettie again.

"That was bad," Margaret agreed. "Maybe as bad as it gets. But what if it happens again—to someone else we care about? It'd be worse this time. If they get their hands on Raven's pot . . ."

"That damn pot. Why does it have to be our responsibility?"

"Someone's got to do it."

"Yeah, and we're doing such a great job of it, too."

Margaret had no argument with that. But she didn't know if it was entirely their fault. There was something about that pot that made it easy to misplace, to forget. Then you'd hold it in your hands and you couldn't imagine ever letting a piece of magic like that slip out of your mind.

"We're going to need everybody's help on this," she said.

Jack gave her a slow nod and got to his feet. He offered her a hand up, then looked out the window—not the one that offered a view of the Tombs, but the one that opened out onto some night, somewhere.

"That's a peaceful dark," he said. "There's not an ounce of loneliness in it."

"I remember."

"It belonged to us once. That's what Cody's looking to bring back."

"I've got friends to ease that loneliness," Margaret told him. "And that's what Cody's looking to take away."

"I said the same thing to Ray."

"Maybe they don't live long," Margaret said. "Not like us. But I figure they're worth fighting for."

Jack nodded, still looking out at the dark.

"You know what scares me?" he said.

Margaret shook her head.

He turned to her with haunted eyes. "If the killing starts again, this time I don't think I'll be able to stop."

Margaret didn't have an answer to that.

6

THE LONESOME DEATH OF NETTIE BEAN

What we want most is a secret
That no one can tell us.
　　　　　　　　—ANONYMOUS

1.

Hazard, Late summer, 1983

There's those that say that Nettie has another breakdown when Lilah and her husband took Kerry away from Hazard. You can understand people's point, if you take the time to look at it from their perspective. Best they can make out is Nettie's just gone feral. She takes to the woods again, but not to collect stories. She's not sketching or keeping a journal—working up something to be published or hung in a gallery, which they think is strange enough. It's like when she was that fox child I first met all those years ago, doesn't matter she's a woman grown. She's running wild, plain and simple. Has a purpose, but it makes no more sense to the locals than when she was looking for some lost daughter that was never born.

She's looking for magic.

She's looking to fly.

She reaches for it the way the crow girls travel, gives herself time to stop and look at everything. Goes tumbling through the wooded hills like an acorn bouncing down the branches of its oak, following the wind, chasing fancies real and imagined, reading portents in the way moss flakes on a stone, mushrooms grow from a stump, a snag points its long length between the trees still standing.

She's tracking down the wild crow boys, climbing up in their trees and trying to talk to them while they're wearing their black feather skins. She's sitting on the porch with that old juju woman who lives at the head of Copper Creek, the two of them listening to the clink of glass coming from the bottle tree in front of the house, the wind brushing the bottles against each other, Nettie asking questions, the juju woman shaking her head, she doesn't know. She's pestering Alberta and Jolene and Bear, but they can't help her. Crazy Crow comes by and tries to talk some sense into her, and later Annie and Margaret, but she won't listen to anybody.

She's got this idea that once she gets hold of some piece of magic she can call her own, once she can fly, she'll be able to bring Kerry back from California to live with her. She'll be able to find her other daughter, the one that got lost before she had the chance to get born.

"It's never going to happen," Crazy Crow tells her, trying one last time.

He's right, but he's wrong, too. In the regular turn and spin of the world, it isn't going to happen. Doesn't matter how deep the fox blood runs in her, canids don't fly. But he should've remembered that nothing's impossible if you want it bad enough—hell, doesn't the story go that the whole reason the world's here for us to mess up the way we do is because Raven was looking for someplace to fly? He couldn't do it on his own, but you put enough heads together and a thing'll get done.

Only Crazy Crow forgot that, so he didn't think he could help. The crow girls would have known what to do, but they were off in Tibet at the time. I know, because I ran into them there, on my way back to the Americas from a summer spent on the shores of the Dead Sea.

"Give it a rest," Crazy Crow says. "Appreciate what you've got."

"I know what you're doing," Nettie tells him. She's looking wild, hair all knotted and caught up with seeds and twigs, wearing a circle of burrs on the hem of her ragged dress. "You're the voice in the wilderness, come to dissuade me. But I won't be dissuaded in this."

Crazy Crow gives up on her then. Most folks do. But she doesn't give up. Not on flying. Not on finding her missing daughter. She just keeps digging, deeper and deeper, further afield, until somewhere she hears about the Morgans and that's when it all goes bad.

In human terms, the Morgans are an old moonshining family that lives back in the hills where no one goes unless they've got legitimate business. If you don't have legitimate business in Freakwater Hollow, you don't come back.

Inbred, folks'd say, seeing how they all have that same Morgan look—tall and lean, men and women both, handsome, dangerous, clannish. They age well, silver-haired and dark-eyed from their teens on, and they don't seem to have children, least no one sees any Morgan children. Story goes that mean as the Morgans are, their children are worse, so they keep them kenneled up somewhere out beyond where they run their stills, deep, deep in the hills. Keep them there until they're old enough to act civilized, if that's what you can call a Morgan's behavior.

We know them better. They don't kennel their children. They leave them in other people's nests like faerie changelings, come and collect them when they're grown. "Grown" for a Morgan usually means they've killed off the family that raised them and are ready to spread their wings. Round about then their birth parents come to collect them and bring them back into the hills.

There's serious bad blood between us. Goes back forever it seems and I've never been able to track down the story of how exactly it all got started. I remember once, before he went away, Raven told me there was no big mystery, we just had to keep them in check because that's the way it was. Someone had to do it and we got elected, same as that pot of his was our responsibility.

"Comes from being the oldest," he said. "Certain things we've got to do. Everybody's got a role to play—world wouldn't turn without us all doing our part."

Maybe that's why things are the way they are now. Raven's turned his back on his responsibilities and the world's been going downhill ever since. I don't know what part it is the Morgans are supposed to play unless it's to catch and skin corbæ and they're too damned good at that.

But Nettie doesn't know any of this. No one's ever thought to tell her. So there she is one afternoon, walking barefoot up Plum Hollow Road, what the locals call 'Shine Road on account of the Morgans and their stills and marijuana fields. They're watching her as she follows that old dirt track up into the wooded hills, some of them pacing her through the trees on either side, rifles in hand, others winging it above. She doesn't smell like the law or trouble, so they let her come, curious about this raggedy woman who doesn't have enough good sense to stay away.

When she finally reaches their place it's nothing like she expected. It doesn't look magic, it just looks rundown. Big old barn up on the hill, wood beams gone the same gray as that silvery Morgan hair, tin sheets rattling on the roof whenever a wind comes up. Junked cars and pickups in the fields. A couple of others that don't look like they're in much better condition parked in the dirt yard that lies between the barn, the clapboard farmhouse, and the outbuildings. There's trash everywhere. Morgans don't keep a clean nest.

It's so quiet it feels like there's a storm building, but the sky's blue for as far as Nettie can see. She looks around some, wondering if maybe the place is abandoned, until she suddenly notices the woman in a rocking chair on the porch that fronts the house, just sitting there, looking at her, smiling. Something about that smile's not quite right, but Nettie, she's not noticing that sort of thing. She smiles back and crosses the yard until she's standing by the porch.

"You lost?" the woman asks.

She's genuinely curious. There's a throaty, hollow-toned ring to her voice, as though the sound of it's coming up from the bottom of a well. Or a crypt. Her name's Idonia and she's the matriarch of this clan, hundreds of years old but she looks the same as any Morgan, late twenties, early thirties, smooth pale skin, silvery hair, dark eyes.

"No, ma'am," Nettie says. "If this is the Morgan farm, then I'm right where I looked to be."

" 'Ma'am,' " Idonia repeats and she has to shake her head. Nettie's politeness is even more puzzling than her being here. "You got a reason for dragging your bony self into my yard?"

"My name's Nettie Bean."

"Oh, I know *who* you are," Idonia says. "I can smell the corbæ on you like a piece of roadkill gone bad—that's a stink that doesn't go away with a bath or two, girl." Idonia's been around so long, any human she meets is a child in her eyes. "What I can't figure is what would possess you to come walking in here."

Nettie doesn't question that Idonia knows who she is, or worry about how maybe this isn't the safest place to be for someone who's known to be a corbæ friend.

While they're talking, Morgans are drifting into the farmyard. Ambling from the barn and outbuildings, ghosting in from the woods, all of them looking pretty much the same, the way a nest of bugs do when you turn over an old stone or stump, you can't quite see what's what as they go skittering away. A few of them are roosting in feathered skins on the roof of the porch and in the twisty boughs of the old crab apple tree growing up along one side of it. But Nettie doesn't seem to notice any of them.

"I've heard you can teach me how to fly," is all she says.

Idonia starts to laugh, she can't help it.

"Where'd you hear that, girl?" she asks.

"I can't remember—it's like I just knew it one day. But you've got to tell me, ma'am. Is it true?"

"Well, now," Idonia tells her. "That's about as true as it gets."

One of the Morgans in the yard snickers and Idonia shoots him a dirty look, but Nettie doesn't catch it. She's got a glow on her from Idonia's news that just won't quit.

"It's not easy," Idonia warns her.

"I'm not a-scared of hard work."

Idonia gives her a solemn nod, fixes a serious expression on that long narrow Morgan face.

"And it can hurt some," she adds. "At first, I mean. But after that you'll be fine."

Nettie just squares her thin shoulders. "When can we start?"

"Right now, girl," Idonia tells her.

She gets up out of her rocker and joins Nettie where she's standing in the dirt, puts her arm around Nettie's shoulders and starts walking her up the hill to the barn. There's maybe twenty Morgans standing around now, smiling at Nettie, and for the first time she starts to feel a little nervous, hesitates. Idonia gives her shoulders a squeeze.

"Don't you be fretting yourself about my family," she promises. "We're going to treat you the same as we do all our guests."

Nettie lets herself relax then, not stopping to think that Idonia didn't say she'd treat her good or bad, just the same.

"Back off," Idonia tells her family as the whole crowd starts to follow them up to the barn. "Give us some room to breathe. None of you got work to do?"

By the time they reach the door of the barn, there's only Nettie and Idonia and a couple of her boys left. Daniel and Washington. Don't wonder how I know their names. I know everybody who was there. I've got their

names chiseled in my heart the way a stonemason works
letters into a tombstone—big and plain, for all to read,
so the weather can't wear them down, so nobody can
forget. So I can't forget.

So they're at the door of the barn and everybody else
fades away, going back to whatever it was they were
doing when Nettie first arrived. The birds that were
perched on the porch and in the crab apple tree fly in
through the doors ahead of them and get swallowed by
the dark lying inside.

"What's in here?" Nettie asks, feeling a little nervous
again.

There's a smell in the air she can't place. Like something died, but not recently. An old dead smell.

"This is where we'll fix you up with your feather
skin," Idonia tells her as she leads the way inside.

Nettie follows her in, blinking at the dark. The smell's
stronger here, so thick it seems to layer like fine dust on
the walls of her lungs. Then her eyes start to adjust to
the dimness and she feels faint, would have fallen except
there's a Morgan boy on either side of her, keeping her
on her feet, fingers holding on to her arms like vises
squeezed tight.

"You're not changing your mind, are you?" Idonia
asks.

"I . . . I . . ."

Nettie can't talk. All she can do is stare up where
thousands of crow skins hang from the rafters, dangling
on long thin strips of leather like herbs drying—heads,
legs, black feathers all still attached. Most of them are
our little cousins, but here and there's a bigger shape,
some corbæ got too close to Freakwater Hollow and
didn't get away fast enough.

"Where'd you think you'd get your feather skin?"
Daniel asks her, his voice a throaty rasp in her ear.
"Outta thin air?"

"Now don't you go scaring her, Daniel," Idonia says.

Washington laughs. "Too late for that."

Nettie finds a last piece of strength, lying there at the bottom of her heart, half-buried by the sickness that seeing all those dead crows has put in her. She tries to pull away, but those Morgan boys just haul her along, deeper into the barn.

It's not Nettie's dying that calls to me, but her need to make her peace. That's what brings me to her where she's lying at the bottom of the craggy point up past the Bean farm. The Morgans left her there, broken like a raggedy doll, made her a skin of feathers and then dropped her off the top of the cliff. They left her for dead but she's too strong for them, can't die until she knows that lost daughter of ours will be looked after.

That need of hers focuses sharp as a knife. It reaches out to me where I'm visiting some cousins on the coast of northern Oregon, puts a fire and a pain in my chest and draws me to her side. I take the first flight out of Portland to Newford and fly the rest of the way under my own steam, but I still don't get to her until late in the day. And then I'm standing over her and all I can do is weep to see what's become of my little wild fox girl.

"God . . . goddamn . . . you . . . Jack . . . ," is what she says when her gaze focuses on me. "Always . . . too late. . . ."

I can't talk. There are no words to ease what's been done to her. I kneel at her side, drop some water between those parched lips of hers, wipe her brow with a wet cloth, and all the time I'm dying inside.

"You . . . you've got to . . . do this . . . thing . . . for me. . . ."

The peace she needs to make isn't with me. It's with that lost daughter of hers.

"You got to . . . promise me. You'll . . . find her. You'll . . . keep her . . . safe."

I haven't got crow girl magic. I can't mend the broken bones, the torn flesh. I don't even know if they can, this is so bad. But I've got to get them to try.

"Let me get the girls," I tell her. "See if they can't—"

"*Promise me.*"

Those sky-blue eyes of hers are cloudy with pain, but their gaze pins me and I can't turn away.

"I promise," I say. "I'll find her, no matter how long it takes. I'll find her and bring her over from wherever it is she's gotten lost."

"Suh . . . safe. . . ."

I nod. "And I'll keep her safe. But right now you've got to let me . . ."

But that's all she was hanging on for. She hears me say what she needed me to say and then she finally lets go. I stare at the stillness that she's become and all the darkness in the world comes swelling up inside me. I can't hardly breathe. I can't think. My hand's shaking as I close her eyes, then I bow my head to the ground and I can't stop crying.

I keep asking myself, over and over, why'd I ever have to come into her life? Why'd I have to make such a mess of everything?

But there aren't answers to that kind of thing.

I lift my head and scream my grief into the sky, scream until my throat's torn raw and all that comes out is a whispery rasp that still holds more pain in it than I ever thought a body could bear.

It's almost dark before I can finally stand up and carry her back to the farmhouse. I take out those feathers, one by one, wash her body, dress her in one of those pretty flower-print dresses of hers. I comb out her hair and then I carry her again, down that familiar path we used to take through the woods.

I bury her in that field of grace, with the stone where we first met to watch over her. With every shovelful of dirt I can feel myself growing colder and colder, like I'm carrying a piece of winter inside me. When I finally get the job done, I stand there in the moonlight and look down at the grave.

"I know I made you a promise," I say, "and I'll keep it. But . . ." I have to swallow, but it doesn't do much for the big lump that's sticking in my throat. "I've got me some other business to get out of the way first, Nettie. I . . . I'm hoping you'll understand."

Grief is a stone in my chest and I know nothing's going to ease the pain because nothing can bring Nettie back. But this isn't something I can let go. Everything's shut down in me, except for this thing I've got to do.

I make a visit to a gunrunner down in Tyson, wake him out of bed around four in the morning. He starts to give me some jaw, but then he takes a look at my face and he shuts right up. I tell him what I need, my voice still a husky rasp, and he sells me an old army-issue U.S. carbine, a .30 calibre M1, throws in a half-dozen boxes of ammo rounds, thirty cartridges to a clip. By four-thirty I'm heading back up past Hazard in a stolen car.

It's getting on to dawn when I leave the car at the foot of 'Shine Road and start walking up toward Freakwater Hollow and the Morgan farm, the same route Nettie took, though I've got different business with the Morgans. The pockets of my duster are weighted down with ammunition clips. The rifle's in my hand, loaded. I'm not making any secret of what I'm doing up here. You don't need to see the rifle—all you've got to do is look in my face.

If those Morgans were smart, they would have hightailed it as far and fast as they could go, left the county, left the damn country. But they're not smart. They're mean, through and through. Bullying, cruel, maybe even cunning. But not smart.

The first guard's dozing under one of those tall lonesome pines. He jolts awake as I come walking past him, starts to get up. My bullet takes him in the throat and drops him back into the pine needles and I keep walking. I kill the second one, too, but the third lives long enough to tell me what I need to know. I engrave the names he gives me on the stone in my chest.

Idonia. Washington. Daniel. Callindra. A half-dozen more. These are the Morgans directly responsible for what happened to Nettie.

"You . . . you're a dead man," he says, coughing up blood.

"You think I don't know that?" I tell him.

He has something else to say, but I pull the trigger before he can get it out.

It goes on like that. I keep cutting down Morgan boys and make my way up that winding dirt road. I take my time, doing a thorough job of it. I shoot some of them out of the air, most of them in the woods that run alongside the road. A few of them get off a round or two, but it's like the cold stone of grief that's lodged in my chest is an enchantment against their bullets. I can't be touched.

By the time I step into the farmyard, I've gone through my first clip and snap another into the carbine. Behind me I've left a trail of dead Morgan boys, but I'm only getting started here.

They don't deserve to die clean and fast like they do, but this isn't just about vengeance. I mean to clean out the whole nest of them, the way you deal with vermin. What happened to Nettie can't happen again to anyone else.

The sun's up now.

Somebody steps out of one of the outbuildings. She's got her hands up in front of her, like she wants to talk, but there's nothing to discuss. The rifle lifts in my hands. There's the loud crack as the bullet exits the muzzle, traveling at six hundred and fifty yards a second. When it hits the figure, it slams her back against the wall of the building.

There's a flurry of gunfire then, coming from all sides, but the charm that's kept me alive this far is still holding. I start picking them off, through the windows, from the rooftops, in the woods.

It's over fast. The quiet that follows is profound. Nothing much lives up in Freakwater Hollow, but you can't hear anything now. No birdsong. No insects. Just the stillness, smelling of death. I drop a second clip onto the dirt of the farmyard and snap in the next. Wait a moment. See a movement alongside the barn. Drop another Morgan.

There's a shout from the house then. Anger or grief? I can't tell. I turn to face the clapboard building and Idonia's standing there in the doorway with a shotgun in her hand.

"How many of us are you planning to kill?" she says.

The barrel of that shotgun's aimed my way. It's a good weapon for a mediocre marksman. Lots of stopping power and the odds are good of scoring a hit if you're in the limits of its effective range. I'm well within the limits.

"How many you got?" I ask.

"Christ, you're such a little pissant," she says. "Can't you take a joke?"

We both know how this is going down. There's nobody left. If there was, she wouldn't be standing there by herself. But if she's got to take a fall, she's going with bravado. The only thing a cuckoo carries more of than meanness is pride.

"I didn't think it was funny," I tell her.

I drop her before her finger can tighten on the trigger, shoot her in the throat like I did the first of her boys down on the road coming up. The impact sends her reeling back into the house. The shotgun goes off, blowing out the upper right-hand corner of the doorjamb, but it's only a reflex of her hand muscles.

I know I've cleaned out the whole nest of them now, but they're not all dead. Not all the Morgans live up here in Freakwater Hollow. But these are the only ones I had to deal with today. These are the ones that hurt my wild fox girl.

That grief swells strong in me again. I let the carbine

fall to the dirt and I can't move. All I can do is stand there, with my heart turned to stone.

I'm still standing there when the sheriff's men come. They don't see a corbæ wearing a man's skin when they pull up in their vehicles, falling over themselves to haul out their guns and train them on me. They see a black man.

Nobody ever had any love for the Morgan clan in these hills—they made about as many human friends as they did corbæ. But the difference is, they looked white, and bad though they were, some things always come down to skin color. In these hills, poor white trash is still a tall step up from a black man.

They take me to the county seat in Tyson to stand trial. There's some more killing as I wait for my court date. The ones dying are Morgans, coming up from other parts of the country, looking for payback, meeting up with corbæ before they can get to me in the jail. Pretty soon those Morgans get the message.

Chloë stands me a lawyer, but there's not much he can do. The only thing I'll say in my defense is, "They needed killing," and that's no defense at all. It leaves everyone to worrying about what's going to happen to me. Except for me. I don't think at all. All I am is empty and cold. All I know is that stone of grief I'm carrying with me. I don't go away like Raven—the grief holds me here—but I don't know much else. Everything goes by fast and I don't pay much attention to any of it, can't seem to focus. Not on the trial, not on the jury's verdict of guilty, not on the judge's sentencing. Makes no difference to me if I'm in the county jail while the trial's on, or sitting on death row, waiting to die.

Because Nettie's still dead. None of their words, nothing they can say or do to me, can change that.

That lawyer Chloë hired me wants to appeal, but I'm not interested. He means well. He tries to argue with me, but all I can think is, when did Nettie get a chance to appeal?

When they finally set a date, I don't even hear them tell me I've got two weeks left to live.

It just doesn't seem all that important.

One winter's night, the week before my execution, Annie comes to see me. I don't know how she gets in. Slips in through some window somewhere, I guess, and ghosts her way down to my cell. Or maybe she finds a fold in the way the fabric of place is bunched up around here. I haven't been looking myself. There's no need for short-cuts where I'm going.

I'm stretched out, taking up most of the narrow bed in my cell when she comes in. My eyes are open, but I'm not looking at anything. It takes me awhile to register her presence. I don't know how long she's been sitting there on the end of the bed before I finally notice her.

"You got a death wish?" she asks.

It takes me awhile to work that through.

"I don't have any wish at all," I say.

Though that's not true. Given a wish, I'd ask for Nettie to be alive. For her not to have died, and died so hard and alone.

Annie shakes her head. "When're you going to tell us what this is all about?"

"Nettie's dead."

"We *know* that, Jack. But what happened? What did those Morgans do to her that'd make you up and kill them all?"

I've never explained. It's bad enough I've got the memory of it, that big stone of grief taking up all the breathing space in my chest, without handing over pieces of it to the rest of my kin. No one else should have to feel this cold I've got in me, like they're walking dead.

Annie leans forward. "Jack," she says. Her voice is soft, soothing. Always was. Lord, that girl can hold a tune. You'd never think she was a jay, to hear her speak. "They're going to kill you next week."

"I know that."

"I'm not even going to argue with you about why you're not putting up a fight," she says. "But you can't let her story die with you."

"Why not?"

"Because it's not right. You've told me yourself, in the end, stories are all we've got. They're who we are and what we are and why we are. We've got to share them with each other, the good and the bad. Maybe especially the bad, you said to me once, because anyone who doesn't remember history is doomed to repeat it. Do you want whatever it was that happened to Nettie to happen to someone else?"

I shake my head wearily. "That's why I killed them all."

"You didn't kill them all," Annie says. "The world's still full of cruelty and meanness—human and blood. Cuckoos are still breeding and dropping their eggs in other people's nests. You think your killing a few Morgans is going to stop all the rest of the misery in the world? You think it'll stop those cuckoos from hurting somebody else?"

"I don't know anymore," I say. "I don't know that the stories do any good. We're all so good at hurting each other, even when we mean well. Even when we know the stories."

"There's a big difference between doing something wrong by accident and doing it on purpose," Annie tells me. "And how're people going to know it, unless someone tells them the stories?"

I'm thinking, she just doesn't understand.

"Talk to me, Jack."

But then I remember what not giving Nettie my story got us.

"Sorrow halved, Jack," she says. "When you share it. Remember that? It's something else you told me."

I remember Chloë pointing at Raven one time and reminding me how we had two choices. We can carry on, or we can go away, withdraw from the world like Raven has, and that doesn't do anybody any good. I realize then that what I'm letting happen to me is just another way of going away.

I open my mouth to speak, but the words won't come. I'm thinking of my Nettie and tears flood my eyes. My throat gets so thick it's like that stone of grief is trying to rise up it. I try to close it all down, to go away, to embrace the cold—this is too raw; this hurts too much— but Annie won't let me. She puts her arms around me and draws my head down onto her shoulder. She doesn't make like it's going to get better, doesn't promise me anything, but just her being there's enough.

Sorrow shared.

It's a long while before I can find my voice. After a time we end up lying together on that narrow bed of mine, she's holding me, and I'm talking, I'm telling her the whole sorry tale, and it's while I'm telling it that I remember the promise I made Nettie.

All that killing I did killed something in me, but I can see a glimmer of it shining bright when I'm talking. It's way off in the dark, flickering and calling to me, but I know the way to chase it isn't to go away like Raven did, but to carry on. I sit up and swing my feet to the floor.

"I've got to find that girl," I say, my voice a hoarse whisper.

Annie sits up beside me. "You can't do that by dying."

"I'm not dying."

"Not anymore you're not," Annie tells me and then she walks me out of that place.

I hear later that the crow girls came by and left a changeling in my place—some kind of jackdaw man they put together out of twigs and mud and moss and things.

Dressed it up in my prison clothes and left it on the bed. It wasn't made to last long, but then it didn't need to. It only had to stay of a piece for as long as it took the guards to walk it down that long hall on death row and execute it. Long enough for them to dig a hole for it and then throw it in.

By the time the gravediggers had that makeshift man covered up with dirt, it was already turning back into whatever it was the girls had made it out of and I was long gone, walking the piney wood hills around the Bean farm, looking for that daughter of Nettie's and mine that never got herself born.

2.

Hazard/Long Beach, Spring, 1984

I spend that winter in the hills around Hazard, but I have no more luck finding the lost girl than Nettie did. I have more to go on in my search than Nettie ever had, access to secret places she never knew existed, long views of the winter woods from high up in those frosty skies, but it doesn't help. I find every hidden fold in the fabric of those hills and check it out, once, twice, a dozen times, just to be sure. I fly over more square miles of wooded hills than you can imagine.

There's no gossip about her the way there was for my little wild fox girl that summer we first met. If the lost girl was ever here, she didn't leave any traces behind her. Nothing. She's got less presence than a ghost, less substance than a memory—though Lord knows there's plenty of them here for me.

I have help from time to time, but nobody's got a reason to stick with it the way I do. When the months go by, nobody tries to talk me out of it, nobody tries to tell me that I did my best and it's time to give it up now. I guess they figure it's better to have Jack out walking these hills on a fruitless quest than stepping out of the world the way Raven did. At least this way nobody's got to care for me the way Chloë looks after him.

There are Morgans back in Freakwater Hollow, but they keep their distance from me, and I keep mine from them. I can't afford to step back into that place where that killing frenzy took me last year. It's not just because being there would shut me away from my search. It's that it's wrong. I don't want to be the person I'd be if I let myself go there again. That's something I know I can't repeat because if I did, I know this time I'd never get back again.

I guess it's close on the end of April when I get the notion to see how the twin that got born is doing, thinking maybe I can find some clue by looking at her, listening in on her life, watching over her.

I fly down from spring in the Kickaha Hills north of Newford to that piece of oceanfront land in California that you humans have claimed from the desert and made your own.

There's no accounting for what some folks'll do. You'll take a perfectly good section of land and ooh and ahh over just how pristine and untouched it is, but then you have to change it out of all recognition before you can be comfortable in it. I've seen you do it over and over again and it makes no more sense to me now than it did when your ancestors were first chipping away at rocks and cutting down the woods to build themselves their shelters. You never build just what you need, the way we would a nest. You've got to spread out as far as you can, cut down a whole forest, irrigate a whole desert, just to make sure that you won't accidentally stumble upon a place that's still in its natural state.

Long Beach isn't much different. Worse than some, not so bad as others. Mind you, I remember what it was like before you got to it and there's no comparison. 'Course I got my own bias—same as you. But living in an environment I can't control doesn't scare me. I'm partial to the surprises.

Doesn't take me too long to track down the Madan household. Maybe Kerry isn't bearing the Bean name, but I wasn't looking by names. I was going by smell and she's got so much of the blood in her—canid and corbæ—that she's not hard to find at all.

I take to sitting on her windowsill while she's sleeping, just looking at the marvel she is. We made that girl, I think—me and Nettie, except Nettie did all the real work. But sometimes when I look at her, I have to ask myself, what for?

Kerry doesn't seem to have what I'd call a good life. No woods to run in. No real friends, human or blood. Not much affection from either Lilah or her husband. They don't treat her mean. They make sure she gets a good schooling, learns her manners, how to carry herself. But they don't give her any love either and that's hard for a child to bear. Even those plants you folks have transplanted to this desert need their water. They need some tenderness and caring. A child's no different. You can't put her in a desert and expect her to flourish without her parents' love.

But then Lilah's her half sister, not her real mother, and Stephen's not really any relation at all. Kerry doesn't know it, but her mother's dead and her father's a no-account jackdaw who follows her around when she leaves the house and sits perched on her windowsill at night, sitting there looking in at her and wishing with all his heart that things could be different.

But they're not. I can't do much to help Kerry—it's not like she'd have any better of a life, wandering around homeless with me—and I have no more luck finding her lost twin sister here than I did back in the hills around Hazard. I toy with the idea of taking on a young boy's shape and finding some natural way to meet Kerry, just so's she can at least have herself one friend, but all I've got to do is think how that worked out with her mammy and the dark cold comes slipping back into my heart, the grief rears up in my chest, and I have to fly off, hard and fast, fly for miles until I can burn off enough of that grief and pain to at least pretend I'm all of a piece.

Finally I realize there's nothing more I can do here. I can't help Kerry, can't find her sister, and I'm ready to take the search back to Hazard again. I sit there on the windowsill for one last time, looking in, drinking in the sight of that sleeping child, and then I see her, the missing twin. She's lying there inside of Kerry, a little bundle of bones and hair, all curled up, sleeping under Kerry's skin.

I even know her name.

Katy.

It comes to me as clear as though someone's whispered it in my ear. The lost girl's name is Katy and she was never lost at all. She just got herself caught up under the skin of her sister and she's too deep asleep to make it out into the world on her own now.

I study the pair of them for a long time, but I can't see a way clear to getting her out without hurting Kerry in the process. But if I can't do it, there's those that can. They just need a nudge to get them looking in the right place.

Flying around to the other side of the house, I perch on Lilah and Stephen's windowsill and put the idea of Kerry needing a checkup at the doctor's office into their minds. Once I get that done, I make sure that doctor twigs to what's sleeping under Kerry's skin. They start in on the X rays, admit Kerry into the hospital, she goes into the surgery theater, but it doesn't work out like I hoped.

Katy's not sleeping—it must have been an echo of Kerry's heartbeat I heard and mistook for hers. The doctor gets her out all right, and they stitch Kerry up again, do a beautiful job of it, except the lost girl doesn't get born, she doesn't get to live. The poor little thing's born dead, if you can call it being born when all they do is take out the fossilized pieces of her that have been hiding there inside her sister for the past twelve years.

Another piece of my heart gets broke when I sneak in and collect that little bundle of bones and hair. I wrap it up in a scarf and put it in the inside pocket of my duster, where it can lie against my heart, and then I take it back up to Hazard, out to that field of grace, where I bury the unborn child beside her mammy, under the watchful presence of that old gray stone.

I don't go back to see Kerry. I couldn't do anything for her before and I still can't do anything for her now.

Some things don't change, I guess. I'm never going to be of much use to anyone in that family and I realize the best thing I can do is just stay out of the surviving child's life. I only wish I'd done that before I ever met my little wild fox girl. The idea of never having known Nettie hurts, but I'd rather suffer that and a thousand more powerful hurts, if it could have meant that Nettie wouldn't have had to endure what she did. If it could have meant that she'd still be alive.

I could've let myself go then, just let that store of grief I carry in me bear me down, but I've taken on the responsibility of my stories again, doing my best to keep history alive so that we don't repeat our mistakes. I end up moving down to Newford, take to living in that old school bus of mine near the junkyard, walking the streets, collecting stories, telling them to whoever will listen.

And time goes by.

3.

Newford, Fall, 1995

Retrospect's a wonderful thing. All those things we could have, would have, should have done, had we only known. Except we didn't. And maybe some things just have to play out the way they do—which isn't exactly a comforting thought. It calls up too many questions I can't answer. All I know for sure is that by the middle of the eighties it looks like the hard times fate has in store for the Bean family haven't ended with Nettie dying.

Chloë's lawyer managed to keep Nettie out of the institution, but some fifteen years or so later, none of us were there to stop Lilah and her husband from putting Nettie's daughter away. And once Kerry's inside, there's not a damn thing we can do to get her out again because Kerry won't let go of her own obsession, and we can't prove it's true.

Hell, Katy showing up the way she does isn't something we can explain any better than you can.

None of us even knew that Katy had survived until Paul was out on the West Coast a couple of years after she'd been "born"—that'd be late in '85, when Kerry had already been committed. Chloë had asked him to check in on the Madans to see how Kerry was doing and he came back with a story that actually takes Chloë out of the Rookery and down to my school bus.

"You told me she was dead, Jack," Chloë says, sitting there at the kitchen table, looking across at me.

We've already had us some snow and the winds are strong outside the bus today, blowing trash across the empty lots, building drifts wherever the snow can get some purchase. Winter's settling in. I have my woodstove stoked with a kettle set on top, boiling some water for tea. I forget about the water when I hear what Chloë has to say. All I can do is stare at her.

"Your water is boiling," she says.

I get up and pour it over the tea bags in the teapot, bring the pot to the table, set out honey and milk, going through the motions mechanically because I can't think straight. For a long time I just can't get my head around what she's just told me.

"She *was* dead," I say finally. "I buried that little bundle of bones and hair up in Hazard, right beside her mammy."

"So what're we dealing with here?" Chloë asks. "A spirit? A ghost?"

You might think this strange, but we don't have much more experience with spirits and ghosts than you do, except for how you put those names to us sometimes. So Katy's about as much of a mystery to us as she is to you, the difference being we're a little more open-minded about that kind of thing.

"Damned if I know," I tell her. "But I'm going to find out."

A gust of wind shakes the bus, rattling the windows.

"What about Kerry?" I ask. "Can you get her out?"

Chloë shakes her head.

"I could get her out," I say.

"I'm sure you could," Chloë says. "But then what? We're discussing a thirteen-year-old girl here, Jack."

I know where she's going with this and I can see her point. I've already been through all of this in my own head when I was down there in Long Beach myself and made the decision to stay out of Kerry's life. I'd realized then that I'd brought enough grief to the Beans and wasn't prepared to bring any more. But that was before she'd been institutionalized.

"I'm not standing by again," I say. "Doing nothing."

"I'm not saying you should," Chloë tells me. "But we have to consider the other child now. What's going to happen to her with nobody even believing she exists?"

I find myself nodding. It makes sense that she'd be more in need of my help. And Katy was the one Nettie made me promise to look out for.

"But I'll look in on Kerry," I say. "Make sure they're not mistreating her."

Chloë's got no argument with that.

I head down the next day.

First thing I do is stop by that Baumert Hospital and check in on Kerry. From how it looks to me, she seems to be doing okay, though you have to understand that I'm not exactly an expert when it comes to these kinds of places. When I see her so calm, I don't realize they've medicated all the fire out of her. I see the doctor talking so nicely to her and I don't know that she's being paid under the table to keep Kerry in that medicated state. I find myself thinking that maybe she's better off here, instead of living with Lilah and her husband. Maybe she'll have a better chance to grow up happy, out of their mean-spirited influence.

So I leave Kerry in that place and I go looking for her sister. I still don't know what Katy is—spirit or ghost or something else entirely that we haven't got a name for yet—but she has the same canid-corbæ smell that Kerry does and she's not that hard to track. I find her a little farther south, down the coast in Seal Beach. She's sitting on the low stone wall of that parking lot at the end of Main Street, down by the pier, watching the tide move the water in and out. Red-haired and brown-skinned with those sky-blue eyes she got from her mother.

She pays no more attention to my approach than she does to anybody else on the beach. I'm thinking she's deep in thought until I sit down beside her and say hello. She looks so startled I think maybe I've left a few jackdaw feathers growing out of my forehead when I shucked my corbæ skin, only then I remember Paul saying she's got our knack of not being seen unless she wants to be. I guess she doesn't realize the trick only works with humans.

But while I surprised her, she's quick to compose herself.

"Who're you?" she asks.

"Nobody," I say with a shrug. "Just some old jackdaw needing a place to set for a few minutes. You mind if I share this piece of wall with you?"

She shakes her head. "Go ahead. There's lots of room." She waits a beat before she has to ask, "What do you mean by 'jackdaw'?"

"It's what I am. Corbæ. You got a piece of the first

people in you, too—bit of corbæ, some fox blood. It's why I came up and said hello. Be pretty rude of me not to pass a little time with my kin when I see one of them sitting on her own.''

She gives me a look like she's not sure if I'm putting her on or what.

''Who're these first people?'' she asks.

''You know—we got here before the humans, when Raven and the crow girls pulled the long ago out of the medicine lands and set the world to wheeling through the sky.''

She gives a slow shake of her head, still unsure about where I'm coming from, but interested now, which is what I'm aiming for.

''I have no idea what you're talking about,'' she says.

So I tell her the story, the two of us sitting there in the California sun, watching the waves, nobody looking at us, nobody paying any attention to us at all. To either of us. I see her note that, too.

''Is that true?'' she asks, the way everybody does.

''Pretty much,'' I tell her.

''And I'm one of them?''

I give her a nod. ''The blood's not exactly first generation, but you can't mistake it.''

''I don't remember any of that stuff you're talking about.''

''That's because you weren't there,'' I tell her. ''Leastways, I don't remember you being there. You got yourself born a little further down the road.''

''I didn't get born at all.''

''Then how come you're here? You had to come from somewhere.''

She shrugs. ''I think I just happened—like an accident.''

''You don't want to put yourself down,'' I say. ''You're better off doing what we all should do and that's making the most of yourself, seeing how that's all there is of you.''

She gives me this sweet wise look, a laugh hanging there in the back of her eyes. "So I come from these animal people, huh?"

"There's no arguing it."

"Maybe that's why I'm so different."

"Different from what?"

She makes a motion with her hand that takes in the other people on the beach.

"From them," she says.

"I reckon."

That steady blue gaze of hers studies me for a long moment.

"So do you have a twin, too?" she asks.

I shake my head.

"I do," she tells me. "We look exactly the same, but otherwise we're not at all alike. She's locked into who she is and won't have any fun. And then she makes me feel guilty when I do."

"So you don't much like this sister of yours?"

"Oh, I love her—you can't not. But I don't understand her. I can't figure out why she lets everybody tell her what to do . . . unless it's because she's one of them." She gives me a sudden smile. "I never even knew there was a 'them' before and that makes me feel a whole lot better. I always thought there had to be something wrong with me."

I'm trying to get a measure of her and it's hard. She seems a lot like Nettie at the same age, only she's running wild through a concrete forest instead of those old piney wood hills, and she's full of more contradictions than her mother ever was. As innocent as she is streetwise. Independent, but she's yearning to be looked after. Thoughtful, with a giddy undercurrent.

The more I think of it, maybe she doesn't remind me so much of her mother as she does Maida and Zia. Lose the red hair and you could almost take her for a crow girl without having to work too hard at it. Has the temperament down pat.

"So do you live around here?" I ask.

She shakes her head. "I don't live anywhere in particular, but I like it here." She grins. "It suits me."

"I can see that." I stand up. "Well, maybe I'll see you around."

"If you're ever looking for me," she says, "this is where I'll usually be."

I feel her watching me as I walk off. I get about a block away and she starts to follow, so the first time I'm out of her line of sight, I shift back into my jackdaw skin and fly up to a perch on the closest telephone pole. She looks puzzled when she comes around the corner, checking up and down the street, but she doesn't think to look up. Most people don't. There's a whole world going on up here above their normal sight lines, but it might as well be invisible.

I'm feeling pleased, looking down from my pole. Things worked out pretty good, I'm thinking. I made a connection, intrigued her a bit, let her know she's not alone, she's not some kind of freak, but didn't open the door to her getting dependent on me. What I want to do is have her get comfortable around us, let us be a part of her life so that we can look out for her, but not get her to thinking we hold all the answers. And I particularly don't want to get too close to her myself.

That's not a mistake I'm about to make again.

It works out pretty well for awhile. We take turns checking in on her over the next few years—Margaret, Annie, Paul, the crow girls, Alberta, and some of the others that Nettie used to know from up around Hazard. We feel kind of proprietary about her, considering her history and all, but no one tells her about her real mother. They leave that up to me and it's not something I figure she has to know. If she asked me straight out, I'd have to tell her, because I'm not about to start lying to my own child, but it doesn't come up.

She doesn't talk about her sister much, but you can tell

Kerry's on her mind a lot—why exactly, I don't find out until years later, when Katy moves to Newford. I try to convince her that whether or not Kerry believes she exists makes no never mind, but it's hard to be convincing when none of us can actually explain what she is. Maybe this idea she's got about Kerry is true, but if it is, it's a cruel trick fate's gone and played on her. 'Course fate hasn't proved too kind to the Beans before this and life isn't fair.

"Imagine if life was fair," she says to me one time. "I think maybe that'd be worse."

"How do you figure that?"

"Well, then we'd deserve all the awful things that happen to us, wouldn't we? It'd mean that at some point in our lives—or maybe some life we had before this one—we were pretty creepy people."

I never thought about it like that before. Seems odd to take comfort in life's unfairness, but I start to feel the same way she does.

For a long time I think she's going to stay on the West Coast, but then one day she gets the traveling bug and starts to wandering. She can't change skin like we can, but she gets pretty adept at some of our other tricks— riding around the country for free and the like. Most of them she picks up from Margaret.

I never ask her what put the itch in her feet until she finally shows up in Newford and makes like she's planning to settle down.

"I had to get away from her," Katy explains.

"From who? Kerry?"

She nods and I see the hurt in her eyes. Then she asks me something that makes my heart want to break.

"Have you ever loved someone so much you don't think you can live a moment without them, but at the same time you know that staying with them is maybe the worst thing you can do to them?"

It takes me a long time to get my voice.

"Yeah," I finally manage to tell her. "It's the hardest decision I ever made and the worst thing is, in the end, I made the wrong one. I had the best of intentions, but all I did was screw things up worse."

"I don't think it's something you can work out," she says. "It doesn't matter if you stay or if you go, you're still going to hurt them."

"I can't answer that for you," I say.

"You don't have to," she tells me. "I know that's how it is for me when it comes to Kerry. But I have to try staying out of her life. I don't really feel like I have any choice."

"There's always a choice."

She shakes her head. "I know for sure that my being in her life wasn't ever any help to her at all."

She takes to hanging around the school bus a lot, bringing me coffee or tea or a sweet pastry, casual, like she was just in the area. All she asks in return is for me to tell her stories. I figure she's got too much affection for me, treats me like her best pal and father all rolled into one— an irony that doesn't escape me. But it's too late to do anything about how she feels now and the truth is, I don't want to. Her company means the world to me and I'll do whatever it takes to keep her happy and safe. It's got nothing to do with the promise I made her mother and everything to do with a father's love for his child.

Lord knows I cherish the time we have together. Not just for how good it is, but because one day it's all going to come out . . . who her mother is, how it was between us, how hard Nettie died.

And then Katy's going to hate me forever.

I won't blame her. Whenever I think of what happened to Nettie, I hate myself.

7

CITY OF CROWS

Jack's crows are in for a murder
a murder is a gathering
some watch, some go a little further
some eat what the others bring
* to Jack's crows, Jack's crows*
where everybody's from, and nobody goes
that's where you're gonna find Jack's crows
                    —JOHN GORKA,
                       FROM *JACK'S CROWS*

1.

Newford, Tuesday afternoon, September 3

Tired from a morning's fruitless search for Raven's pot,
Annie found herself a perch in between two gargoyles,
high above the rose window of St. Paul's Cathedral. It
was an old thinking spot of hers that she'd claimed from
the pigeons years ago. She shifted from her blue jay skin
and sat with her back against the thick stone wall behind
her, legs dangling into space. From her vantage point she
could look past the sweep of the cathedral's steps below,
over the roofs of the buildings on Battersfield Road,
across the river and all the way up the wooded slopes
that backed the high-priced real estate of the Beaches.

It was a spectacular view, but today her gaze was
turned inward, scanning landscapes of memory and conjecture.

There was something wrong about all of this.

It wasn't that the pot had gone missing again. The up-

heavals it brought into their lives occurred with such reg-
ularity that Annie had decided a long time ago that the
pot must have a mind of its own, that its periodic dis-
appearances served some private agenda, one only the pot
understood. They were related to the constant discrep-
ancies in its appearance, she was sure, and just because
she was the only one ready to assign sentience to it, it
didn't mean it wasn't true.

So what was it after this time?

Chloë seemed to think that Rory's friend Lily might
have inadvertently come into possession of it—and the
interest that the cuckoos, with their gift for finding things,
had taken in Lily appeared to bear that out—but what
would be the point? Whatever plans the pot might have
for her, Lily couldn't do anything with it. That required
more than the thin trace of grackle blood running through
her veins. And anyway, Annie had gotten no sense of the
pot's presence when she'd flown by Lily's apartment after the meeting last night.

She'd tried talking to the crow girls about it, but they
were as oblique as always. That wasn't particularly unusual either. They pretended indifference to everything,
more often than not, or offered up contradictory advice
as they had last night at the gathering when the pair of
them had come in and suggested they try to smell out the
pot's whereabouts. A fine idea, except the pot didn't have
a smell. It had an aura, but no odor.

Of course, they were at least willing to pitch in. Chloë
hadn't come to the meeting, nor was she helping in the
search. She claimed she couldn't leave Lucius, but Annie
suspected Chloë was simply becoming more and more
agoraphobic. Another few years and she'd be as withdrawn as Lucius.

And that, for no good reason, reminded her of Paul,
who'd been as outgoing as the crow girls, but sensible.
A deep melancholy settled in her. She missed Paul terribly at times, more than the others did, she was sure, but
then she'd been closer to him than anyone. Sometimes,

if she closed her eyes and listened hard, she could still hear his piano.

She did so now, but all she heard was the sound of wings. Opening her eyes, she found that the crow girls had come spiraling down from the sky and joined her. They were perched on the backs of the gargoyles, one on either side of her, regarding her with serious expressions.

"Did you have any luck?" she asked.

But the girls didn't seem at all interested in the missing pot.

"You're looking veryvery sad," Maida said.

Zia leaned forward so that her chin was resting on the broad brow of the gargoyle she was straddling. "Very-very."

"I was thinking about Paul," Annie told them.

"We liked Paul," Maida said.

"He was always nice to us."

"And ever so wonderfully musical."

Annie sighed. "I know. I used to leave my apartment door open so that I could listen to him practice. We always planned to do some recording together, but we never made the time and now it's too late."

"Too late," Zia echoed.

"Those are two of the least fun words in the world," Maida said.

"When they're put together."

Maida nodded. "And in that order."

Annie had to agree. How many lingering regrets weren't born from missed opportunities that could never be recalled?

"About the pot," she said, trying to get the conversation back on a less depressing track, though chasing after that damned pot of Raven's was hardly the most cheerful of occupations. "Have you heard any news?"

"Nothing interesting," Zia said.

"Have you been swooping about, trying to sniff it out?" Maida asked.

Annie nodded. "But it doesn't have any scent. You know that."

"I thought it was a good idea Ray had," Maida said.

"Ray's the one who suggested that?"

Both girls nodded.

"I don't believe this," Annie said. "Yesterday you were ready to stick a knife in him and now you're having little chats?"

"Oh, he's all changed," Maida told her.

"Mm-hmm," Zia said. "He's gone very corbæ now and ever so tasty looking." She put a hand over her mouth and shot Maida a quick glance. "Or was that supposed to be a secret?"

"I don't think so."

"Why's he disguised as one of us?" Annie asked.

"Well," Maida said, drawing out the word. "It could be because we're all so very intriguing and he wants to be just like us."

"But we think it's so that he can follow Kerry around and maybe we won't notice him."

"But of course we did."

"Because we're very observant."

"Of all the corbæ, we're probably the most observant."

Annie had to laugh. "But then you don't know where the pot is either."

"No," Zia said. "But we're not in such a hurry to find it."

"Why not?"

Zia shrugged. "Because it'll just get lost again. Don't you find it all sort of boring?"

"Except it's not really," Maida said before Annie could reply. "Because every time it gets stirred up, the world changes."

"This is true." Zia gave Annie a considering look. "Maybe we should be trying harder."

"Chloë thinks that Lily has it," Annie said, curious as to their reaction.

But of course that simply sent the crow girls off on a new tangent.

"Now Lily's very interesting," Maida said.

Zia nodded. "She has a new boyfriend."

"A very nice boyfriend—all sort of gruff and tumbly."

"But kind."

"Oh, yes," Zia said. "Veryvery kind."

"And she has new enemies, too."

"*And* new friends."

"Like the pair of you?" Annie asked.

Maida shook her head. "We only kind of know her. In a mostly peripheral sort of a way."

"But she's met Margaret, you know," Zia put in.

"And they like each other fine."

"We knew they would."

"That's why we suggested that Margaret go see her in the desert."

Sometimes Annie thought she'd go mad trying to sort out any sort of linear sense in a conversation with this pair.

"In what desert?" she asked.

"You know," Zia said, as though everyone had the same access to what they knew. "For her job."

Maida pretended she was taking pictures with an invisible camera. When she lost her balance, Annie caught her by the scruff of her collar and pulled her back onto the ledge.

"I can fly," Maida said.

"I know."

"Don't get grouchy," Zia told Maida. "She was being nice."

"I wasn't being grouchy."

"You were."

"Well, maybe a very little." Maida gave Annie a sweet smile. "Thank you for catching me."

"Do *you* think Lily has the pot?" Annie asked.

"You were supposed to say, 'You're welcome,'" Maida told her.

"What?"

"When I said, 'Thank you.' If you were polite, you'd say, 'You're welcome, but it was nothing, really,' and then I could say, 'No, really, thank you,' and we would go on smiling and being polite and not asking boring questions."

Annie sighed. "You're welcome," she said. "Now can we be serious for a moment?"

The crow girls exchanged looks that Annie couldn't read.

"The pot's wherever it's supposed to be," Zia said then. "That's how it works."

"Wherever it's supposed to be," Annie repeated.

Maida nodded. "So there's no point in looking for it, really, unless you're planning to write a book about it and you have to write down everything it does—you know, where it's been, who's been carrying it, that sort of thing."

"You've been looking for it," Annie said.

"But only because you asked us to," Maida said.

"And we haven't been looking very hard," Zia added.

Annie began to speak, but Maida leaned over and put a finger against Annie's lips, almost losing her balance again in the process.

"Raven understands," Zia said as Maida regained her perch. "That's why it doesn't matter if he goes away inside himself."

"So everything'll be okay?" Annie asked. "No one's going to get hurt?"

The crow girls both frowned.

"We don't know about that," Maida said.

Zia gave a slow nod of agreement. "Only the pot knows that."

"I thought I was the only one to think it has a mind of its own," Annie said.

"I don't know if it's a mind so much," Zia said. "It's

more like an idea. The way a wind or a view is both a thing and an idea.''

"I think it's more like a storm," Maida said. "You can't hold on to it, but you can't pretend it's not there."

"And the only answers you can get from it are what you'd get from a storm."

Maida nodded. "They wouldn't make any sense."

"But . . ."

"The only way no one gets hurt when the pot's stirred," Zia said, "is when whoever's doing the stirring understands exactly what the pot is and what they're doing, but that means you have to give up a piece of yourself to it."

"It's like trying to break it," Maida explained.

Zia nodded. "But if you do understand it, you can stir up whatever you want."

"I don't understand," Annie said.

"Most of us don't."

"It's like what happened to Paul," Maida added.

Annie gave her a sharp look. Paul had died in his sleep, though she'd always suspected that the cuckoos had poisoned him in retaliation for keeping them out of the city. He'd always worked the hardest of all of them to stop them from leaving their eggs in Newford nests or settling in themselves.

"What happened to Paul?" she asked.

"He stirred up a dream in the pot, but he lost himself in it and never came back."

Annie shivered. "Back from where?"

"The medicine lands."

"But that's . . . impossible, isn't it? The medicine lands are long gone. They only exist in our memories."

"That's why he never came back."

"I always thought it was the cuckoos," Annie said. "That they'd poisoned him."

"Oh, no," Maida told her.

Zia nodded, a dark look in her eyes. "We always kill cuckoos when they even try to hurt someone we love."

"Why . . . why did you never tell me this before?" Annie asked.

"You never asked."

Annie's gaze went from Zia to Maida, searching their unfamiliar solemn expressions for a flippancy that wasn't there.

"No," she said finally. "I guess I never did."

2.

Dominique Couteau picked up Raven's pot as she had dozens of times since she'd finally acquired it this morning. She studied the chalice against the window of her hotel suite, noting the way the light played against the facets of the crystal and the small figure curled up where the stem met the bowl, and was no closer to understanding how it worked or what the figurine was than when she'd first held both in her hands.

Cuckoo lore concerning the pot said nothing about its ability to change into a shape such as this, nor that there would be anything inside it. It frustrated her to no end to know that now she'd have to ask Cody about it. She'd expected Cody to be out of the equation by now. They'd only needed him to find the pot and he hadn't even been able to manage that, tangling everything up in complicated plans involving far too many others. The corbæ weren't even supposed to know that her people were in the city, but Cody appeared to have mismanaged that as well. It was no wonder his plans never resolved as he expected them to. The man was a walking advertisement for incompetence.

But audacious, she thought. She'd have to give him that. Cody walked large, with more to him than first met the eye. In that way he was much like this pot of Raven's. She'd always known it was potent, but who would have thought it could also be such an object of beauty? The only anomaly was the figure curled up in its bottom.

She tipped the chalice, as she had before, but the figurine never shifted. It was the same when she'd tried holding it upside down, tapping the chalice against the suite's plush carpet, or tried to poke at the figure with the end of a clothes hanger. She hadn't quite been ready to risk putting her hand inside to try to pluck it out. There was too much enchantment caught up in this pot of Raven's for her to chance that. All the stories concerning it revolved around one's stirring it—not with a ladle or any other object. It was always one's own flesh and bone.

She could be patient, she thought as there came a knock at her door. But not for too much longer.

Setting the chalice down on the mahogany side table once more, she crossed the room and opened the door to find her son Armand in the hall.

"What is it?" she asked, easing the sharpness of her question by patting him lightly on the cheek.

"I'm sorry to disturb you, *Maman*," he said, "but Gerrard called up to tell me that Cody is in the lobby."

She sighed. "Ah, Cody."

"Should we deal with him now?"

"Unfortunately, no," Dominique told him. "It seems we still have need of his services."

The disappointment in his features was obvious.

"Oh, don't look so put out, *mon cher*," she said. "Soon you will be able to have your fun."

Armand nodded and touched the "Hold" button on his cellular phone. "Send him up," he said into the speaker. Returning his attention to Dominique, he asked, "Shall I wait in the suite with you, *Maman*?"

"No. Let him think we still trust him. I have left the connecting door unlocked. And, Armand?" she added as he began to turn away.

"Oui, Maman?"

"What word on the blackbirds?"

"Still nothing."

"Bon."

The trick to leadership, she'd long since discovered,

was to always appear assured of oneself and in control. So she hid the worry that the corbæ had yet to move against them. So many of her people in their city—when had the crows ever allowed such a thing before? What could they be planning? She was not so foolish as to imagine they weren't planning something.

She walked back to the table and sat down, gaze drawn back to the chalice.

Or were they still too busy searching for this lovely jewel that she'd managed to pluck from under their beaks?

"It's open," she called when there was another knock on the door.

Cody stepped inside, his handsome presence filling the room as it always did. It was easy to see how so many could fall under his spell with no more than a kind word and a smile from him. But she'd taught herself to see through his charm.

"Now's that really so smart?" he asked as he closed the door behind him, then engaged the lock. "This isn't New Orleans, darling. You're sitting in crow city now and nobody's got any reason to love you here. I'd lock my doors if I were you."

He leaned with his back against the door, tall in his cowboy boots, coyote grin in the dark eyes that were half-hidden under the brim of his hat.

"I am not unprotected," she told him, her voice cool.

Her gaze flicked to the door connecting her suite to that of her sons before she could stop herself. She returned her full attention to Cody to find him smiling at her.

"Just so's you're playing it safe," he said.

So he knew, she thought, her features giving nothing away. He'd probably always known that they would turn on him. Fine. She could be patient in dealing with him as well. She would treat him as a trusted ally for as long as it took for him to let down his guard.

So she smiled back at him, guilelessly, as if to say, I

know I should consider you my enemy, an ally for only as long as we need to work together, but you've charmed me too thoroughly.

"We have reason to celebrate," she told him.

"That's nice. About anything in particular?"

She hid her impatience and gestured toward the chalice. "We have it."

His reaction was nothing like she'd supposed it would be. She'd expected anger, since he'd made it clear when he first approached her that no one was to touch the pot if they managed to find it. It was too dangerous, he'd told her. Only he could handle it safely.

But now Cody merely tipped his hat brim up with the tip of a finger and ambled over to where she was sitting. Taking a chair, he turned it around and sat down, arms folded across the back. His gaze rested for a long moment on the chalice, then finally rose to meet hers.

"And what is it that you think you've got?" he asked.

"Don't play games with me."

"That works two ways, darling. Why don't you explain what I'm supposed to be so excited about?"

"The photographer had the pot all along," she told him. "It was a moment's work to acquire it from her."

Cody nodded. "Well, I can see how it would be . . . considering this isn't Raven's pot."

"What do you mean?"

"You know," Cody said with a grin. "Cast-iron, big-bellied, has some weight to it. Not all delicate like this, though I will give you it's pretty."

"The pot has never kept to one shape."

Cody shrugged. "Maybe. But it's never had something lying at the bottom of it either. What is it you've got in there, anyway?"

He leaned closer, then sat back and gave a low whistle.

"Now what?" Dominique asked.

Cody's dark gaze lifted to settle on her. "You've got Jack's little red-haired girl in there, darling. How'd you manage that?"

"She was there when we acquired it."

"Uh-huh."

"It's true."

"That's not going to mean diddly to Jack. I heard he's been out looking for her and if he finds out you've got her, you better pack your bags, darling, and start in on running as far from here as you can."

"What are you talking about? If you think—"

"You just don't get it, do you? I was the first one of all of us to wake up in the long ago, but who do you think I saw looking down at me from the trees? Corbæ, darling. Not your little rooks and jays and 'pies, but the big guns: Raven and the crow girls. And old Jack Daw."

"And your point is?"

"Didn't you folks learn nothing from what happened in Freakwater Hollow? They don't just live forever, darling. They can't die. They're not like us. You can fire a half-dozen notched slugs into his head and he's still going to be coming for you."

Dominique shook her head. "Everybody can die."

"Then how come all those Morgans are gone and he's still walking? I heard there were some real crack shots living in the hollow, but they're all dead and not even you can believe he snuck in and killed them in their sleep."

"No, but—"

"So the *point*, darling, is you don't want to piss him off."

"You're afraid of him, aren't you?" Dominique said.

Imagine. Cody as much as admitting to a fear. Who would have thought his bravado would let him even hint at such a thing. But then he surprised her more.

"Damn straight," he told her. "But the important thing to remember here is, I've got no quarrel with him. Never had and don't plan to."

He rose from the chair and looked down at her.

"If I were you," he said, "I'd have a real careful think on what you're doing here."

"What is that supposed to mean?"

"Well, darling, call me naive, but I really thought we were working on the same wavelength—you know, we'd get the pot and then I'd give it a stir, return everything back to the way things were before I started screwing it all up. But I can see now you've only got a hard-on for some corbæ blood, and I don't want any part of it."

"You hate them as much as we do."

"Wrong. We disagree some—I'll give you that—but I don't hate them. That's like saying you hate the moon and stars, things that just are. Things that are bigger than any of us."

"But you wanted—"

"I was sincere, darling," Cody told her. "I do want this world to end."

"But the corbæ—"

"Have nothing to do with how it got screwed up. How can you not get that?"

"Because you're not making a great deal of sense," Dominique said.

"That's because you never made much of an effort to get to know me, darling. See the thing is, I'm tired. Tired of all the pain I hear and see and feel. Tired of being on the road, of having nobody I can call a friend to walk beside me. Tired of people being so damn ugly to each other. It gets to be like broken bottles in my head, grinding away against each other. I'm tired all the time. Tired of trying to help and just making things worse. Tired of the lonesome dark. But mostly I'm tired of the hurt and pain. There's too much of it and I can't stop it. I can't even bear to look at it anymore."

This was a Cody that Dominique neither recognized nor understood.

"So I wanted to put an end to it," he went on. "Get things back to a time and place when things could be good again. I thought that was what you wanted, too. To get your people to stop playing all their little hoodlum games and regain the dignity they had in the long ago.

But you know, when I look back in my head to that time, the corbæ are there. Truth is, I'm not all that sure there'd still be a world, you take them out of the equation.''

Dominique's lip curled in a sneer. ''You're pathetic.''

''You're not the first to call me that, darling, but the funny thing is, it almost feels like a compliment, coming from you.''

''I won't let you stop us.''

''I'm not even trying. This is between you and the corbæ. Me, I'm heading back out into the high country to wait for the fallout to settle down. Maybe we'll see each other again, but I'm doubting there'll be much of you left to sweep up once the crows get done with you.''

''How charming,'' Dominique said. ''Go then. But not before you explain how the pot works.''

Cody shook his head. ''Maybe you've got the genuine article there, and maybe you don't. But there's one thing you have to know about the pot, darling. Everybody's got to figure out on their own how it can work for them.''

''It wasn't a request,'' she told him.

She knew Armand had been listening. Now the door connecting to her room opened silently and Armand stepped through.

''You see,'' she began. ''We can't simply let you—''

She blinked in sudden shock. One moment Cody had been empty-handed, now he stood with that pearl-handled .45 of his in his hand, the muzzle of its long barrel pointed at her head.

''I guess you don't hear too well,'' Cody said. ''When I told you I was out of it, I meant it. Now I'm no corbæ, so I figure that little jackass boy of yours might put a couple of shots in my back and do me in, but I'm still going to live long enough to kill you and probably him. So what's it going to be? Am I walking out of here, or are we all leaving in body bags?''

Looking into that flat dark gaze of his, Dominique knew he wasn't bluffing. She found herself thinking of how only moments ago she'd called him pathetic for be-

ing afraid of Jack Daw. But now, with death staring him
in the eye, he seemed, from the twitch that now touched
his lips, to be almost amused.

She swallowed dryly.

"Is that a clock I hear ticking?" Cody said.

"*Maman*?" Armand asked.

"Leave us," she told her son. "Everything is under
control."

"But—"

"Do as you are told."

When the door clicked shut behind Armand, Cody's
.45 vanished back under his jacket as magically as it had
appeared.

"I'll be going now, darling," he said. "Can't say it
hasn't been fun."

"The blackbirds . . ."

"I told you, I'm out of this."

"You won't warn them?"

Cody tipped a finger against the brim of his hat. "You
have my word on that."

"Then there will be peace between us," she said. "If
you keep your word. . . ."

Cody smiled. "I'm like the devil, darling. I always
keep my word—right to the letter."

When he left, she turned to look at the chalice once
more, troubled by Cody's parting comment, though she
didn't know why.

3.

Crossing the foyer of the hotel, boot heels clicking on
the wide expanse of marble floor, Cody spotted Gerrard
glaring at him from a chair by the door. Cody knew all
about cuckoo pride, but he couldn't stop himself from
making a gun shape with his fingers and pointing it at
the man. He made a firing motion with his thumb as he
went by.

"Bang," he said.

Then he went out the big oak-and-brass doors, tipped the doorman a ten-spot, and got into his long white Lincoln.

He hadn't lied to Dominique. He *was* finished here—let the crows and cuckoos sort it out while he headed straight for the high country. And he'd keep his promise, too, just like he said he would. He wouldn't be talking to any crows on the way out of town—not that they'd listen to him anyway. But that didn't mean there was nobody else he could talk to.

Picking up his cellular phone, he flicked it open with one hand, then pulled the short antenna out with his teeth and hit the speed-dial for Ray's number. He was a little surprised when Ray actually answered. Cody'd thought for sure Ray would have thrown that phone away by now.

"It's Cody," he said into the mouthpiece.

"I told you," Ray replied. "I'm out of it."

"Now, Ray. Is that a friendly way to answer the phone?"

"What do you want?"

Cody touched the control for the driver's seat window and stuck his elbow out the open window.

"Funny thing," he said. "Turns out, I'm out of it, too."

"So why're you calling me?"

Cody could hear the suspicion in his voice.

"Well, that's the other funny thing," he said. "I'm just on my way from Dominique's hotel room and you'll never guess what she's got in there."

"I'm in no mood for games," Ray said. "Just tell it straight."

"Straight it is. She's got herself something she thinks is Raven's pot. Looks like a crystal chalice, but I didn't put my hand on it so I can't say for sure."

"Why are you telling me this?"

"Well—and this is something you might want to share with Jack, you two being so chummy and all lately."

"I'm hanging up, Cody."

"You'll regret it."

He heard Ray sigh. "Okay. What's this big news?"

"She's also got one of your granddaughters up there with her and her boys."

"She's got—"

"Don't say I never did you any favors, Ray," Cody said.

He touched the "End" button and tossed the phone out the window.

"Maybe now you'll know we really were friends," he added as he headed for the freeway.

4.

Kerry could feel her newfound confidence begin to wane as they crossed the long stretch of empty lots that lay between the school bus where they'd met Paris and the junkyard she was leading them to. It was hard to feel self-assured, let alone bold, right about now. She hated to be the center of attention and wasn't especially comfortable meeting new people in the best of circumstances. Knowing that Paris's friends would probably greet her with the same animosity Paris had at first only made her feel worse. But it was too late to back out now.

They walked three abreast, the tattooed woman on one side of her, Rory on the other, the dogs ranging ahead of them. When they approached the front gate that appeared to be the only break in the chain-link fence enclosing the junkyard, a larger pack of dogs appeared and the two groups barked at each other from either side of the fence, snarling, jaws snapping against the links.

Kerry moved a little closer to Rory. The dogs sounded so fierce her pulse had begun to race.

"Don't worry," Paris told her when she noticed Kerry's nervousness. "They just like to carry on. It'd be different if you were trying to break in or something, but you're perfectly safe with me.''

She pushed open one half of the gate and the dogs that had accompanied them slipped through the widening gap, immediately beginning to tussle with the ones that had been inside. Kerry let out a breath she hadn't been aware of holding when she realized that there was no real animosity between them. More importantly, none of them appeared to be all that interested in taking a bite out of her.

Paris waved them through ahead of her and then she and Rory were being introduced to her friends.

Everybody only seemed to have one name. There was the grizzled old man simply called Moth who owned the place. He merely nodded at them when he was introduced, regarding both Rory and especially herself with a suspicious eye. Much friendlier was an older woman named Anita in grease-stained overalls, her hair pulled back in a loose ponytail. Kerry noted the same recognition in her face as there'd been in Paris's when they first met, but it wasn't followed by anger.

"I can't believe how alike the two of you are," she said after wiping her palms on her jeans and then shaking hands.

Kerry couldn't suppress a shiver. After having finally convinced herself that Katy was only a figment of her imagination, it was awful to discover that her twin actually did exist. What made it even more distressing was that she herself was responsible for Katy's current disappearance. She should have welcomed Katy when her twin had appeared in the new apartment, instead of turning her away. Having come to understand that she'd been lied to about so many things in Baumert, why should she have believed them when it came to Katy? Why couldn't she have accepted what her own senses were telling her?

When she put it to herself like that, Kerry thought she deserved Moth's animosity. She didn't much like herself right now.

She forced herself to concentrate as Paris's introductions continued. Anita had been working on a car with a man named Benny who looked more like an accountant than a mechanic so far as Kerry was concerned. He gave Kerry a shy nod, then immediately returned back under the hood of the car.

Last was Paris's brother, Terry, a very good-looking Oriental man about Kerry's age with none of his sister's tattooing—or at least none that Kerry could see. He didn't get up from his lawn chair, but he had a ready smile and flashed her a peace sign.

It didn't take Kerry long to see what Paris had meant about her family. While it was obvious that none of the people sitting around in the junkyard were blood-related, there was still far more of a connection among them than she'd ever felt with her own parents.

"So you're saying the crow girls are vouching for her?" Moth asked after Paris had finished explaining what had brought Kerry to Jack's bus.

"You mean they're real?" Terry said, sitting up a little straighter. "I always thought they were just something out of one of Jack's stories."

"We only know them from the stories," Paris explained. "They must be so awesome."

"Actually, they act like little kids," Kerry said.

But then she reconsidered, remembering the touch of Maida's fingers on her brow, how they'd pulled the anxiety attack right out of her to help her face her problems the way normal people did. She made herself focus on the flicker of that candle, deep inside. While it didn't ease the guilt she was feeling over having chased Katy away, it did make it a little easier for her to deal with all these strangers.

"But they're pretty magical, I guess," she added.

Terry shook his head. "You guess? Man, that's like saying you just met Elvis and he's not so bad a singer for a guy who's supposed to be dead."

That woke smiles from everyone except for Moth. He wasn't ready to be sidetracked.

"So you've only been here a few days, is that what you're saying?" he asked.

Kerry nodded.

"Which is when all the trouble began."

Kerry gave him a nervous look. This man didn't like her at all.

"Oh, for God's sake, Moth," Anita said to him. "Will you stop glaring at her like that. None of this seems to be her fault."

"She says."

Anita gave Kerry a reassuring look. "Don't mind him. There's been a lot of strange things going on for the past week or so and everybody's a little on edge." She turned back to Moth. "Give me that phone of yours. I want to see if I can catch up with Hank."

"Who's Hank?" Kerry asked.

"He works for this lawyer named Marty Caine," Rory said, speaking up for the first time. "And apparently here as well."

"How do you know that?" Moth asked.

"I worked with him in Caine's office."

Moth nodded. "I remember you now. You're a journalist, right?"

"Some of the time."

"What do you do the rest of the time?"

"I'm a jeweler."

That made Paris perk up. "No kidding? What do you work in?"

"Gold, silver—when I can afford it. Whatever comes to hand when I can't."

"I'd like to see some of your stuff."

"Drop by the apartment sometime."

The small talk was driving Kerry crazy. They should be out looking for Katy. Instead she felt like they were sitting around in some sort of bizarre combination of a kangaroo court and an afternoon social, junkyard style.

"Okay," Anita said. She had walked a few feet away from where they were all sitting in front of Moth's trailer to make her call. Rejoining them, she tossed the cellular phone back to Moth and sat down once more. "He was still in Caine's office, but I was able to leave a message."

"Hank'll be able to straighten everything out," Paris said, obviously confident in his abilities.

But when Hank did arrive, he was no more able to help her than the others had been. Jack was still missing, Katy was still missing, and Hank's animosity level lay somewhere between Moth's and Anita's, a slow distrustful burn, which only added to Kerry's feelings of guilt and left her no closer to making some sense out of this confusion. Adding yet more to her discomfort was that Hank seemed to be having his own problems.

Kerry supposed he was nice enough and might have liked him under other circumstances. But in this place, he was a little scary, a little too tough-looking for her to feel entirely at ease with him. When he started talking to Moth about some man named Eddie putting the arm on the D.A.'s office and how Moth was going to have to have a talk with him, she began to feel as though she'd stumbled onto the set of some gangster movie.

Why are they talking about this kind of thing in front of us? she wondered.

The same thought must have occurred to Hank for he suddenly broke off and an uncomfortable silence settled over them all. Finally Kerry stood up. There was no point in her staying here. While Paris and Anita had been friendly enough, it was obvious that she and Rory weren't really welcome. Hank had been surprised to find Rory here, but it hadn't felt like a nice surprise—more an intrusive one.

"We should be going," she began.

She was interrupted by the arrival of another car, which pulled up beside the black VW bug Hank had arrived in.

"Hey, Lily!"

Rory and Hank called out a greeting at the same time

to the woman as she stepped out of her car. Then they looked at each other.

"We go back a long way," Rory said.

Hank only nodded.

"I was over at the bus looking for Jack," Lily started to say to Hank, "but then I saw your car so I thought I'd . . ." Her voice trailed off when she noticed Rory sitting beside the lawn chair Kerry had so recently vacated. "Rory?" she added, obviously puzzled to see him here.

There were more introductions to be made then and Kerry tuned them out. She shifted from one foot to the other, trying to listen to what was being discussed, but then the conversation got far too confusing as Lily started talking about magic chalices and cuckoos. What Kerry found even more confusing was how everyone seemed to take what she was saying so seriously. Back in Baumert this kind of talk would have earned Lily a visit to the seclusion room for acting out.

Kerry moved a few steps closer to where Paris was sitting and touched the tattooed woman's shoulder.

"Do you think you could show me that car where Katy was living?" she asked.

"No problem," Paris said. "But she wasn't actually living there. I don't think anyone knew where she was living. That was just the last place Anita and Moth saw her."

"I'd still like to see it."

Paris nodded. "Sure. I understand."

Kerry was going to tell Rory where she was going, but since he seemed to be as caught up with Lily's strange story as everybody else, she didn't think he'd even notice the few minutes she'd be gone.

"C'mon," Paris said.

She led the way down a narrow lane with fifteen-foot-high stacks of rusting vehicles and other metal trash on either side until they reached a bright yellow Volvo that was in marginally better shape than most of its neighbors. It still wasn't going to run, not with its engine dropped on the dirt out of the rusted front end, but it had most of its windows and the seats inside were all in one piece.

"So do you have a tattoo like Katy does?" Paris asked.

"I didn't even know she had one."

"Yeah, it's this cool Japanese ideograph on her upper arm. I found out it means 'little sister.' "

The idea that Katy would have a symbol of their relationship permanently etched into her skin made the ache in Kerry's heart hurt more.

"No," she said softly. "I don't have one."

"I guess you two aren't much alike except in looks."

Kerry nodded. "Do your . . . do all those tattoos mean something?"

"They're like a diary for me—one that no one can take away."

Kerry had known girls in Baumert who'd cut themselves, or put out cigarettes on their arms and legs, for much the same reason. They could tell stories about each one. It had struck her as terribly sad and she felt the same way about Paris's tattoos. There was such a darkness to the images that they couldn't be to remind her of happy times.

"What do you do when you run out of room?" she found herself asking.

"I guess that's when I die," Paris said. "I'm joking," she added quickly when she caught Kerry's shocked expression. "I don't think I'm ever going to run out of room—not anymore. These represent the high—or maybe I should say the low—points in my life. I'm on a lot more even keel these days and don't really feel the urge or need to add to the story anymore." A pensive look touched the features. "Though I guess that could change. . . ."

Kerry put a hand on one of the tattooed arms. "Don't let it," she said.

That was what the patients, at least those who were with it enough to hold up their end of a conversation, told each other in Baumert. It usually didn't help, but it was always worth saying.

"I'm working on that," Paris said. "One day at a time."

Kerry nodded. She put her hands in her pockets.

"Look," Paris said. "Do you want to head back? I'd like to hear more about these cuckoos and everything."

"Would it be okay if I stayed a little while longer?"

Paris smiled. "Hey, stay all day if you like. Just don't go climbing around in the stacks. Those wrecks may look like they're solidly stacked, but I've seen them come down a time or two."

"I was only going to look in the car where you said Katy was sleeping."

Paris gave her an understanding look.

"Don't worry," she said. "We'll find her."

You don't know that, Kerry thought, but she took comfort in being told all the same.

She waited until Paris had started walking back toward the others before she returned her attention to the car. Poor Katy. Reduced to sleeping in a junked car when she could have been sharing the futon back in the apartment on Stanton Street. Of course that hadn't exactly been Katy's choice.

She stepped closer to the car and trailed her hand along the hood.

"I guess saying I'm sorry wouldn't mean a whole lot at this point," she said. "You probably can't hear me. Maybe you don't even want to hear me and I wouldn't blame you."

Bending down, she looked inside the car. There was a blanket lying on the backseat. She could imagine Katy sitting in there, the blanket wrapped around her against the cold. It was unseasonably warm today, but she remembered it had been cool last night. She couldn't imagine not having a home or anyplace at all to go except for an old abandoned car in some junkyard.

The tears she'd been keeping in check since first meet-

ing Paris filled her eyes now, making it hard to see. She
fumbled with the door handle. Finally getting the door
open, she crawled into the back of the car where Katy
had been sleeping and held the blanket against her chest.
She imagined she could smell her sister in its musty folds
and the tears came in earnest then, her shoulders shaking
as she cried into the blanket.

Once she started she didn't think she'd ever be able to
stop. She wept for Katy, but she wept for herself as well,
for all that they might have shared but never had.

"I . . . I'd give anything for . . . for one more . . .
chance," she managed to get out between sobs.

5.

"Am I missing something here?" Hank said.

Lily gave him a puzzled look. "What do you mean?"

"Well, it sounds to me like we've got what we wanted.
We mind our own business and the Couteaus—cuckoos,
whatever they are—are going to leave us alone."

"You didn't see that chalice," Lily told him. "I can't
let them keep it and use it for something horrible—not
in good conscience."

Moth shifted in his lawn chair, catching their attention.

"I don't know from cuckoos," he said, "but I know
too much about the Couteaus as it is. These are seriously
dangerous people. If they say stay out of their business,
it's good advice."

"But—"

"Besides, you're coming out ahead. You say Eddie put
ten grand in your bank account?"

"I don't know who put it in there."

"Well, if your bank says it came from the Newford
Investment Group, that's the same as saying Eddie Prio
put it in there. The NIG's the legit side of his business."

"I don't care where it comes from," Lily said. "I
don't want his money."

"She's got a point," Hank said. "I wouldn't accept it either. Eddie's not the kind of guy I'd want to be owing any favors to."

Moth shook his head. "That's not what this is about. It's just Eddie being generous. You had a problem with the Couteaus and he couldn't fix it, so he did the next best thing."

"It's causing more headaches than fixing anything," Hank said.

"The girl's out of jail, isn't she? The charges are all dropped?"

"Yeah, and Marty's seriously pissed off."

"Why? Because he didn't get to make the deal?"

"You know it's not like that."

"Right." Moth turned to Lily. "And as for the ten grand. That seems to me to be a pretty fair compensation for having your place trashed and the trouble you've been put through."

"I'm missing something here," Lily said. "Is he partners with them or something?"

"Not likely."

"Then what's he get out of all of this?"

"He's doing it," Anita put in, "because he couldn't fix it. It's that Italian machismo of his showing through. Friend comes to him for a favor and it looks bad when he can't help out."

"I don't want a gangster for a friend," Lily said.

Moth shook his head. "No one's asking you to—"

"And I'm not going to stand by doing nothing about that chalice either," Lily added, before Moth could finish. She settled her gaze on Hank. "It's not something I can walk away from."

"But it's just a piece of crystal," Hank said.

"No," she told him. "I don't know what it is, but it's a lot more than that."

"It's not our business. Let them sort it out."

"But it is my business. I was carrying it around for all that time. I'm the one who handed it over and that makes me feel responsible for them having it. So I'm going back to Jack's bus and if he's still not there, then I'll have to see what I can do on my own.''

"Lily," Hank said. "Be reasonable. Forget the danger for a minute and think about what you're saying. Where would you even begin to start looking?"

"I don't know. I just know I have to give it a try. And I'm sending that money back to your friend as well."

"That's not such a good idea," Moth said. "You don't want—"

"You asked for the favor," Lily told him. "I didn't. He's your friend, so it's your problem."

"Lily," Hank began again.

He stopped when she held up her hand, palm out.

"I don't want to talk about this anymore," she said, "so let's just stop it now before we start saying things we might regret later. I'm not blaming you for wanting to keep out of this. I know you have your own problems. You still have to find this missing girl and you've got the safety of your other friends to consider. Well, I don't have either of those worries."

She stood up and looked around.

"Nice to have met you all," she said. "I'm sorry you had to listen in on all of this." Her gaze rested finally on Rory. "Do you need a ride back?"

He glanced down between the rows of junked cars where Kerry had gone earlier.

"I have to wait for Kerry," he said. "But call me at the house later. Maybe Chloë'll have some ideas."

"Who's Chloë?" Moth asked.

"She lives with my landlord. They're the ones who lost the chalice in the first place."

"When it looked like a tin?"

Rory nodded.

"Is it just me," Moth said, "or does anybody else feel like we should be calling in a reporter from the *National Enquirer* to help us make sense of all of this? It's like we're stuck in one of Jack's stories."

"What makes you think we're not?" Anita asked.

No one had an answer for that.

"I'll call you," Lily told Rory. She turned to Hank.

"Look, Lily," he said.

She put a finger to her lips. When he fell silent, she kissed the pads of her fingers and blew the kiss to him.

"I'm sorry things turned out this way," she said, then she walked back to her car.

Hank stood up, but he didn't follow. He watched Lily start up her car, back it onto Gracie Street, then pull away.

"I should go collect Kerry," Rory said.

Paris got up with him and offered to show him the way.

"What do I do?" Hank said. "If the Couteaus are everything Eddie says they are—"

"No question there," Moth put in. "If they make Eddie nervous, you know they're serious."

"Then how can I put all of you in danger? Because you know that's how it works. They're not just going to come after me if I start messing with them—they're going to want a piece of everything and everybody I care about."

There was a long moment's silence.

"Well, now," Anita said finally. "We're all pretty much grown up around here." She shot Moth a look. "Or at least as grown up as we're going to get. Why don't you let us worry about what happens to us."

Moth nodded. "Yeah, kid. If you care about her, you've got to help her."

"Like you did us," Terry put in.

"You sure?" Hank asked.

The question was for all of them, but he was looking at Moth.

"I know," Moth said. "I didn't think I'd be saying what I just did either. But I meant it."

"Okay. Then I'm going—"

He broke off when Paris came running back to them from between the junked cars.

"She's gone!" she cried. "Kerry's disappeared as well."

"What the hell?" Moth said, getting to his feet. "Have we got a sinkhole someplace back there or what?"

"All I know is I left her by the Volvo and she's not there now. Rory's still looking for her, but I don't think he's going to find her."

Moth put his fingers in his mouth and gave a sharp whistle. The dogs lounging nearby jumped to their feet. Others came running from various parts of the yard.

"Judith. Ranger. Find," Moth told the pit bull and German shepherd.

When the two alpha dogs tore off to search the junkyard, the others followed their lead, fanning out down the various lanes that led between the junked vehicles. Moth turned back to Hank.

"Go help Lily," he said. "We'll be okay here." He turned away before Hank could reply. "You better check on the girl's friend," he told Paris. "Make sure the dogs don't give him a scare. Terry and Benny, you check the perimeters of the fence—look for signs that someone's been tampering with it, or maybe got themselves hung up in the barbed wire up top. Anita, as soon as Hank's through the gate, throw up the electricity, then we'll check the rows ourselves to make sure the dogs haven't missed anything."

He turned to look at Hank. "What're you still doing here?"

"Thanks, Moth."

"Time's wasting, kid," was all Moth said.

Hank nodded and started for the gate. Behind him he could hear Moth muttering, "And when I find the sonovabitch who's snatching girls from my 'yard, I'll have the dogs . . ."

Hank didn't hear the rest of the threat, but he could fill it in.

Maybe the Couteaus would be biting off more than they could chew if they decided to make a run at the junkyard. Lord knew, Hank wouldn't want to have Moth that pissed off with him.

6.

There was a small dark-haired figure sitting on the sofa in front of Jack's bus when Lily pulled up. At first she wasn't sure if it was a boy or a girl. What she was reminded of most were those two bird girls who'd rescued her in that alley last week. The stranger had the same exotic quality. The slender frame engulfed by the bulk of the sofa appeared ethereal, delicate, yet strong and resilient at the same time. The presence of an otherness clung to the figure, as though an aura of dark angel wings rose up behind it. But when she got out of the car and the figure quickly stood up from the sofa, she soon realized it wasn't either of the bird girls. Instead, it was a rather androgynous male and no one she knew.

"Have you seen Jack?" they both said at the same time.

Lily had a lot on her mind. She was depressed about how things had gone with Hank—she'd *really* expected more from him—and she was worried about the deep trouble she might be getting herself into by chasing after the chalice, but the way the small, boyish man stood blinking in surprise couldn't help but wake a smile from her.

"No, I guess you haven't," she said. "I'm Lily," she added, offering him her hand.

"Ray."

"You look like some friends of mine."

"It's a good time to be looking like a corbæ, considering," he said.

"Considering what?"

Ray gave her a sharp look. "How do you know Jack, anyway?" he asked instead of replying.

"I just—"

She broke off as behind Ray she saw Jack and Margaret literally step out of nowhere. The air in her lungs felt as though it were suddenly expanding, making her chest go tight, and the ground seemed to shift under her feet. The sudden sense of vertigo made her legs go all jellyish.

I am *never* going to get used to this, she thought.

Before she could speak, Margaret pointed at Ray and started to laugh.

"Oh, Lord, Ray," she said. "Now I've seen everything. What the hell are you doing, going about looking like a crow girl?"

"The man has no shame," Jack said.

Jack looked drawn and worn out—maybe "haunted" was a better word, Lily thought—but a thin smile touched his lips as he looked at Ray. Lily didn't know what was so funny, but she took the opportunity while they were being so amused to make her way to the sofa, where she gratefully sat down.

Ray gave an embarrassed shrug. "I was keeping an eye out on Kerry and just trying to fit in."

"Oh, you fit in, all right," Margaret said. "But into what, I don't know. How're you doing, Lily?" she added, dropping down onto the couch beside her.

Margaret's action made the sofa's old springs bounce and worsened Lily's vertigo.

"The crow girls like this look," Ray said.

"Well, they would, wouldn't they?"

"Okay," Ray told her. "Enough with the jokes already."

Margaret gave a throaty laugh. "Oh, I'm just getting started."

"I'm here on serious business."

"Right," Margaret said. She sat up and leaned a little

closer to him. "You know, I think you might have missed a few red whiskers."

Ray lifted a hand to his chin.

"Gotcha!" Margaret said and fell back onto the sofa, laughing harder.

Lily had to grip the arm, but she was getting her sense of equilibrium back.

"Let the man speak his piece," Jack said.

He pulled up a barrel and sat down, waving Ray over to the sofa. Ray gingerly took a seat beside Margaret, but she was done with her teasing, her expression serious now.

"Tell us what's on your mind, Ray," she said.

He gave a short nod. "Like I said, I've been watching out for Kerry when I got this call from Cody. He says the Couteaus have got both Raven's pot and Katy." He hesitated a moment, then added, "I know what you're thinking, Jack, but Cody says he's out of it."

Jack's face went grim at the first mention of the Couteaus.

"What's he playing at now?" he said, his voice soft, as though he were thinking aloud.

"I don't know," Ray replied. "But I thought it was worth passing along. If it's true . . ."

"I'll kill them," Jack said flatly.

Lily cleared her throat. Jack turned to look at her and Lily wanted to crawl under the cushions of the sofa to get away from the dark look in his eyes. She had to clear her throat again before she could speak.

"It . . . it's true," she said.

Jack nodded thoughtfully. "You know, I never did ask what you were doing here with Ray."

His gaze was milder now, but the darkness was still in his eyes. The difference, for Lily, was that it no longer seemed to be directed at her.

"We didn't come together," she said.

"But you've got the same story?"

She had to clear her throat yet again. "They got the

chalice from me. I didn't even know I was carrying it around, because it looked like an old tin. . . ."

She told an abbreviated version of what had happened to her, finishing up with Dominique Couteau's appearance in the library that morning.

"You got those juju charms I sent along with you?" Margaret asked.

Lily nodded. "I'm not wearing them, but I had them in my camera bag."

"You were smart to keep them close. I put a little spell on them—something to make you seem innocent and ineffectual—and it's a good thing I did. The Couteaus don't usually leave loose ends lying around behind them."

Lily shivered. She *was* innocent and ineffectual so far as all of this was concerned.

"Looked like a chalice, did it?" Jack asked.

"Made of crystal."

"And you're saying there was a little statue lying in the bottom of it?"

Lily nodded. "It was hard to tell what it was made of. It didn't move at all, except for the hair, and I'm not even sure if it really moved or it only seemed to because the figurine was so lifelike."

"That's where she went," Jack said to Margaret. "Into the damned pot. No wonder we couldn't find her."

"But why would she climb in there in the first place?" Margaret asked.

"Better ask how'd she even know to manage the trick. It's nothing I've ever heard of before."

"Maybe the Couteaus . . . ."

Jack looked back at Lily.

"The woman seemed surprised that there was anything inside," Lily said before he could ask.

Jack nodded. "Which leaves Cody."

"Or Katy herself," Margaret said. "Give the girl some credit."

"How would she—"

Margaret broke in. "She's not exactly a known quantity, Jack. Who knows what she is or what she can do?''

"Maybe you're right," Jack allowed, "and they're not connected. But Cody had a hand in it, somewhere along the line.''

Margaret shrugged. "All Cody wanted to do was set the world back into the long ago. Maybe when he found for himself what the Couteaus really want, he got an attack of conscience.''

Lily looked at Jack and Ray to see them nodding in agreement. They all seemed to know what Margaret was talking about except for her.

"What *do* the Couteaus really want?" Lily asked.

"To get rid of the corbæ," Margaret explained. "Not just little spirits like me, but the old ones.''

Jack nodded. "Raven and the crow girls.''

"And you, Jack.''

He shrugged. "Whatever.''

"Why's it so important to them?" Lily asked.

"Well, we've had trouble between us for about as long as anyone can remember," Margaret said.

Lily glanced at Jack, but quickly looked away. He was looking too grim for her again.

"Cody once told me," Ray said, "that without the old corbæ in it, there can't be a world.''

For a long moment, no one spoke.

"Is that true?" Lily asked.

"Who knows?" Jack said.

"But if we don't get the pot back, we're going to find out," Margaret said.

"I know where the Couteaus are staying," Ray said. "They're booked into the Harbor Ritz, downtown.''

Jack rose to his feet. To Lily's eye, he was moving slow, as though he wanted to put off what was to come, but knew he couldn't. When he was finally standing, he seemed impossibly tall, as though his hat could brush up against the clouds.

"Time we paid them a call," he said.

On the heel of his words, the ground started to tremble

and a rumbling sound rose up from deep underground, like a subway passing, except there were no subways running out here in the Tombs. The sky darkened, not all at once, but slowly, the way ink clouds water. Lily thought it was Jack's doing and she was more scared than ever, but then she caught a glimpse of the pained expression that had settled across his features and realized that he was no more responsible for this than she was.

"Too late," he said, his voice no louder than a whisper.

The rumbling came from under their feet again. Louder. And the ground began to vibrate steadily.

"What . . . what's happening?" Lily asked.

From beside her, Margaret reached over and took her hand.

She's as scared as me, Lily realized and that only made it worse.

"Somebody's stirring the pot," Margaret said.

Jack nodded. "Got something pulling on me. . . ."

This was all her fault, Lily thought. Maybe she hadn't known she was carrying it, but once she did, she should have put up some sort of a fight, tried to do *something* to stop that woman from taking the chalice.

Jack tilted his head, turning his face up to the dark skies. He spread his arms wide. His crows lifted from the roof of the bus and began to circle above him.

"Raven!" he cried.

His voice boomed like thunder.

"Raven!"

A wind came up out of nowhere and touched only him. It made the tails and sleeves of his duster flap wildly, blew his hat from his head, shook him where he stood. Margaret's fingers tightened their grip on Lily's hand. Lily heard a doggish whine come from where Ray was sitting.

"Raven!" Jack cried a third time.

He took one step forward, another, and then it was like the wind lifted him up, blowing him from the world, and he was gone. All that was left were the crows, still circling above the place where Jack had been standing, cawing and shrieking now in a way that Lily had never heard crows cry before.

The sky went darker still and the rumbling underground was so close that the sofa began to shake under them. Behind them Lily could hear the contents of Jack's bus rattling about, pots and pans falling from the shelves. She could hear the crows, flying higher than before, invisible against the blackening sky. And she could hear the wind, stronger now, carrying with it an otherness that was so alien it stole away the foreignness of the animal people, making them appear almost normal in comparison.

That wind.

It seemed to be all around her, but it had no physical presence. It didn't touch them, didn't touch the bus, didn't rage across the empty lots of the Tombs, blowing refuse and litter ahead of it.

But she could hear it all the same.

She put her hands over her ears and the sound of the wind only intensified. That was when she knew that it was blowing inside her, a storm front moving across an inner landscape she hadn't realized she was carrying until now.

When she lowered her hands, the sound was less intense, but she knew it was still inside her, she was still aware of that strange landscape swelling into life somewhere under her flesh and bones. She turned to Margaret, barely able to make out the woman's features in the dark. Past her, Ray was only a smudge of darker shadow.

"It's the voice of the pot," Margaret told her. "That's what we're hearing. The voice of Raven's pot."

"I feel like it's . . . inside me."

Margaret nodded. "Blowing across places you never knew existed."

"It's happening to you, too?"

"It's happening to everybody who can hear it."

"What . . . what is it telling us? I don't understand it."

"Don't even try to," Margaret told her. "The only ones who can understand it are the mad and the dead."

"But Jack . . . ," Lily began, remembering how the wind they could only feel inside them had had enough physical presence for a brief moment to take him away.

"Now Jack," Margaret said. "He's somewhere in between the two. Not quite mad, not quite dead."

"What do you mean?"

Margaret shook her head. "That's not my story to tell."

7.

Earthquake, Hank thought when he first felt the ground shake underfoot. But then the sky darkened and that didn't jibe with what he knew of earthquakes. You might get a cloud of dirt and debris when buildings collapsed, but that would be a localized phenomenon—nothing like what was happening now. This wasn't natural. It was night coming too early, a storm front appearing out of nowhere to blanket the entire sky.

The tremors came again, stronger. They became a steady vibration and he could hear a dull rumbling rise up from under the ground. He glanced back toward the junkyard. Because of the poor light, it was already hard to make out more than hulking shapes. If some of those stacked vehicles started coming down and anybody was under them . . .

He was ready to head back until Anita's words returned to him.

We're all pretty much grown up around here. Why don't you let us worry about what happens to us.

Reluctantly, he decided he had to take them at their word.

Giving the junkyard a last worried look, he pressed on toward Jack's bus. The going was slow. The constant tremors underfoot made it hard to keep his balance. The sky continued to darken. Visibility worsened until he had to feel his way through the rubble and trash. But what made his skin prickle with goose bumps was the sound of the wind. A gale raged all around him yet he couldn't see or feel it. He could only hear it—the wind and the cawing of Jack's crows, the latter sounding more distant with every step he took.

When he suddenly came up against the brick wall, he knew he'd gotten turned around. It was so dark now that he couldn't tell what building he was standing beside or where Jack's bus lay in relation to it. There were no reference points. He couldn't even use the graffiti that covered every structure in the Tombs since it had all been washed away by the dark.

He pivoted slowly and put his back to the wall, trying to get his bearings. Logically, he had to be facing Gracie Street. Which would put the bus over . . . there. Unless he'd gotten more turned around than seemed possible. That pulled a humorless laugh from him. None of this felt possible. The dark. The wind. Getting lost in the empty lot that lay between the junkyard and Jack's bus.

He couldn't hear the crows at all now while the sound of the wind made it hard to think clearly. It felt too much like it was blowing inside him.

He wished he hadn't thought of that. The situation was eerie enough without adding to it. The next thing you know, he'd started imagining spooks or—

Something cold and wet touched his hand.

"Ye-aah!" he cried, jumping back.

He banged his head on the bricks behind him and almost lost his balance. A large furry shape pressed up against his legs and he almost cried out again, but then he realized what it was. That monster dog he'd been feeding for all these mornings. The one that followed him on his runs but never came up close.

Lowering his weight onto his heels, he put out a hand and felt the large broad features.

"That you, boy?" he asked. "What happened? Did you get lost, too?"

The dog made a low grumbling sound deep in its chest. As though in reply, a deeper echo came reverberating from below.

Years ago an earthquake had leveled much of the city and parts of it still remained underground, pockets of hidden streets and building remnants that the present city had simply been rebuilt upon. Hank tried to remember if any of those sections were near this part of the Tombs. His suddenly overactive imagination could picture all of them tumbling into some lost piece of the old city—he, the dog, the junkyard, Jack's bus, all of them. The ensuing rubble would close in on top of them and nobody would ever know where they'd gone. Who would even look for them?

He made himself stop before he got too carried away. Concentrating on the dog helped.

"Or did you come looking for me because you missed out on breakfast?"

The dog moved its head, dislodging Hank's hand. Before Hank could pull his arm back, the dog closed its massive jaws around Hank's biceps and gave them a gentle tug.

"What?" Hank asked. "What do you want?"

The dog tugged again, firm, teeth not breaking the skin, until Hank started to stand up. It let his arm go then, pushing its head up against Hank's hand. It repeated the motion a few times. Finally Hank tried grabbing a fistful of the dog's rough hair. As soon as he did, the dog began to step away. When Hank let go, the dog repeated its earlier actions.

"So now you're Lassie?" Hank said. "I guess the next thing you're going to tell me is that little Timmy's stuck in the well."

As soon as the words were out of his mouth, he regretted them. All he could picture was some dark hole that this strange earthquake was about to drop them into.

He didn't know what was making the unnatural grumbling and shaking that was coming from the ground, but he wasn't in the least bit interested in coming face-to-face with its source.

The dog barked. Once. A low, gruff sound that made Hank feel a bass note deep in his own chest. Again it bumped its head against Hank's hand. This time Hank held on to the dog's fur and let it lead him away.

They could have been walking through limbo, for all Hank could tell. He couldn't judge one direction from another. If he hadn't had the ground underfoot, he'd have been hard-pressed to pick an up or a down. The strangest thing was how there were no lights anywhere—not from the buildings in the city or from the vehicles on the streets. He knew if he'd been near a light source, he'd have turned it on as soon as the darkness came flooding in.

Maybe there was a power outage as well? But while he could imagine the whole city being blacked out—that was the sort of thing that could actually happen in the world he knew—a problem with the power company couldn't explain the lack of car headlights.

"You got a destination in mind?" Hank asked as he followed alongside the dog, fingers tangled in its fur. "Because I'll tell you the truth, I can't make out a damned thing."

But the dog seemed sure of its destination, whatever it might be. It led Hank, winding through the rubble and trash at a slow, steady pace that Hank couldn't have managed on his own. The ground underfoot wasn't trembling so much anymore, though he could still hear a low resonating mutter of sound coming from deep below. The dark hadn't let up at all—if anything, it was now more pronounced—and the unfelt wind still blew, somewhere deep inside him.

"You know," Hank said, "I was heading for Jack's bus myself. . . ."

Then he heard the sound of the crows again, somewhere overhead. Loud. Insistent.

"I'll be damned," he said in a low voice.

Ahead of him he could make out the flickering light of an oil lamp. It was held aloft by a woman he didn't recognize—casually dressed and dark-haired except for two white streaks running back from her temples. In the light cast by her lamp he saw what he took for a boy and then Lily. The dog shook its head, dislodging his hand, but he didn't need its guidance anymore. He hurried forward.

"Are you okay?" he called to Lily.

She turned in his direction. "Hank?"

She seemed relieved as he came into the circle of light until her gaze fell on the enormous dog padding at his side. Her eyes widened.

"Well, now," the woman holding the lamp said. She, too, was looking at the dog. "You're not exactly a puppy are you?"

"It's all right," Hank told Lily, sensing her nervousness. "I know he looks mean, but he's a friend."

Lily gave the dog a dubious look.

"This is Margaret," she said, gesturing to the woman. Hank nodded, remembering the name. "From Tucson."

"From everywhere," Margaret said, smiling. "That is, if you want to get specific."

"And this is Ray," Lily finished, introducing the boy.

Up close he didn't seem so young anymore. There was a sense of antiquity in his gaze that you'd never mistake for a street kid's assumed worldliness.

"Hey, cousins," Ray said.

"Cousins?" Hank asked.

"Well, sure," Ray replied. "You think I can't smell the wolf in you? Though your friend's got more'n canid blood. Bear maybe?"

Margaret nodded, the motion making the lamp bob slightly in her hand.

"Grizzly," she said. "Though it goes back a long way."

Hank looked slowly from the dog to Lily's companions.

"They're animal people," Lily explained. "Like in Jack's stories."

"Animal people . . . ," Hank began, then he shook his head. "And you're saying I'm . . . that is . . ."

"Well, it's thin, cousin," Ray said, "but we can smell it. You've got some old lobo back there in the bloodline, same as your friend."

"But he's . . ."

"A dog? Sure. But when we're in animal form, we hang with the animal cousins." Ray grinned. "Family trees can get a little complicated."

"So what does it mean?" Hank asked.

Ray laughed. "You people are always asking that. Find out you've got a little bit of the blood in you and it gets all these questions rolling around in your head."

"Well, wouldn't you—"

"It doesn't mean anything, cousin. It's like saying you've got brown hair or an overbite—you follow me? It's just something that is."

Hank tried to digest that, but had to put it aside until later.

"Does anybody know what's going on?" he asked.

"Somebody's stirred the pot," Lily told him.

Margaret nodded. "And unless you've got the blood, the world's standing still, which means except for you and about five percent of the people living in this city, everybody else is living in one piece of time right now. It took us awhile to work it out, but it's the only thing that makes sense."

If this made sense to her, Hank thought, he'd hate to see what confused her.

"We were just about to leave," Lily said. "Margaret says we've got to wake up Raven."

"That's got to be what Jack was trying to do," Margaret said, "before he got pulled away."

"Pulled away to where?" Hank asked.

"We don't know," Lily told him. "Are you going to come?"

He nodded. He had no idea what was going on anymore, but if Lily was going, he wasn't going to punk out on her again.

"Then I'll explain along the way."

Hank followed Margaret and Ray to Lily's car, Lily walking at his side.

"I'll drive," Margaret said.

She opened the car door and blew out the oil lamp when the interior light came on. Hank got into the back with Lily while Ray took the front passenger's seat.

"How come we can't see other car headlights?" Hank asked. "Or lights from the buildings?"

Margaret glanced at him in the rearview mirror. "We're outside of time. The world the way we know it has stopped, only not for us. We're moving on. Light doesn't just exist, remember. It needs time to travel from its source to our eyes and it's not getting that time right now."

"But our headlights are working."

"That's because they're moving with us."

Hank settled back into his seat. Between the wind blowing in his head and the confusion that deepened every time someone told him something, he was having a hard time of it.

"I'm glad you came," Lily said.

When she gave his fingers a squeeze, he held on to her hand.

"About what happened earlier," he said. "In the junkyard."

"It's okay. I understand. But I'm happier that you're with me."

Margaret started up the car. The headlights seemed abnormally bright when she turned them on, throwing

Jack's bus into bright relief. The dog stood in their glare, blinking, eyes flashing red.

"So here's what we're thinking," she said as she backed the car out onto Gracie Street.

There were cars, but they were all stationary. Dark shapes on the road. When their headlights slid across them, Hank could make out blank-eyed people sitting in the vehicles. Occasionally he caught glimpses of furtive movement—figures ducking down alleyways at their approach, crouching low behind cars. Some of that five percent who hadn't been dropped out of time, he assumed. They'd be more scared than he was, having no explanation at all as to what.was happening to them.

Not that having an explanation helped all that much.

Margaret wove a slow, winding path in between the vehicles, talking the whole time about things that just made Hank's head ache. Cuckoos. Raven's pot. Animal blood.

"See," Margaret was explaining, "the crow girls couldn't have helped either you or Lily if you didn't have it. Which is the same reason you're not stuck out of time like most of the people are. There has to be a connection or the magic can't travel. It's simple physics. Or is it genetics? Anyway . . ."

Hank tuned her out.

He glanced out the back window. In the rear lights— which also seemed abnormally bright to Hank—he could see the dog loping along behind the car. The red glare of the car's lights made the dog's coat turn the color of blood. It looked like a hellhound with its red fur and enormous size, some damned creature that escaped from the nether regions.

Maybe we're all damned, Hank found himself thinking. He faced the front again.

"The dog's following," he said. "What do you think it wants?"

Ray turned to look.

"Maybe it just wants to see how it all ends," Margaret said.

Ray shrugged. "It's just going to have to wait in line like the rest of us."

"What's its name?" Lily wanted to know.

"Bocephus," Ray said before Hank could tell her the dog didn't have one.

"How do you know that?" he asked.

"How come you didn't?" Ray replied. "You being related and all."

"How can I be—"

"It goes back a long way," Margaret said.

"And what's so bad about carrying canid blood?" Ray asked.

Margaret glanced at him. "If you're so proud of it, why're you walking around pretending to be a crow girl?"

For a long moment, Ray glared at her, then suddenly he changed. Gone was the small, dark-haired man sitting in the passenger's seat. In his place was a red-headed stranger, tall and pointy-featured. All Hank could do was stare. Beside him, Lily gasped.

"Happy now?" Ray asked Margaret.

"Oh, yeah," she said. "Like that's supposed to be an improvement."

Lily tightened her grip on Hank's hand, moving closer to him for comfort. Hank was in need of some himself. He forced himself to look out the window of the car, away from the pair in the front seat. The blackened streets only drove home how far removed he and Lily were from the way they'd always supposed the world worked.

"It could've been worse," Lily said softly.

He turned to look at her.

"You could've found out you were related to a cockroach."

With all they'd been going through, they surprised themselves to find that they could still share a laugh.

* * *

A half-dozen blocks away from the Rookery on Stanton Street they finally ran into a traffic snarl that Margaret couldn't finesse her way around.

"We're close enough that we can walk from here," she said.

Bocephus was waiting on the pavement when they got out of the car. Hank reached out to give him a pat, then reconsidered when the dog gave him a look that said in no uncertain terms, back off.

Yeah, Hank thought. I wouldn't want someone giving me a pat on the head either, no matter how related we might be.

"Nice to have you with us, Bo," he said instead.

The dog replied with a rumbling sound from deep in its chest that made both Lily and Hank back away.

"He's just being friendly," Ray said.

Hank nodded.

"What's he sound like when he's not being friendly?" Lily said.

"I don't think we want to know," Hank replied.

Margaret killed the engine, but left the headlights burning until she got the oil lamp lit once more. The circle of light it cast when she held it aloft seemed smaller than it had been before, by Jack's bus.

"Is it getting darker?" Hank asked, though it didn't seem possible.

Margaret shrugged. "Probably."

She took the lead and they fell in alongside her. Bocephus kept pace for awhile, then ranged on ahead, obviously impatient with their slower pace.

"You give any thought as to how we're going to wake Raven?" Ray asked. "I mean, he's been gone down inside himself for a long time now."

"I'm thinking of banging a brick up alongside his head," Margaret said. "This is all his fault. If he didn't want to take care of the pot, he should've passed it on to someone else."

Ray laughed. "Like who? You? Me? How long would

it be before we gave it a stir, just to set some little thing right?''

"I don't know. Maybe the crow girls then.''

"Like they wouldn't be a hundred times worse than Raven? They'd probably trade it to someone for a lollipop or a Cracker Jack ring. When's the last time they ever did anything that made sense?''

"They saved our lives,'' Lily said.

"I'm talking global here,'' Ray told her. "Maida and Zia are great with the details, but they can't seem to step back and take in the big picture.''

Margaret shook her head. "Like you know them so well.''

"You're saying I'm wrong?''

"No. What I'm saying is, when it comes to the old corbæ, we're talking about people who think as differently from us as we do from humans. None of us know what they can or can't do.''

"That's like—''

Margaret cut him off. "Are you forgetting who it was that made this world?''

Hank didn't like the sound of that at all.

"Wait a minute,'' he said. "Are you telling us—''

"That's right,'' Margaret said. "It was Raven and the crow girls who pulled us out of the medicine lands and made the long ago, and Jack was there to watch them do it, to hold the story of it so that we wouldn't forget. Things were pretty good until Cody came along and screwed everything up—just like he's doing again.''

Ray shook his head. "You can't blame Cody this time.''

"Oh no? Who brought the cuckoos into Newford?''

Hank and Lily exchanged glances. Hank could tell from the look in Lily's eyes that she was feeling the same as him, trying to come to grips with the idea that the two punky-looking girls who'd rescued them in that alley were immortal creation goddesses of some kind.

"Well, why not?" Hank muttered. "It makes about as much sense as anything else."

"No," Ray said, thinking that Hank was contributing to his argument with Margaret. "The cuckoos were going to make a move sooner or later—everybody knows that. Cody was only using them to create some confusion so that he could make his play for the pot. The only thing I don't get is what he was expecting my granddaughter to do."

"You haven't figured that out yet?" Margaret said. "It costs big time to use the pot—why do you think Cody keeps screwing it up? He can't make the commitment to give up enough of himself to use the pot right."

"What do you mean?" Lily asked.

"You have to give up a piece of yourself to make the pot work," Margaret explained. She gave Ray a sidelong glance. "All the corbæ know that. The more you try for, the more you've got to give. If you're not strong enough—haven't got enough of the blood—the pot'll just swallow you whole."

"He was going to use Kerry for *that*?" Ray said.

"Get with it," Margaret told him. "Cody uses everybody."

"I'm going to kill him."

"You'll have to stand in line. I've about had it with his idea of fun and games."

"But I thought Cody was the one who told you where the pot was," Lily said.

Margaret sighed. "Okay. He gets points for not bailing on us totally. And to tell you the truth, I can't help but liking him for all that he's a stubborn jackass. But still. When you add up the history of everything he's put us—"

A low rumbling growl rose up from the dog, cutting her off. Hank looked up to see a tall black man step out from behind one of the massive oak trees lining Stanton Street. He was carrying a shotgun, the muzzle pointed their way. A long steady rumble came from deep in the dog's chest as it stood its ground.

Hank wouldn't want to be on the receiving end of the dog's attack, but the man with the shotgun didn't seem to be in the least bit fazed. When he moved a little closer and the light from Margaret's lamp illuminated his features, Hank recognized him. It was Brandon Cole, the sax player he checked out at the Rhatigan whenever he could.

Hank had to shake his head. "What?" he said. "Is everybody one of these crow people now?"

"Brandon's a rook, actually," Margaret said. She stepped closer and pushed the barrel of the shotgun away. "And would you stop pointing that thing at us?"

Brandon lowered the muzzle so that it was aimed at the ground.

"Sorry," he said. "Chloë in such a twist she's got me jumping at shadows." He looked from her to Hank and the others, eyes narrowing when he noted Ray and the dog. "So what's going on here?"

"We're here to see Raven."

"You're kidding."

"Do I look like I'm kidding?"

Brandon regarded her for a long moment, before saying, "Chloë's not going to like this."

"Why don't you let me worry about Chloë," Margaret said.

Brandon gave them all another considering look.

"You have a problem with this?" Margaret asked.

"Nope," Brandon said, standing aside. "I just want to be there to see it."

"This Chloë," Hank asked Ray as they followed Margaret toward the house. "She runs the show here?"

"She likes to think so," Brandon replied from behind them. "It's getting so that even she believes she's first-born."

Hank remembered Moth telling him once, you get more than two people together in any one place, and right away you've got politics. Looked like it held true for animal people as well.

When they reached the porch, a woman was waiting for them. She cut a tall and stern figure, her hair a massive cloud of dark curls that simply merged with the surrounding shadows. Hank assumed she was Chloë.

"We've come to wake Raven," Margaret said.

Hank could hear in her voice how she was bracing for an argument, but now that they were this close, it was plain that the woman on the porch had no fight in her. She looked drawn and worn out.

"You're too late," Chloë said.

"He's already awake?"

Chloë shook her head. "Something took him away. One minute he's sitting there at his window, the next he's gone."

For a long moment no one spoke. It was, Hank thought, as though they simply couldn't believe what they were hearing. Well, welcome to the club.

"Just like Jack," Ray said finally.

Margaret sighed. "It's that damned pot. Every time things go bad, that pot's right in the middle of it."

"Don't be so quick to judge what you can't understand," Chloë said, her voice mild. "The pot's not good or bad—it's only what we do with it that makes it one or the other."

"Well, the cuckoos have it this time," Margaret told her.

Chloë's features sagged. She lowered herself onto the wicker bench on the porch and leaned slowly back against the wall of the house.

"Maybe Annie's right," she said. "Maybe it does have a mind of its own."

"What's that supposed to mean?" Brandon asked.

"She means it's perverse," Margaret said. "The way it keeps disappearing and then showing up again in the wrong hands."

Brandon looked back and forth between them in confusion. "But I thought it was on our side."

"The pot doesn't take sides," Chloë told him. "It just is, Brandon."

"So what happens now?" Hank asked. "What are the cuckoos doing with it?"

"Well," Chloë said, bitterness heavy in her voice. "This is no more than wild conjecture on my part, but I'd say they're trying to do what they're always trying to do: get rid of the firstborn corbæ."

"And that means?" Hank continued when she didn't elaborate.

"The world can't exist without the corbæ," Margaret explained. "It'll either end abruptly, or it'll go on like this, an endless night that'll only last until everything finally runs down."

"But don't the cuckoos know this?" Lily said.

Hank nodded. "They've got to know they're just shooting themselves in the foot."

"Cuckoos don't listen to the same kind of reason as normal people do," Chloë told them. "They don't consider cause and effect. When the world ends, they'll be the most surprised of anybody."

Hank looked around at the others. "So we've got to stop them, right? Ray says he knows where they're holed up."

But Margaret was already shaking her head.

"You don't get it," she said. "We're already too late."

Chloë nodded. "Once the pot's been stirred, all we can do is wait it out."

"No," Hank said. "Maybe you're ready to quit, but I'm not."

"There's nothing you can do," Margaret said. "Whatever's happening with the pot has got to play out and your confronting the cuckoos isn't going to do a thing to stop it. Besides, any one of them could break you like a twig without even needing to work up a sweat."

"I don't give up."

Chloë regarded him thoughtfully. "I'd forgotten how tenacious your kind can be. Though perhaps I shouldn't be surprised, considering it was Cody who brought you into the world and I don't think I've ever met anyone more stubborn."

Hank couldn't tell whether she admired that stubbornness or not. The truth was, he didn't particularly care. He turned to Ray.

"Where'd you say they were staying?"

"The Harbor Ritz."

"Then that's where I'm going," Hank said.

"Me, too," Lily added.

Hank looked at the others. "You can tag along or stay here. Your choice."

As though the dog had been following the conversation, Bocephus padded over to stand beside him.

"What the hell," Margaret said. "I always said I'd go down fighting."

In the end, they all went.

8.

The Aunts had joined Annie and the crow girls on their perch above the cathedral's rose window, stopping long enough to report on the general fruitlessness of the search so far before flying on again in their rook skins.

"Everybody's looking, looking, looking," Maida said. "It's so funny, really."

Annie had been watching the Aunts' flight, shading her eyes with her hand. Now she lowered her hand and looked at the crow girl.

"I don't get the joke," she said.

"Not funny ha-ha," Maida told her.

Zia nodded. "Which we like."

"But funny strange."

"Even a little sad."

"*What* are you talking about?" Annie asked.

Maida shrugged. "You know, that it takes something like this for us all to start paying attention to each other again."

"*Doing* something together," Zia put in.

Annie settled back against the wall and sighed. "Oh," she said. "Now I know what you mean. I suppose you're right." She was about to go on when the cathedral shook and they all had to cling to their perches. Annie looked at her companions.

"What was—" she began.

"Oh, look," Maida said.

But she didn't have to point. Annie could see the darkness flooding across the sky. She knew what was causing it, too—the darkness, the tremors that shook the building and the deep rumbling underground, the wind that had risen up that they could only hear, not feel. This wasn't the first time she'd been near Raven's pot when it was being used. But she'd never been this close before, so near the epicenter. She'd heard how disorienting it could be, but never actually experienced it for herself.

It was a very disconcerting feeling. She had the sense that if she didn't get down to the ground right away, she might lose her perch and be too disoriented to shift to her blue jay skin. She was about to suggest that they all fly down, but the crow girls had both suddenly gotten odd, surprised looks on their faces.

Maida blinked. "Oh . . ."

". . . my," Zia finished.

And then they were gone.

Annie sat very still, holding on to the ledge. She tried calling their names, but there was no reply. She knew they hadn't slipped into some shortcut or a fold in the world, because there were none up here. That was one of the things she liked about this spot—it offered safety from surprises. Nobody could sneak up on you. By the same token, nobody could slip away unseen either.

Except that had changed, hadn't it? Just like that.

And now she wished there was some hidey-hole she

could slip into, some quick shortcut to safer ground, because this perch of hers suddenly felt like the least safe place she could be.

Where had the crow girls gone? Or more to the point, what had taken them away, because what had just happened wasn't another one of their little tricks. They'd been just as surprised as she was when they'd vanished.

A wave of vertigo touched her, something she'd never experienced before. Wouldn't that be strange, to die falling from the sky?

Don't wait any longer, she told herself.

She shifted skins and lifted off before she could change her mind. The wind blowing inside her head threw off her equilibrium, but she forced herself to concentrate on her flight, gliding on the faint air currents, dropping downward in long, wide circles. When she finally touched the ground, she tumbled, wing over head. Shifting from bird to human form, she lay breathless on the pavement.

It was a long time before she could sit up without feeling nauseous.

Finally she managed to get to her feet. She staggered at first, then caught her balance. She called for the girls again.

"Maida! Zia!"

But they were well and truly gone.

It was so dark that she couldn't see anymore. Shifting her principle concentration to her olfactory senses, she began the slow trek back to the Rookery, hoping it was still there, that it hadn't disappeared along with the crow girls.

The idea of being all alone in a world gone black made her shiver with dismay.

She thought of the crow girls' gentle reprimand and promised that if she got through this, she'd look up from her work more often. She'd connect more with the world, make the effort to spend more time with the other corbæ.

Then she remembered what they'd told her about Paul,

how he'd lost himself in Raven's pot and had never come back.

The pot had taken them. She was sure of that. Taken them, but not her. Why? Because they were oldest?

What if it kept them?

She didn't even want to imagine a world without the crow girls in it, but she couldn't stop the thought, now that it was in her head. What if the pot had taken them and they were never coming back?

Would there even be a world without them in it?

9.

Before the darkness flooded the skies and the world fell out of time, Dominique Couteau sat with her chin cupped in her hands and stared at the crystal chalice she'd taken from the woman in the library.

Raven's pot. She didn't care what Cody thought. She knew what she had and with it, she finally held the fate of the corbæ in her hand. And yet she hesitated to use it, all because of Cody and his parting comments.

She was no longer alone in her hotel suite. Her two surviving sons had joined her, along with her brother Auguste, some of the Morgans from Hazard, and representatives from a half-dozen other cuckoo families. Dominique was the oldest of them, although it wasn't obvious from her looks. A stranger entering the room would have been forgiven in thinking that he had stumbled into a secret meeting of animated department store mannequins—they were all so indistinguishable from one another. Men and women. The old and the young. They weren't simply of a type, but identical. All of them tall and handsome. And ageless.

The next oldest after Dominique was Tatiana Morgan, Idonia's sister. She'd been living in Mexico when Jack Daw decimated her family in Freakwater Hollow. Self-exiled at the time from the endless feuding between

cuckoo and crow, the slaughter had brought her back into
the conflict with a hatred for the corbæ that rivaled Dominique's.

"Well?" Tatiana said, stirring impatiently. "What're
we waiting for?"

Dominique kept her gaze on the chalice. There was
something odd about it. When she looked at it from a
certain angle, the figure inside appeared to double.

"There is a problem," she said.

She was only half paying attention to Tatiana. The
chalice and its contents mesmerized her. The way the
light from the window played on the facets of the crystal
created a gleaming pattern that almost seemed to shape
pictographs. And then there was the puzzle of the figurine
inside, solitary from one angle, doubled from another.

"Cody claims the world won't survive without the
firstborn corbæ in it," Auguste explained when his sister
didn't elaborate.

"Bullshit," Tatiana said. "Where'd he get that idea?
From one of Jack's stories?"

Dominique finally looked up. "He didn't say."

"But you're still buying into it?"

"It seems worth considering," Dominique told her.

Tatiana shook her head. "I don't believe what I'm
hearing here." She looked around the room. "If the
corbæ are so powerful why's Raven spent the last sixty
years sleeping like some fat hog in its trough? Why does
Jack live like a bum in an old school bus in the Tombs?
And the crow girls . . . weeping Jesus. If they had anything to do with the making of the world it'd be a circus
fun house with every street a carnival ride and jelly beans
growing from the trees."

A murmur went through the room, heads nodding. Tatiana appeared to take it as a general agreement that she
remain their spokesperson. She turned back to Dominique.

"If you don't have the balls to get this show going,"

she said, "pass that crystal spittoon over to me and tell me what to do with it."

"Be careful you don't overstep the bounds of my patience," Dominique told her.

For a moment it seemed that Tatiana would continue the argument. Dominique met her gaze steadily until Tatiana had to look away.

"So," Dominique said. "Tatiana has been kind enough to share her views on the matter with us, but what of the rest of you? Do we proceed?"

She looked at them one by one, holding their gaze until each of them had nodded in agreement. A moment's silence followed, then Auguste cleared his throat. Dominique gave him her attention.

"Without Cody . . . ," he began.

"Yes?"

"It's just, I was under the impression that he was the only one who knew how to operate that . . . that . . ."—Auguste waved a hand toward the chalice—"device."

Dominique smiled. Device. That was an eloquent description.

"Cody told me all I needed to know before he made himself redundant," she told her brother.

It wasn't entirely true, but Dominique's pride wouldn't let her admit that she'd allowed Cody to simply walk out, unharmed, the working of Raven's pot unexplained. No, that wasn't entirely true.

There's one thing you have to know about the pot, darling. Everybody's got to figure out on their own how it can work for them.

Fair enough, she thought. How difficult could it be? She was sure she knew the basics from the stories. What it seemed to boil down to was that one had to be utterly focused on what one desired. And then one stirred.

Stirred what, she wasn't entirely certain. The air inside the pot? And what did one stir with? Presumably one's hand—if something Cody had told her when they first embarked upon this partnership was anything to go by.

She could call up his voice without needing to try very hard:

"So there I was, darling," he'd told her after his last botched attempt to use the pot. "Up to my elbows in the primordial goo, and then I don't know what it was. Maybe a skitter flew up my nose, or maybe it flew into my ear, but all of a sudden I've got this humming in my head, like a wind coming down off the mountains, and I lose my concentration."

That wouldn't happen to her. She could maintain her concentration, it didn't matter how many bugs tried to fly into whatever orifice. Her hatred of the corbæ was so singular and focused that it didn't require attention. It drummed in time to her heartbeat, a constant nagging reminder of their dominance, despite—as Tatiana had so readily pointed out—their obvious unsuitability as a ruling class. Although that wasn't the worst of it. The worst of it was their damned indifference to their position as the ruling class.

So the problem wasn't focusing on what she wanted from the pot, nor even a fear of thrusting her hand into it. She'd dare that and more to rid the world of the crows once and for all. What troubled her was Cody's parting remark in reference to the corbæ earlier today.

Truth is, I'm not all that sure there'd still be a world, you take them out of the equation.

He'd lied about the chalice not being Raven's pot. She knew that. But she wasn't as certain that he'd lied about the firstborn corbæ's place in the world. What if they truly were its anchor, if the world couldn't go on without them?

That was one possibility. The other was that it would simply be a different world. Radically altered, it was true, but that wouldn't necessarily be a bad thing. Not if the cuckoos were finally in ascendance.

At any rate, the questions were irrelevant. It was too late to back out now and still retain some semblance of pride.

Before some new argument arose, she thrust her hand into the open mouth of Raven's pot.

There was time for a moment of surprise. Earlier she had stuck various objects into the chalice and met no resistance, but now the air inside the pot was thick and cold, clinging to her skin like wet, runny mud. More confusing was how the relatively confined space inside appeared to be far larger than should be physically possible.

Then came the pain.

Her mouth opened, lips twisting, but no sound came forth. The pain was beyond articulation. It flared up from her hand and wrist as if she'd plunged her fist into a vat of acid, a burning that seemed to strip the flesh from her and leave all her nerve ends raw and bare.

She knew a momentary admiration for Cody, that he could dare this not once, but time and again.

And then she cursed him for what he hadn't told her.

The pot had a mind of its own.

The knowledge came to her through a swelling wave of agony. And as soon as she understood that the pot was sentient, she also realized that one was expected to approach it as a supplicant, not a master. That the pot decided whether or not to grant one's request. That the pot admired a creative petition, but abhorred destruction and turned such negative impulses back upon the supplicant.

The pain that ravaged her hand and wrist was the acidic boiling of her own hatred.

She could feel her arm being pushed up out of the chalice, clamped her mouth shut against the torment that grew in intensity every moment she remained in contact with the damned pot.

"No," she muttered from between her gritted teeth.

She forced her hand more deeply in and continued to stir whatever invisible muck it was that filled the pot. The raw heat of pain spread up from her lower arm, encompassing her shoulder, moving across her chest and into her neck, but instead of allowing it to weaken her, she used the pain to combat the will of the pot, used her hatred to make it submit to her command.

The sound of a hundred winds filled her head. The room went black. The chalice rattled and bounced on the table and she used her free hand to keep it from falling to the ground. But it wasn't simply the chalice that was banging about on the tabletop. The whole building trembled and shook.

"I will not submit to you!" she cried and thrust her arm up to the shoulder into the pot.

The pot lunged from the table. She threw her free arm around it, hugging it to her chest. Her body arced with a new blaze of pain.

Then the pot came apart in her arms.

She was thrown back against the windows. Glass shattered and only the sash bars kept her from being thrown outside. She could hear the cries of her family and the others—wild shrieks that rose above the screaming winds. Her body slid to the ground, all her muscles in spasms so that she jittered and bounced on the floor. Blood oozed from her nose, her ears, her eyes, filled her throat, choking her.

What have I done? she cried soundlessly. What have I done?

Though she clung to every tattered vestige that was being spun and torn away, she could feel her life ebbing away. It was too dear a price to pay, and yet, and yet . . .

She could sense that she had succeeded.

It was costing her her life, but the corbæ were no longer in the world.

10.

One of the worst stories Rory had ever written had been about "the last man on earth." It was an awkward, seriously juvenile effort, but then he'd only been fifteen when he'd put it down on paper, so perhaps he could be forgiven its stolen premise, faulty logic, painful storytelling, and other excesses.

What he'd really been writing about was how disassociated he felt from everyone around him. His character hadn't been so much the last man on earth as an anxious teenager trying to make sense of his raging hormones and loneliness. It hadn't been much of a success on either level, but at least he'd been wise enough to throw it out and move on. Still the idea, once awoken, remained with him, resurfacing not in his writing, but in his dreams. The scenarios varied, the world ending in everything from bangs to whimpers, but he was always the one man left alive while everyone else was gone.

All of which was to say that he was perhaps overly familiar with the concept. So when the sky flooded with darkness and the ground under the junkyard began to tremble, making the junked cars shake and rattle, he actually knew a moment's relief.

Everything was suddenly explained. All the weirdness of the past few days was only part of a dream, leading up to this familiar place where he was, *da-dum, da-dum,* the last man on earth once more. All he had to do was wake up and everything would be back to normal.

Except dreams didn't go on for this long, did they? Stringing together day after day of such detailed mundane activities along with the strange.

Nor were his dreams ever lucid. He never *knew* he was dreaming until after he'd woken up.

"Oh, man," he said softly as the realization hit home.

His voice seemed so small in the sudden vastness that surrounded him. He'd never felt so alone before in his life. And then there was this wind blowing in his head, inside, whining in his ears. A wind he couldn't feel on his skin.

This wasn't a dream. This was the strange times cranked up another notch, like the difference between watching *The X Files* on his television set and actually being a character in the story. Stepping from the known all the way into someplace no one had ever gone before. Into the impossible.

A stronger tremor made him jockey for balance. He looked up at the rattling cars, junked heaps piled one upon the other, already losing their definition in the growing dark.

If one of those stacks came down . . .

He headed back toward the front gates while he could still see, while the ground was still relatively stable underfoot, before some huge crack opened up underfoot and swallowed him whole. Halfway back down the lane between the stacked cars he saw Paris standing motionless, a couple of the dogs at her heels. He called out to her, but got no response.

The sick feeling that had started up in the pit of his stomach intensified.

"Paris!" he called again as he closed the distance between them.

Still no response.

"C'mon," he said. "Stop screwing around. You're really creeping me out."

But it was no use talking to her because she wasn't really there. Her body was standing in the dirt in front of him, but there was no one home. Her gaze was vacant, refusing to track his hand when he moved it back and forth in front of her eyes. He touched a tattooed shoulder and shuddered. The skin didn't feel real. It was spongy and cool to the touch.

He pulled his hand back and wiped it on his jeans. Hard. Backed away, desperate to put distance between them, but unable to take his gaze from her. One foot, two. By the time he was a half-dozen feet away, he couldn't see her anymore. Couldn't see anything, the darkness was so profound.

He stood perfectly still, listening for something, some sign of life, anything, but all he heard was the wind in his ears and the rattling and clanking and grinding of metal as the wrecked cars jostled in their stacks.

He couldn't stay here.

Hands held out before him, he shuffled slowly back the way he'd come, half-expecting to come into contact with Paris again, bile rising in his throat at the thought. Instead he bumped into one of the dogs that had been standing by her. Under its fur, the flesh was as spongy as Paris's had been.

Swallowing thickly, he circled around the motionless dog and continued his snail's pace toward the junkyard's front gates. At one point he heard a car engine start up, not close, but not that far away either. He thought of calling out to whoever it was, then realized they wouldn't be able to hear him over the sound of their engine. Standing quietly, he listened to the motor rev. A moment later he heard the vehicle moving away.

Oddly enough, the receding sound comforted him.

He wasn't alone.

He wasn't the last man alive on the earth.

When he could no longer hear the car, when there was only the wind in his ears and the rattling metal of the stacked cars again, he started forward once more. Hope made the sick feeling subside in his stomach, made him feel stronger, more able to cope.

He wasn't alone.

It was odd how quickly he lost his sense of time. He had no way of gauging how long he'd been shuffling down the lane before he finally stumbled into one of the lawn chairs they'd been sitting on earlier.

What he wanted most was light.

He slowly felt around the chair he'd just knocked over until he came to another one, then a third. By the way they were facing he was able to make an educated guess as to where he remembered seeing the two cabs parked. Taking a deep breath, he started in what he hoped was their direction, counting his steps.

Seventeen . . . eighteen . . .

When he hit twenty, a sinking feeling rose in him. He

became convinced he was off on his angle, heading to who knew where in the darkness. Everything was so disorienting. He was about to try to retrace his steps when his questing hands came into contact with the hood of one of the cars. He felt like kissing the smooth metal. Feeling his way along the side of the car, he reached the door, opened it. The flare of the interior light seemed blinding. He looked away, letting his eyes adjust through his peripheral vision. When he could see without spots dancing in front of his eyes, he got into the cab and checked the ignition.

The keys were there.

The engine turned over smoothly. Closing his eyes, he flicked on the headlights. He waited a moment, then slowly eased them open. His pulse jumped into sudden overtime when he saw the man standing a half-dozen feet away from the front bumper.

Who—?

He calmed a little when he realized it was Moth, the junkyard's unfriendly owner, but the rush of adrenaline had put him all on edge again. Moth was standing as motionless as Paris and the dogs had been, a frozen cloud of cigarette smoke hanging by his head—a grim reminder of how much the world had turned upside down. Everything was unknown territory now.

Rory put his foot on the clutch and shifted into reverse, backing the cab up a few feet so that it would be easier to circle around the motionless figure caught in his headlights. He had to stop at the gates and get out to open them. Once he drove through, he didn't bother to close them again.

Heading slowly down Gracie Street was a surreal experience. Frozen figures on the sidewalks. None of the cars moving, the drivers sitting with their hands on the steering wheels, staring vacantly out of their windshields. The traffic had been light before it was abruptly frozen, so it wasn't too hard to make progress through the maze of stopped vehicles, but he still took the first side street to get away from them. He couldn't bear to look at all of those uninhabited faces.

He was making for home, because he didn't know what else to do, where else to go. And now that he had the glare of his headlights to cut away at the darkness, the solid metal body of the cab giving him a sense of protection from whatever might be out there haunting the streets, he could think a little more clearly about what had happened. The trouble was, being able to think more clearly didn't help, because the questions he had didn't have answers.

What had become of the world he'd always known?

Why had he been spared?

And who else was out here in the dark with him?

He thought of Kerry then, how she'd disappeared. Was this where she'd vanished to? Was this some parallel world set next to their own where when you were drawn into it, you could still see an aspect of the world you'd left behind, but they couldn't see you at all?

All these frozen people and vehicles. He wondered if the world had actually stopped, or if he was only looking at something like a snapshot of the way it had been when he stepped out of it.

It all made his head ache. He had a sharp throb behind his eyes that wasn't helped at all by the wind that was still inside him.

Blowing.

Endlessly blowing.

It was hard not to just pull over to the side of the street and simply give up. The world, the wind, the frozen people . . .

It was all so insane.

That made him think of Kerry again, locked up for ten years in an institution when there was nothing wrong with her. But because of that, because of how the experience had left her so unprepared for life outside of the institution, she'd ended up having all sorts of trouble functioning in the ordinary world.

He shook his head slowly.

Christ, if she *was* in this world, would she be able to cope at all?

He wished he could help her, but if she was here, where would he even begin to look?

Get back to the Rookery first, he told himself. Maybe there'd be somebody there who could help.

Twice he came to side streets that were completely blocked with stopped cars on either side of the road and he had to back up to the last intersection he'd passed. The back lights were far dimmer than his headlights, making the procedure that much more nerve-wracking.

Occasionally he caught glimpses of people. They were always darting into an alley or lane, away from his head-lights. He thought their caution was a little extreme until he put himself in their position and decided he'd be just as leery of approaching a stranger himself if he was out there, alone and on foot, with no light. The world had gone so off-kilter, who knew what you might run into?

A half-dozen blocks from the Rookery he came around a corner and spied a figure on the street ahead of him. A woman, walking slowly along the side of the street, one foot scuffling against the curb, using it as a guide. She stopped and turned, shading her eyes against the glare of his headlights. Rory's heart lifted. He rolled down his window and called to her.

"Annie!"

When he pulled up beside her and put the car in neutral, she climbed in the passenger's side, her familiar features oddly lit in the lights from the dashboard. But Rory didn't care how strange she looked.

"Oh, man," he said. "Are you a sight for sore eyes."

Annie leaned back in the seat as though all her muscles had gone limp. She turned to him and managed a half smile.

"Now that's what I'd call an understatement," she told him. "What are you doing with this car?"

He was so glad to see her that he began to babble, the

words coming out all in a rush. "I took Kerry up to see Jack, except he wasn't there. Instead there was this tattooed woman with a bunch of dogs who started off being really pissed off with us, but then she took us over to this junkyard and . . ."

He gave her the abbreviated version. Annie listened without interrupting—a first for her, Rory thought, but these were weird times.

"Did Kerry disappear before or after all of this"—Annie waved her hand toward what lay outside the windshield—"happened?"

"Before. Why? Is it important?"

"I don't know. It's just that the crow girls disappeared as well, right when everything started to shake and the sky went black."

"Do you think they're in the same place?" Rory asked.

"I don't know that either."

"Because I thought maybe this was where Kerry had disappeared to."

Annie gave him a blank look.

"You know," he said. "Because it's like we're someplace else, too, aren't we? The way we can move around but everybody else is frozen like time stood still for them or something."

"This is still our world," Annie told him. "It's only like this because Cody got his hands on Raven's pot again."

Rory shook his head. "Lily said these cuckoos have it."

"Shit. That makes it even worse."

For a long moment neither of them spoke. Rory stared out at the endless night that had fallen across the city, broken only by the headlights of the cab. They lit the street ahead of him, but in comparison to the darkness that lay beyond their reach, they seemed woefully inadequate.

"Annie, what's going on here? I can't tell the difference between what's real and what's not anymore.''

"Take us home," she said, "and I'll try to explain while you drive."

But it didn't help. The things she was telling him were too divorced from life as he knew it—never mind that life was no longer even remotely the way he knew it. The corbæ, magical cauldrons, Cody, the cuckoos . . . it was all too much like walking into the middle of a particularly convoluted foreign film that had no subtitles and was already half over.

"So . . . everybody in the Rookery," he said. "They're all bird people?"

Annie gave him a tired smile. "Even you—though your blood's pretty thin."

"Even me."

She nodded.

"We're all bird people."

She nodded again. "In the house, at any rate."

"I guess that's why it's called the Rookery," he said.

A mild hysteria was building up inside him. The only thing that kept him from losing it completely was Annie's calmness. He was able to accept, if not understand, all the strange things she was telling him because he trusted her implicitly, because she'd never lied to him and had no reason to be lying to him now.

The absence of normality outside the cab did much to help convince him as well.

"How could I have lived with you all for nine years and not known any of this?" he said.

Annie shrugged. "There was never any need for you to know."

She gave him a look that reminded him of the old Annie, the one he'd always thought he'd known. The one who'd been as human as he was—though of course he wasn't entirely human himself, was he? He had this bird blood running through his genes, too.

"Besides," Annie said. "What would you have thought if I'd told you all of this before?"

"That you were just being Annie. Putting me on."

"Well, I'm not."

"Yeah, that's kind of obvious now."

They'd reached Stanton Street, but soon their way was blocked with stopped cars. Rory backed up the cab again and took a side street. From there he turned into the lane that ran behind the Rookery.

Rory glanced at his companion. "So you figure Lucius—who's really this Raven guy—will be able to make things right?"

"If we can bring him back."

"And he's gone where?"

Annie shook her head. "I don't know. Maybe it's a matter of waking him up. He's just gone, you know? His body's here but who knows where his mind is roaming? You have to understand, Rory. I'm not one of the firstborn. I've no idea what makes them tick."

If, as Annie had told him, the crow girls were also firstborn corbæ, Rory knew exactly what she meant.

The lane was clear all the way to the Rookery. When he got to the coach house, Rory pulled in, pointing the car into the backyard so that the headlights illuminated the back of the house. Two tall figures, all in black, were standing in the yard, looking back at them. It took Rory half a moment to recognize them. The Aunts. Eloisa and Mercedes.

"So they're crows, too," he said.

"Rooks, actually."

"Rooks. Right."

Annie got out of the car and crossed the lawn toward them. Rory sat for a moment, then put the car in neutral, engaged the hand brake and stepped out as well. He left the engine running, the lights on.

"We're too late," one of the Aunts was saying as Rory approached.

As usual, he didn't know if it was Eloisa or Mercedes. Some things didn't change, even when the world went crazy. He took a small measure of comfort from that.

"Everyone's gone," the other Aunt said.

The first one nodded. "We made our way home—"

". . . through the endless dark—"

". . . across the trembling ground—"

". . . and they were all gone."

Rory had never realized how much like the crow girls they were—if the crow girls were to speak with less modulation in their voices and looked to be in their sixties, that is.

"Gone how?" Annie asked. "I was at St. Paul's when Maida and Zia simply disappeared. Are they gone like that, right out of the world?"

"We don't know," one of the Aunts replied, her voice mournful.

The other nodded. "All we know is everyone's gone—"

". . . and nothing will be the same again."

Annie had explained to Rory that what was happening now wasn't the usual effect that came from this cauldron of Raven's being used. The other times there'd be a shift in the world, but it was transitory. Over in minutes. Nothing like this.

"So what do we do now?" he asked.

Annie slumped on the steps of the back porch.

"I don't know," she said. "Pray?"

"Who would you pray to?"

Her only response was to shake her head.

Rory'd never seen her like this. Annie wasn't even remotely prone to depression. She was always the one who jollied him out of bad moods, made him smile when he was feeling down.

He sat down beside her and put an arm around her shoulder. When she leaned against him, he reached up with his free hand and stroked her arm.

"I don't know what's going to happen," he said, "but whatever it is, you're not going to face it alone."

"Thanks," she said, her voice so soft he had to bend down to hear her. "Thanks for being here."

"Works both ways," he told her. "I'd be going seriously crazy by now if I hadn't run into you."

She put both arms around him and burrowed tight against his side.

He glanced up to find that the Aunts were looking up at the house once more, holding hands, heads cocked like the birds they were supposed to be able to turn into. They seemed resigned, simply waiting now for what was to come next, comforting each other the way he was comforting Annie, the way his having to be strong for her made all of this easier for him to bear.

That made him think of Kerry again. Kerry who was out there somewhere, alone, with no one to turn to.

11.

Kerry wasn't alone.

But she had been alone, weeping in the backseat of the Volvo earlier, and she had been alone when she first found herself drawn into this strange place by her need to make amends with Katy.

Now I've gone all the way, she thought as she slowly turned in the gray space that surrounded her. Stepped all the way through how things are supposed to be into . . . what? Madness or magic. The line between them had never seemed so blurred and thin as it was now.

Junkyard, car, tattered blanket, the world she knew was gone. She'd been spirited away into otherness, into an eerie, but oddly calming, place. The ache in her heart was soothed, though she couldn't have said how or why.

She should have been panicking, because this was worse than any anxiety attack. It was impossible to differentiate directions. Turning slowly on the balls of her feet, she saw the same unchanging vista on all sides, an endless gray haze that held nothing except . . .

She paused, focusing on a tiny spot of color half-hidden in the distance.

There was something. . . .

She began to walk in its direction, feeling as though she were stepping on clouds, the surface underfoot having the give of soft down. It would be so easy to stretch out and nap, but she knew she shouldn't. In this place a nap seemed too likely to last forever.

There was no way to tell how long she walked until the spot of color she was aiming for became a recognizable shape. A reclining figure. Red-haired. The features as familiar as her own. She might have been looking at herself, finally having succumbed to the lure of the yielding surface underfoot, but it wasn't of course, because she was standing here, only . . . only . . .

As she drew closer, she saw there was not one redhaired woman sleeping there, but two. The second had been hidden behind the first and she was wearing the same dress that Kerry had put on this morning, the same one she was wearing right at this very moment.

This is strange, she thought. How can I be in two places at once?

But even that thought wasn't as troubling as it logically should have been. All it managed to wake in her was a faint itch of curiosity.

"Kerry?"

She turned to find her sister sitting cross-legged nearby, regarding her with obvious surprise. Katy wore the same yellow jeans and sleeveless purple top that her sleeping double did. Her hair was an untidy red tangle. Kerry found her gaze drawn to her sister's tattoo. She remembered what Paris had told her, that the symbol meant "little sister" in . . . was it Japanese?

Katy stood up and smoothed down the fabric of her jeans where they had bunched at her thighs.

"What are you doing here?" she asked.

"I . . . I'm not really sure. I was in the junkyard, sitting in the back of that car where you'd been staying and wishing I could make things right between us, and the next thing I knew I found myself here." Kerry paused for a moment, then added, "Where are we anyway?"

Katy didn't reply to her question. "What do you mean, you wanted to make things right?"

"I don't want to chase you away anymore," Kerry told her. "I don't know exactly what's real anymore, but even if you're not real the way the world judges real, I know that I'd rather be crazy and have a sister than not have a sister at all."

Katy sighed and sat back down. Kerry hesitated a moment before joining her.

"You're spoiling everything," Katy said.

Not even the soothing qualities of their surroundings could stop the sudden stab of hurt that went through Kerry when she heard those words. Her lower lip began to tremble and tears welled in her eyes.

"I . . . I guess I deserve that," she said. "I've been so awful to you, haven't I?"

Katy shook her head. "No, your reactions have been pretty normal, considering. I mean, what're you supposed to think when I don't let people see me and whenever you try to say that I really do exist, they lock you away and dope you up until you finally start seeing the world the way they want you to? I'm the one who should be sorry. And I am, Kerry. I truly am. That's why I came here."

Kerry wiped her eyes on her sleeve. "What . . . do you mean?"

"It gets pretty complicated. Do you know about the corbæ?"

"Not really. I mean, I've heard people talking about them but it's all kind of confusing."

Katy nodded. "I guess magic is, when it all comes flooding down upon you."

"But it's real, isn't it? Just like you are."

Katy smiled. "You're here, aren't you?"

Unless I'm dreaming, Kerry thought.

Her gaze went to the two sleeping figures, each of them curled up, the head of the one at the feet of the other.

They looked like some curious yin-yang symbol.

She returned her attention to Katy as her sister began to talk, telling her about the corbæ and Cody and Raven's pot and all.

"So that's what I'm doing here," Katy said, finishing up. "The pot's always causing trouble, but Jack said if you could really understand it, then you could destroy it, or send it back to where it came from. And that's what I've been trying to do. I was trying to understand it, but instead it swallowed me."

"We . . . we're inside this pot?"

Katy nodded.

"But how big *is* it?"

Katy held out her hands about eight inches apart.

"Magic," she said in response to the confused look that came over Kerry's features.

"I guess." Kerry looked at the sleeping twins. "Are they us? Are we sleeping somewhere in the real world and only spirits here?"

"I don't know," Katy told her. "The pot's way more complicated than I thought it would be. It's not so much an object as an idea—or an object holding an idea—and it's really hard to figure it out. You remember those Chinese puzzle boxes we used to have?"

Kerry nodded. She'd had a set of them that Katy had loved to play with, putting a precious something in the smallest, a pebble, a braid of grass, a piece of jewelry stolen from their mother, and closing it up in box after box, each one larger than the next.

"That's sort of what the pot's like," Katy explained. "Every time I think I've figured it out, I find a new, smaller box that I have to puzzle out."

"But I don't understand why you're doing it," Kerry said.

"See," Katy went on, "I thought I could fix both my problems. Get out of your life and get rid of the pot."

Kerry shook her head. "I still don't get it."

"I figured it out—from all of Jack's stories. It costs

big time to get the pot to do exactly what you want. The only reason no one's ever gotten rid of it or sent it back is that no one wants to pay the price.''

Understanding began to dawn on Kerry.

"You were going to . . . sacrifice yourself?" she asked.

Katy shrugged. "I don't think anybody knows if it's actually dying that happens. I think you just go back to where the pot came from." She gave Kerry a rueful look. "And maybe that's a better place."

"But—"

"And the thing is, of everybody, I've got the least to lose."

Tears welled in Kerry's eyes again.

"It's all my fault," she said. "If I hadn't kept believing people when they said you weren't real—"

Katy shook her head. "Don't say that. I'm the one who doesn't fit in. I should never have been born. I don't think I was *supposed* to be born, or I would have popped out at the same time you did."

"But you *did* get born . . . eventually."

"And I haven't been happy. And I've only brought misery into your life."

"That's my fault, not yours."

"No," Katy said, her voice gentle. "Who's the one who always got you into trouble? Who's the one who let you take the fall for everything? Who's the one who let you spend ten years in an institution because I wanted to be a secret?"

"Why?" Kerry asked. "Why did you want to be a secret?"

Katy shook her head. "I don't know. Maybe there's too much crow girl in me."

"That's not a bad thing," Kerry said. "I like the crow girls."

"Me, too. Though I've only ever met them in Jack's stories."

For a long moment neither of them spoke. Finally Kerry asked the question that had made her forgo her first day at the university and eventually brought her into this strange place.

''Who were our parents?'' she asked. ''Who were they really?''

''You haven't figured that out yet?''

''How could I?'' Kerry said. ''Everybody I talk to about it gets all vague and . . .''

Her voice trailed off. Behind Katy, a rich golden, amber glow was rising up around the figures of their sleeping doubles. Katy turned to look. Goose bumps ran up Kerry's arms and she could feel the hairs prickling at the nape of her neck. The light reminded her of the glow Maida had shown her how to find inside herself. It had that same luminous, soothing property. But at the same time, its presence put an electric charge into the air. There was an untamed, almost feral quality to its presence that made her want to simultaneously celebrate its existence and hide from its view.

''What . . . what's happening now?'' she asked.

''I'm not sure. I'm just kind of winging it myself. . . .''

Kerry moved closer to her sister and gripped her arm when a tall, dark-haired man began to materialize on the far side of the sleeping pair. His arms were widespread, making his long black overcoat drape like wings. Under the brim of his hat, his eyes were so dark they seemed to swallow the golden light.

''Who . . . ?'' Kerry began.

She felt Katy relax.

''It's okay,'' Katy said. ''It's only Jack.''

The man had been looking down at the sleeping figures at his feet. Now he lifted his gaze to regard Kerry and her sister. He'd seemed so scary when he first appeared, but now he only looked confused. Behind him, the amber glow intensified.

''You're here?'' he said, his attention on Katy. Then he included Kerry in his gaze. ''Both of you?''

When Katy rose to her feet, Kerry quickly scrambled up to stand beside her.

"Hello, Jack," Katy said.

"Tell me this isn't where I think it is."

"I can't do that."

"Did you bring me here?" he asked. "Are you the one who stirred the pot?"

"Is that what happened?"

Jack shook his head slowly. "There's something seriously wrong here. I've never heard of . . ."

His voice trailed off. All he seemed to be able to do was shake his head. Kerry wasn't sure if he was simply denying what was happening or trying to marshal his thoughts. She understood exactly how he felt.

"Jack," Katy said. "This is Kerry—though I guess you already know that. Kerry, this is our father, Jack Daw."

Kerry stared at him, wide-eyed. "Our . . . father . . . ?"

"You knew?" Jack said. "How could you know?"

"C'mon, Jack," Katy said. "Do you think you're the only one who tells stories?"

"But the other corbæ said they wouldn't—"

"Who said I only listen to corbæ stories?"

"But . . ." He looked from one of them to the other. "And you . . . you don't hate me?"

Kerry was still trying to adjust to his being their father. But now she focused on what he was saying.

"Why would we hate you?" she asked.

"Because Jack carries guilt like a 'pie steals treasures," a familiar voice said.

They all turned to find that the crow girls were now here as well. It was Maida who'd spoken. Beside her, Zia nodded.

"It's what he does," she said.

"He can't let go."

"Not ever."

"Not even when it makes things go worse."

Jack was frowning at them, but the crow girls only smiled back, unrepentant.

"Oh, look," Maida said, turning to Kerry and her sister. "Now there's two of them."

"Just like us."

"Is that why you brought us here?"

Zia grinned widely. "This is so very much fun."

"Be serious," Jack told them. "We're in a load of trouble here."

"We're always serious," Maida told him.

"What gets confusing," Zia added, "is that we're often serious about different things."

Maida nodded. "To what other people think is serious, that is."

"But we don't get confused at all," Zia said. She pointed to the amber glow. "Oh, look. Isn't it pretty?"

It rose up like a candle's flame now, bright, burning, reminding Kerry more than ever of the glow she carried inside on such a smaller scale. Jack turned to look at it and retreated quickly, his eyes filling with wonder.

"The Grace," he said.

"Oh, it is, isn't it!" Zia cried.

Maida smiled. "What a good name for it, Jack."

Jack shook his head, still retreating. "How can it be real?"

"What does he mean?" Kerry asked.

"There's a place near where you were born," Maida explained, "that's Jack's heart home."

Zia nodded. "That's what he's seeing in its fire. The home of his heart."

"Maybe even Nettie," Maida added.

"My grandmother?" Kerry asked.

Zia gave her a sad look. "No. Your mother. We remember now."

"My . . . mother . . . ?"

Kerry turned to her sister for help with this new revelation, but Katy's gaze was locked on what Jack called the Grace. The crow girls fell silent, their own attention as riveted as Katy's and Jack's. When Kerry looked herself, shapes flickered in the Grace's amber glow. It looked like a tree. A woman. A man. A bird. A dog, or maybe it was a wolf. A turtle. A spider.

And then a woman again. Sweet and fey, but oh so strong. You could tell that rivers changed course at her word. Forests would part before her. The wind would carry her hair. The sun and moon would stop for her. Mountains would bow to offer her fealty. The ocean would whisper her name.

Kerry was so entranced by the woman that it took her long moments to realize that behind her, one more dark-skinned figure was taking shape. He was an enormous Buddha of a man, the largest man Kerry had ever seen. She searched for and found her sister's hand. Katy squeezed her fingers with as tight a grip as Kerry did hers.

"Raven," she heard one of the crow girls say and knew from what Katy had told her earlier that this was her mysterious landlord.

He knelt with his immense weight resting on his legs, his eyes closed, his hands clasped loosely on his lap. His features were placid, almost expressionless. Kerry would have taken him for a statue, except when the Grace stepped toward him and touched his brow with a glowing hand, his eyelids flickered, then opened to reveal eyes so dark that the deepest night, the blackest raven wing, paled in comparison.

He looked upon them with deep curiosity before letting his gaze settle on the Grace.

"Is it time?" he asked.

His voice was so low-pitched and resonant Kerry could feel it vibrating deep in her chest.

The Grace made no reply. None of them spoke.

Raven looked slowly at each one of them, then spoke again.

"Has this world finally reached its end?"

12.

They were maybe a half-dozen blocks from the water-front when Hank noticed that they no longer needed the oil lamp Brandon was carrying. Out past the reach of its light, an amber-gold glow was creeping over the pavement and spreading across the sides of the buildings. The glow wasn't exactly bright, but it continued to swell inside. At this rate Hank thought it would soon feel like dusk in the countryside, or that they were walking out under a full moon.

Lifting his head, he looked for the source of the light.

It wasn't hard to find. The tall towers of the Harbor Ritz were pulsing amber-gold. As he watched, the light swelled into the shape of an enormous hardwood tree—an oak, or an elm, with broad spreading branches and a seriously huge canopy. You could still see the hotel through the tree, but as the light continued to stretch upward, the thirty-story building began to look like a child's toy in comparison.

"Jesus," he said. "Would you look at that."

But his companions' attention was already fixed on the scene. Lily's reaction seemed to be a lot like his own—relief that there was finally some real light to combat the oppressive dark, mixed with a good dose of awe as to the shape it was taking. Hank would have thought that the others, since they were supposed to be these magical beings themselves, would be taking this latest piece of strangeness pretty much in stride. Instead, they looked like they'd just found out that Elvis was not only alive, but a couple of hundred feet tall and wearing a halo.

They'd all stopped walking and were just staring up at that tree of light. Brandon blew out the oil lamp and set it down on the pavement at his feet. When he stood up again, he went right back to being as mesmerized as the rest of them.

"It's so beautiful," Lily murmured.

Hank nodded. He turned to Margaret, who was standing closest to him, Brandon's shotgun held loosely in her hands.

She's going to drop that, he thought and took the shotgun from her. She made no protest. Didn't even seem to be aware that he'd taken it.

"What do you see?" he asked.

It had to be more than he could.

For a long moment she didn't answer and he thought she hadn't heard him.

"A forever tree," she said just before he could repeat the question. "Made of the light of the long ago."

"The long ago?"

She nodded, not taking her gaze from it. "That was the light that was waiting for us when Raven first called the world up out of the medicine lands."

Hank glanced at Lily but all she could do was shake her head. It was making no more sense to her.

"And is it a good or bad thing?" he asked. "Us seeing it like this, I mean?"

"It's not good or bad," Margaret said. "It just is."

The others nodded in agreement, but nobody added anything to explain the puzzle. The corbæ seemed to be good at that. Hank gave the source of the light another considering look.

Okay. It was a forever tree. Whatever that meant.

"What do we do now?" Lily asked.

"I don't know about anyone else," Hank replied, "but I'm going on."

Lily nodded, but nobody else responded. Hank looked down at Bocephus, sitting on his haunches, also staring up at the source of the light.

It even had the dog spellbound, he thought, but then Bocephus shook his head and made a rumbling, querulous sound deep in his chest. Hank followed his gaze to see what had distracted him.

"Heads up," Hank said.

Only Lily looked away from the big glowing tree to see what Hank and the dog had already noted. They were no longer alone.

In some ways, nothing had changed. The buildings were all still dark. Cars, buses, cabs, delivery vans . . . nothing was moving. The drivers and passengers remained immobile in their vehicles. Pedestrians were still frozen in the positions they'd been in when the world went strange.

But now dozens of people had joined them on the street, all of them looking up at the glowing tree that lit the skyline and was banishing the dark that had swallowed the world earlier. Slowly they started walking toward the waterfront. Hank waited a beat, then took Lily's hand and they started walking again as well. Bocephus immediately fell into step beside them. When they'd gone a half-dozen steps, Hank looked back to see that the corbæ and Ray were following.

With the stronger light to guide their way, they made much better time than they had coming from Stanton Street. It only took them a few minutes to reach the Harbor Ritz, where a large crowd had already gathered. Hank estimated there were at least two or three hundred, maybe more. They appeared to come from all walks of life. Men, women, and children. Black, white, Asian. Everybody with a drop of animal blood in them, he figured.

There was little conversation and no one paid much attention to them, even when they made their way through to the front of the crowd. Hank craned his neck. This close, the glowing tree was beyond impressive. He stared up until he got a crick in his neck, then made himself look at the building itself, enclosed by the glow. Katy was in there somewhere.

He gave the crowd a once-over. No one was making any effort to get any closer or trying to get in. He didn't blame them. The whole situation was completely out of his experience as well. But he didn't see that he had a choice.

"I'm going in," he said.

"There's no point," Margaret told him.

He glanced at her in surprise. This was the first comment she'd offered freely since the tree appeared.

"Katy's in there," he said.

She nodded. "But there's nothing we can do about it now. It's out of our hands."

"But—"

"Trust me, Hank. All we can do is wait."

Hank shook his head.

"You don't understand," Brandon said. "But we've been here before—when the world began. That light is the place the music comes from. You can't mess with it. You can't talk to it. So what's going inside it going to do?"

"What do you mean it's where the music comes from?" Hank asked.

"It's where everything comes from," Brandon said. "Music. Art."

Chloë nodded. "Intellect. Dreams."

"Hope," Ray put in. "Compassion."

"Heart," Margaret added.

"So tell me this," Hank asked. "What kind of heart would I have if I just left Katy in there on her own without trying to get her out?"

"The light won't harm her," Chloë said.

Hank turned to her. "You know that for a fact?"

Chloë hesitated for a long moment.

"No," she said finally.

"So I'm going in."

Hank walked toward the building, Bocephus padding along at his side. Lily waited a heartbeat before she started to follow. Margaret caught her by the arm, her strong grip holding Lily back. Hank paused, turned to look at them.

"You don't have to do this," Margaret said.

But Lily shook free. "Yes, I do. The only reason Hank got caught up in all of this is because he stopped to help me. I can't let him go on now by himself."

Hank was going to tell her that it was okay, she didn't have to come, but Margaret spoke first.

"He's going in because he's worried about Katy," she said, "and Katy has nothing to do with what's going on."

"But I do," Lily told her. "Remember who handed the pot over to the cuckoos. If it weren't for me, if I'd just held on to it better or hidden it or something, none of this would be happening."

"You didn't know."

Lily glanced at the building. "What are you so afraid of?"

"It isn't fear," Margaret said.

"Then what is it?"

Hank nodded. He wouldn't mind knowing that himself, since however this conversation turned out, he was still going in.

"Do you believe in God?" Margaret asked.

Lily looked confused. "I . . . I'm not sure. I guess so. Or at least I believe there's something, some kind of spirit or force. But when I was a kid I believed in God."

"So you can remember those feelings you had about God when you believed in him?"

"Sure."

Margaret pointed to the light. "Going in there for us would be like the child you were meeting God."

"Oh."

Hank looked at the building, then back at Lily. When he held out his hand, she walked over to him and took it. With the dog at their side, they went up to the revolving doors of the hotel, pushed on them, then stepped through.

Into the light.

13.

"Oh my goodness," one of the Aunts said.

Rory looked up from the steps where he and Annie were sitting. He still didn't know which was Eloisa and which was Mercedes. But one of them was pointing south, toward the lake.

He stood up to get a better look. "It's some kind of light," he said.

As he watched, the distant glow took the shape of an enormous tree that almost seemed to fill the entire skyline above the roofs of the neighboring buildings.

"Not just any light," Annie said, coming to stand beside him. "That's the light from the first day—what Raven brought across from the medicine lands to make the long ago."

"It looks like a tree."

"That's the way it looked back then, too."

Rory gave her a considering look, then walked slowly over to the idling cab. Reaching in, he turned off the engine and the headlights. The sudden silence was eerie. The dark came washing in on them, but it was only their eyes adjusting to the change of light. After a few moments he realized that he could see as well as he normally could in the twilight.

"We have to go," one of the Aunts said.

The other nodded.

"But Rory won't be able to keep up," Annie said. "And," she continued, "he can't take the car because the streets are probably even more blocked up downtown than they are here."

The Aunt who'd first spoken shrugged. "But that's where the others are."

"Let him take his pedal bicycle," said the other one.

Annie nodded. "Good idea."

Rory went up the steps to the back door and brought

his mountain bike out of the shed where he stored it. When he had it down on the lawn, he looked at the three women.

The Aunts leapt into the air, arms outspread. Instead of coming back down on the ground, the way he would have if he'd tried to do that, they shrank, were transformed, kept rising, and two small crows—no, he corrected himself numbly, they're rooks—were circling above his head, under the boughs of the elm.

"Oh, Jesus," he said, staring up at them.

He turned slowly to Annie.

"You didn't really believe me, did you?" she said.

"Well . . . that is . . . I just thought it was . . . um, some kind of metaphor. . . ."

Annie laid the palm of her hand against his cheek. "Don't freak out on me now."

"I . . ." He cleared his throat. "I won't."

"Good." She smiled and stepped back, making a motion toward his bike. "So let's go."

Rory slowly straddled his bike. He looked south, to that giant tree of light that rose up from somewhere near the waterfront, then back at Annie. But she wasn't there anymore. A blue jay had joined the two rooks in the air above him. Seeing they had his attention, the rooks flew out of the yard, southward. The jay dropped down to land on the handlebars of his bike.

"Uh . . . Annie?" he managed.

The bird scolded him until he set the bike in motion and started down the lane. The rooks were no longer in sight.

I'm going insane, Rory decided.

He really didn't see another logical explanation.

14.

"What does he mean, about the world coming to an end?" Kerry asked.

Katy gave her sister a sympathetic look. Kerry looked scared and Katy couldn't blame her. By all accounts, Raven wasn't exactly the easiest of the corbæ to warm to and while he might look like a Buddha, he added a grimness to the image that the statues of the real Gautama Buddha never portrayed. When you put that up alongside his stern pronouncements, uttered in that deep bass rumble of his voice, it was hard not to be nervous around him.

Though he didn't seem to faze the crow girls at all.

"Oh, don't pay attention to Raven," Maida said.

Zia nodded. "He just loves to sound dramatic."

"The more dramatic the better."

"As if the world would end on his say-so."

Maida shook her head. "As if."

Raven shot them a dark look, obviously intended to silence them, but all it did was make them giggle.

"It would not be my decision," he said. He nodded toward the Grace. "But hers."

That quieted the crow girls.

The reactions of the corbæ surprised Katy. They all seemed to be, if not nervous about the Grace the way Kerry was, nevertheless very much in awe. But what surprised her more was that none of them seemed to know why the Grace had gathered them to this place.

"That's not why she's here," she told them.

Dark corbæ gazes settled on her.

"The cuckoos broke her vessel," Katy explained. "And because of that a door's opened and it's drawing her back." She gave them an apologetic look. "One of us has to accompany her—to close that door after her— or the whole world's going to get sucked out through it."

"How can you know that?" Raven asked.

The resonance of his voice made it feel as though her ribs were vibrating against each other. She felt Kerry's fingers tighten on her own. Raven made her nervous, too, but she was too stubborn to let it show. Her way of dealing with it was to be more aggressive.

"How can you not?" she shot back.

Raven frowned. "The light has no voice. She doesn't speak."

"Not in words exactly," Katy said, "but that doesn't mean she isn't communicating."

It was hard to explain. When she quieted the inner chatter of her own thoughts and let the warm, amber-gold glow swell inside her, she simply knew what the Grace wished to express.

"I have never heard of such a thing," Raven said.

"So that makes it a lie?" Katy asked.

"I did not—"

Katy made a movement with her free hand toward the figure of the woman in the light.

"Tell her about it," she said. "Not me. I didn't come here to argue with you."

For a long moment no one spoke.

"The door," Jack asked finally. "What does it open into?"

"To . . ." Katy had to think a moment. "What you call the medicine lands."

"But without her . . . if she's drawn out of the world . . ." Jack's voice trailed off.

Raven turned to the crow girls. "Was I so wrong? Without her light, the world might as well cease to exist."

He's like me, Katy realized. He doesn't fit in either. The difference was, he wanted to take everything with him when he went.

"That's not how she puts it," Katy said. "The world will be different, that's all. Not over. We'll just have to make our own grace."

Raven gave a short, humorless laugh. "And what a world it would be if its grace were to be dependent on the good nature of its inhabitants. Every year the world becomes more dour, more hateful. Kindness has become a myth."

Katy regarded him thoughtfully, trying to understand

why all the animal people held Raven in such esteem. He was certainly large enough, with a big voice, but there didn't seem to be a whole lot of compassion in him. Maybe he'd been asleep for too long. Maybe he'd forgotten what it was like to live, to care about other people.

"It doesn't have to be like that," she said.

The crow girls nodded in agreement.

"We're happy," Maida said. "We're ever so veryvery kind."

"It's true," Zia added. "We bring grace wherever we go."

"Or at least we try to."

"And that counts, doesn't it?"

"Of course it does," Jack said.

"Which of us has the Grace chosen for her guide?" Raven asked.

"That's not actually up for grabs," Katy told him, "because I'm doing it."

"You can't!" Kerry cried.

Katy let go of Kerry's hand. Putting her hands on her sister's shoulders, she looked her in the eye.

"But I told you," she said. "That's why I came here."

"And why are we here?" Raven asked. "Simply to wish you bon voyage?"

Maybe, Katy thought, the real reason no one disturbed him was that it was better when he was asleep. At least then you didn't have to listen to him.

"No," she said, turning away from her sister to face him. "The cuckoos were trying to use the Grace to kill you, but she's a life-giver, not a life-taker—remember?"

"She brought death into the world," Raven said.

Katy looked to the Grace, quieting her thoughts so that she could find an answer in the amber-gold light.

"No," she said after a moment. "Cody was using the pot that time and death was attracted by the light. He woke from it."

"There has to be some other way," Kerry said.

Katy could only shake her head. "Maybe I'm not the

only one who wants to go, but I'm the only one who should go. The world loses too much if one of you goes, but it's not going to miss me. It's not like I've been pulling my weight.''

"Don't say that, Katy," Kerry said. "It's not true."

"Listen to your sister," Jack told Katy. "You can have a lot worse sins hanging on your soul, and unlike myself, you're not guilty of any of them."

15.

Once they were inside the hotel, Hank and Lily walked across the wide marble floor of the lobby, Bocephus padding at their side. The light was brighter in here than it had been outside, but the hotel's patrons, bellboys, desk clerks, and all were as immobile as were the rest of the people in the city who didn't carry a trace of the blood.

"How are we going to find out what room she's in?" Lily asked.

"Well, normally I'd bribe the desk clerk," Hank said, "but considering she can't stop me . . .''

He went around behind the counter, laid down the shotgun he'd taken from Margaret, and flipped through registration cards until he came across the name "Couteau." There were two cards, one for Dominique, the other for her sons. They'd taken connecting suites.

"Here we go," he said. "They're all the way up on the top floor. Do you want to trust the elevator?"

"Well, my car worked, didn't it?" Lily replied.

The bank of elevators was on the far side of the lobby. The only sound was the sound of their shoes and the dog's toenails clicking on the marble as they wound their way in between the frozen people to reach it. Hank pressed the "Up" button and they waited a moment for an elevator to arrive. When it did, there were people in it.

"Oh, this is too creepy," Lily said, looking at their blank faces.

Hank nodded. "I know. But it's this or thirty flights of stairs."

Bocephus made the decision for them. The dog padded into the elevator, then sat on its haunches, regarding them with a patient gaze.

"Okay, Bo," Hank said.

They joined the dog inside. Hank pressed the button for the thirtieth floor and the elevator doors closed with a hiss. Lily couldn't suppress a shiver.

They immediately noticed a change in the light when they arrived at Dominique's floor. Where before it had been a rich amber-gold, now it held a red tint that grew darker the farther they progressed down the hall to the Couteaus' suites. A low growl woke in Bocephus's chest.

Lily wished she could be as brave as Hank and the dog, but it wasn't the same for them. They'd never seen the cold light in Dominique's eyes while they were told that they were only alive at her sufferance. Dominique had been very clear to Lily about what would happen if she tried to interfere. Any minute she expected one of the Couteaus or the other cuckoos to step out into the hall, gun in hand. This time there were no crow girls around to magically kiss them back to life.

This time they'd die for real.

But she couldn't back out now. The need to at least make an effort to retrieve Raven's pot had become an obsession akin to the solemn promises the knights had made in old medieval romances she and Donna used to read when they were supposed to be studying for their classes. It lay on her like a geas—a compulsion. Leading her on to her doom, no doubt, but there seemed to be only one path lying in front of her and she had to take it.

She could choose to ignore the compulsion, but she wasn't sure she'd be able to live with who she would be if she did.

Ahead of her, Hank had stopped in front of the door to the suite registered in Dominique's name. Pooling around the carpet in front of the door, the amber-gold of the light was almost entirely swallowed by a flood of dark red.

Blood, Lily thought. This is the light of blood.

The air held a vague metallic taste.

Hank put his ear to the wooden panels and listened. Bocephus stood stiffly beside him, hair bristling at the nape of his neck. The dog was silent now, gaze fixed on the door. Lily's legs were trembling so much she had to lean against the wall, afraid that they'd give out from under her.

"I can't hear a thing," Hank said quietly, straightening away from the door. "It's like there's no one there."

Lily swallowed.

"But I've got a bad feeling about it," Hank added.

She nodded. "Me, too."

He tried the handle and looked surprised when it turned.

"Stand back," he said.

She nodded again.

When he opened the door, the dog slipped in ahead of him. Dark red light poured out of the room, washing over Hank's features. Lifting the shotgun, he took a step in after Bocephus, then stopped dead, leaned a hand against the doorjamb. A numbed look settled over his features.

"What . . . what is it?" Lily asked.

He waved her back. "Don't come any closer."

But she was already beside him, looking into the room. It was like a slaughterhouse inside. The ceiling and walls were splattered with blood and feathers. Along the bottom of the walls, the floor was littered with the bodies of men and women, except they weren't entirely human. They had died in various stages of metamorphosis. In among the human faces and bodies she could see bird heads, wings, clawed scaly legs, talons instead of feet.

Before she could stop herself, she turned away and

expelled the contents of her stomach. She flinched when
Hank touched her, then realized who it was, let him hold
her.

"Wait out here," he said.

She shook her head. "I . . . I'm okay," she lied.

She knew she might never be okay again. The contents
of the room were going to haunt her forever. But she
steeled herself and followed Hank back inside all the
same. She waited by the door, staring resolutely away
from the walls and the bodies, while he and the dog
checked the rest of the suite to make sure there was no
one hiding anywhere. Bedroom, closets, toilet. When
Hank stepped back into the main room, Lily pointed to
the table that stood by the window.

"Look," she said.

A piece of the chalice lay there. Two other pieces lay
on the floor. It seemed beyond reason that it could have
caused so much damage and only be in three pieces. But
however many pieces it was in was irrelevant. The simple
fact was that they were too late.

Bocephus padded slowly over by the far side of the
table, snuffling at a body that lay there. He gave a low
bark and they crossed the room to where he was standing.
This one was in human shape, a woman, but covered in
blood and obviously dead.

The dog repeated its low bark.

Hank went down on one knee. Laying the shotgun
aside, he put two fingers to the woman's neck.

"She's still alive," he said.

It was hard to tell, because of the blood and the way
the Couteaus all looked so much the same, but Lily
thought she recognized the woman.

"I think . . . I think that might be Dominique."

"Well, she got what she deserved," Hank said, standing up again.

"What are you doing?"

Hank looked at Lily in surprise. "What do you
mean?"

"We can't just leave her there."

"Lily, this woman's the cause behind all of this damage. She broke the pot and Christ knows what she did with Katy. You think I'm going to spend any time nursing her back to fighting strength so that she can come after us again?"

When he put it like that, it did sound stupid, but it was still wrong.

"If we let her die," she said, "that makes us no better than them."

"If we let her die, we have a better chance to live to a ripe old age."

Lily shook her head. She went into the bedroom off the main suite and returned with a pillow and sheets. Kneeling down beside the woman, she put the pillow under her head and began to tear up the sheets.

"Could you get me some warm water?" she said.

"This is not a good game plan," Hank told her.

The dog made a grumbling noise in its chest as though agreeing with him.

"You're being as bad as your friend Moth," she said.

"What's that supposed to mean?"

"You know. You said he'll do anything for his family, but the rest of the world can just fend for itself."

"This is the enemy we're talking about here," Hank said.

"I thought you were different. I wouldn't even be here if you hadn't stopped to help me. You didn't know me at all, but you still stopped."

"You hadn't been trying to kill me either."

"Could you just get the water?" Lily said. "Then you don't have to stay. I know you want to look for Katy."

He hesitated a moment longer before taking the ice bucket and going into the washroom. Lily listened to him run the water while she continued to tear strips from the sheet. When he returned with the warm water, she dipped a piece of the sheet into it and began to bathe the woman's face, trying to be gentle. At the touch of the cloth, Dominique's eyes flickered open and she stared uncomprehendingly up at Lily. Slowly recognition came to her.

"Wh-What are . . . you . . . ?"

"Hush," Lily said. "Don't try to move."

But Dominique wouldn't let it go. "Are . . . are you . . . mad?"

"Don't try to talk either. Save your strength because you're going to need it."

"Ask her where Katy is," Hank said.

But Dominique had heard him. "Don't . . . know . . . any . . . Kuh . . . Katy. . . ." Her gaze returned to Lily. "Dying . . ."

"Maybe we can get one of the corbæ to help her," Lily said to Hank. "Like the crow girls did us."

"I don't think so," Hank replied.

He was probably right. But Lily still thought they should try to—

She cried out as Dominique suddenly grabbed her hand. The woman's strength surprised her, her pale fingers digging into Lily's wrist. Before she could pull free, Dominique's whole body went stiff, spasmed, then her head lolled to one side, her body limp.

"She . . . I think she just . . ." Lily swallowed thickly.

Hank knelt down beside her. He checked Dominique's pulse again, but this time he moved his hand to her face and closed her eyes.

"She's dead," he said.

Lily turned away. She knew Dominique had been the enemy—of the corbæ and herself. But she still mourned the woman's death. Mourned all the deaths. What was the point of it all? It was so stupid. So senseless.

Hank stood up once more. Lily hesitated a moment. Then she rose to her feet as well.

"You were right," he said.

"About what?"

"It would have been wrong to not have tried to help."

She nodded. But being right didn't change what had happened.

She was dealing with being in this room of slaughtered cuckoos only by keeping her vision narrowed and focused, trying to see no more than she had to. But it was hard. The longer she stayed in here, with the red light washing over her, the strange inhuman bodies scattered all around, the more dislocated she felt. But she couldn't leave yet. Not without what she had come for.

As she bent down to pick up the two pieces of the chalice that lay on the floor, she also saw the little statue that had been lying at the bottom of it when Dominique had taken the chalice from her. Putting the pieces of the chalice on the table, she bent down again to pick up the statue and found not one, but two of them.

"Look at these," she said.

Hank stepped closer and took one from her hand. "It looks just like Katy." He turned it over in his hand. "What are they? Some kind of voodoo dolls?"

"I don't know. But the detailing's incredible—right down to the cloth used for the clothing."

She gave him the other one so that he could stow them both away in his pocket.

"Here," she said. "Help me fit the pieces of the chalice together. I want to see if there are any other pieces still missing."

"Do you think it can still be fixed?"

Lily shrugged. "I'm so far out of my depth here I have no idea what is or isn't possible anymore. Maybe the corbæ have some kind of magic glue they can use."

"Crow girl spit."

Lily nodded, remembering how effective it had been in helping them.

"Or something," she said.

She fit the first two pieces together and Bocephus barked. She almost dropped them as she looked up, expecting some new danger to be coming in the door, but there was no one there. There were only the bodies. Her stomach churned and she looked away, quickly, before she started to gag.

"What's wrong, Bo?" Hank asked.

"Probably just . . . nerves," Lily said. "Here, see if that other piece'll fit."

As Hank brought it toward the pieces Lily was holding in place, the dog barked again, more urgently.

"I think he's telling us not to do this," Hank said. He looked around the room. "Maybe he's got a point. We don't know what we're messing with here. We might be making things worse."

"The pot won't hurt us," Lily said. "Because we don't want anything from it."

"You know that for a fact?"

Lily slowly shook her head. "It's just . . . under this red . . . there's the other light. I can't see it ever causing anyone pain. Not deliberately."

Hank regarded her for a long moment, then shrugged.

"I've been with you this far," he said. "I'm not about to back out now."

When the dog whined, he added, "Don't worry, Bo. We're being careful."

Bocephus turned his head away when Hank turned his attention back to the chalice, bringing his piece in close again to check its fit.

16.

Rory stopped across the street from the Harbor Ritz hotel, using the height of the curb to make it easier to steady the bike with his foot. A large crowd of people had gathered on the street in front of the hotel. Old, middle-aged, teens, children. And not only people, he realized as he looked more closely. There were cats and dogs, rats, raccoons, a fox, and birds of all kinds, mostly crows and other corbæ. Ravens, rooks, jays, magpies. All of them staring at the light that had sheathed the hotel with its amber-gold glow.

"Who are all these people?" he asked Annie, then realized he was talking to a bird.

She regained her own form and made the bike wobble with her sudden weight as she leaned back over the handlebars to look at him, upside down. Where he felt all on edge and anxious, the situation only seemed to be making her giddy.

"They're like you. They've all got the blood."

"And the animals? I suppose they've got it, too?"

"Well, of course."

Of course, Rory thought. Like it's an everyday thing. Though in her version of the world he supposed it was.

Annie straightened up and got off the bike. Leaning on the handlebars, she studied him for a long moment.

"So how come you've never made a pass at me?" she asked.

"What?"

"You heard me."

"Is this really the time to get into something like that?"

"For all we know," she said, "the world could be ending. So I'd just like to know before everything goes away."

"That . . . that could happen?"

She shook her head. "Haven't you figured it out yet, Rory? You're walking under the surface now, seeing the world the way we see it. Anything could happen."

"Oh."

"So are you going to tell me?"

Rory took a steadying breath. "I was too scared to."

"Scared of *me*?"

"Not exactly, though at first you kind of intimidated me."

"So you didn't like me playing the strong-woman card."

"And then, when we started getting along so well, I didn't want to screw up our friendship."

Annie smiled. "I guess I know that feeling. It's kind of sad, isn't it? I mean, lovers should be best friends, too, don't you think?"

Rory nodded.

"But then there's the trust factor, I guess. The problem is, if you don't believe it'll happen, it won't. It's like everything."

"What do you mean?"

"Well . . ." She shrugged. "If you don't believe in magic, then it won't happen for you. If you don't believe that the world has a heart, then you won't hear it beating, you won't think it's alive and you won't consider what you're doing to it."

"I don't—" He had to stop and correct himself. "I didn't believe in magic. This all still seems like a dream to me."

She smiled. "I know. But just because you don't believe in something doesn't mean it's not real. Sometimes it just sneaks up on you all the same. Like love."

Rory nodded, wondering if she was talking to him as a friend, or if there was something more happening here. But before he could take it any further, one of the Aunt's came flying back. The sounds she made as she circled above them were only so much gibberish so far as he was concerned, but Annie seemed to be understanding her.

"What . . . uh . . ." This was so weird. "What's she saying?"

"Apparently the pot's inside the hotel and the cuckoos have been using it."

"That's bad, right?"

Annie nodded. "And your friend Lily and her boyfriend went inside."

It took Rory a moment to figure out who she meant.

"You mean Hank?"

"If that's his name."

"What are they doing in there?" he asked.

"Nobody knows."

"What about Kerry? Have any of them seen her?"

The Aunt replied, but Rory had to wait for Annie to translate for him.

She shook her head. "No, but apparently her twin's supposed to be inside."

"But she's . . ."

Imaginary, he'd been about to say. Except, so was all of this. Or at least it should be, if the world made any sense.

"It's a long story," Annie said.

Rory looked up at the hotel, craning his neck to take in, first its height, then the enormous canopy of the tree of light that had swallowed the building.

"How long have they been in there?" he asked.

"I'm not sure. Awhile."

Rory swallowed. He didn't want to do this.

"We have to go in after them—"

He broke off as a spot of the amber-gold light flared bright white at the top of the building. Around him the crowd suddenly stirred. He glanced at Annie and saw that the giddiness had finally left her. She gazed up with a solemnness he'd never seen in her features before.

Awe, he realized. She's awestruck.

Oh, and like he wasn't?

But somehow it wasn't the same.

"Annie?" he tried.

There was no response, not even when he touched her arm. He looked for the Aunt who'd been flying above them, but she was perched on a lamppost now, as entranced as Annie.

They see something we don't, Rory thought.

The crowd was still shuffling restlessly in place. Flocks of birds suddenly rose into the air. They weren't corbæ, he realized, but birds with the blood. A vast cloud of blackbirds. Like him, they were nervous. Anxious. Nearby a dog began to whimper. Then another. A child cried. He saw a woman that he didn't think was the little girl's mother go down on one knee beside her to offer comfort.

Annie's words from a few moments ago returned to him now, heavy with the possibility that they weren't so much a consideration as a promise.

For all we know, the world could be ending.

The building dragged his gaze back to it. The white light on the top floor made his eyes tear.

Your friend Lily and her boyfriend went inside.

Jesus, he thought. Kit's in there.

He laid his bike down on the curb and moved forward through the crowd, heading for the front door of the hotel.

17.

Jack's words hung in the air.

You can have a lot worse sins hanging on your soul, and unlike myself, you're not guilty of any of them.

"What's that supposed to mean?" Katy asked finally.

"I've brought too much pain into the world as it is," he told her. "It's time for me to move on."

"That is so not true. The world needs you, Jack."

He shook his head. "It needs Raven and the crow girls, but not me. What I do, any storyteller can do. All you need is an ear to listen and a voice to pass them on."

They spoke as if only the two of them were here in this place, gazes locked on each other, not at all aware of Kerry, the other corbæ, or even the Grace.

"Look," Jack went on. "If the world's going to need us to make our own grace from here on out, I'm just going to bring everybody down. I've got too many sins hanging on my soul. If you know I'm your father, then you've got to know that."

"What happened to our mother—"

"Should never have happened, period. No one deserves that kind of a fate. No one."

Katy nodded. She couldn't think of a more awful thing.

"But it wasn't your fault," she said. "You didn't do anything."

"That's just it," Jack replied. "I didn't do anything. If I had, none of that would have happened."

"But—"

"And then after—that's nothing I'm proud of either."

"They deserved to die," Katy said.

"But so many? For the sins of a few?"

Maida spoke up then. "All cuckoos are guilty of something."

"Maybe," Jack agreed. "But that doesn't make me judge, jury, and executioner."

"The Grace is my responsibility," Raven said. "I will do what needs to be done."

"I don't think so," Katy told him.

The other corbæ regarded her in surprise. Maybe the crow girls could get away with teasing him, but it was obvious that normally no one would think to contradict Raven. Katy didn't care. This had to be said. He had to hear it.

"You claim to be responsible," she went on, "but how can you even say that when you've been asleep—or whatever it is you've been—for the past fifty years or more? You don't even know what the world is like anymore. Maybe things are getting worse, but there are still people trying to do good. There's still hope. Maybe if you were pulling *your* weight, things wouldn't have got to where they are now."

"But they have."

"That still doesn't give you the right to decide whether the world goes on or ends."

"You forget. I brought the world out of the dark."

"With the help of others."

Raven glanced at the crow girls and Jack.

"With the help of others," he agreed. "But I have carried the burden of the pot since the first day."

"And done such a good job of it, too."

He frowned, dark eyes flashing, and gestured toward the light.

"You see for yourself," he said. "She has always had a mind of her own."

Katy sighed. "That's not what this is about. It's not about trying to control what can't and shouldn't be controlled in the first place. The pot only holds her—keeps her in this world. All you were supposed to do was guard it."

"You came here to destroy it."

"Or send it back," Katy said. "But that was before she let me know that the pot's only a vessel to hold her to this world. Now I know."

"And yet *I* was supposed to have intuited—"

Katy cut him off. "Yeah, you *should* have known. You've had the pot long enough. But you've never even tried to communicate with her."

"It is not such a simple—"

"Don't you see? You've tried to hang on to that pot for all these years, tried to keep it under your tight control, and then, when you finally realized you couldn't, you just gave up on it."

"No one else would accept the burden."

"That's not true," Katy said. "You chose to be responsible for it. Maybe if you hadn't laid such a strong claim to it, other people would have taken responsibility for it and come to understand what it really means to be its guardian. It's always been the mythic 'Raven's pot' instead of what it really is: the vessel of the Grace. Instead of thinking of it as an object of power, you should have been celebrating it, cherishing it. Thinking of it as an object of wonder instead of some scary thing that had to be hidden away."

Raven hesitated for a long moment, then slowly nodded. "I see your point."

"Except now it's too late."

They shared the sorrow of it, argument forgotten.

Kerry suddenly tugged on Katy's sleeve. "Something's happening to her. . . ."

Katy turned and the warmth of the Grace washed over her anew.

"There's nothing . . . ," she began, but then her voice trailed off.

"What is it?" Raven asked.

They peered at the light, corbæ and twins, and this time they could all read the wordless voice in the light. They all felt the pull of the medicine lands, the world being drawn back through the door the cuckoos had stirred open.

And there was something more.

"She doesn't have to go," Maida said softly.

Zia nodded. "Not anymore."

"But the door still needs closing."

Katy moved forward, but Jack was quicker. He stepped into the light and it enveloped him. Spreading his arms, he became . . .

A dark angel, winged.

A jackdaw, blue-black feathers gleaming in the light.

A shadow in the heart of the Grace that shrank to the size of a pinprick.

The light blinked. For one moment an awful dark swallowed them. Then the light was back. But diminishing. Leaking away. Returning to the state it had been in before the cuckoos had called her up with their hate.

They could see in her dwindling light that the door was closed, the world was safe.

But Jack was gone. Forever gone.

Turning to her sister, Katy burrowed her face in Kerry's shoulder and wept.

18.

As Hank brought his piece of the chalice toward the two Lily was holding together, he felt a sudden pull and the piece in his hands jumped toward the others, fusing with them. He had long enough to see that the chalice was whole once more, with not even a seam showing. Long enough to lift his head and exchange a surprised look with Lily, then a flare of brilliant white light blazed up from the chalice, blinding him.

"Oh, shit," he heard himself say.

His voice seem to come from far away, as though he were talking from across the room, or from another room, or from somewhere else entirely where he didn't even exist anymore.

A deep vertigo grabbed him and held him hard. He could no longer sense the floor under his feet, the walls around him. Outside of his body the only things he could sense were the smooth warm crystal of the chalice and the blinding white light that came out of it. All other physical sensation was gone.

He tried to pull back from the chalice, but couldn't.

Tried to close his eyes against the light, but couldn't do that either.

Then he saw something, deep in the glare. A black spot. A hole.

The sound of the wind that had accompanied the first fall of the darkness returned. Until that moment, he hadn't really thought about its having gone away.

He knew now where the sound came from. That hole. It was the sound of the world being drawn down into the hole. Drawn where, he didn't know. The hole was somewhere inside the chalice, that was all he knew.

No, that wasn't true. He also knew the hole was hungry. Not the way he thought of hunger, but a more primal appetite, what the vast canopy of space must feel when it tried to swallow the light of the stars. It was the oldest hunger there was, a desire that could never be appeased because no matter how much light the darkness swallowed, it always wanted more.

This was their fault, he thought. His and Lily's. Messing with things they had no hope of understanding. They should have let well enough be, gotten out of that room and left the pieces of the chalice lying there, just like they'd found them.

Except the door had existed all along, hadn't it? He'd heard the light being sucked into it since the darkness first fell back in the junkyard, sucking at the world's light, drawing it into itself so that the light spun like water going down a drain. And it was still going down, taking him with it.

Taking him, and Lily, and maybe the whole world along with them.

Taking . . .

He saw a tall dark figure walking toward the hole. The man had his back to him, but Hank recognized him by the wide brim of his black hat, by the flapping tails of his black duster and his rolling walk.

Jack.

The pull of the hole exerted an incredible force, but it didn't seem to bother Jack at all. He just kept walking toward it at a steady pace, like he was strolling from his school bus to the junkyard, getting ready to tell another night's worth of stories.

Seeing Jack was weird enough, but now he could see the hole better, too, see it right up close as though he were walking at Jack's shoulder, and it wasn't so dark anymore. Wasn't dark at all. It didn't seem so much like a hole as a door and through it Hank could see the side of a meadowed hill with trees ranging up the sides of it and along its crest. There was a big old stone there in the middle of the tall grass and wildflowers, little flecks of mica glinting in the sun that poured down on stone, meadow, hill, trees.

He saw Jack pause, hesitate.

He wasn't expecting that either, Hank thought. Whatever Jack had thought he was walking into, it wasn't that field.

A shadow crossed over the rock and all of a sudden Hank believed in God again, because if that wasn't an angel then what was? He'd had it wrong, thinking the bird girls had been angels. This was the real thing. There was no halo and she wasn't even wearing white. But she had wings, big angel wings that rose up from behind her back that were the same russet color as her tangled hair. And she had a look in those sky-blue eyes of hers that told Hank she knew the way to heaven, because those eyes had looked upon it.

She smiled at Jack, and Hank found himself wishing somebody would smile like that at him, like she'd been waiting all her life for him to get to this place.

Jack started walking again.

There was something familiar about that angel, Hank thought. Jack had taken the angel's hand and was stepping through the door before he knew what it was. The face of that angel. She looked just like Katy. Not Katy now, but the way Katy'd look when she got older.

He wanted to ask how that could be. He wanted to call after Jack, to say good-bye if nothing else, but the hole, door, whatever it was, closed behind them, closed like the lens of a camera. Just shrank down into itself until there was only a dot left.

Then, blink, it was gone.

And he was standing back in Dominique Couteau's hotel suite, hands still on the chalice, but looking over the top of it at Lily instead of into some strange otherworld. The wind was gone again, too, and this time he was aware of its going, but there was a rumbling sound coming up from deep underground. He looked down to see Bocephus crouched with his belly against the floor, scared for all his size. There was something in the dog's eyes that Hank had never seen in an animal before, like he had looked onto the same piece of heaven Hank had, and like Hank, he remembered and thought maybe he was never going to feel completely satisfied with anything in this world again.

"I . . . did you see . . . ?" Lily began, but couldn't go on.

Hank could tell that she was having as much trouble working this out as he and the dog were. They'd all been touched by something that was so much bigger than they were, they just couldn't seem to hold on to it, never mind figure it out. But now wasn't the time to worry about it anyway.

"Let's get out of here," he said. "Before something else happens."

He picked up the chalice, took her by the hand, and headed for the door. Like Lily, he didn't look at the bloodstained walls or the bodies of the dead cuckoos, just focused on what lay straight ahead, moving across the room and out the door, Bocephus on their heels.

They got most of the way down the hall toward the elevator when the building gave a shake, like it was clearing its head, and all the lights came back on again. They stopped, feeling off-balance. A weird hum filled the air, an uncomfortable buzzing that Hank realized was the building's electronic and mechanical functions starting up again along with the lights. Air conditioners. Electricity. The elevator, where people were moving in time again.

The elevator's doors closed before they could reach it, but not before Hank caught the shocked looks on the faces of the people in it.

Christ, we must look a mess, he thought. Blood all over our clothes, carrying this crystal chalice that they must think we stole from one of the rooms, a dog the size of a small bear padding at our side.

"We've got to get out of this building," he told Lily. "I figure we've got a minute, minute and a half tops before all hell breaks loose up here."

She looked nervously around.

"No, it's not something supernatural this time," he said. "It's just . . . well, you can bet the people on that elevator are going to come tumbling out of it as soon as they reach the lobby, screaming about Bo here and us all covered in blood. Security'll be hightailing it up to this floor and we don't want to be here when they show up."

"But—"

"Think about it, Lily. When they find that room full of bodies back there, who're they going to blame? It's not like we have answers that'd make any sense to them."

Understanding blossomed in her eyes. She nodded and they started to run for the stairwell at the far end of the hall. Hank counted off the rooms as they hurried by them, half-expecting one of their doors to open and some poor sap attending a convention, or in town on a holiday, to blunder into them.

But their luck held. At least in that regard.

"I don't know how much good this'll do," Hank said when they were just a few rooms away from the fire door. "They're not stupid. They'll be sending some of their people up the stairwell."

He silently corrected himself as he saw the handle working on the door. It seemed too soon, but it looked like they already had. And he'd gone and left the shotgun behind in the Couteaus' room.

He pulled Lily to a stop but Bocephus kept right on running. The fire door started to open inward. Whoever was pulling it open was about to have a couple of hundred pounds of dog at his throat.

"Bo!" Hank cried. "No!"

Because it wasn't necessarily hotel security coming through that door. It might be some poor putz who decided to get some serious exercise and do the thirty sets of stairs. And whoever it was, letting Bo attack them was only going to complicate the problems they already had.

Bocephus skidded against the door, knocking it further open. The man in the stairwell lost his balance and fell back against the wall. He looked seriously rattled and Hank didn't blame him. Bocephus wasn't exactly some yappy little lapdog that you could push away with your shoe.

"It's okay," Hank started to say, but Lily had stepped past him, moving toward the door.

"Rory?" she said.

Hank recognized him as soon as Lily said his name.

Rory straightened up from the wall. He gave the dog a nervous glance, then let his gaze settle on them.

"Jesus," he said. "What happened to you? Are you all right?"

Hank twigged to what he meant before Lily did. It was all the blood. He touched his shirtfront.

"It's not ours," he said.

"Then whose . . . ?"

"This isn't a good time to get into it," Hank told him. "We've really got to get out of . . ."

His voice trailed off as he realized that Rory was no longer looking at them, his attention completely swallowed by something in the hallway behind them. Bocephus growled and Hank slowly turned to see the biggest, baldest black man he'd ever seen filling the hall where they'd just been. With him were two pairs of twins: the crow girls who'd rescued Lily and him in that alleyway what seemed like forever ago, along with Katy and a girl that was her exact double except she looked a lot straighter. He remembered seeing her in the junkyard earlier. Her name was . . . Kerry.

He looked from her to Katy, and the angel he'd seen welcoming Jack into that other place flashed through his mind.

"I will take that," the man said in a deep low voice that was resonant as Bocephus's growls.

He plucked the chalice from Hank's hand before Hank could think to protest.

"I've never seen it in this shape," the man said.

The chalice seemed tiny as he turned it over in his large hands. After a moment, Hank realized that he wasn't so much admiring it, as trying to figure out how it was all still in one piece. Bocephus was still growling, but he immediately stopped and lowered his head when the big man gave him a sudden stern look.

"It's veryvery pretty," one of the crow girls said.

The other one nodded. "The prettiest it's ever been, don't you think, Raven?"

Raven? This was the Raven from Jack's stories? Jesus, but he was big.

Hank stuck his hands in his pockets and discovered that the statues Lily had given him were gone. He must have dropped them in the cuckoos' room. Except, looking at Katy and her twin, the pair of them dressed exactly the same as the little figurines had been, he wasn't so sure.

When he thought about where they'd all come from, appearing as if out of nowhere . . . His gaze went to the chalice and the strange idea came to him that they'd come out of it. He made himself look away, not wanting to go where that train of thought might take him. Instead, he concentrated on Katy.

Her eyes were rimmed with red from crying and there was a hollow look in them that broke his heart. She leaned against her sister as though she couldn't support her own weight.

"Katy," he said. "Are you okay?"

She shook her head.

"We . . . we just saw our father die," her sister said.

"Your father?"

That came from Rory, surprise in his voice.

Kerry nodded. "I know who my parents really were now. Jack Daw was our father."

Jack had kids? Hank shook his head. He was going to need a scorecard to keep everything straight.

"And now he's dead," she said.

Is that what we saw? Hank thought. Did we really see Jack walking into heaven?

"I'm so sorry," Lily said.

Hank nodded slowly. He couldn't imagine the world without Jack and his stories in it.

19.

Kerry had never been in the position where she had to be strong for someone else. Being able to do it made her guess that she was more resilient than she'd thought. Or maybe she'd just been through so much in the past few days that nothing could really surprise her anymore, though she wasn't entirely immune to being taken unawares. The difference was, instead of letting traumas immobilize her, she was learning how to roll with them, to not let them render her completely dysfunctional.

Finding out that Nettie was really her mother, the mysterious Jack Daw her father, wasn't something she was allowing herself to deal with at all. It was an amazing step forward for her, that she was actually able to set the confusing puzzle of her parents aside and concentrate on the more immediate concerns that couldn't be set aside.

What she really wanted more than anything was to be able to do more for Katy, only Katy couldn't be consoled.

She looked around at the others, crowded together with them in the hallway. Surely someone here could help. Perhaps the crow girls would work their magic on Katy, the way Maida had helped her back at her apartment. But before she could ask them, Raven was turning his attention to Katy. Kerry shivered. Maybe he wasn't a bad guy, but he still scared her.

"Katy," Raven said.

His voice was pitched remarkably soft. But still deep. Still so resonant you could feel it vibrating way down low in your chest. Beside her, Katy lifted her head to look at him.

"I know this is not the time to speak of celebrations," he went on, "but I have been considering what you told me earlier. Of all of us, you would seem to be the best choice to guard her vessel and teach us how to celebrate her existence."

Katy started shaking her head as soon as he began to speak, but Raven handed her the chalice and it was take it or drop it. Kerry squeezed Katy's shoulders, trying to lend her sister strength.

"I . . . I can't . . . ," Katy began.

She tried to hand it back, but Raven wouldn't take it. Such a small thing in his hands, Kerry thought, so big in her sister's. Then Katy looked down at the crystal she was holding and a strange thing happened. It grew smaller, changed. The crystal darkened, became opaque, turned into a metal like tarnished silver. The goblet shape shrank in on itself. For a moment it was a formless lump in the palm of her hand, then she was holding a small crudely rendered bird figure.

"It's a crow," Kerry found herself saying. "A crow pendant."

Katy gave a slow nod. "The Grace." She weighed it on her palm. "I think it's hollow."

Maida peered closely at it. "I had one of those once and it was hollow, too. You just screwed the head off when you wanted to peek inside."

"Here," Zia said. She pulled a knot of strings and threads and unidentifiable items out of her pocket and managed to work free a length of leather thong. "You can have this."

Kerry threaded the narrow strip of leather through the hole in the back of the pendant, then she slipped it around her sister's neck, tying it off for her at the back. Katy fingered the pendant, rubbing a thumb along one wing. Kerry didn't know what her sister was feeling, but the pendant seemed to be giving her the comfort that no one else had been able to give her. And then Hank surprised her, offering up the one thing that Katy needed to hear.

"We saw Jack go," he said. "When the chalice fused back into one piece, we saw a door opening into a meadow with a big stone in it. There was an angel waiting there, with red hair and red wings. Waiting for Jack, it looked like, because when he walked up to her, she took his hand."

"And then the door closed behind them," Lily said.

Katy's free hand claimed one of Kerry's, squeezing tight. Kerry didn't mind. Katy could squeeze as hard as she wanted, if it'd make her feel better.

"That angel looked like you two," Hank said. "Like you'd look if you were older. In your forties, maybe."

"You . . . you really saw this?" Katy said. "You saw them together in this field?"

Hank nodded.

"And she had wings?" Maida asked.

Hank nodded again. "Big ones. Like an angel's."

Zia and Maida smiled at each other.

"You were so right," Zia said. "Nettie did learn how to fly."

"The angel was our mother?" Kerry asked.

"That'd make sense," Hank told her. "Definitely related."

Kerry could feel the tension easing in her sister, the sharp edge of her sorrow softening.

"Um, heads up, people," Rory suddenly said. "We've got company."

Kerry hadn't even heard the elevator open. When she turned, she saw a half-dozen men in suits step out of it into the hall.

"Hotel security," Hank said. "Now we've got a problem."

"It's okay," Zia told him, taking Hank and Lily by the hand. "We know a shortcut where they can't follow."

She led them for two steps, then the three of them vanished. Kerry stared. Even after all she'd been through, she wasn't quite ready to believe what she'd just seen. She was still trying to adjust to it when Maida took Rory's hand, grabbed a handhold in the thick fur of the big dog standing near him, and walked them away into thin air as well.

"How . . . ?" Kerry said.

"It's okay," Katy said, lowering her hand from the pendant. "It's just another way of walking. You can learn how to do it, too."

"But—"

"You down the hall!" one of the hotel's security people called. "Stop where you are!"

One of his companions was talking into a cellular phone. The rest had all drawn handguns from under their suit jackets.

Katy took her hand. "Come on. I'll show you."

But she hesitated a moment, looking at Raven.

"You go on," he said, turning away from them. "I still have to remove the cuckoos."

"What does he mean?" Kerry asked.

"I guess he doesn't want their bodies found. Probably because it'd start the wrong people asking questions."

Kerry watched him move down the hall, soft-footed now despite his bulk, where at the Rookery, the simple act of crossing a room made the whole building shake. For some reason the security people didn't see his approach. He stepped right by them and proceeded to the open door of the cuckoos' suite.

"How does he do that?" she asked.

"I can show you that, too," Katy said.

Three of the security people were coming down the hall toward them.

"Okay, ladies," the foremost said.

The gun in his hand was shaking and the eyes of all three were wide. Kerry knew just how he felt.

"Let's . . . let's just take it easy," he went on, "and no one . . . no one has to get hurt."

"Time for us to go," Katy said and she walked Kerry into the same thin air that the others had vanished into.

~ 8 ~

THE LIGHT WILL STAY ON

And if you bury me, add three feet to it
One for your sorrow, two for your sweat
Three for the strange things we never forget

And long after we're gone
The light will stay on
The light will stay on
　　　—CHRIS ECKMAN,
　　　　　FROM "THE LIGHT WILL STAY ON"

1.

Hazard, Thursday afternoon, September 5

Maida and Zia are forever friends—the way I always wanted my sister Kerry and me to be. Maybe we'll get there, too, once we finish putting all the baggage of our lives behind us. But I don't know if we'll ever be so merry. I guess I mean that in all the ways the word can be taken. Merry, happy, the way we define the word now; and merry, fey, one of things it used to mean a long time ago.

I heard about the crow girls for years but it wasn't until this past week after they finally came into my life that I can really understand what Jack meant about them. They really are irrepressible. It's like that rhyme, "two for mirth." Even when they're trying to be serious, they can't seem to stop smiling and neither can you.

So it's funny to see them at Jack's funeral—funny odd, I mean. Funny to see the smiles gone away, like they're gone to stay. The pair of them dressed in black, but I'm told they're always in black, standing here in the meadow with the rest of us, faces solemn, eyes shiny, Maida biting her bottom lip, Zia with her hands stuck so far into the pockets of her jacket it's like she's making wings out of the cloth.

We're all here today, gathering under the watch of those piney wood hills, everybody—Margaret and Annie, Raven, Chloë, the crow girls, Kerry, me. Humans, too, without the blood and with. Rory and Lily, Hank and our friends from the junkyard. But it's mostly corbæ and their black-winged cousins.

More of them keep dropping from the sky or walking out of the woods all the time. I lose count after a hundred. The bare branches of the trees are clothed in blackbirds, grieving. Nobody's talking. We're just standing there in ever-widening circles around the small still figure Jack makes lying there in the browning grass, wearing his first skin again, jackdaw feathers stark against the pale ochres and browns.

Jolene found him here, lying like this, and sent down word to us with one of the wild crow boys. They're here, too, along with a lot of the other wild folk. Bear, Alberta, Crazy Crow, and the rest. Even Ray.

I'm standing by the old stone where my parents first met, on the grass above my mother's grave. There's a gray sky overhead that makes it feel like all the color got bled out of the day, went away with Jack, or maybe it's just in mourning like the rest of us. And still there's more of them coming, corbæ and cousins. After awhile you can't see the grass for the blackbirds. All the autumn colors are swallowed by blackbirds, the heavy fruit of their bodies filling every branch, and the air lies still under the pressure of our heavy hearts.

"How'd he die?" somebody finally asks.

"*Why'd* he have to die?" Zia says before anyone else can answer.

It gets real quiet then. If you listen hard you can hear

the shuffle of someone's feet, the slow flap of wings as another latecomer arrives. But mostly the quiet holds, a deep silence that swells from the small body lying in the grass at our feet and washes out across this field of grace.

Finally, I clear my throat.

"Before he died," I say, "before he knew it was coming so soon, Jack once asked me to tell you a story if I was still here and he'd gone on."

Sad smiles flicker here, there. Nobody groans. There's no teasing Jack now. He's gone. The fingers of my right hand rise up to close around the silver crow pendant that hangs from my neck. It's becoming a familiar gesture.

I go on. "He said he thought one or two of you might show up today and he didn't want you going away empty-handed."

"It's not the one about the porcupine again, is it?"

I don't see the speaker, but it sounded like one of the wild crow boys. Sad smiles wake in memory of that crazy, tangled story.

"I liked that one," Bear says.

I nod. "Me, too. But I've got another one for you today."

"It won't be sad, will it?" Maida asks.

She and Zia are holding hands, looking at me like their hearts are going to break. Mine already has. I'm working on the mending of it now, but I get the feeling that might take as long as the crow girls have been friends.

"Just say it won't be," Maida says.

All I can do is shrug and tell it. Not like Jack would have, because I'm not Jack. I have to use my own voice and hope it'll be enough.

2.

The thing you have to remember about those days is that Jack wasn't always so good at holding on to who he was. More than any of us, he was a wan-

derer, and that only makes it harder to hold on to yourself. Because the thing about wandering is, you don't put down roots, and without roots, without history, without the stories of who you are and where you come from and how you fit in, you can slip out of context.

A place knows who you are. I don't mean simply the people who live there, but the place itself. If you go walking in the old neighborhoods, the streets or fields where you grew up, it comes back to you. Those old haunts remind you of the stories of who you were. Which makes it easier to figure out who you are.

Now I'm guessing most of you go a lot further back with Jack than I do, and you're thinking, the one thing Jack always had was stories. And that's true. He always remembered the stories. They were so much a part of him, he couldn't not remember them. What he'd forget sometimes was his part in them. That the Jack in the stories was the same Jack telling them.

One day Jack's walking along a dry riverbed, following it up into the mountains. I don't know where he's going or if he even has a destination in mind that day. Could be he's only rambling.

Come nightfall he's up around the tree line where the air's thin, but the stars feel so close he figures he could reach out and pluck one and not even have to stand up from the stone he's using for a seat. He sits there awhile, enjoying the dark and the starlight, listening to some of Cody's cousins singing to each other in the distance. Some time passes like that before he finally gets up to build himself a small fire and sets to boiling water for tea. He boils that water right in a tin cup with a wooden handle, keeping the handle turned away from the fire.

"Let me finish fixing that tea for you," someone says.

He looks up and there's a woman standing there in the dark that lies just outside the circle of his firelight. He guesses that she thinks he can't see her, but he can see just fine, corbæ's eyesight being as good in the dark as it is in the day and all. She's a slim, tall woman, maybe as tall as him, dressed in traveling clothes, split skirt with a man's white shirt tucked into the waist, a canvas jacket overtop, sturdy boots on her feet. Her face is long and narrow, dark chestnut hair pulled back into a ponytail, gray eyes. There's a journey sack slung from one shoulder and she's carrying a birdcage, covered with a piece of cloth. Jack can't see through the cloth, but he can smell there's someone inside, been spelled back into their animal skin, and that's when he knows she's a witch.

Now the thing with witches is, you can't let them do a thing for you because that puts you under their power. You've got to turn them down, every time they offer you a helping hand. It's like inviting one into your home. You do that and you've only got yourself to blame when they spell you back into your first skin and fry you up in a skillet.

So Jack, he smiles at her, but says, *"No, thank you, ma'am. I can fix my own tea. But you're welcome to have some with me."*

"I'm not really all that thirsty," she tells him.

He drops a handful of dried chamomile into the water because it's well and hot now and sets it aside to steep. Glances at the witch, still standing in the dark, frowning to herself, and he starts to making some flatbread. Well, the witch comes into the light then, that frown wiped right off her face.

"I hate to see a man trying to make bread," she says, putting down her sack and the birdcage. *"Let me do that for you."*

"Well, now," Jack says, "I'm partial to making my own bread. But you're welcome to have some with me."

He sees her gritting her teeth. Only thing witches hate more than not getting their own way is kindness.

"I'm not really all that hungry either," she says.

And it goes on like that for awhile. The witch offering to clean up after his meal, and he tells her he likes cleaning up and does she maybe have anything dirty that he can wash while he's doing his own? When he pulls out his pipe, she offers him a light, but he tells her there's no need, he's got a fire right here and did she want some tobacco? When he pulls out a needle and thread and starts to mending a hole in his jacket, she offers to do it for him, but he tells her he likes to sew and did she have anything that needed mending?

"I never knew people were so friendly in these parts," Jack says after awhile of this. "Tell you the truth, I never knew there even were people in these parts."

"I'm just passing through."

"Story of my life," he tells her. "I'm always just passing through myself."

They sit there for awhile, him sewing and smoking his pipe, her looking at him from across the fire, stroking the cloth on her birdcage.

"So you got a name?" she asks him then.

He nods. But he's no fool. Telling her his name'd be the same as letting her give him a helping hand.

"Well, what is it?" she says when he doesn't offer it up to her.

"What's yours?"

"I'll riddle you for it."

Jack smiles. "Well, now. I never had much of a head for working out riddles. Only ever could remember one, you know, 'What's the strongest of all

things?' That being love, because iron is strong, but
the blacksmith is stronger, and love can subdue the
blacksmith.''

"Never much cared for that one," she says.

Jack shrugs.

"You play the bones at all?" she asks then.

"You fixing to pull out a fiddle?" he says right
back.

She just looks at him, waiting him out. Jack smiles
to himself. He's starting to enjoy this now.

"I'm talking gaming bones," she says finally.

"Dice or dominoes?" he asks.

"Either one, makes no difference. Winner take
all."

Jack shakes his head, like he honestly regrets
having to say this.

"I don't gamble either," he tells her.

She nods. "You figure you can wait me out, don't
you?" she says, straightforward about it now.
"Well, let me tell you something, boy. I was walking
these mountains before you were even a gleam in
your mother's eye. I know a thing or two about waiting. I'm as patient as that rock you're sitting on. As
untiring as time passing. Sooner or later you're going to fall asleep and I'm going to be there, tuck
you in maybe, make up your knapsack into a pillow,
ease the boots off your tired feet. And you know what
happens then?''

"You that hungry?" he asks. "All I am is gristle
and bone. Doesn't seem worth the wait."

She gives him a feral grin. "I'm always hungry,
boy.''

Now Jack doesn't remember he's a corbæ that
day, that he could sit there wide awake till the world
comes to an end and still not be tired, were he to
put his mind to it. And she doesn't know what he is
either, or she wouldn't have stopped by his fire in
the first place. She thinks she's got herself some little

wild jackdaw traveling man, instead of a full-blooded corbœ. So she's ready to wait him out, probably watched him walking up that dry riverbed all day, climbing higher and higher up into the mountains, and figures he's got to be tired from all that exercise. He's got to nod off sooner or later.

Well, maybe Jack doesn't remember who he is, but he's still about as stubborn as they come and he's thinking about whoever she's got under the blanket in that birdcage of hers. Knows that whoever she's got caged, he's that person's only chance. So he starts in to telling her stories—not the kind he'd be telling us, but long pointless stories, the ones that go on for so long by the time you get to the end you can't remember where it was he started, only you don't want to ask in case it starts him telling the whole thing all over again.

And some time goes by.

I'm not talking hours, I'm talking days. It's like when Margaret and Cody got to playing billiards, or Zia got into that face-pulling contest with one of Sleepy Joe's kids.

By the time dawn finally came around at the end of that first night, the witch knew she was in trouble, but it was too late to back out now. Not without forfeiting her prize. Like a cuckoo, she was too swollen with pride to allow herself to do that. Truth is, she had cuckoo blood, somewhere back in her family tree. It's what made her a witch in the first place, gave her the finding gift and all.

So by morning she was worrying, but that was like nothing as the days went by. Got to be where neither cuckoo blood nor witcheries could keep her awake anymore and one cool evening her eyelids are so heavy she decides to let them close, just for a moment. Jack's in the middle of some confusing story about porridge, partridges, and an otter with a wooden leg and she figures he won't notice. She's right, too—or she would've been, if closing her eyes just for that moment didn't trick her body into thinking it could finally have some rest. She topples over, fast asleep, and the next thing you know, Jack's jumped across the fire and he's laying a blanket over her to warm her from the night chill.

That wakes her up.

"Damn you," she starts to say.

But it's too late. He's already done the favor for her, turned her witcheries back on her, and quick as you can say hickety-split, he's got himself a little cuckoo bird wrapped up in that blanket. She'd have maybe fought a little harder against the folds of prickly wool, but the tiredness that was her undoing didn't go away with her becoming a bird. She struggles a few moments, then goes still, exhausted, falls asleep.

Jack builds up the fire and takes the cloth from the birdcage to find that she hasn't got a bird caught in there, but a toad. A toad girl, actually. An old spirit who'd never heard about avoiding the kindness of witches. Didn't pay attention to the learning stories when they were told to her, I guess, or maybe she was just never in the company of anyone who knew them, which is probably more likely.

Well, he takes her out of the birdcage and puts the cuckoo witch in, lays the cloth over the cage again. Then he sits by the fire with that little toad in the palm of his hand, considering her, not like the witch did, weighing what she might be worth to him, but taking into account what she's worth to herself. He thinks he's trying to discover her name, but that's only because he doesn't remember that once on a time, back on that first day, he knew everybody. What he's really doing is trying to remember her name.

When it finally comes to him, he says it aloud.

"Charlotte."

*And that lets her shake off her toad skin. He sets
her down on the ground and the next thing you know
he's got himself a brown-skinned toad girl sitting
there with her broad face smiling at him.*

" 'Cept my friends call me Tottie," she says.

"I guess I knew that," Jack tells her. "But nam-
ing you Tottie might've brought you back as a hot
drink."

"That's a toddy."

*Jack shrugs, which makes her giggle and him
smile. But that toad girl's good humor doesn't last
long. After a moment she turns to look into the fire
and sighs.*

"What's the matter?" Jack asks.

"Guess I'm pretty much a dumb old toad," she
tells him.

"What makes you say that?"

"Letting myself get taken in the way I did."

Jack shakes his head. "Smartest person in the
world can still be tricked—especially when she
doesn't know the rules. You don't want to start on
belittling yourself, Tottie. You've got a good heart
and that's more important than just about anything."

"Doesn't stop a witch from catching you and fixing to fry you up in her skillet."

"Maybe not. But the evil people do, that's their
responsibility. The burden they have to carry. Sure,
when we see 'em starting on causing some hurt,
we've got to try and stop 'em, but mostly what the
rest of us should be concerning ourselves with is
doing right by others. Every time you do a good
turn, you shine the light a little farther into the dark.
And the thing is, even when we're gone, that light's
going to keep shining on, pushing the shadows
back."

"You really think so?" Tottie asks.

Jack gives her a solemn nod. "There's a lot of

things in this world I've got to guess at, but that's one thing I know for sure.''

3.

Long after everybody else is gone, Kerry and I are sitting in the grass by that old stone in Jack's field of grace. I'm feeling a little strange, being here. This is where Jack buried that little bundle of bones and hair that the doctors took out of Kerry all those years ago. There's no marker with my name on it, though. There's no marker for our mother's grave, either. The only one Jack has for now is a small plot of turned earth, but soon enough the grass and wildflowers will grow up and cover it over. Which is how they would have wanted it, I tell Kerry when she asks why there's no gravestones.

"I didn't get that story Jack wanted you to tell," Kerry says after awhile. "I mean, I understand about treating people right—the way you'd want them to treat you—but there seemed to be more to it that went right by me."

I lean back on that stone so that I can look up into the sky. I've never been to this place before, but I understand now why it meant so much to our parents. It's one of those places where the Grace can shine, untouched by meanness or spite. If they come into this field, it's only because we brought them. Which is pretty much how it works everywhere, when you think about it. The difference is, this piece of grace hasn't been spoiled yet.

"I think the other part of what he was saying," I tell her, "is that everything has an existence separate from ourselves. People, animals, trees, art . . . everything. So when you're interacting with something—it doesn't matter what it is—you shouldn't be concentrating on how clearly you see yourself in it. The trick is to recognize the worth of a thing for it's own sake instead of recognizing its worth to you."

"Jeez, I didn't get that all."

I give her a small smile. My hand lifts, clasps the crow pendant hanging at my neck.

"Or maybe that's just what I see in it," I say.

4.

Newford, Sunday, September 8

```
Sender: 1carson2@cybercare.com
Date: Sun, 8 Sep 1996 19:32:16-0500
From: 'Lily Carson'
<lcarson2@cybercare.com>
Organization: Not very
To: dgavin@tama.com
Subject: Re: How I spent the day af-
ter Labor Day
```

Hey, Donna,

Thanks for getting back to me so quickly. I mean, I only got up the nerve to finally send my letter off to you a couple of hours ago.

>how crazy all of this sounds?!?

Yes, I do know. And that makes me appreciate how supportive you've been all the more. To tell you the truth, if you came to me with a similar story, I don't know if I'd be as supportive. I'd want to be, no question, and I'd try, but I don't know if I could.

But that's one of the main problems when you're dealing with something

like corbae. Katy says that people
have a natural gift of denial, some
sort of a genetic thing that lets us
retain our safe view of a normal
world no matter what. We can forget
the most momentous, bizarre experi-
ences like they never happened. Because if we couldn't, we wouldn't be
able to operate efficiently in the
world that most of us have agreed is
real. We'd always be looking under
the surface, around the corner, paying more attention to our peripheral
vision than what's right in front of
us. So we forget it instead.

I remember that happening after Hank and
I first met the crow girls in that alley.
The whole experience kept sliding away
from me--partly, I guess, because it was
so upsetting to remember Philippe
Couteau's attack on us, but also because things happened that night that
shouldn't be able to happen.

It's like all those people who were
drawn to the Harbor Ritz when the
Grace's light enveloped it. Katy says
none of them remember it. They might
dream about it sometimes, or catch
the way light falls in a certain way
and have one of those niggling feelings of deja vu, but they won't con-
sciously remember.

I don't know if that's true or not,
because I don't know anybody who was

there. But I know it's true for Rory
and he saw a lot more than any of
those people ever did. It's impossible to talk to him about what happened. He just gives you this blank
look, or smiles, like he knows you're
putting him on.

It drives me crazy because this is
something I can't *not* talk about. I
have to keep it alive and fresh because it's important to me. I don't
want to lose the knowledge that the
world really is a bigger, stranger
place than we ever thought it was. Or
that there really is a thing called a
spirit inside us. That's why I wrote
it all down in the first place.

I have to tell you that I really had
to think long and hard before sending
you a copy. I didn't want you flying
back here to have me committed or
something. :)

But I'll tell you now, the next time
you do come back--Thanksgiving? Xmas?--
I've got some stuff to show you. I don't
know if you've got animal blood or not,
but for some things it doesn't matter.
Margaret's been teaching me how to find
those shortcuts I was telling you about,
and those little pockets of the world
that got trapped in a fold and can't be
seen unless you know how to look. Those
are things I *can* share with you.

Oh, jeez. Listen to me. I sound like
I was born again, or have started
selling Amway or something. Look,
just tell me to shut up if I'm getting on your nerves.

>And how are things working out with
Hank?

Well, it hasn't even been a week
since we first slept together, you
know, but so far it's good. Forever?
I don't know. He's an odd contradiction. On the one hand, there's this
whole street-smart tough guy that he
is. I mean, you wouldn't want to mess
with him--at all!!--and he obviously
had a really hard time growing up as
a kid. Seriously bad home life, on
the streets when he was really young,
in trouble with the law, in prison.
He's been through stuff that I don't
think we could ever understand. I
mean, it makes having been tormented
in high school like we were sound
like a cakewalk.

But he came out of it with such a big
heart and a positive attitude. And
he's really bright. Actually, his
whole 'family' at that junkyard is
really sweet and smart, once you get
to know them. You keep wanting to
tell them to do more with their
lives, but then you realize that they
see things differently and you have
to remember to respect the choices
they've made. I don't know as much

about them as I do Hank, but just
from stuff I've overheard, I know
that they've all had really hard
lives, so if this is how they want to
deal with that past pain, who am I to
tell them different?

Truth is, I kind of admire the way
they live outside regular society. In
that way, they're kind of like the
corbae--invisible people that the
rest of us don't normally see because
we're not paying attention. Getting
to know them the little I have has
sure given me a different perspective
on street people, I'll tell you that
much. I mean, not to romanticize them
or anything, because some of them
just are losers or broken people that
can never be fixed, but they're still
people. They just deal with things
differently than we do. Sometimes by
choice, sometimes not.

Anyway, getting back to Hank. He's
very sweet and attentive, but we move
in such different social circles that
I don't know what's going to happen
in the long run. I think I'm more
comfortable with his family than he
is with the people I know. The weird
thing is, I'm starting to see through
the pretensions more myself. It's not
anything he says--he's got to be the
most circumspect person I've ever met
in some ways. But I can tell what
he's thinking and it makes me think
about things differently, too. Which
is a good thing, I suppose.

Now you're probably thinking that
it's that falling in love syndrome,
you know, where you suddenly take a
great interest in, oh, say reggae music because your new sweetie's so
into it, but I don't think that's entirely it. For one thing, there are
people like Christy, who Hank immediately liked and respected, which
makes me trust my own reactions more,
because he's always been one of my
favorite people, too.

>gangster's money?

I don't know what to do with it. Giving it back will just cause problems
for Moth and since he's starting to
loosen up around me, I don't really
want to get him irritated with me
again. But it doesn't seem right to
keep it either. Maybe I should just
give it to some charity.

Well, I guess I've run on at the
mouth long enough. Thanks for being
so patient with me. And now it's your
turn. You haven't told me *anything*
about what you've been up to lately.
Whatever happened to Peter? Or are
you seeing that Andy Parks fellow
from work now?

You have to come home for a visit
soon. (I know, I know, Boston's home
now, but you know what I mean.) It's
just that I miss you and right now

```
I've got *no* money or I'd fly out to
visit you.

Or  maybe  we  should  just  use  that
$10,000 for  travel  money  to  ferry  us
back  and  forth  when  we  *really*  need
a  visit!  :)

Love you.

Lily
```

5.

It was early evening and Hank was watching the sunset from one of the lawn chairs in front of Moth's trailer. He had a tape in Moth's boom box of some classic tunes from the mid-thirties, Lester Young playing with a quintet that included Count Basie on piano and Carl Smith on trumpet. On the ground beside the tape player was a thermos of tea, in his hand a half-full mug. There were dogs sprawled all around his chair, but Bocephus wasn't among them.

Hank couldn't see the sun anymore from where he sat, but the sky behind the deserted tenement buildings of the Tombs was still smeared with pinks and mauves. Bo was out there somewhere, haunting the streets that ran between the empty lots and buildings.

He liked this recording a lot. The basic Kansas City grittiness of the playing, particularly Young's staccato style on his sax. The understanding expressed between Young's horn and the piano. They were just finishing up a version of Gershwin's "Lady Be Good" when Moth's cab pulled into the junkyard, dirt crunching under the tires. The dogs jumped up, but didn't bark. Like Hank, they'd recognized the car by the sound of its motor. Moth came over to join him and the dogs crowded around the chair he took. Hank reached over to the tape player, turning off the music.

Moth smiled. "And here I was hoping to catch you playing one of my Boxcar Willie tapes."

"You think that's going to happen in this lifetime?"

"Hope springs eternal in the human breast," Moth told him.

Hank raised his eyebrows.

"Comes from something Alexander Pope wrote," Moth said. "You'd know that, too, if you'd spent more time in the prison library."

"You know me. I was always too busy planning my big escape."

Moth laughed. He shook a cigarette free from his pack and lit up.

"Saw that dog of yours when I was driving up," he said. "You forget to feed him this morning?"

"He's not my dog."

"Whatever. He looked hungry."

"Bocephus always looks hungry."

Moth blew out a wreath of blue-gray smoke. Beyond the tenements the sky was losing all of its color and the shadows grew long.

"Bocephus," Moth repeated. "Now I would have thought you'd name him after one those horn players you like so much instead of after Hank Senior's boy."

"I didn't name him."

"Yeah, you told me that."

Lily had pointed out an odd fact to Hank, though she hadn't needed to since he'd already twigged to it himself: Nobody really remembered anything about the corbæ. In her case it was Rory. In his, except for Moth, what personal experience the rest of his family had had with the corbæ had slipped out of their memories; everything else was just stories Jack had told. Katy and Kerry hadn't vanished from the middle of the junkyard. They'd only wandered off. Hank hadn't had a bullet hole miraculously heal. It was just some old wound he'd been carrying from before he and Moth had met up in prison. Jack wasn't a magic man, and he certainly wasn't dead. He'd hit the road like he'd do from time to time and he'd be back. The cuckoos were only a bunch of mob-connected punks from New Orleans. Dangerous, sure, but not magical either.

Hank had already given up trying to argue any of those points with Paris and the others, and he and Moth didn't bother to talk about any of it around them anymore. There was no point.

"So where is everybody?" Moth asked.

"Lily's at her place writing some letters and that's about all I know. There was nobody around when I got here."

"I think Benny's been hitting the track again."

Hank nodded. "He's about due. What's it been this time? Two months without laying a bet?"

"Two and a half."

Moth took a last drag and butted his cigarette out under his heel. His gaze traveled over to where the dark bulk of Jack's school bus was slowly being swallowed by the encroaching night.

"I miss Jack," he said after a moment. "Without him and his stories, it's going to make the winter seem long."

Hank sighed, remembering that last look of Jack he'd seen when the chalice came back together in his and Lily's hands. Remembered the things that Katy had explained to him. Like Lily, they were things he kept repeating to himself, holding them in his head so he wouldn't lose them like the others had. Trouble was, that remembering also made him know that Jack wasn't coming back.

"Yeah," he said. "I miss him, too. But Katy knows a lot of those stories of his and she'll be around."

"Won't be the same."

"Won't be bad either—just different."

Moth nodded. "I suppose." A smile touched his lips.

"I even miss those crows of his, though I don't guess the dogs do."

"No, I guess they don't."

Moth went and got himself a beer, sat back down, lit up another smoke.

"I'm thinking of getting an apartment," Hank said.

" 'Bout time," Moth told him.

"What's that supposed to mean?"

Moth shrugged. "I always thought you could do more with your life. Getting yourself a place you can call home's a good first step."

"You never said anything before."

"Didn't want you to take it wrong. So are you going to be moving in with Lily?"

"It's a little early to be thinking about that kind of thing. We're taking it a day at a time for now. But it's good."

"You hold on to that," Moth said. "There's little enough of feeling good around as it is. You find some, it's worth keeping a hold of."

"I know," Hank told him.

Moth dragged from his cigarette. "I didn't warm to Lily right away, you know, but then I guess I don't warm to most people first time I meet them. It's an old, bad habit that I don't know if I'll ever break. Can't seem to hang on to a faith in people the way you do. I look at a stranger and I see trouble. You, you see someone who could be a friend."

Hank didn't know if it was exactly so cut-and-dried, but it was something he worked at, trying to see the good in people. To see the Grace in them.

"Don't be too hard on yourself," Hank said. "You didn't exactly grow up in an environment that promoted trust."

"And you did?"

Hank shrugged.

"I mean, I hear what you're saying," Moth went on. "It's hard to have much faith in people when all your life everybody, starting with your own family, betrays that trust, but Christ. What a way to live."

"You do what you have to survive."

Moth took another drag. "Older I get, the more I wonder if that's enough. If it's really living, or just getting by. And then I start to wonder if the walls we put up are to keep others out, or keep ourselves in, and what we lose by walling ourselves away like that."

"That's something you can only answer for yourself," Hank said. "Same as everybody."

Moth nodded. "So how do you do it, kid?"

Hank thought for a moment.

"I guess what it comes down to in the end," he said, "is that I don't want to live in the kind of world where we don't try to look out for each other. Not just the people that are close to us, but anybody who needs a helping hand. I can't change the way anybody else thinks, or what they choose to do, but I can do my bit."

Moth dropped his butt on the dirt and ground it out. He looked out into the night that now lay deep around them.

"You think it's enough?" he asked.

Hank shrugged. "Nothing's ever enough. I know there's crap out there, waiting to fall down on me. I know there are people looking to take advantage of me, who'd rob me blind and leave me to die in an alleyway. I just don't want to be like them."

"Makes you think about the work we do," Moth said. "Some of those guys Eddie has us ferry around . . ."

Hank nodded. "Maybe it's time for a career change."

Moth shook out another cigarette, lit it up. He took a long drag.

"Maybe you're right," he said.

6.

Saturday, October 26

"You moved again," Kerry said.

She'd managed to get Rory to sit for a portrait but he wasn't having an easy time of it. They were in her apartment, Rory on a kitchen chair by the window where the strong sunlight accentuated the shadows on his face, she on the other mismatched chair, drawing board balanced upright on her lap, a stub of charcoal in her hand.

"Sorry," he said. "It's not as easy as I thought it'd be."

"Why do you think professional models get paid for what they do?"

"I can't honestly say it's something I ever thought about."

"Do you want to stop?" she asked.

He shook his head, then shot her a guilty look. "Whoops. Sorry again."

"It's okay. Lift your head a bit . . . now move it to the right. No, your right, not mine. There. Perfect."

The worst thing about this was that he was going to be so disappointed with what she was drawing because it was, in a word, awful. But that was why she was using him for practice. The odd thing she'd discovered about her art courses at Butler were that life drawing and portraiture seemed to have fallen completely out of favor. The profs were far more interested in having the students "express themselves," which basically boiled down to slapping paint and whatever else was at hand onto a canvas and then being able to talk about it in such a way that it sounded like you knew what you were doing. Making a statement.

All Kerry wanted to do was learn how to draw properly. To be able to get down on paper what she saw in front of her. She figured there'd be time enough to express herself once she got the basics down. As soon as she could afford it, she was planning to take some actual drawing courses at the Newford School of Art to augment the art history that made up the bulk of her studies at the university. The history courses fascinated her, but they weren't enough. She wanted hands-on experience as well.

It was Katy who'd suggested she use people around her to practice on for now.

"Like who?" Kerry had said.

"Well, for starters, you could ask Rory. Maybe it'll get his mind off of Annie."

That was easier said than done. The only thing Rory seemed to recall out of all the strange things he'd experienced was a conversation he'd had with Annie during the blackout when she'd asked him why he'd never made a pass at her. He didn't even remember the things Kerry had told him about her time in the institution or Katy. He thought she'd only discovered that she had a twin sister after moving to the city, that Katy had been adopted by other people than she'd been, and wasn't it cool?

But he did remember the conversation with Annie and decided it meant that he should actively pursue more than a platonic relationship with her. Annie's reaction was to immediately embark on a tour.

"I know what you're thinking," Annie told Kerry the night before she left. "That I'm making the same mistake Jack did with your mother, but this kind of thing never works out in the long term. It's better he gets hurt a little now, than hurt a lot later on."

"But then why did you talk to him the way you did?" Kerry had to ask.

"I don't know. I thought the world was ending. Or maybe that it was beginning again, starting fresh. I've always liked him. I was giddy with the light of the Grace and I thought he'd finally be able to accept that there's more to the world than what's sitting in front of his nose. But he doesn't. He can't. And I'm tired of shifting into

my corbæ skin and going through all the shock and dis-
belief over and over again. It gets old real fast.''

Kerry had nodded, understanding all too well. She'd
come up against the same baffling wall herself whenever
she tried to talk to Rory about any of it. And she couldn't
even confront him with physical proof the way Annie or
the crow girls could. She tried taking him through some
of the shortcuts and into the hidden folds that Katy had
taught her how to find, but they only left him confused
and disoriented and she'd finally given up as well.

But she liked Rory, so she accepted his foibles the way
you're supposed to with a friend. She did her best to
cheer him up when he got too glum about how it hadn't
worked out for him with Annie, though that got a little
hard sometimes. She liked having him as a friend, but
she kept finding herself wishing they could be more. All
that meeting other people at the university had done was
remind her of how much more she liked him.

"I think I'm getting a crick in my neck," he said now.

"That's okay," she told him. "I'm pretty much done
anyway."

She turned her drawing board around so that he could
see what she'd drawn.

"I know, I know," she said before he could try to find
a polite comment to make. "It's awful. But that's the
whole point."

"To draw awful pictures?"

She had to laugh. "No, to practice until I get to a point
where they're not awful anymore."

"You should get the Aunts to give you some tips."

Kerry did spend time with them and she loved their
art, but it wasn't what she wanted to do. That realization
came as a surprise because in many ways, the Aunts'
watercolor were very much in the same mode as her
mother's art had been. She'd thought that was what she
wanted to do until she began to seriously apply herself
to practicing and discovered what she wanted to draw
were people. Wildlife, landscapes, plant studies . . . they

were all interesting and she liked looking at them, but
they didn't call out to her the way the human face and
figure did.

"I would," she told him, "but their work's not really
my style." She put down her drawing board and
stretched. "Not that anything seems to be my style at the
moment. But that's okay. I'm enjoying the process. Do
you want some tea?"

"Sure."

He followed her into the kitchen, sitting on the counter
while she got the water boiling, took the canister of tea
bags down from the cupboard, set out their cups.

"You're really different now," he said.

She gave him a questioning look.

"I mean, in a good way. You were so shy when you
first moved in a couple of months ago."

"Oh God, don't remind me. I can still remember how
shocked I was when I realized the apartment was unfurnished."

Rory smiled. "But you're way more confident now. I
told you. You just had to give it some time. Everybody
feels overwhelmed when they first move to the big city."

"I know," Kerry said.

Though that wasn't really it at all. Who she was today
had started with that morning when Maida had shown her
how to look inside and use the echo of the Grace that
everyone carried in them to stabilize herself. But there
was no point in explaining that to him.

"And having you and Annie helped a lot," she added.
"I would've been lost without you guys."

She regretted bringing Annie up as soon as the name
came out of her mouth. But Rory seemed to be dealing
better with it these days. He only got a wistful look.
Maybe there was hope for them yet, she thought. But she
wouldn't push it.

"The house sure is quiet this last little while, isn't it?"
was all he said.

Kerry nodded. Annie was away on tour. Chloë and

Lucius had gone to Europe for an indefinite period of time. The only people in the house proper were Rory and herself. And of course the crow girls, who still came and went pretty much as they pleased, though Kerry had been waging a mostly unsuccessful campaign to have them respect her privacy and at least knock instead of wandering into her apartment whenever the fancy took them.

As though thinking of the pair had been a summons, there was a knock on the door and the crow girls were there, standing in the hallway, grinning, little cloth sacks held up in front of them.

"Trick or treat!" they cried.

Kerry smiled. "You're a bit early, aren't you? Halloween's not until next week."

"We're practicing," Zia told her.

"I see. And where are your costumes?"

Maida laughed. "We're wearing them, silly. We're pretending to be crow girls."

"But you are crow girls."

Zia gave Maida a poke with her elbow. "See? I told you we should have better costumes."

Maida ignored the poke. "What are you going as?" she asked Kerry.

"I'm a little old to go trick-or-treating."

Zia shook her head, very emphatically. "Oh, no. We asked Margaret and she told us that no one asks your age when you come to their door."

"I just can't believe we never knew about this before," Maida said. "Who'd have thought that you can go around all dressed up and people will just give you sweets when you knock on their door?"

"But only on the one night," Kerry told her. "Which isn't until Thursday."

"So we can't practice?" Zia wanted to know.

"Well, you could practice the dressing up part."

They both looked a little glum.

"Does this mean we're not getting a treat?" Maida asked finally.

Kerry laughed. "Of course not. Come on in and we'll see what we can find."

"Ah, the sisters incorrigible," Rory said when the crow girls trooped into the kitchen ahead of Kerry.

"We're not sisters," Maida said.

Zia nodded. "Kerry and Katy are sisters. We're just friends."

"Of course," Rory said, giving Kerry a wink.

Kerry could only wonder what it would take to make him wake up and really see the world as it was, instead of how he supposed it should be.

The only thing she had to give the girls was a hazelnut chocolate bar that was in her fridge. She broke it in two and handed the halves to them, but they both immediately raised their bags instead of taking them from her hand. Smiling, she dropped the chocolate into the bags.

"Can we see the tattoo again?" Zia asked.

Maida nodded. "Oh, yes, please." She grinned. "Do you see how veryvery polite we are getting to be?"

"I'm very impressed," Kerry told her.

"What tattoo?" Rory asked.

The tattoo had been Katy's idea. Kerry had been a reluctant participant in the scheme until they got to the tattoo parlor and Hank's friend Paris had shown her the design she'd drawn up from Katy's instructions: a fox's head with a black feather behind it. Kerry had immediately fallen in love with it and had it done that afternoon.

The crow girls crowded close as Kerry lifted up the sleeve of her T-shirt to let them see the tattoo on her shoulder. For some reason they never got tired of looking at it.

"I'm getting a thousand of those," Zia announced. "All different."

"I'm getting two thousand," Maida said.

Zia shook her head. "You don't have room for that many."

"Yes, I do. They'll be veryvery tiny. So tiny you'll need a telescope to see them properly."

"You mean a periscope."

Rory wasn't listening to the girls chatter. He had an odd look on his face as he looked at the tattoo himself.

"What's it mean?" he asked.

"It sort of symbolizes my parents."

His gaze lifted to her face. "What, like a fox and crow were their totems or something?"

"Jackdaw," Kerry said.

"What?"

"It's a jackdaw feather, not a crow's."

"I'm getting crow feathers," Zia said. "Hundreds of them. I'll have them tattooed all over my back."

"I'm getting mine tattooed on my bum," Maida said.

They both giggled, but their conversation continued to fall on deaf ears.

"It's funny," he said. "I don't know why I'm remembering this, but I had a dream about you one night—not long after you first moved in. You were sleeping in the back of this abandoned car and there was a blackbird and a fox watching over you, like they were protecting you or something." His gaze returned to the tattoo. "When I woke I started sketching some designs, mixing the fox and bird images up. . . . I wonder what I did with them."

"I'd like to see them."

Rory nodded, still bemused. "I remember telling Chloë about that dream, which is weird since Chloë and I never talked about anything that didn't have to do with the house. She was looking for this tin that had gotten accidentally thrown out. There were these weird black stones in it." He looked up at her. "I should show them to you. . . ."

His voice trailed off.

"Do you . . . remember anything else?" Kerry asked.

"What do you mean?"

"You know, strange things. About crows and ravens and jays. . . ."

For a moment she saw something stir in his eyes. A memory. An image, perhaps. Then he blinked and smiled.

"What would I remember about them?" he asked.

Kerry let her sleeve fall back down, covering the tattoo

"Nothing," she said with a shrug.

That night Katy came by to find her sitting in her window seat, looking out at the dark leafless shape of the crow girls' elm. Kerry lifted a lazy hand as her sister crossed the room and came to sit at the other end of the window seat. They pulled their feet up and put them in each other's lap.

"I saw Ray earlier tonight," Katy said.

"I didn't know he was back in town."

"He just got in. He wants us to all go for dinner some place tomorrow night."

Kerry shrugged. "I don't have anything happening."

She didn't know their grandfather nearly as well a she'd like to. He seemed to have the best of intentions i their doing things together like a real family, but whe they actually got together for a meal or an outing, h never seemed very comfortable. It was as though the intimidated him or something, Kerry thought. Katy sai it was just that he felt guilty for having abandoned thei grandmother and Nettie.

"But at least he's trying," she'd always add. "S we've got to give him points for that."

Kerry did, which was why she always agreed to gettin together with him, even though it got so awkward some times.

"Look at these," she said, picking up the jar of blac stones that Rory had brought up earlier. "Rory gave ther to me."

Katy took the jar and held it up to get a closer look a the stones. "Where'd he get them?"

"I think they were in the pot—before it ended up wit Lily."

Katy touched the crow pendant hanging from her neck She took one of the smooth pebbles out and rolled it o her palm.

"I think they're pieces of the long ago," she said.
"Like in Jack's stories."

"What do you think they're for?" Kerry asked.

"Well," Katy drawled. "I'm guessing they're like the
corbæ answer for all things strange and mysterious."

"They're not for anything," Kerry said, having heard
it often enough in the past couple of months. "They just
are."

"You've been taking notes."

"I've got a lot of catching up to do."

"You and me both," Katy said. She wiggled her toes
in Kerry's lap. "You know what I'd just love?"

Smiling, Kerry began to massage her sister's feet.

"What makes people not believe?" she asked.

"Not believe in what?"

"Corbæ. Magic. The Grace. All of it."

Katy shrugged. "Maybe the same thing that makes
them not believe in love. Because it scares them. Or they
don't want to be laughed at for believing it can be real.
What brought that up?"

"I was just thinking about Rory and Annie. He doesn't
believe in magic, but he believes in love, and she's just
the opposite. It's so sad."

"You should just tell him that you like him—that'd
make him forget all about Annie. I mean, it's not like
they were ever really an item or anything."

"That wasn't what I was talking about."

"I know," Katy said. "But I still think you should do
it."

"I'm going to let him work through this business with
Annie first."

Kerry stopped massaging her sister's feet. They both
pulled their legs up and looked at each other over the
tops of their knees.

"It makes you think about our parents, though," Kerry
said after a moment. "How could our mom *not* have
believed in magic? Where did she think all those people
came from? That they just lived in cottages in the forest

somewhere?''

"How could Jack not believe in love?" Katy asked in reply.

Kerry sighed. "Is it going to be like that for us?"

"Only if we let it," Katy said.

Katy fell silent then and Kerry saw her eyes were filling with tears. Swinging her feet to the floor, Kerry scooted in close. She moved Katy's legs out of the way and put her arms around her sister.

"I just miss him so much," Katy said with a tremble in her voice.

Kerry didn't have to ask who.

At least you got to know him enough to miss him, she thought. I didn't even get that.

But she didn't speak the words aloud. They'd only make Katy feel worse. Instead, she took Katy's hand and curled her sister's fingers around the crow pendant that dangled between them. Then she held her close, letting Katy cry.

She took her own comfort from having a sister she could still get to know. At least it wasn't too late for that.

7.

Bighorn Mountains, Wyoming

Cody sat by a small fire in the high lonesome, way past the tree line, so far up in the mountains that there was only the sky left to climb. It was a quiet night so he heard the footsteps from a long way off. Smelling the air, he knew he was meant to hear them because the person approaching his fire could be as silent as the nightfall when she wanted. He looked up but didn't speak as Margaret came into the firelight. She waited a moment, then lowered herself down onto a stone across the fire from him.

"How're you doing, Cody?" she asked.

He shrugged. "You're a long way from home, darling

Come to have yourself a laugh at how I screwed up again?"

She shook her head. "When're you going to understand that nobody's got a problem with you. You're the one with the chip on his shoulder and the only person who keeps stepping up to knock it off is your own self."

"You reckon?"

"I think that pretty much sums it up."

"Except you're forgetting something," Cody said. "You're forgetting all the people who get hurt in the process."

Margaret made no comment.

"Like that little granddaughter of Ray's," Cody went on. "What was I thinking?"

"What were you thinking?" Margaret asked.

"Damned if I know." He looked out over the lower ranges of mountains, then slowly returned his gaze to her face. "No, I know what I was thinking. I was thinking, if the world's going back to how it was in the first days, then it didn't matter if one little girl with some of our blood in her gave up her life to make it happen. I told myself I wasn't really sacrificing her. She was never going to have existed in the first place anyway—not if things had worked out the way I was thinking they could."

"That's hard," Margaret told him.

Cody gave a slow nod. "I can't even say that realizing how I was using her even changed my mind. That didn't come until I finally figured out what Dominique was really after. Once I knew she wasn't working on a return to the old days like I was, that she was only hungry for corbæ blood, I couldn't be a part of it. We've had our differences, but even this old dog knows that the world doesn't turn without the firstborn in it."

They fell silent for awhile. Looked at each other through the thin trail of smoke that rose from the fire. Listened to the crackle of the wood as it burned.

"Raven says you're not to blame," Margaret said finally. "Says you're just susceptible to things that move outside the world."

"And what kinds of things would those be, darling?"

Margaret shrugged. "Spirits, I guess. Whatever they are, Raven says they were around before him. Says they've got their own agenda. Usually they just leave us alone, but every once in a while they start in on scheming, make plans for us that we can never understand."

"Well, I sure don't understand."

Cody pulled a silver flask out of the inside pocket of his jacket and offered it to her.

"Sure," she said.

He poured a couple of fingers of whiskey into a tin mug and passed it over, then took a swig from the flask.

Margaret took a sip. "Did you hear about Jack?" she asked.

Cody gave a slow nod. "Word travels fast." He sighed. "Every time I get my hands on that damn pot I come away regretting what I've done, but I think maybe I regret this time the most."

"I was told he chose to go."

"There wouldn't have been a choice necessary, darling, if I hadn't been messing with things. I'm going to miss him."

"We'll all miss him."

"That story his daughter tells, about him and Nettie finally meeting up in the medicine lands. You think it's true?"

Margaret shrugged.

"Because I don't remember the medicine lands."

"No one does," she said. "Not even Raven."

"I didn't even think it was, you know, a place. Not really."

Margaret had another sip of whiskey.

"So what do you think, darling?" Cody asked. "Is that where we go when we die?"

Margaret looked up into the vault of stars that hung above them. "I'd like to think so."

"Yeah. Me, too."

He capped his flask and returned it to his pocket.

"Well, darling," he said. "I want to thank you for coming by and sharing your thoughts with me. But I'm guessing you've got places to go, people to meet."

Margaret set the tin mug down on the dirt by the fire.

"You just don't get it, do you?" she said. "You always want people to think the worst of you."

"What were you expecting from me?"

"Nothing I guess. I thought maybe we could travel while together, get to know each other. See if we couldn't leave some of these bad feelings in the past where they belong and make a few better ones."

Cody cocked his head. "Raven sent you to keep an eye on me, did he?"

Margaret regarded him for a long moment. Then she stood up.

"I see I'm wasting my time," she said.

As she started to walk away, Cody jumped up from where he was sitting. She stepped out of the firelight before he was able to catch her arm. She shook his grip off. But what startled Cody was that she seemed genuinely mad.

"You really mean this, don't you?" he said. "You really just came along to say how-do and be friendly."

"It doesn't really matter anymore, does it?"

Cody gave her a long, penetrating look. "Damn right it matters. I'm just not that good at having people treat me kindly."

Margaret didn't move.

"What I'm trying to say, darling, is I'd be honored if you'd sit with me a spell, maybe walk down the road with me a ways. I could sure use the company. Hell, who knows? Maybe a corbæ and a canid can be friends."

"There was never any reason that they couldn't."

Cody shrugged. "The only thing I ask is, if I start to get a yearning after that pot of Raven's again, you just give me a slap across the back of my head and knock some sense into me.''

That got him a smile.

''You don't have to worry about Raven's pot,'' she said. ''Way things worked out, it's not something to be used anymore. It's something to celebrate.''

''So that part of the story's true, too?''

Margaret shook her head as if to say, didn't he get it yet?

''That's what Raven figures it was all about, Cody,'' she said. ''Keeping the Grace in this world. Maybe her light's not as strong as it once was, maybe the world's gotten darker since the first day, and it's still getting darker, but something's shining on. In you. In me. Everywhere you look, if you take the time to pay attention. So we've got two choices. We can let the darkness win, or we can celebrate the Grace and shine her light stronger.''

Somewhere in the lonesome dark that Cody thought of as his heart, he felt an ember stir. Maybe it was only a glimmer of hope. Maybe it was the novel idea that loneliness didn't have to be his lot. Or maybe it was a flicker of the Grace's light that could be fanned into a brighter flame.

''You reckon?'' he said.

Margaret gave him a light punch on the shoulder. ''Yeah, I reckon. So what do you say, Cody?''

He stepped back and gave her that coyote grin of his.

''I feel like dancing, darling,'' he said.

''Dancing.''

He held out his arms to her. ''Like you said. Celebrating the light.''

She looked at him for the space of a few drawn-out heartbeats and shook her head before she let him waltz her back into the firelight.

And long after the coals of Cody's fire had burned down to ash, they were dancing still.